Dedication

This novel is dedicated to those Medievalist
friends and teachers and colleagues who
tolerate my tendency to write fiction and
make bad jokes at inappropriate moments.

LANGUE[DOT]DOC 1305

UNCORRECTED PROOF

LANGUE[DOT]DOC 1305

GILLIAN POLACK

To Nicole
My secret is that
this is a time travel
novel (?)
hope you enjoy it!
Gillian Polack

UNCORRECTED
PROOF

SATALYTE PUBLISHING

VICTORIA, AUSTRALIA

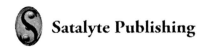

First published in Australia in 2014
This edition published in 2014
By Satalyte Publishing
ABN 50 145 650 577
satalyte.com.au

ISBN: 978-0-992XXXX-X-X (Paperback)
       978-0-992XXXX-X-X (eBook)

 Satalyte Publishing

6 Reserve Street, Foster VIC 3960, Australia

ACKNOWLEDGMENTS

First and foremost, thanks to Van Ikin for mentoring me (and my novel) during a rather difficult few years. Thanks also to Stephen and Marieke, for the obvious (championing the book) and the not-so-obvious (sometimes my ideas are a bit unusual...). Thanks also to the University of Western Australia for its financial support and to ArtsACT for a 2011 grant.

Sometimes it takes a village: this novel was research intensive and covered many disciplines. All real errors are my own, though some apparent errors belong to my characters and are quite intentional. Thank you to all those who gave me help and advice on this project: Lara Eakins created my skies and checked my astronomy and explained the importance of delta T; Guy Micklethwait introduced me to methods of time-travel; Samantha Faulkner checked Geoff Murray's background for me; Mark gave me explosives advice and Pixie help with the blacksmithery.

Of the fine scientists of CSIRO and the writers of CSfG special thanks to Cris Kennedy, Linda Karssies, Wendy Welsh, Barbara Robson, Stuart Barrow, Elizabeth Fitzgerald and Simon Petrie. Of my wider world of historians and writers, thanks to Kathleen Neal, Kari Maund, Jonathan Jarrett, Katrin Kania, Brian Ditcham, Amy Brown and Elizabeth Chadwick.

I owe a very particular debt of gratitude to all the friends who pushed me towards this project I swore I would never undertake, but particularly to Lucy Sussex and to Ian Nichols.

Thank to Sean Sidkey, for naming Ben Konig as part of fundraising to help people inundated by the Queensland floods.

CONTENTS

This is the year when human horizons will grow again. We've looked outward. We've looked inward. Now, for the first time, we're about to look at our past with new eyes and new technology. For the first time, we will understand who we are and how we came here.

Theodore Lucas Mann

Chapter One: Arithmetic

"You have to say something." Harvey had said this to Luke six times before and he would explain six times more if he had to. He relaxed back in his ostentatious black chair and explained patiently, "We need a ceremony to mark the moment. We also require words for the great unwashed. If you don't want the floor, just say so: I'll cobble something together." Behind him, the Melbourne skyline stretched towards the bay.

Luke grunted and fidgeted. He wanted to leave the ceremony behind and get on with changing the world.

"Something that we can translate into a press statement," Harvey continued, gently and implacably. "That Timebot is new. That Timebot is part exotic matter and part mechanical and part computer. That Timebot will set up a platform so that we can travel into the Middle Ages. That there are many questions that Timebot will answer, but one is very dangerous: is Timebot reliable?"

"Oh God, that'll make everyone happy, won't it?" Luke interrupted, his voice gruff with frustration. "More doom and gloom. I'll do the talking. You can stay behind the scenes. Pay the bills, or flutter some paper."

"I'll be glad when you're gone, you know," Harvey said, leaning forward and posing his elbows on his oak desk, confidentially. His posture reminded Luke that every time, Harvey won and Luke ended up doing something he hated.

* * *

"No chance of another contract?"

"None," the Chair was polite but firm. "You're good, but we simply don't have the money. It's not just the Department of History the whole university has been hit by these budget cuts. No three-year teaching contracts. Not even a one-year one." Artemisia found her eyes had crept over the Chair's shoulder, to the bridge beyond. The coathanger shape of the bridge dragged her mind ahead of her body.

"Back to Australia, then." Artemisia stood up, ready to leave at once.

"There's no hurry. Your visa gives you a bit of time."

"I have that research booked in France." Artemisia was almost apologetic. "If I'm to go back to Melbourne straight from there, I'll need to rearrange." She moved towards the door, determinedly dragging leaden feet.

"We could fix something…help you get research contracts, see if the London group are taking editors…it will only take a few weeks."

"I wish I could take you up on that." Artemisia turned fully back and smiled, her face brittle.

"Damn it, woman, sit down!" Artemisia's obedient feet lost their lead and she returned and sat. "Now tell me what's changed. Two weeks ago you would have turned this into a career opportunity."

"It's my sister."

The Chair nodded. "She needs you?"

"She needs money. Her cancer's returned and all that the experts can promise is that they'll spend a great deal of money."

"And?"

"Lucia says she'll cope. She says she'll never forgive me if I don't finish my research project. I'm so nearly done, and I've a grant to cover it."

"But if you stay past that last bit of research, then you're not earning any money to send her."

"Right. If I go back sooner, I can get a job as a check-out chick or something. I can help."

"That email address you use for friends, it's still active?" Artemisia nodded. Every microsecond, her face became tighter with tears. She just wanted to hide in the toilets until they passed. "Check it every day. Every single day. And if anything comes up, I'll send it."

"There's not much of a chance."

"Not much," the Chair was fierce. "But whatever there is, whatever I can find, I'll send it your way."

"Thank you," Artemisia said, her voice still under pressure from tears, but her face able to open up just enough to give a minute smile. She was so near the edge that talking to even the most well-intentioned person was a strain.

She didn't stop at her office. She didn't stop for milk. She went straight home and shut herself in the bathroom.

* * *

Luke walked into the tiered lecture hall, a sheaf of papers fluttering. The pages were more for decoration than anything else, like his speckled beard and the slight narrowing of his eyes and the use of his full name. It was what he would say that was important. The tremor of the papers showed how he felt, deep inside to the world, he was magnificently confident.

Only half the seats were full. The doors were closed. Security guards slumped outside, bored.

Luke had a flair for the dramatic. He stood and looked out and up, those slightly narrowed eyes roaming the hall, making it seem as if he were noting everyone there. It was the smile that caused the room to go quiet. It was a big smile. An intensely happy smile. A smile that suggested great things.

"We've done it," he said. "Timebot is no longer with us in our present. It's somewhere near the end of the Medieval Warm Period, in Languedoc. It triggered the beacon exactly on schedule. The time, ladies and gentleman, is right."

There was a silence. The news was expected, but somehow beyond comprehension.

"Do we know the date?" A lone voice in the wilderness. It didn't break the silence: it confirmed its intensity.

"All we know is that Timebot arrived safely, unpacked, and set up the beacon. We can go to that place, that time whenever we want. We have a platform. The exotic matter at the far end is stable and we can trigger wormholes. We can maintain a wormhole for almost half an hour.

"Now," he continued, "we're ready for humans to travel. We want to go soon. Very soon. The set-up party and all the equipment will follow immediately after we have the power for a second trip. We're stripping the State of Victoria and half of New South Wales of their energy. If everything continues to run smoothly, we should have four people in Medieval Languedoc by this time tomorrow night."

He was grandstanding. Everyone present was part of the project and knew all the details. Except that it had worked: a machine had travelled backwards in time and space. Across the world and into the past. It had unpacked itself into a platform that accepted teleportation data and had reconstructed itself perfectly, almost every time. Now anyone could travel.

A moment later, Luke regretted having given into his desire to make that extra flourish, to present that swirl of information. It had broken the intensity of the moment. Worse, it had created a space for The Ancient Mariner. The old man was about to speak. From the front row. Luke could see it. He couldn't stop it. The hushed silence changed from awe to the verge of laughter. The Ancient Mariner was an institution: brilliantly gifted and there, him and his long white beard, forever, at the precise moment when he should not be.

"And then?"

Everyone looked at the Ancient Mariner.

He was an older man with a riveting gaze. He was the unwelcome guest at the wedding. The one that was there because the university had insisted. His voice, as ever, was querulous. He was demonstrating to the whole room that he felt, as ever, neglected. "And then?" he repeated.

"Sir," Luke's voice was respectful but the way his right shoulder jutted forward just a little showed he still owned the universe. He intentionally echoed his voice, like a boombox through his ribcage. *That should make it clear. This is my day. My year. My journey.* "I can go through the process again, if you want."

"Not the process. I understand the damn process. I helped with the maths, if you'll remember. I just want to know the order of things."

"If everyone else will bear with me?" A murmur of agreement from the floor.

"All right, then. Timebot has gone back to the end of the Medieval Warm Period. We send the set-up team in two days. Four people and all the equipment. The first humans to travel backwards in time. A triumph for humanity. They will have three months to prepare. Three of them will come on home. Cormac Smith will remain with the rest of the team. He'll be back-up. The handyman, if you will. The first team is almost ready, in fact, just got to sign a few more forms. The specialists also have to sign a few more forms, but they have a bit of time up their sleeve for briefing and so forth. The second team is full of knowledgemakers. Let's see, we have an astronomer, a biologist, an atmospheric scientist, two agricultural experts, two historians, and, of course, myself. Once we get together, seven hundred years ago, we'll have serious science."

"Travelling seven hundred years into the past isn't serious science?"

"Trust me," Luke said, his eyes shining, "Travelling seven hundred years is just the beginning. Our research program will change the world."

* * *

The Montpellier archive had closed early, so Artemisia had taken a bus to see an abbey and its town. Artemisia looked up at the twelfth century castle, her tatty twentieth century handbag ironically hiding her natty twenty-first century mobile phone. The ruins were from her kind of period, but not of her kind of place. Jagged edges at the top of the pile of rocks were all that were left. It was as if the craggy peak had a crown. Those edges loomed over the old town in its valley. Cast its old shadow. Spiked. Wary. River below, castle above and abbey dominating it all, gently, from within the town. Greens and creams and the sound of wind and water and the streets lined with the Middle Ages. She recognised the shape of some doorways and the curve of the road. Even though it wasn't the region she knew, the buildings still had the right feel to them.

It was a bit like coming home. Home was faded and exhausted and crumbly, but comforting.

* * *

As Artemisia walked into the abbey of Gellone to pay her respects to the bones of Saint William, her path crossed with someone else's. They didn't see each other, for they were removed in time. Guilhem left as Artemisia arrived, however. He had already paid his respects to his dead kin and was ready to make his home on the slopes of the town and do his duty to his family and to give up his dreams of Jerusalem. He wasn't ready to let go of his anger. Not yet. It showed in the size of his stride and in the way his gaze disrespectfully refused to lower itself before his seniors.

Timebot's presence in Guilhem's 1305 had created a synchrony between the two people.

Chapter Two: Solving Problems

"We can't do everything," Sylvia said. "These contractors simply won't be able to deliver on time."

Luke frowned. "Harvey warned us about this. If it's money" His office was big and full of sunshine. Whiteboards everywhere. Formulae everywhere. Papers everywhere, even on the stands of the fake tree ferns. The scent was plastic and paper, old dust and faint ammonia. It smelled as if Luke had lived in it forever, put down institutional roots. He had not. Luke had moved to Melbourne three years before, specifically for this project.

"Not money." Dr Sylvia Smith's voice was firm, despite its softness. "There were problems with the orders, with follow-through when personnel dropped out. And the contractors, as I said. The ones dealing with the scientific databases. All of them. Every single library supplier was waiting for confirmation from us about one element or another. Our history people walked out. Some of our scientists walked out. Follow-up never happened. This means that the library suppliers are running late. We can prioritise and get more than we have, but not everything. Not in time. There's no way around it. We can't change the launch date: our expedition will be short."

"Not of supplies."

"No, the Director was wrong. Supplies are mostly local and are all clear. It's the databanks. Everything electronic. Mostly for research and reference."

"How bad is it?"

The two sat down and spent an unhappy hour trying to work out what was most important. What could be improvised. Which project relied on what sort of electronic material. How the whole thing could be made to work.

"That's most of it, then. Not so bad after all." Sylvia was cheerful; her own research program was completely covered. Sylvia's voice communicated her confidence. "If we hire a couple of students, get them to download publicly available material for the next four days, not even the library will suffer."

"I wish you'd brought this to my attention earlier, Dr Smith." Luke turned formal when he was unhappy.

Sylvia just let it flow over her. "We'll manage."

* * *

Artemisia found a café that had wifi. She set up her Skype account. She ordered a drink and waited for the call from Australia. It didn't take long for Harvey to appear on her computer screen.

"Sorry to bother you. I was looking for you. I was given your email by your Department Chair," he had explained. "It's been a long time. I wanted to talk."

That was why, here in Nîmes, Artemisia was nattering on the net. The Chair had already let her know all this, by email. Not a job, she had commented, but it might lead to something. Artemisia couldn't take anything seriously today, not this chat and not France. Her mind was in a hospital in Australia, recovering from the last round of chemotherapy. She had perfected polite babble, however, and it helped her cover her hurt.

"My research was half an excuse. I came here on a kind of pilgrimage," Artemisia explained, "Then I discovered this is the country of heroes. I came to see Saint William and Saint Gilles and found that William was a lot more than that. It was wonderful. This whole region has been special for a thousand years. More."

"You're going to stay and explore, now you've finished your research?"

"Can't," Artemisia almost sounded regretful. "I'm in between jobs, as you know, and my sister needs medical care. I'm back to Melbourne to lose my academic career as quickly as I can. Sorry — that sounded flippant. It's just that losing a career is such a strange thing to do."

"Do you want to?"

"Go back to Melbourne? Of course. It's where my sister is. Where I have contacts and can find a job. In a whacking great hurry."

"To dump your career? I might be able to help you avoid that. I need a medievalist. Right away."

Artemisia looked across at the stranger on her screen. Until this moment he hadn't been a stranger. He'd been a friendly voice in a foreign land. He'd been an old flame she'd almost forgotten whose email had popped up in her in-box the day before.

His face was serious. He didn't look as if he was asking questions that would undress her soul.

Artemisia took a sip of her citron pressé and the tartness of it and the golden light undid the floodgates. She told Harvey everything. About her sister fighting cancer, about there being no permanent jobs in her field anywhere and none at all in Australia and not even a contract job around for months. "Who needs an expert on Anglo-Norman and Norman hagiography?" she asked, denying the obscurity of her knowledge with her face and hands even as she claimed it with her tongue, paying no attention to Harvey's reassurance that he had a job for her. He was a scientist there was no job. Besides, he wasn't the sort of person to race into employing anyone without due planning and calculation.

Melbourne would give her some sort of job, any sort of job, and those experimental medicines would be paid for and her sister might survive.

She suddenly realised that Harvey was a stranger. Three dates ten years ago. Several friends in common. She felt raw.

"I must go," Artemisia said. "It was lovely to talk to you again. Sorry about the confession."

"You needed it," Harvey still had his sunshine-laden, sympathetic voice. It had, perhaps, grown warmer with age. She would date him again, if life were different. "When do you arrive? What flight?" She told him and they left it at that. Normally Artemisia would have reflected on Harvey's words, but she really didn't care.

After she left that odd conversation, she went to the Roman temple. Its perfect proportions would soothe her, as they had last time she passed this way. There was nowhere to pray. The temple was denuded and full of tourists. She knew this. She also knew that the shape of stone would be gentle on her, make life easier. Telling Harvey had been a release, in a way, but not the one she needed.

After the temple and its perfect proportions, she collected her baggage and made her way to Montpellier, where she left her hire car at their bright little airport and took the first part of the wearisome journey back to home and her sister.

* * *

Two tired days later and she emerged from Immigration. "Home," she thought. "I'm home."

"A taxi," was her next thought, when she took in the white brightness of Tullamarine and the damp chill of Melbourne in winter. "Get home fast. Damn the cost."

"Can I offer you a ride to Carlton? It's still Carlton, isn't it?" asked Harvey. Artemisia was too tired to be astonished. She merely accepted. She accepted everything he said and everything he suggested. That was how she agreed to go to Saint-Guilhem-le-Désert twice in a subjective two-month period. She hadn't quite processed, even once she accepted, that the second visit was for nine months, and that it started sometime in the early fourteenth century and that she couldn't quit if it didn't work out. All she knew was that Harvey had promised her work as an historian.

Artemisia was mainly concerned about her sister. The initial sum she'd be paid would more than cover the experimental treatment Lucia's doctor recommended, and would still leave enough to outfit Artemisia herself for her little expedition. Her main feeling was relief.

She went to see her sister the first thing the next morning. Lucia was at home, in bed, looking determinedly cheerful.

"You know," Artemisia said, "you don't fool me."

"I don't?" Lucia was amused.

Artemisia took a long look at her sister, slender beyond sanity, pale as a vampire, hair sharply short. She didn't look too bad, but this was because she was between treatments. Resting up so that her cure didn't kill her.

"I know what you get up to in your spare time."

"What spare time?" Lucia challenged her sister.

"The time when you're not colouring your hair that unnatural brown. The time when you're masquerading as...as..."

"Your imagination is failing you, my life."

"Jetlag," Artemisia claimed. It had to be jetlag. It couldn't be because she had just noticed that Lucia's infamous eloquent hands had been silenced by exhaustion. "Which reminds me, I need to give you your presents now."

"Afraid I might die on you," Lucia mocked, her voice gentle.

"I got a job. Nine months incommunicado. So you get your presents now."

"What sort of job is that?" Lucia's voice was full of wonder.

"A completely bizarre one. But it pays a lot."

"No," said her sister.

"Yes. It will make me happy."

"But your career…"

"Would you believe that I'm participating in a scientific project as a bloody medievalist? And it's only nine months. The worst it will do is give me a break from undergraduates. If you won't let me pay for that damn treatment, I'll say 'no' and get a job as a…"

"Check-out chick," Lucia supplied. "You always say 'check-out chick.'"

"Well, I will."

"You'll write to me in the nine months."

"Can't."

"Then I need my presents, now!" They smiled at each other, remembering the same demand over many years of birthdays. At Easter, she always ate her eggs first. At Christmas she always opened the first package. Nine months would be hard on her, but Artemisia saw her sister lean her head back as if her neck was no longer strong enough to hold it and she wished that she could know that Lucia would get through. This is why she was going to the past. Not because of the excitement, but because she wanted her sister to be able to hold up her head, walk down the street, tear into wrapping paper, talk with her hands: she wanted her sister to live.

* * *

After she had seen Lucia, Artemisia went to see her new boss. She was covered in jetlag. What Professor Mann had to say was hardly reassuring, but whenever she thought she might back down, she remembered Lucia's head, resting against the back of the couch. Mann talked about the great science and the progress for humankind. He extolled the physics and the crack team of scientists at both ends and the government support.

"And the history?" Artemisia prompted.

"It's all history," Mann said, expansively.

"And what if we change the people in the region? What if we change history?"

"It's all covered. We're living in a cave system," he said, carefully, as if to a first year student. "Self-sufficient. No impact.

Troglodytes. Our protocols cover everything outside those caves. History will be fine."

Artemisia accepted, but not because of Mann's reassurances. She accepted because she wanted Lucia to live.

Chapter Three: Assembling the Team

"So," Luke ran his hand through his hair for the fifty-first time. "We can't get anyone else?"

"Lucky to get the people we have," Konig said, picked up his briefcase and left Luke's office. Not a word of farewell. Ben Konig assumed that they knew each other well enough. That he could take liberties. "Don't know how we even *have* a historian, to be honest."

We, Luke mouthed after him, his mental powers so exhausted that he couldn't even think the word across the desk Konig's French Government support had nearly cost them the expedition. Ben Konig didn't deserve to be 'we' he was the evil other.

Luke blamed the evil other in its amorphous mass for the formidable clauses that had scared half the expedition away after training, so close to departure. Everyone had known the risks: those clauses had created confusion.

Then Professor Theodore Lucas Mann realised something. He prided himself on not being petty; he was a big man and had a vast soul. Sometimes, however, he allowed a smallness into his munificent existence. Professor Theodore Lucas Mann leaned back in his big chair and he smiled.

Not everyone had signed the waivers and forms. Not everyone had been able to get to the briefings. One of the team members was going into the past gloriously unprepared by the bureaucrats. If it weren't the night before the most momentous day in human history, Luke would be thinking about the expedition and the need for preparation and would snap his fingers and call Dr Artemisia Wormwood in and have her working the whole night long, making up lost ground. He was so annoyed with Konig, and he so longed for the last sleep in his own bed, that he merely copied the briefing to his data file for transmission back.

Wormwood could be briefed *in situ*. And Konig could be blamed for not having ensured that she had signed his stupid French forms. Luke went home for one last night with his partner.

* * *

Artemisia lay in bed, thinking about her situation. *Living underground, in a cave. And the local saint is, of course, Benedict. Patron saint of speleologists.* This was the first thing she'd checked. Straight after she'd transferred almost all of her advance to her sister's bank account. Before she'd bought the things the expedition shopping list had suggested.

The saint. His patronage. Not enough time to check out the state of his hagiography, but there was a library waiting for her in the Middle Ages. It was promised.

She had a sudden urge to check Benedict's saint day. Something was niggling. Something that Professor Theodore Lucas Mann had said about them knowing the locals and timing the start to fit local customs. He thought he knew everything, this man in charge.

He knew something, she soon discovered. *It's the vigil of Benedict,* thought Artemisia. *Tonight is my last night in the world I know and tomorrow the first day in the world I've studied and which I don't really know, not at all. The only thing I know about it, for certain, is that Lucia won't be there.*

* * *

With the exception of Professor Mann, the group was assembled along with the possessions they would carry. It was the first time the group had been together, and even now it lacked Cormac Smith and Luke Mann. It was in a conference room at Melbourne University. A nothing-room that could have been anywhere on the planet, furnished with nothing-chairs devoid of all specific nature. Smith had been on the far side for three months, living ancient time while the others lived modern. They were still living modern, but were dressed in clothes that were suitable for nine months underground, their backpacks leaning ready by the door. Poised.

"We only have twenty-five minutes, and that includes provisioning," a harried young man explained. His hair was white and rumpled and he looked thirteen, but the nametag he wore suggested he had a doctorate. "Wait here. Don't leave. Be ready to move quickly."

The group of strangers looked around at each other. Artemisia knew what she saw. Aliens. Scientists. People she would live in a hole underground with for long enough to drive them all mad. Her late night thoughts had been along these lines and the crowd she was looking at was not reassuring.

Artemisia hated meeting new people. It took her a while to relax and to get to know anyone. *It will pass,* she told herself. *It's just nerves.*

She'd met Mann the day before. "Call me Luke," he'd said, jovially. He'd called her Artemisia once and Wormwood twice, not bothering to ask which she preferred. It almost made her regret the name change eight years ago. But without the name change, she would still have family and Lucia was the only family she was willing to own.

The harassed young man passed around a sheet of paper with names on it. Suddenly each of them was looking up and down and across, trying to work out who was whom.

"This'll keep us busy till the time comes," joked a tall lanky bloke with the most shaven scalp and the most soulful brown eyes Artemisia had ever seen. "I'm Geoff." Geoff Murray, meteorologist and atmospheric scientist. *Must be my age,* Artemisia realised. *Or a couple of years older.* Like the harassed young man, he didn't look it. He lounged lazily. She envied him his temperament. She herself was wound to almost breaking point.

"Artemisia," she added, quickly, then just as quickly looked down at her paper, hiding behind her hair, like a teenager. Life in fast-forward was not comfortable.

"Pauline," an older voice added. "But call me Doc." Cook, it said on the sheet, Pauline Adamson. Artemisia looked up at the woman, in her sixties with shoulder length hair, beautifully kept, and wondered where the nickname came from.

"Tony," said an Asian Australian, short and deep-voiced. He was a plant genome expert. His hair was almost as non-existent as Geoff's, but not quite. He had the most alert gaze Artemisia had ever seen his eyes soaked everything in. It was almost uncomfortable.

"I'm Ben," and a rather gorgeous man in his mid-thirties gave a small bow. Dark hair and pale grey eyes. Germanic cheekbones. A bit Prince Valiant. He obviously knew he was gorgeous, too. Ben Konig, the sheet said, biologist and zoologist. Whatever did they need a zoologist for?

"Dr Sylvia Smith," the last woman said, abruptly. She was so very small. Compact and pretty and even winsome, with a soft voice and a gentle manner and sweetly waving short hair. The sort of woman who mostly got what she wanted, Artemisia guessed, noticing how the soft and gentle manner had switched on when Smith realised she was under observation. She was Mann's offsider, apparently, also a planetary astronomer and a geologist. More power to her. Though why she needed a title when everyone else was happy with first names or nicknames...maybe it was something to do with the manner. *I have to try to stop disliking her. Disliking someone at first sight will make it difficult to work in a closed environment. I have to stop disliking her.*

Artemisia sighed. Apart from that sigh silence prevailed.

"Hell," said Ben Konig, when the silence went on for too long, "Just because most of us haven't met before, doesn't mean"

At that moment the door opened. "It's time," said the young man, harassment transformed into a jubilant grin. "Time for Botty to beam you down to the Middle Ages!"

Chapter Four: New Residents in the Languedoc, March 1305

"Sir," said Guilhem, formally, and gave the proper bow. "My respects." He didn't remove his hat. Not quite polite, but sufficient. Not a hint of homage, for homage he would not give. Enough courtesy to show how reluctant those respects were and how he hated being made to travel from the back of beyond to report to a commander whose knowing look showed that he was going to exploit the politics of it all.

The Templar commander was a shade more polite. Only a shade. The big man was obviously not yet certain that he wanted to have Guilhem reporting to him, much less to recruit him.

Guilhem smiled to himself. The recruitment was his own idea, to push away some other notions his aunt had. He was playing on the concept his aunt possessed about his profound spirituality, based largely on the emotions he had brought back from that pilgrimage to Jerusalem.

Guilhem was not above using his own foibles to save his skin. A year or so in a hermit hole in the middle of nowhere was better than marrying a foul-mouthed turd or entering a monastery. If it redeemed his honour in the eyes of the family, then he would be satisfied. If he chose to join the Templars, then his uncle would be satisfied. Someone was going to come out of this happy.

There was no report to give this time. Just a wary game to be played, setting things up for the rest of the year. Guilhem intended to delay all the encounters with his new Templar friend and to give him as little information as possible.

His new Templar friend wasn't stupid. This year of considering joining the Templars and licking his wounds was going to be lonely and fraught with politics. Guilhem could tell that from the way Bernat kept an eye on him even as he turned away to talk to a servant. They both had to be careful not to make enemies of the other. Guilhem didn't need more enemies at this moment. And Bernat? No-one wanted to make an enemy of someone from Guilhem's family.

For the whole meeting, neither was humble and neither offended the other. It was a very courteous and cold dance.

Guilhem set out with his packhorse and his poor-man's palfrey. He wanted to leave Pézenas which was a misery of a place, despite the nice, plump partridge he had recently devoured and be well clear of its Templar Commanderie, because he wasn't sure about what had happened and he needed distance to think. Also, he wanted to travel. Ever since his pilgrimage, travel had become easier than finding solutions. Nevertheless, he didn't really want to return to that hermit hole in the middle of nowhere his aunt had consigned him to. It was inglorious and unmanly and, frankly, dull.

Guilhem was an experienced traveller. If a brigand had encountered him and had overcome his sword and dagger, Guilhem might not have been able to rip the hind leg off a pack animal as his namesake had done and defend himself with that, but he would have coins as long as he had even a single item of clothing. He'd learned the hard way to secrete coins everywhere. Also inglorious, but practical. It had been easier when he'd been a man with an army or a man with his peers.

He spent much of the long path from Pézenas to Saint-Guilhem-le-Désert hating his aunt.

Sometimes he rode his horse and sometimes he led both horse and packhorse. *I look like a dealer with a string of animals on long leads.* When he reached Saint-Guilhem and passed through the boundaries, the turns into his street made the packhorse all but invisible. *All the townsfolk will see,* Guilhem thought, *is a man and his paltry animal, walking together across the narrow path at the end of the road, with the shadow of a half-castle behind him and the powerful menace of the abbey in the valley.*

The abbey could swallow him if he let it, just as the Commanderie could see him eaten up in service to the Templars. But what were his options? He'd burnt many bridges when he had spoken out three years ago. He'd done worse since. This was reparation and penance and a possible future. It felt like disaster.

He reached his home. His own house. He was welcomed by his people. His own people, no matter what his aunt said. He smiled at the three of them and gave them small gifts he'd bought in Pézenas. They were his, even if all they did was clean his house and feed him and take care of his equipment and, at this moment in time, bring him water for a bath. *Not everything in life has to be noble.*

After he'd bathed and after he'd eaten, he collected his coins and his own trinkets. He'd bought an astrolabe, even though he had no idea how to use it. It was beautiful and graceful and inscribed with incomprehensible flowing words and he enjoyed holding it and peering round it at the sky. It had cost rather more than he should spend.

Money might bear thinking upon soon, since along with the loss of glory in war came the loss of spoils in war and his aunt was parsimonious in sending him income from his northern holdings. There were other possibilities. Not yet. Nothing yet. Guilhem hated the long path, the slow wait.

He added the astrolabe to his Saint-Jacques shell and his blessed oil from Jerusalem and the bone that the seller swore was from a virgin martyr. He kissed the bone, even though he was positive the seller was a liar. One must be careful, walking this earth. Careful and courteous and calm.

* * *

"I'm here." Artemisia was surprised. One moment stepping onto a glowing platform in a big, empty room and the next moment standing on another glowing platform in a very crowded storeroom. She'd never seen so many boxes and whitegoods in her life.

"Not bad," said a male voice from behind her. "I'm writing down what everyone says for posterity, and 'I'm here' is certainly better than 'What a dump' and 'It's full of stuff.' Not as good, but, as 'Oh, God, why did I do this?'"

"I should get down," Artemisia said uncertainly, turning to look at the gentleman who spoke. He was big and muscular and full of smiles. His voice ought to have been baritone. Instead it was a wispy tenor. His hair was messy and his clothes looked lived-in.

"Cormac," he said, holding out his free hand. Artemisia shook it, because that was what he seemed to want. Once Cormac had shaken her hand, he put down his notepad and he helped her off the platform.

"Artemisia Wormwood," she said, feeling the name was redundant.

"That really is your name?" This man was like an inquisitive puppy.

"I chose it myself," she smiled up at him. "And I'm the last, aren't I?"

"Watch," Cormac said. He turned them both around and they looked at the platform blinking out. "I wanted to see it properly this time. Last time was too rushed," he confided. "They told me the light isn't intrinsic, but it helps us know if we have a live wormhole. Or whatever it is that got us here."

"We have everything, by the looks of it. Except people."

"The rest of the crew's unpacking. I assigned rooms on the Prof's orders, by discipline, to prevent squabbles. We meet in the dining room once you're all done."

"I guess I'd better take my stuff." Artemisia looked around.

"Some of it came three months ago," Cormac began. "You'll find"

"I wasn't on the project three months ago."

"Oh," said Cormac. "That's why I didn't recognise your name." He nodded to himself. "I'll rustle you out the basics, then. We have spares and spares of the spares, so you'll be fine." While he led her around boxes and crates and storage containers until they came to a second room, he kept up a constant dribble of chat. "D'you know why you're here? I mean"

"Why not the person on your list?" Artemisia helped him out to cover the awkwardness. "There were last minute losses. No-one's told me why the others resigned, but I'm replacing one of them."

"You're double the value, heh?"

Artemisia didn't know what to say. She looked down, to break eye contact. Underneath the floor was wire mesh below it was pale stone.

"We're standing on solid rock!" Artemisia couldn't help sounding pleased.

"I know. Isn't it great! Sacred ground, you know. Borrowed time. Winds of change. All of that. Don't drop anything through the mesh, but it's a bugger getting stuff out."

Cormac methodically collected bedding and a couple of towels and a little bag of toiletries. Also a mirror. "I'll find you other stuff later. This'll set you up." He led the way down cold corridors, curved limestone on one side, a pool of darkness above, light partition wall on the other. "Don't go down that way." Artemisia couldn't tell how serious he was, as he jerked his head towards an unlit tunnel.

"Why not?" asked Artemisia, half-expecting cave bears.

"It's mud, mud all the way," said Smith. "Once you go down just a little. And by go down, I mean down. It gets really sticky."

"So we're living in the dry section."

"Above the big wet."

"We should call it Darwin down there, then," Artemisia joked.

"Not a bad idea," nodded Smith. "Be careful down there, but. Don't drown. Gotta preserve the ecosystem also can't leave your bones behind." They started moving again. Small lights at regular intervals made the whole surprisingly pleasant. The temperature was a little chill, but not bad, either. Fluffy slippers and warm socks, Artemisia thought, thankful she'd packed both. "You're one of the historians, right? This must be yours."

"I thought I was the only historian."

"Ah," said Cormac. "More changes." He nodded, amused. Then he opened a door and gestured, "Your home for the next nine months, ma'am. Be grateful you're the only historian you get an empty room between yourself and the evil scientists." Artemisia laughed. Cormac looked thoughtful. "Let me give you a hand setting up. Theo expects us to do things instantly. Like the army."

"Theo?"

"The Prof."

"Oh. Luke."

"Theo," Cormac was insistent.

"Why Theo?" While they were talking, Cormac made the bed and Artemisia unloaded the contents of her two packs into the single chest of drawers. A hook for the mirror above the chest of drawers. It was a very Spartan room. Limestone on one side, with a single bed hard against it. A canopied single bed. Iron. Cormac had draped a cotton spread over the canopy for warmth, presumably, since there was no heating in sight.

Everything else was white partition or soft cream tile underfoot. Not mesh, thank goodness. Artemisia hung the mirror and pulled out her little bowl and put her earrings in it. Now it felt like home.

"He called me McGyver. Until he stops calling me that, his

name's Theo."

"I bet McGyver takes. You're the guy who can do everything, and you have 'Mac' in your name."

"Smith?"

"Cor*mac*."

The others were in the dining room. It was a very odd space. The kitchen was on one side, slotted into the limestone like a child's toy. When Artemisia looked up, she saw frayed rock and half-formed stalactites and a symphony of light and curve. When she looked across, she saw metal and fake veneer. At the table, it felt like a real dining room except that the air reflected its passage through the stone. Tomblike. The scent of calcite was tempered by the smell of bad coffee.

Luke was drawing directly on the table. He half-noticed Artemisia and Cormac and he gestured them to sit down.

"Welcome all," said Sylvia brightly, the perfect second-in-command. "We're getting right into it. Luke's already working on data the transit spawned. That's the big project, of course. The rest of you are with the global warming and environmental science mob. And I'm refining delta T, of course." Most of the team nodded sagely. Artemisia had no idea what delta T was, but this was not the time to ask. Besides, she found herself the surprised recipient of a cup of instant coffee. Foul stuff, sweetened beyond belief, but she nodded thanks to Pauline, who had deposited it in front of her. "God," Sylvia said, her right hand dragging her pretty hair out of shape. "I'm so nervous. This is so big. Can we just skip the introduction and set up our computers?"

"Fine with me," said Geoff Murray, obviously amused.

"Go for it," said Luke, waving his hand again. He hadn't once stopped drawing on the white tabletop. Artemisia caught a glimpse of impossible mathematical formulae as she edged past.

She wondered if she'd ever feel less lost in the Middle Ages. She thought she was coming to her intellectual home, but there was nothing homely about this arrival. In fact, the only saving grace so far was Cormac Smith and his sense of humour.

"Can we talk about schedules first?" Ben Konig's voice was persuasive and his manner apologetic. Luke waved his hand in vague agreement and those who had begun to stand up, sat down again, their faces denying that movement.

It was different, when Konig stood before them, explaining how their work fitted together and how the seasons would impact the schedule. It confirmed that they were in the Middle Ages.

* * *

The next morning was when the project really began.

After breakfast, the whole team assembled in the big room that served as the main office space. Artemisia blinked twice as she entered the office. By daylight it looked much larger. So much stone. And golden light pouring through the massive triangular opening. Light and warmth and an open plan office. Hardly troglodytic.

"This is Day One," announced Luke, stroking his beard and leaning forward into the light. "St Benedict's Day. March 21, 1305. We're in the hills near Saint-Guilhem-le-Désert."

Artemisia noticed that the gorgeous Dr Konig winced a little when Luke pronounced 'Désert' in pure Strine.

"We have a calendar that we'll fill with our projects," and Luke handed it to the now straight-faced Ben Konig, who stuck it on one of the big office dividers that passed for internal walls. "Dr Wormwood will brief us on current history on the computer system, for easy reference. The history is important because those people outside are the past us. We won't interfere with them and we won't touch their lives. Dr Wormwood is our resource for enabling this. Lots happening in town. Lots happening here. Let's keep them separate. Remember your contracts and your ethics briefings. Always keep in mind that we are guests in this foreign time. We do our work and when we're not working, we're here," he gestured back to the rest of the cave, "underhill. Like hobbits. We're neutral observers and we never, ever touch people's lives." He gave them a moment to appreciate the importance of this statement, then he moved on.

"All the rest of you will update your data files regularly and we'll send data back monthly. Konig'll put the dates for transmission on the calendar: these dates are crucial. There will be actual transfers of goods a third through the project and again at two-thirds. We'll be reprovisioned then. You'll note that we're down one historian, one scientist and one general staff member. Sylvia will handle day-to-day administration, with help from Ben, who is the French Government amongst us," Konig smiled wryly. "Go to McGyver for general needs, and to Doc for medical problems. She can cure everything short of plague. This isn't 1320, or even 1348, so there should be no plague." *My God,* Artemisia thought, *He made a Connie Willis joke.* "When she's not saving you from imminent death, she's our live-in gourmet chef. Sylvia, have I missed anything?"

Sylvia then said what Artemisia thought was a lot of positive nothings about everything. She didn't learn much from it. But then, she didn't have the background and she didn't like Sylvia. This really wasn't fair on Sylvia.

Ben Konig was also ambivalent about Dr Smith, Artemisia suspected, as he spent the whole of her pep talk watching, face inexpressive, arms crossed, leaning against the cold wall of polished limestone. Geoff Murray's feet were tapping and his eyes looking towards his computer terminal.

Tony Dargentueil was in his own world, somewhere deep. His own world; that was funny. Here they were in the past and their agricultural scientist was on another planet entirely.

* * *

Guilhem was fascinated by this land. It was his mother's. He knew it from her stories, but he had never been here. He knew the stories of his namesake as well as he knew the earth underneath his feet, with its dry, crumbly ground and its olives and its twisted pines. Rich in the way his northern kin never understood. Rich in legends and in the farming of the desert, where man didn't live on top of man and the sun was always there, ripening the olives and grapes to rich harvest. That wine and the olive oil were the wealth of the Languedoc. The sunshine on his skin was its gold.

He walked towards the caves, intending to explore. His mother had told him the usual childhood stories. She had said those caves were forbidden and dangerous. She told him stories of the humanlike creatures that lived in the dark under the hill, about lights at night. The uncanny excited him. His feet wanted to carry him to that excitement and search out monsters and secrets, but he firmly turned back. It was too close to Sext.

* * *

Cormac issued torches and led the company on a stumbling tour of the caverns. "Watch your toes and knees," he would say, after someone hit the wall with their knee or a partition with a big toe.

"We couldn't make this bit work. It's got a slope and a bump and a step." He led them up and down and round about, showing them every human-size space in the complex of caves and tunnels. "Our water supply," he'd say, proudly, as they stood over a fissure filled with clear liquid. "Look, it goes on forever. I need a snorkel, but, to find out where forever ends."

"You need to be an intrepid cave explorer," Geoff Murray suggested. Cormac's eyes brightened and the tour continued.

When the team was bewildered by the maze of limestone walls and caverns, Cormac led them to the stores. Artemisia realised that the system wasn't nearly as big as it felt. *It's because it's unfamiliar, and that mesh leads our eyes down to the rock underneath. We feel every footstep. When we've been here a few weeks, the same big space will probably be claustrophobically tiny.*

Cormac handed each of them a pack with the equipment they would need for their specific work.

"This is it?" asked Tony Dargenteuil.

"This is what you need when you go outside. Standard stuff. The computers are set up in your workspace, which you already know and me telling you is stupid but Theo said I had to. So I might as well tell you that your workspace is next to the big opening. The workspace you've already sat down in and worked in," Cormac replied. "Come back for outside clothes separately," he added, as an afterthought. "Some of you were prefitted and some not, so it's easier not to do it all at once."

"Pity," said Pauline, "No displays of naked manhood."

Ben laughed. Every single woman looked at him, with Pauline's comment in mind. *He'll look good in Medieval clothes,* Artemisia thought. *He really is rather splendid. I wonder what he's thinking, though. That laugh was not a conformist laugh.*

From stores they went to the living area. There was one big chair "Specially brought in for Prof. Mann," Smith said, his tone disrespectful. "Be nice to it. It's the only chair like it in the whole world." The others would sit on less sumptuous furniture. Ikea in cane.

"We set this up so you're all facing outwards." Outwards was a small opening that looked onto a twisted tangle of bushes. "The TV screen is solar-powered and this was the best set-up for it. Also, you can pretend there's a view. And you don't have to look at your workspace all the time." The office area was directly behind them, past a rather spectacular stalagmite formation.

"Why is the furniture all cane?" asked Artemisia.

"I hate cane," Tony said, firmly. "Not comfortable."

"Cane burns quickly," Cormac was apologetic. "Less to take back in nine months. Our bums'll get used to it."

Cormac led them back again, through to the dormitory, which was really a wide straight tunnel divided into a narrow corridor and slightly wider rooms. Spartan, but private, was Artemisia's thought the night before, and it was her thought again today.

He was taking them in circles when he could. She laughed to herself. Someone was going to get confused. Possibly the good Dr Smith.

"You already know this," Mac said. "Kitchen and medical area and bathrooms. And toilets. Very Japanese. Also development of waste products for the garden." Cormac was enjoying himself.

"Good," said Tony.

"I really didn't want to know about that," said Sylvia.

"Me neither," agreed Artemisia. Her feet wanted to dance jigs of excitement. They, her feet, knew where she was, even if the rest of her was repressing the understanding.

"You're both wusses. It's very cool and we leave nothing behind us except a fertilised garden bed," Cormac Smith was irrepressible.

Bathrooms were each side of the kitchen. The kitchen/dining area with a little room off the side for medical procedures was Pauline's domain. The caverns weren't the right shape for the use being made of them, unlike the wide tunnel that had been transformed into the dormitory. If she looked at the whole, Artemisia saw a sad case of Gaudi gone wrong: graceful rockflows and astonishingly gentle colour schemes interrupted by mesh walkways and inserts and dividers.

The others were looking at the walls.

"It's melted," Ben Konig commented.

"Very artistic," Geoff Murray agreed.

Artemisia tried to discover which of them was serious. She suspected that they were joking and that the jokes were their way of hiding their fizzle of excitement. She took a look at Sylvia Smith's body language and shut herself up small there was something about that woman that just did that to her. Made her not belong. Like when she visited Lucia, and Mum was there.

The main office had that giant triangular opening. Outside was warmer and brighter. Outside was where the Middle Ages began.

"In our time this was partly bricked up someone lived here in the nineteenth century."

"So we're not the first."

"We're the first, not the only."

It was the work area and the office area and the area with natural light.

"Don't move the tables we need to be stingy with energy. We want to supplement light in this area, not depend on the artificial stuff."

"Unlike that bank of fridges in the storeroom."

"They're different. They've got our frozen comestibles now and will go back with our samples. And they're low energy. Deep cold in the bottom section. They can maintain their temperature for a very long time if the power fails."

Artemisia suddenly realised how much money had gone into this expedition. It made her feel very small, to be the tail end, the afterthought, in something so very big.

They had seen the little indoor waterfall and the twisty tunnels that were too small for habitation. They had seen holes and dips and the never-ending well that was their source of water. The only thing the group hadn't seen was Cormac's toolroom.

"Mine," he said, proprietarily. "Keep out."

Then they returned to the common room yet again for still more briefing, while Pauline got their first main meal together. Every now and then she would pop into the lounge area and ask Cormac for something; apart from that, she seemed already settled.

Artemisia felt even smaller.

Chapter Five: Where Nobody Talks

The space was too small and the outside world too unknown. Above their hilltop, Orion shone, and Canis Minor. There was no Southern Cross.

Each member of the time team did what they could to make things comfortable. This included using the computer to converse. It also included exploring Mac's medieval reproductions. He and Geoff called them 'toys'. Artemisia retaliated by calling him 'Big Mac'. Geoff laughed, Ben looked at her consideringly.

All the girdles being handed out for their outdoors costume had the same clasp.

"Outdoors is all Medieval, all the time," noted Mac, as he distributed them.

"Copper alloy," observed the geologist.

"Looks like it was copied from that Museum of London book," said Artemisia. She noted that the cloak pins, likewise, were all the same: large and circular with a horizontal pin. Whoever commissioned the clothing was short on inventiveness. *One day I'll find out who made these things*, Artemisia thought, *and if they used London models.*

The belts came in two kinds, leather and linen. "Don't make them too tight," said Artemisia. "They go over several layers and you need to hang things from them."

"Things?" Ben Konig was curious.

"Beltknives and stuff. I always think of the belt as the Batman aspect of the Middle Ages. Tighten it with the buckle and let that metal strap end work with gravity to hold the hanging bit straight."

"That's not a useful system," said Luke.

"Well, it is. If you want to take small stuff with you and want your hands free and you're not carrying a bag, then you tie it to your belt."

"That's why they're so tough," said Cormac.

"Yep. Utility-belt tough."

Geoff Murray laughed. He had a nice laugh. It was strange coming out of such a bald head.

Cormac then hauled out shoes for everyone. Most people had been pre-measured, but none fitted Artemisia.

"You'll have to go barefoot," Luke said.

* * *

Father Peire's hand was raised in blessing. He held himself formally, straight, head slightly bowed. It was a declarative statement. What the declarative statement said was that he was not a part of the mess that was still happening on the steps of his church. You could fortify a building against invaders, but you could not fortify it against stupid parishioners. All you could do was bless them and hope that the blessing stuck.

Fiz and his two best friends were the cause of the pile of people who were just now disentangling themselves, with much noise and acrimony. The boys had needled Sibilla about her reluctance to let a pawned brooch return to its owner. Sibilla had pushed Fiz. Fiz had fallen down the steep stairs and had made a great cry. Sibilla had secrets, everyone knew. One didn't jostle in and out of the crowd to tell her those secrets in loud whispers. Not that Sibilla was right to push the boy: he might have broken his neck.

Bona and her small brother stood hand in hand on the street below, watching in wide-eyed astonishment. Peire found it hard to believe that Bona was only a year younger than Fiz. Bona was like her family, quirky, but a good member of the community. Fiz was Fiz and a law unto himself. Peire prayed that the children had not heard what Fiz had whispered so loudly. He suspected they knew. The town was so small that everyone must know, but he could dream of innocence, and hope that theirs would last a little longer.

Father Peire was above, while Berta was below comforting Sibilla. Berta had a self-satisfied look on her face. One reason she was Sibilla's close friend was because Sibilla made her feel superior. Peire thought of a very good sermon that would address Berta's pride and resolved to deliver it, soon. But Berta wouldn't listen. That was the trouble with the seven deadly sins. They took over lives.

Pride was Berta, lust was obviously Sibilla, but what of the others? *SALIGIA*, he thought, and used the mnemonic to call up the seven: superbia, avaritia, luxuria, invidia, gula, ira, acedia. If superbia was Berta and luxuria was Sibilla then gula was Fiz. He would eat anything, that boy. Invidia was himself. He was a rampaging mess of envy. He rather suspected that avarice might be the new knight, Guilhem, who hid his greed behind gift-giving. Or Sibilla again, with her collection of objects that had touched relics. She held onto them all as if they would save her soul. If Guilhem wasn't avarice, then he was wrath. Such an angry young man. That left only sloth. Acedia. He wanted to think that the abbot was guilty of that, but, really, he was not. Berta's husband, then, who no-one ever saw and no-one ever saw working. Berta claimed that he sold her cloth at the fairs, but Pézenas and Montpellier were not here.

Peire's hand, he realised, was still raised. He decided it meant admonition, not blessing. And no-one had noticed. Fiz's outcry and Sibilla's wails absorbed everything. He gave up and went inside, to the cool and dark safety of his big stone church.

A little later and the town was still not dignified.

Berta sat outside her house, right beside the double door, her legs lolling apart as if it were one of those sultry days of summer where dignity was irrelevant. She was fully aware that she looked like a peasant: she was making a point. She could have been inside, working, the big door flung open to drag in the light. She could have been chasing her always-errant husband. Instead she sat in the cold, the wind blowing up her skirts, pretending it was a summer day and that she had all the time in the world and that reputation was not worth a candle.

Guilhem-the-smith passed her and sighed. He didn't say anything, simply nodded politely and doffed his cap. This was not the first time Berta had expressed herself thus. It would not be the last. It would probably take one of the priests to get her to behave with dignity and proper modesty. He sighed again, and walked on by.

His sighs were all Berta had needed. Her face expressionless, she stood up, brushed her skirts down, smoothed them, and straightened her back. Within moments she was her proper self, all restrictions and decorum. She dragged the bench indoors and used the last of the light to finish her weaving.

Berta's timing was perfect. As the smith walked down the street he fell over an argument. *That's the trouble with bent streets*, he thought, as he disentangled himself, *you can't see, and the stone muffles sound.*

He could walk down to check his land in Aniane and there would be no Berta and no messes such as the one that had just given him a bruised left shin. He contemplated moving to their neighbouring town for good, as he mechanically separated the two young men. It was not the first time that the big smith had sorted out a fight, and it would not be the last. He acted without thinking, from separating to scolding to sending the boys on their ways. *The inhabitants of Saint-Guilhem-le-Désert may live in the shadow of the holy abbey,* he thought, *but that doesn't make us holy. Perhaps all the sin the monks vanquish with their prayers creeps out through the garden gate and into us. Especially into the young ones and the women of a certain age.*

Friendly, the folks of his hometown were, and kind, but unruly. Self-willed. Impossible.

* * *

"Technically," Artemisia interrupted, "we're not even speaking Old French in 1305. This is the start of the glorious period of Middle French." She was trying hard to find a polite way to express her complete dismay. While the theory was that no-one would meet locals, the reality was that someone could run into one at any time. Until this moment, she had not realised that none of the team had language training. None. It was inconceivable.

"Frenchly, my dear," said Luke, jovial but not pleased, "I don't give a damn."

"Except that it's a good idea that people learn. Unless language training was one of the things I missed?"

"It's not necessary. We won't be mixing with the natives. It'll interfere with the research." The superiority of the scientist at work.

Artemisia argued, but Luke refused to change his mind. She wasn't to know that he had never successfully learned a foreign language in his life. It was an area of vulnerability and he would not admit it. The decision about languages had been his, from the start, and he was sticking to it.

* * *

Guilhem met Guilhem. Guilhem-the-smith felt that it was necessary. So many people had said, "There's a new knight with your name. Here in the town. Not one of the abbot's boys. You should speak with him." So he did.

This disconcerted Guilhem. He had accepted that his name was common down south, just as Guillaume was up north, but being Guilhem-the-knight made him uncomfortable. His name should stand alone, a touch exotic, referring to himself.

He was also disconcerted to discover the importance of a blacksmith. Guilhem-the-smith was the person who others thought should meet the newcomer and serve as a conduit between himself and them; he was someone around whom things revolved. In short, he was of rank. This explained perhaps the coldness at the castle and the disdain at the abbey. It explained how the world operated in this little valley. His contact point was Guilhem-the-smith, since he himself had not made the proper approaches to one of the priests.

Guilhem didn't like it. He showed his dislike by thinking of himself as himself he would always be Guilhem and never Guilhem-the-knight.

* * *

Artemisia needed a role; tasks that were hers; legitimate work she could do during normal working hours. At the first briefing, Luke had given her one; at the second, he had taken it away. *Damn it,* she thought rebelliously, *I shall make my own. Carefully, following official guidelines. I shall analyse everyone and everything. And I shall educate.*

She set up a little pro-forma for herself, and she set up a place on the intrawebbed bulletin board and from then on each and every saint's day (which was most days, in 1305) was ornamented with the details of that saint's life. It was like her favourite email list. The re-enactment of those saints' days made her less homesick.

She read Cormac's policy regarding found objects and the logging system he'd set up. She footnoted his note saying that prayer times would be the best times to be out and about. Konig added a curt comment to her footnote, *Dr Wormwood, please provide schedule.*

"It's not that simple," she turned to the next desk and told Konig, to his face. "Prayer times aren't that simple *at all*. Can I be given a few minutes next meeting to explain time measurement?"

Sylvia Smith leaned over from two desks down. She snapped, "This is your job. Just do it. And email it. We don't need chapter and verse only data."

Ben corrected her, his voice black velvet and convincing. "It's her job," he said, slowly, "And I do realise you're second-in-command, but you might wish to take changes in work through me. It affects everyone, each decision like this." He was very polite, almost diffident, but also firm.

Artemisia suspected that Konig didn't give a damn about prayer times. Sylvia Smith had threatened Konig. What use was she, if her work was to be disregarded? Why did they bother bringing an historian if they assumed that historian's stupidity? Besides, data was never, ever *only* data. It had contexts. It didn't select itself. Artemisia talked herself into a giant sulk. It was the easiest way of handling it.

* * *

There was a christening at Saint-Barthelmy's. The most notable thing about it was that everyone was there. For a wonder, the two halves of the town had come together. *It happens*, thought Peire, who was setting an example by bringing his own priestly self into the other church. *It doesn't happen very often, but it happens.*

Saint-Barthelmy had a superior font, he had to admit, even though in every other respect Saint-Laurent was the better church. Saint-Barthelmy wasn't fortified, and one couldn't stand tall on the high steps and watch congregants walking up those steps and symbolically attain the heights. The font, however, he had to admit, was special. Red stone on top and dark stone underneath even in the black church (for it stood in shadow at this hour not, perhaps, the most auspicious time of day to celebrate the sacrament) it was visible.

Peire noticed Fiz and his friends giggling, and frowned. What were they up to this time? They were looking at the font. If this were his church, he would investigate, but all he could do was wait for events to unfurl. He hated helplessness.

All went well, until the baptised baby was brought into a ray of sunlight. At this moment it became obvious that Fiz and his friends had taken dye from Berta's cloth workshop and had added enough to the holy water to turn the baby's face undeniably green. A particularly vile yellowish-green. Peire wished he could have that pilgrim back who had told the story of green children and could give him a penance worth remembering.

Father Louis didn't identify the culprits. *He's sometimes blessed, and sometimes blessed with stupidity,* reflected Peire. In the end, both priests and two townsfolk bailed the water from the font and washed the red stone thoroughly. It wasn't easy, in the shadow, to see if the dark red was clean, so they scrubbed everything twice.

While they did that, the whole town watched, amused. While they watched, they gossiped. It was noted by several that Father Louis had been sleeping with Sibilla again, and that the public embarrassment of a green baby was suitable recompense.

Guilhem noticed the fuss and the time and the entire boring length of it all and made up his mind that the other church would be his spiritual home while he was in Saint-Guilhem-le-Désert. It was a walk, but it was properly run. There was no-one who would tell him that he should go somewhere else: he was his own man in unexpected ways.

After the water was blessed, the whole christening started over. The child would remain green, but at least it would be green and properly Christian.

* * *

"Don't spoil the sediment," Mac worried. Sylvia was prodding the bottom edge of a cork board into the dirt floor.

"The bulletin board will fall over," she pointed out, "if I don't stabilise it."

"We were given warnings," Mac said. "Don't dig unless it's essential. And even then, don't dig much. You're about to dig a swimming pool."

"I'm not digging. Just needling around a little."

"Lots of people won't speak to you if you needle, ever again."

"Oh," scoffed Sylvia. "Who are these lots of people?"

"Palaeontologists, archaeologists, cavologists, good looking male scientists..."

Sylvia laughed, but she balanced the bulletin board with rockfall. As Mac helped her, Tony walked past, looking for the wide outdoors.

Cormac Smith had given Tony a map. He wanted to go straight to his garden plot and check it out and start work. He walked towards the big triangular opening that led to sunlight and 1305, but he was stopped by Konig.

"Tomorrow is soon enough, Tony. We need to finish here before we can start work off-base." Tony was silently unhappy, obedient in a sad-puppy fashion.

* * *

Fiz was bored beyond anything he would ever, ever remember. The flatness of the pale pilgrim path bored him. The steepness of the cliffs past the vineyards bored him. The little lizard he couldn't catch even though he tried and tried and tried bored him. He was bored right until he could see the castle, looming over the path into the town. The men in the castle couldn't see his face. Not from here. Fiz amused himself by pulling faces at the man whose torso half-showed through the crenellations.

The only person to see those faces was Guilhem-the-silent, busy tending his vines next to the pale path. He looked up at Fiz and then stretched. He watched the boy until the path wound out of sight. Fiz, however, pulled faces right until he reached the curtain wall. Bored is bored.

Fiz broke into a run at the last, because he felt energy well up within him, unable to be suppressed, and because he was impatient to get home. He was impatient to get somewhere, always, but home was the best of all. He owned those streets and the gardens were his for the plundering and the stream was his playground. Nothing would change that.

* * *

26 March. The weather was cold and bleak, but the sky was clear, which was all that mattered. Sylvia had dragged them all to the flatness above the caves in order to take advantage of the new moon and to introduce the team to their new horizons, and explain delta T and how she was improving its accuracy and hoped to refine the description of the processes that governed Earth's rotation. Pauline had cooked an early dinner.

What struck them all was the brightness above.

"It's like being in the desert back home," Geoff said.

"No cities," Ben replied, "and even the village is dark."

"No electricity," Cormac pointed out.

"And this place is a desert," Artemisia said, gently. "That's why it was named that way. That's why we're here. Even in our time there are only six people to a square kilometre. It was never a dry desert. It was always a desert of souls. It's about how people describe their realities. The people below see this land as empty."

After lunch, Artemisia settled down and worked. That afternoon, she found two different ways of calculating prayer times, broadcast them to the rest of the cave dwellers in an e-briefing then settled down to read *Tristram Shandy*, which had been included in her library by a wonderful error. She loved *Tristram Shandy*. It didn't make up for the total impossibility that was her research library, but it did give her a refuge when she was unable to contemplate or work with that library any longer.

Whoever had designed this historical resource was pathetic. She would have prayed for them, if she had still been ten and wildly innocent. Now all she could do was despise their stupidity and cheapness.

Over dinner, Luke emerged from his world-changing mathematics and top-secret project to remind everyone to look at Artemisia's list of prayer times. Sylvia made her own little protest at Artemisia. She ignored the double set of calculations and she went out after breakfast the next day, both contrary to specific instructions. Luke said nothing.

And so they all settled down into an odd, half troglodyte existence. Sylvia continued to ignore Artemisia's work and Artemisia continued to mock Sylvia in her mind.

Within five days, Artemisia had a second set of biographies of saints on the go, but they were hidden behind hyperlinks. Anyone who actually clicked on the hyperlink found a satirical version of the same life. Artemisia had mastered these during her various studies: it was almost impossible to be an expert on the lives of saints (even those of Clemence of Barking) and not master the daft satire. If anyone else underground read them, they didn't say.

* * *

The next day was cold and bleak within the slender valley-town surrounded by that desert. The wind blew sharply across street corners and people clustered as if closeness would protect them from the headache and the tears that the sharpness brought. Berta and Sibilla were not talking. They walked past each other, heads turned aside, the wind whipping their cheeks to tears. Guilhem-the-smith heard their confidences and their complaints.

"Why does she do that? She always sweeps like that and it always moves the dirt right outside my house. I hate it."

"Why can't that woman mind her own business? Do some work for a change?"

The complaints were the same every time. They always made up. Until they did, however, Guilhem-the-smith turned to his forge for comfort.

Today, it wasn't only the two women who fought. Everyone was at odds.

The only person who had any cheer in the whole town was Fiz's youngest friend. He was boasting about his diving prowess. "I can dive into the Verdus and come up in Saint-Jean-de-Fos, or even further. I can swim longer than anyone and hold my breath longer than anyone and I know all the currents."

Despite the wind and the black weather he offered to prove himself. Fiz, naturally, called his bluff on this. The whole of Saint-Guilhem was spared the bravado for an afternoon as the young man demonstrated that he could indeed dive into a particular pool and come up, miles away. It was a distraction, and a relief to everyone except the boy himself, who came up shivering and freezing and had to walk a long way home.

"Spring," Peire thought, "they'll calm down when Spring is here. It's the season that makes them turbulent." Until then, daily life was full of potential fraught moments. Small towns in enclosed valleys, even with thick walls and private courtyards and many, many places to which one could escape, small towns in enclosed valleys hurt when they could only look inwards.

"Up to the hills, whence cometh the pilgrims," Peire thought. Seldom as holy as they thought they were, but a distraction. Certain townsfolk would focus on milking those pilgrims and complaining about the whims and fancies of the religious traveller. Less mischief against each other, in pilgrim season.

Chapter Six: The Month of Small Things

It was April. April in the northern hemisphere. The air was full of the scent of spring flowers and of herbs and of hope. Summer was most definitely coming soon. The person most affected by this was Ben Konig. He stood just outside the big opening and drank in deep breaths of the fragrance before strolling downhill to collect data points for his biomass project.

Even Sylvia found him easier to work with, although this was partly because they had adopted an almost forced charm with each other. Sylvia flirted. Ben flirted back. Together they kept things going. Artemisia noticed, however, that after Ben had spent a significant time flirting, he was at the main entrance, looking out on creation and swilling the air.

Artemisia looked at his back, which was just visible from where she sat, and she considered. Ben and Sylvia were both 'I' people if they weren't in the picture then there was no picture. *Ben hides it better*, she thought, *and contextualises himself using the weather and the air. He stays saner than Sylvia, perhaps, because he can go outside and breathe in lavender and thyme and come back smiling. Either way, the universe doesn't need either of them at its centre, and they both think it does. How odd. Whoever recruited didn't do a good job with that one. They're going to fight. Sure and sure. And I'm not going to fight, no matter how much Dr Smith goads me.*

Luke walked into the office area at that moment. She didn't have to turn to see him. He had a palpable presence. This was why Luke didn't have to struggle to get that centrality that Ben and Sylvia squabbled over all he had to do was enter a room. It wasn't because he was Great Leader. In fact, he shirked his Great Leadership on a regular basis. It was his charisma. Artemisia felt shamefully glad that he hid himself and his equations in his office so much of the time. She was much more relaxed when his presence didn't take over the room. It gave her space to breathe.

* * *

Fiz had constipation. He had had constipation for so long that it felt eternal. To the whole of Saint-Guilhem-le-Désert it felt eternal, too, for wherever Fiz went, whether it was gambling with his friends by the Verdus or trying to steal from someone's narrow garden, when he caught sight of any person at all he told them loudly of his suffering.

One day, in church, he finally gave thanks and explained to each and every person near him at the end of the service that God has saved him from the constipation.

"But He hasn't yet saved us from you," muttered Guilhem-the-smith mostly to himself.

Peire said to the metalworker, "Tu cognovisti sessionem meum et resurrectionem meum." Everyone within earshot nodded sagely. "Psalm 138," added the priest.

"Of course," said Guilhem-the-smith, ironically.

"The Lord sees everything," the priest continued, looking at Fiz directly, "even your shitting."

Fiz excused himself, very quickly.

He didn't even notice Guilhem leaning against the church, staring at him neutrally, staring at everyone neutrally. Guilhem ought to have been dwarfed by the huge round tower, but he wasn't. He was simply there, leaning against the rough boulders at its base, wearing his sword effortlessly as if he were a part of the church's fortifications.

Sibilla was too busy complaining about her feet to notice, and Berta too busy arguing with her. She had been complaining for the last month.

"It's so far to walk," Sibilla started her litany.

Berta interrupted before she could finish. "Go to Saint-Barthelmy," she said.

"I hate Saint-Barthelmy. I may have moved house, but I've always come here and I always will. My ancestors and their ancestors have been in this parish since the very first Guilhem. Since the saint himself."

"Then stop complaining. Every time you go to church, you complain."

"My feet hurt."

"If you hadn't bought those second hand shoes"

"They're lovely," and she paused to admire them. "I bought

them from a pilgrim, for a good price. Hardly worn. When I wear them I feel as if I'm in Montpellier, walking along the streets like one of those lords from Aragon."

"They don't fit."

"I might be in Paris, strolling past a palace. Living the life of the city."

"They still don't fit. You'll get bunions."

After almost everyone had gone, Guilhem was still standing there, not walking through town, but standing arms crossed, leaning against the fortified wall, defending his space. Peire said admiringly to Guilhem-the-smith, safely out of earshot at the top of the stairs (and just around the curve of the wall), "Ensuring he doesn't belong."

"He doesn't want to belong. He doesn't want to change and become one of us. He tells me every day that his mother was from the south, but if she was, her affiliations are with Montpellier, not here. And I'm not even certain about that. He speaks with the accent of the Ile-de-France and he walks with the swagger of the Ile-de-France. And we all know what they want, up there in Paris."

"They want to own us," said the priest. "They want to own everything."

"And they never will."

"Nothing changed when the king claimed us, after all."

"It changed for the cities. We're lucky we're a little place."

"In the middle of nowhere," the big Guilhem laughed.

"In the middle of the pilgrim route, with the abbey to protect us. While the abbey's strong, we don't have to fear secular lords."

"You believe the abbot, then, that Jesus protects us?"

"No, I believe the abbot that the abbot protects us. We make him rich with a quarter of our harvests and with our hard work and olive oil, and he keeps us from the king and his politics."

"And Guilhem?"

"He has to stay a stranger." Peire peeked around the wall and looked down at the man lounging arrogantly, and wondered what it was like to be him. Better not. Better to never be a noble. Better to have one's place here, in one's own country than to be a wanderer and alone.

* * *

A typical day in the hellhole (as Mac called it, to the right ears) consisted of Tony gardening and computing and stashing samples and recording developments. When Tony wasn't working, he was watching. Artemisia watched him watch: it was her new hobby. She noticed that everyone reacted differently to it. Sylvia and Pauline developed nervous tics, for instance, while Luke puffed himself up and became magnificent.

Luke always wrote on everything. His main goal was the Big Project that would Change the World. His main tools were his brain and his whiteboard marker, which were obviously connected at some deep level. He wanted the first datastream to arrive more than anything. Whenever he was stymied, he craved that datastream with its twenty-first-century view of the transit. His brow would lower and he would bang his fist on random objects, urgent for answers. *One day,* Artemisia thought, *he will break something.*

He didn't talk about his work. He was either on show and influencing the world, or he was, like Tony, deep in his own thoughts, the Big Brain working. Every now and again, he'd remember he was head of the expedition and take charge, or stop at someone's desk and force them into conversation. The whole team was happiest when these moments passed.

Sylvia was a splendid multi-tasker. She made her observations of the sky, and added her measurements into her delta T work; she evaluated rocks for erosion data, and she did about half the everyday administration. Whether it was half or less than half depended on the state of her tussles with Konig. Artemisia loved watching these.

Konig was a mystery, but an amusing one. He was very easy on the eye and had a splendid voice, and she never fell for either. Lucia had taught her that. "Never believe externals," she had said, often and over. Artemisia determined early on that he genuinely cared about the expedition's success and so she did what he asked. He wasn't a real person to her, however, until the occasion he came in with a question.

"Is it a bad year this year?" he asked. "The grapes are slow. It could affect vintage."

That was when she realised that his love was wine. Not science. Not world domination. Science and world domination were things he was prone to, merely. Not his passion. It gave him a different intellectual footprint to the others he approached his work with a different mindset. This fascinated her.

"I have notes on vintages," she said. "On my thumb drive. I'll hunt them out for you."

On that typical day, Mac might be doing almost anything, and Geoff Murray would be wandering around, whistling, or lounging in a comfortable chair, pretending not to work, his eyes noticing everything. He especially noticed Konig's lists and maps.

Konig was made of lists and of maps. 'Laundry lists', he called the one, and 'Distribution' the other. Lists of species from the region, from similar regions, from regions that might have been similar at different periods. Maps showing distribution. He was a man of lists and a man of maps.

If you wanted to see the questing knight show from under the administrator, you asked him if something was on his list, and when he found it wasn't, he would add it in half a dozen places. Then he would update a map. And he would be supremely happy. And every single woman in his vicinity would bask in that happiness. *There's something about a good-looking man radiating dynamic joy,* Artemisia thought, as she handed over a sample.

She noticed that Tony also handed samples over, though he did so without drawing attention to himself. Tony didn't flirt with anyone, male or female. But he did make sure he had extra plants to give Ben, always. How much of this was because they both worked with plants? Both she and Mac speculated, but out of the way, where no-one could hear. They didn't speculate for long. Tony was so very private; it was impossible to know anything about his sexuality.

"It's very frustrating," Mac said.

"It's very cool," Artemisia retorted. "His face is so expressive."

"No it isn't."

"Yes, it is. He's an inward soul. He's maybe the most inward person I know. He internalises everything. He's not a verbal person, either. He doesn't need to talk."

"You're right about that."

An hour later Luke had everyone perched on the hillside, watching travellers. The man was consistent only in his inconsistency: his policy was as the cock on a weather vane. "Just this once," he'd announced, "we'll watch the travellers and get a handle on what we're avoiding. We can't minimise knowledge of us by our environment without knowing that environment."

There was an irregular traffic of pedlars, merchants, specialist traders, linking the town with Aniane. A few headed through the back paths, past the time team's hideout and into the mountains. These were the ones of whom the team had to be wary, and it was these they were poised to analyse.

Nothing happened. Artemisia used the binoculars and then the camera when Luke wasn't watching. She took pictures of the castle and the wall flowing down from it and the towers that hobbled the wall right to the village. She talked herself through the castle and its relationship to the town, yearning to talk it out loud, to hear it spoken. Her big surprise was how very small it was. It was a castle that protected by looking dangerous. It saw; it was seen: it did nothing.

No need for impossibly long mule trains to supply, because there was no big garrison that needed provision. One visible person (no mail glinting out from beneath very ordinary clothes) wandered around the walls. She pored over every single bit of castle material she could find and finally came to the conclusion that it might be a variant on an old-fashioned motte-and-bailey structure, with the town itself being part of the defences, or the whole thing might be a deception intended to persuade people not to invade in the first place.

"I don't know castles," she despaired, "I only know saints' tales. And I don't even know the right saints' tales. Wrong region, wrong stories, wrong century. It's all wrong." And she went back to her research into castles, knowing as she did that anything she thought was likely to be a complete waste of time. Except the pictures. At least, this once, she had pictures. She processed the photos for sending, hoping that Sylvia wouldn't disallow them as taking up too many valuable megabytes. Artemisia was hungry for answers.

* * *

Guilhem had his eye on the fortifications. They were good, and practical, he thought, but not handled well. Sporadic checks of the pilgrim paths did not equal a proper watch.

Since the castle was out of bounds (by order of the abbot, who really didn't like Guilhem's cousin), Guilhem asked around to find out who had the keys to the towers. He knew that they were managed separately to the castle, for they had been used twice as prisons since he had arrived. Once Fiz had cooled his heels overnight and the other time a pair of drunks had been restrained.

A villager had the keys, he discovered, but no-one would say who. The abbot was the one who made these decisions and the abbot, as Guilhem had already discovered, refused to talk. This was very clear: Guilhem should stay out of the abbey's business. Saint-Guilhem-le-Désert was not for the nobility or for the king, it was for the Church.

"We are of Saint Guilhem, not of Charlemagne. We do not need the scions of Charlemagne to protect us. Look around we have protected ourselves for five hundred years. Find other uses for your time. Praying for your immortal soul, perhaps. I'm certain your soul is in need of prayer."

* * *

It was a bad day.

In a small place, deaths hurt everyone. In Saint-Guilhem-le-Désert, deaths hurt for a long time.

Old Guilhem (the oldest Guilhem of the many by that name) had been expected to die for years. No-one knew who would take his place as the town memory. How was that dispute settled? Where is that boundary marker? How much do we give the abbey, the church, the person in Aniane who owns this triangle of land? There was a power vacuum and it would be hard to manage. Everyone would jostle to change the public memory and grab a few more small rights and privileges. And everyone would be on the watch for such jostling and such greed. Written records would be very important for a while.

The other loss was unexpected. It was Fiz's friend, the diver. He was showing off his skills in the steep slopes overlooking the Hérault. He wanted to find out how long he could hold his breath and how far downstream he could go. He was certain he could go farther than anyone had ever been before.

The Hérault and its main tributaries were not safe waters. He hadn't watched out sufficiently and he was caught up in the stream. As other times (although this time unintentionally) he was drawn underground by the current. He washed out at quite another village, miles away. Drowned.

Young boys should never die, however full of vainglory and boast, thought Guilhem.

He thought on his Book of Hours and was not able to recall if the day was red or black. He decided against opening it to check. Some days were black no matter how they were drawn.

Chapter Seven: Memories

2 5 April, St Mark
They did not commemorate ANZAC Day in the Hellhole. Mac felt that this was vaguely wrong. He found some beers and created his own two-up game from a carved bit of wood and his lucky twenty cent piece.

"Why do you have a lucky twenty cent piece?" asked Artemisia, when he invited her to join. "And why is it here, in the wild past?"

"Wouldn't want an unlucky one," was Mac's reply. "Fight Club rules. Don't talk about the game. See you up top in fifteen minutes."

It was her and Murray and Mac. Murray wore a cap with a green and blue and black and white pin. He always wore that badge, somewhere on his clothes, but it moved according to his mood. They drank beer and played a token game, but it was too dark and the sky was too clear and soon they found themselves on their backs.

"What are we looking at here, Murray?" Cormac demanded.

"Cepheus just peeking out over the horizon," Geoff said, promptly. "Then there are the bears and the dogs and the usual suspects. D'you want to learn?"

Mac was offended: "I was making polite conversation!"

When they returned down their little ladder, Artemisia finally caved in. She asked Mac for help with the communal calendar. They drew all the red-letter days in red letters.

"It's important," she explained to him. "We're living in 1305. We need to have a sense of it, even if we're here, underground. Otherwise we're joining the zombies."

Mac didn't understand her explanation, but he was delighted to make mischief. He also understood Artemisia's frustration. He was a re-enactor and himself was feeling somewhat repressed in matters Medieval. He had expected excursions, not untold hours fixing water hammers, finding supplies, and explaining yet again to Sylvia and Pauline why heating was not an option.

When daylight came, Sylvia looked at the defaced calendar. She marched into Luke's office. A moment later Konig was called in.

Artemisia was asked to explain. She pulled up a picture of a page from a book of hours and told them that red letter days were the good ones.

That was it. No punishment. No big drama. From then on, everything was red or black to the team, on screen or in real life. It became part of who they were, along with logging finds and testing samples and overwhelming Ben's and Sylvia's databases with information.

Chapter Eight: Shifting Views

S aint-Guilhem-le-Désert was in the process of reshaping itself after the deaths. Boundaries between people were being redrawn, memories were being consolidated, relationships were being reaffirmed. The only thing that didn't change was Fiz. He and his friend defiantly acted as if they were still three, still rulers of the earth on which they walked. They wanted no help. If they cried alone, they didn't tell anyone. They played pranks and they raided gardens and they earned odd bits of money through occasional jobs of work. They were not going to accept that the world had changed.

Having had its focus shifted by the loss of the one who knew all the ways and all the traditions, the rest of the town felt differently. It was as if the main street bent now at a different angle and all the vistas were new. Many town dwellers started to wonder about the people who lived under the hill. They'd noticed the hill dwellers (Artemisia would have pointed to this as evidence that not all ancestors were zombies), but now their presence was remarked upon and discussed.

"These people," said Berta, adamantly, "these people," she reiterated, for what she had to say was important. "These people are not going to go away."

"I thought they'd go away," confessed Sibilla. "Why do they live under the hill, anyway? What do they eat?"

And so discussion began. Initially, it led away from the hill folk and to someone closer: Guilhem.

"He is a problem," Berta stated, still adamant in her opinions.

"He's a young man who needs to do a bit of work," Guilhem-the smith shrugged.

"Can't terrace, can't grow olives, no craft skills, doesn't work with or for the abbey," Sibilla, as always, sided with Berta.

"What can he do, then?" asked the big smith.

"Maybe our new knight can help us? Maybe we have a good job for him and he doesn't know it."

"How? What job?"

"We need someone expendable to talk to the hillfolk."

"Why expendable?" Guilhem-the-smith worried when anyone thought that any individual could be sacrificed in this way. Jesus had done that, but ordinary men should not.

"We don't even know what they are. Human, fairy, demon, something else entirely."

"True. And if any of us talk with them and our souls are lost then the whole town has another hole."

"Like the one we have from that idiot diver. He was a pest, and stupid, but death and his soul in Purgatory"

"It was too harsh. It always is."

"How do we do it?" Berta entered the conversation again, enthusiastically, with Sibilla standing next to her, very close, very intense. "How do we make sure that the knight is the one who talks to them?"

"Watch," said Guilhem-the-smith. "He's lonely and needs to find his place. If we continue to exclude him from our daily lives, but if we talk to him and make him care a bit, then he will do it himself."

"We should discuss it with him then," said Sibilla.

"No. Let him think it's his own idea."

* * *

Sylvia was flirting with Konig. Again. The Prince Valiant look, Artemisia supposed, lured Sylvia into constant temptation. This time, Konig's face was intent. Artemisia knew that look. It was exactly the same as her sister's. Konig was up to mischief.

Her experience with Lucia made it all too easy to spot those changes in expression. He might lie and look as if he were telling the truth, or he might be truthful and sound as if he were devising a fanciful fiction. She always caught him out: he'd stopped trying it on her.

Sylvia was less expert.

Mac was also alert to Konig's mischief. It was Mac, in fact, who had first alerted her. He hated Dr Benjamin Konig, even as he wished he could be like him. Artemisia determined that, if their caverns were full of ancient gods, Konig would be Coyote.

"I get it from my great-great-great-great grandfather," Konig said this and looked directly into Sylvia's face. Very confrontational, Artemisia thought, except that Sylvia didn't seem to find it so. His voice was gentle. "He was a notoriously rakish late Georgian poet."

"Oh," said Sylvia, obviously enchanted.

"On my mother's side," Konig continued, his hand cupping Sylvia's chin, as if he himself were the Regency rake, "I'm the descendant of an overly verbal Victorian novelist who also wrote anonymous broadside ballads." What was incredible was that Sylvia believed him. Stars shone in her eyes.

Artemisia made those stars wink out with just two words. "Anonymous, huh?"

"Sprung bad, Konig," and Geoff stepped out from the corridor. He walked blithely through the still tableau, carrying his kit, his flag-pin attached firmly to his backpack.

If he walks straight ahead at that pace, Artemisia thought, *he will walk right off the cliff.* He almost did. He strode out the main cave opening as if it were paved and turned to the left barely before the edge. *Show-off,* Artemisia thought, half-admiring. *Everyone here has the biggest need to make a spectacle of themselves. Everyone except what's his name.* He was at the next desk to her and she knew him as well as she knew everyone and still his name escaped her. She could see in her mind the way his dark hair was growing as stubble and the size of his eyes. Everyone knew those watching eyes. He had a French name and a Melbourne accent. That didn't help. Finally. *Tony.* She said it aloud.

"What?" he said from behind her.

"I was trying to remember your name…." Artemisia wondered if it were possible to feel more embarrassed.

"Oh," said Tony. "It doesn't matter. Sylvia called me Bill yesterday."

"Bill?" Artemisia couldn't see where Sylvia got that from.

"Bill was the person I replaced."

"I didn't realise you were a replacement too. We have something in common."

Tony's voice was non-committal. "Yes," he said. He sat down at his desk and lost himself in the embrace of his computer.

* * *

Outside was Geoff's world. He loved walking by feel and discovering the changes in texture of the rocks underfoot. He loved the shifts in the air and the scent of herbs that reached even the caves. Geoff had moved to a friendly place and time. It enfolded him in his warmth. He measured the temperature and the rain as much with his body as with his gauges.

Back home he had a thousand and one tools to help him. Here he did his job without satellites and without weather stations and he carried bits of other peoples' tasks with him, thanks to Theo's policy of the fewest possible team members being out and about. The challenge filled his lungs bigger and made him want to sing.

Geoff was so absorbed in the joy of noting precipitation and taking samples and in trying not to sing and in the scent of wild thyme and lavender that he entirely failed to notice that he was being trailed by a girl and a boy. They poked each other and they giggled in the way that only an eleven year old girl doing something slightly naughty in the company of her nine year old brother can do.

"Fairy," said the boy.

"Not," his sister was valiantly trying to keep quiet.

"Fairy," he said more confidently, "very big fairy. Dark and tall and *fairy*."

"If you don't shut up, we'll go home," Bona warned.

"Fairy," the boy whispered obstinately to himself, where his sister couldn't hear.

They followed Geoff until Bona heard the bells. "Now," was all she said. Her brother turned with her and they went home.

"I don't want you to go," he said, when they came close to the wall. "There won't be any fairies with you gone."

"I don't want to leave you," she said, her arm around his shoulder. "You're my favourite person on all the earth. I want to be in Montpellier. I want to learn how to smith. Maybe I'll have my own business, one day. I want my own business. I want to make beautiful things. Anyway, it's a long way away. Months and months and months. Maybe not until next Lady Day."

"I know," but his voice was sad.

"Bread," she suggested.

"Yes!" and it was as if wistfulness had never been.

Chapter Nine: Sylvia

Sylvia still ignored the rules about checking with Artemisia's schedule and about not being seen. Each time she ignored the rules, she took her daring a bit further. Partly, this was boredom. Partly it was because she defined her main task as astronomical observations and these depended on factors outside the caves. Partly it was the sense that the historian was a nonsense addition to the team and that what she said was not relevant.

Thus, when Artemisia asked her if she could explain how they were limiting their environmental impact, she ignored the historian and went about her business as if a fly had passed. Geoff answered Artemisia, and so did Ben, walking her through the careful processes that had been planned from Melbourne.

"Where are the people in this?" she asked.

"We avoid them," said Ben, "so they don't feature." *Like Lucia's chemotherapy bod,* Artemisia thought, *where everything is about the science and humans don't come into it.* She was so very lonely for Lucia.

* * *

Guilhem had been in the habit of taking his Book of Hours with him when he was out and about. No-one knew that he had a small book in his bag, and he himself was reassured that one of his most valuable possessions was there, with him, no matter where he found himself.

When he took the long route home because he didn't want to be there, he forgot that the path beyond the End of the World was not as fine as the main pilgrim road. He arrived home to find that his book had slipped out of his pack, probably during a particularly complex navigation around rocks and a rather worrying drop. His bookbag was empty, its ties loose.

"I'll be back soon," he told his people, and went to find it.

He was close to where he thought he might have dropped it, when he saw a woman bending over. She had no veil, no wimple. And she held his book in her hand.

"Mine!" he shouted, "That's my book! Thief!" He crossed the distance quickly but she was gone. He searched until it was too dark, and cursed the crescent moon for not providing the light to search further. He had missed prayers and the evening meal, and he was torn up inside.

The book was illuminated by a master. It was the one possession he could not, would not lose.

* * *

Sylvia strolled in through the big office opening, looking flushed but triumphant. Luke took one look at her, and another at what she carried. He confiscated the book and quietly took it to Artemisia.

"What's this worth?" he asked.

Artemisia looked at it very closely and with mounting awe. "It's exquisite," she said. "Where did it come from?"

"What's it worth?"

"About as much as a Rolls?" she guessed. "A classic car, anyhow. An unaffordable one."

"And whoever has lost it will want it back?"

"God, yeah," Artemisia searched for oxygen. "You'd look for a diamond ring in the street if you lost it, and diamond rings are harder to find in a street than Books of Hours on a barren hillside."

"Sylvia was seen taking it."

"Fuck."

"Language," admonished Luke.

"This is bad," Artemisia said.

"She's put all of us in danger," said Luke.

"I'm afraid so."

"I need to think."

The great man thought. He ate in his study that evening. He thought some more. The next morning he had a long interview with Sylvia. She walked out looking pale but unrepentant. Then Luke called for Artemisia.

Artemisia was designated to return the book and to persuade the owner to keep silent about the team. Luke turned on his charm and power to persuade her. Finally, Luke admitted that the team needed its historian. That she was not an optional extra. Artemisia didn't find this reassuring. *Sylvia,* Artemisia decided, *is a greedy, reckless toad.*

"She has drawn you a sketch."

"Me? A sketch?"

"Of the owner. I want you to give it back. Make amends. Ensure our safety and security and privacy. I've explained already."

"Why did Sylvia do it?"

"I'll find out," Luke promised. "And she won't do anything this stupid again, because I'm going to rein her right in. She thinks she owns the expedition and she most certainly does not." In other words, Artemisia reflected, Sylvia had given the boss cheek.

The Book of Hours puzzled Artemisia. It was a real gem. New. Beautiful. Some sort of late Gothic bookhand.

Artemisia turned for Brown's book, so that she could check the hand out and give it a proper name, but Brown's book was in the distant future. The Book of Hours was of the present. Fabulous illuminations. Expensive illuminations, too, with that glorious blue and that rich gold. A truly exquisite hand. A single hand, for the whole book.

"This is so early," Artemisia thought. "We aren't in the Book of Hours' heyday and yet someone carries this." A museum piece from the moment of its creation, except that it wasn't. They were living in the museum. Who on earth would own a volume like this here, at the end of the world?

She would have to take the tiny book and the picture Sylvia had drawn and look for the owner tomorrow. Artemisia stopped. Realised. She was terrified. All her knowledge was going to be tested and likely fail. She wasn't ready. She would never be ready. It was already six and the sky was about to be full of sunset.

Tonight she had another task. Artemisia didn't like the assumptions that the rest of the team had about what historians knew and what historians did. Her role could become impossible if she didn't clarify things. She needed to write a briefing. That would get everyone thinking, and maybe also help them understand that her knowledge came couched with explanations and caveats and sources. She even had an excuse for this.

* * *

Historical Briefing 1 — an introduction (file from Artemisia Wormwood)

Ben suggests I commit the answers to your questions to internal communications. I'll try to make this user-friendly. If you have more questions, either ask me directly or send me a note and I'll put together a briefing on it.

I can't guarantee to answer everything. Even with all the resources of, say, the British Library, I couldn't answer all your possible questions. I can answer some, and I can suggest where we might find information for others. As we work together, I hope to understand your perspectives and scientific cultures better. The briefings will be more targeted to your needs then, with your help.

Today I want to talk about the sources of information I have available to me and about my own background. Three people have assumed that I'm an archaeologist or linguist like the ones you see in SF shows, who knows everything about all there is to know and is only stumped when the plot requires it. The truth is so far removed from that, it's laughable.

I'm a medievalist. I'm a card-carrying member of ANZAMEMS and other scholarly associations. I read several dialects of Old French, Middle English, Latin both Classical and Medieval various Italians, some modern Spanish, some Old Castilian, a little Old Occitan and a bit of German. I have training in the subsidiary disciplines, things like codicology, palaeography and diplomatics. I spent the last year and a bit in England, lecturing at a perfectly respectable university.

Just because I can't answer your questions doesn't mean I'm incompetent. It means that I, like most academics, am a specialist. I'm not the right specialist for this region, but I'm the specialist you have. Like all specialists, I know about a very particular area. If you want to know the structure and interpretation of saints' lives in Old French, I'm the go-to person. My doctorate was on Clemence of Barking.

My interest in saints is how the Director found me. I was visiting Saint-Gilles and Saint-Guilhem-le-Désert and Nîmes to pay respect to Gilles and William. William is more known for his politics and his epic legends than his saint's life, but since the best and most famous of his epic legends is in Anglo-Norman and since he actually does have a hagiographical record, I know it and so I am here. William was quite a hero and is absolutely the reason the town is what it is, both now and in our century.

At this moment in time, he's quite dead. Being dead doesn't make him less important. This is the Middle Ages. Death is not the same here. I don't mean that there are zombies: there are no zombies. There are saints. Also ghosts. The saints are the important ones. You're already getting notes on some of the saints when their day comes round. It will help you get a feel for the medieval calendar.

Sources

My electronic library is quite different from yours. I don't know if the library was intended to be more up-to-date but time was of the essence (a joke!) or resources were directed elsewhere, but the very large library you see under the History of the Region tag in your database is mostly eighteenth and nineteenth century books. There's a lot of repetition, as several appear to plagiarise unmercifully. I had no time to collect material of my own to add to the library. You have the library and you have my thumb drive and you have my personal notebook that I carried in my backpack and that is the full extent of what I can draw on for briefings without doing live-action research.

Questions I can't answer at this stage

I've been asked several questions that appear to have no answers in the database. One of them is how the castle is run (there appears to be no surviving documentation for the castle government in our time we might want to observe and work it out for ourselves). Medieval mortar you're better off sneaking into town at night and scraping some (as I said, live-action research I know, it's against protocol and therefore illegal I'm not actually suggesting you do it) than asking me about it. There may be thousands of articles written on the subject, but none of them are in our database. Modern research. This needs to be high on our requisition list. Until I have that research, I don't have your answers. Even then, if a subject hasn't been researched or if we don't have that journal, I won't be able to answer you. Human lives are so complex that there are a million questions one can ask, and modern historians aren't necessarily asking the ones that puzzle you personally at this precise moment.

Population: I know there were 849 people living in the town in 1837, thanks to the *Guide pittoresque, portitatif et complet du voyageur en* France (p. 437). This is not a reliable number for our use in any way. In the same volume that castle you see on the nice mountain round the corner was called the 'Giant' and was supposed to be a casualty in a fight between Gellone and William. Right now, as you know, it's a very fine castle.

This brings me to:

Historical events

By a quirk of your wonderful maths and time-travel calculations, we're on the cusp of some dark times. I don't know whether the civilised world we're hiding from is safe or not.

Until I explore our lovely library a bit further, I only know the political history as it affects Northern France and England. Expect my views to change as I learn more. Don't be put out by this this is pretty standard for history. If historians don't revise things as they discover more and understand more, then they're just not doing their job. Not unlike scientists.

Historical method is something you will no doubt get heartily sick of, but it's important. We can't understand things easily or absolutely. History isn't fixed in stone, even if it's carved in stone (a joke!). Anyway, the key things we need to be aware of, because they're either happening or about to happen, are:

1. North-South divide. This is the South. It's powerful. Or it has been powerful and still makes the king a bit jumpy. This is despite the fact that there was genocide here not so long ago. I'll get to that.

The king in the north (Philippe the Very Pretty) doesn't like the South, really. Philippe IV who was often described as *le Bel* rules from October 5, 1285 to November 29, 1314. His father was Philippe III. His grandfather was a saint. He himself has been described as a very beautiful marble statue. He's hungry for everyone's money. Throws all the Jews out of France next year just so that he can own what they own. Did I say his grandfather was a saint?

2. The pope right now is Clement V. He's the one who got rid of the Templars. Or will, in our near future and in cahoots with the beautiful Philippe (first the Jews, then the Templars pretty much for the same reason, too money made Phil's world go round). How might this affect us? The Templars were very active on pilgrim routes (why they existed, as I understand it) and our little town is a part of the biggest pilgrim route of all. I might do you a bigger briefing on both the Templars and the pilgrim route one day: they're very important.

3. There is no such thing as an atheist. Lack of belief in God is probably defined as heresy and could get you burned alive. Also, anti-Semitism. It exists. It's nasty. You might try to throw people out

because you want their money, but without the anti-Semitism it ain't gonna happen. Members of this party could be in serious danger if they start talking to locals. This is why I'm being sent to return that little gem of a Book of Hours. It's not going to be safe for me, but at least I know a little more than the rest of you. We need to know the right words and thoughts, the right mindset. Staying out of reach of people in this isolated place is for *our* benefit.

All I can do is warn you: it doesn't matter how much you think you know about this period and how human everyone looks, it could be very dangerous to break protocol. Not just dangerous in that time paradox sense. It could get one or more of us *killed*.

There is rule of law here, and if any of us gets murdered it will probably be investigated. Isn't that nice to know? It's not lawlessness or lack of civilisation that's the problem. It's a fundamentally different world view. Medieval cosmology doesn't permit of atheism. And Jews are still suspected of killing Christ.

Chapter Ten: Children all

Whenever there was a lull in thought, someone brought up the subject of the strangers. Their behaviour was odd and their appearance ranged from normal to very peculiar indeed. It was entertaining to watch them, but it was also a worry.

The biggest concern was, of course, the drowning. No one said directly, "They killed one of us." Many tussled with the idea. Were the strangers responsible? The matter was tugged about in conversations bit by bit until all its ramifications had been explored. In the end, most people realised what Guilhem-the-smith patiently repeated over and over again, that when a very young man insists on doing dangerous things, it was not unlikely that he would die doing those dangerous things.

Berta held out.

"Don't be an idiot," said Peire.

Everyone was surprised into silence. He was such a careful man, and such a good priest. He never told people to not be idiots, even when they were.

Behind Peire's back, however, the matter was soon discussed again. His parishioners decided, and argued very strongly that it was the other half of the town that ought to take some responsibility. It ought to be a Saint-Barthelmy matter, "Since their parish abuts the end of the world."

Life continued.

It was hard to believe that Berta's husband was a cobbler, when he cobbled so seldom. Mostly he repaired or remade old shoes. He was the laziest man in the whole region, his wife thought, and most people agreed with her.

He finally repaired Sibilla's shoes. She was able to walk to church without hurting. Berta didn't trust her husband, however, and bought herself a new pair of shoes from the cordwainer, who lived in Aniane but visited his brother in Saint-Guilhem from time to time. They were elegant and fine and a perfect fit. She walked around in them looking very smug.

She needed all the superiority she could get, for her best friend was caught sleeping with Guilhem-the-smith's first cousin (again). Father Louis was most unhappy, and insisted that Sibilla confess to him, in his church, even though she belonged to Saint-Laurent and Fr Peire. Everyone knew what that was about. Berta needed those new shoes.

The whole town was in an uproar. Was Father Louis suddenly holy, or was he jealous? And when would Sibilla learn?

"Let their priest deal with it," said Guilhem-the-smith, tired of it all. He wanted to disown his cousin. He wanted someone else to arbitrate. He wanted, in fact, the town to have formal self-government, with properly appointed consuls this arrangement with the abbey might be their inheritance from times of old, but it was not effective and he hated it.

It wouldn't change in the lifetime of the current abbot. He enjoyed his power too much. Never relinquished an iota. Never did anything, but refused to hand rights over. Even the keys to the towers required an argument, every single time. Guilhem-the-smith was so exhausted by this thought that he went to bed early.

Guilhem missed the gossip entirely. He didn't know anyone was talking about him because he was busy telling his household (and especially his page) that he still felt as if he were travelling.

"Half the goods I have here are in that big travelling chest. Most of my possessions are at the other end of the country."

He drew sketches of two small wooden chests and a dresser, to make life less impossible and told his young man to see about ordering them, first thing in the morning. His whole household went to bed somewhat later than they should have.

"It would be easier," was the last word over the fire, once Guilhem had finally taken himself to bed, "if he took that travelling chest and went back the way he came."

* * *

Tony was a creature of habit, so everyone watched as he broke that habit. He was hunting Cormac Smith. Konig insinuated himself into the background, fascinated.

"Cormac," Tony announced, "I like the place you found for me, but the soil is poor. I need good soil."

Cormac looked Tony up and down (mainly down and down, given the height differential) and explained that the soil was bad everywhere. "It's limestone, all around us."

"What am I going to do?" Tony's world was obviously destroyed.

"We can improve the soil, using the waste from the settlement. That's what the planners planned."

"But now? I need to run my trials."

"Let's take a look in stores and see what we can find." Cormac took Tony's hand, like that of a child, and walked him into the stores area.

Chapter Eleven: The Traps of Responsibility

Ben Konig was torn. He was torn between the master that was Luke and the administrator that was Sylvia, and that he had to somehow make their actions meet. He loved making mix-ups into good sense, but he wasn't enamoured of the pressure.

The ethics worried him, too. He'd seen Luke totally ignore discussions about the team's effect on the period and place, and Sylvia entirely unconcerned about the effect of time travel on the people involved. Between them, they were a disaster waiting to happen. And he was the one who had been delegated to prevent it. To save everyone from Luke and Sylvia and save Luke and Sylvia from themselves.

It had been a matter of much amusement to the Australian scientists that the French Government wouldn't grant permissions without him. "Ethics," he had heard Luke saying, "Like Mururoa?" That didn't help. Knowing that he was a laughing stock for trying to follow through on policy and ethics formulations. Knowing that he didn't really fit in with the Australians.

Ben made it his job to keep everything operational. To seduce Sylvia into trust. To woo Luke into acceptance. To listen to everyone. He managed it all with charm and even elegance. And it hurt.

There was no recourse for him inside the caves. The moment he made anyone his confidant he would turn the whole thing into a nasty ballgame. The recruitment was fucked because Mann liked academic papers more than he liked ability to work with others. Konig knew that. He knew politics. That was why it was him. Because he knew politics. Politics was supposed to save the team from self-destruction. Or from Luke. Whichever was more active at a given time.

He had been surprised when he had been asked. He was less surprised when he had met Luke and his second-in-command and assessed who they were and how they would manage things.

Harvey had spent those last months troubleshooting the

impossible, because if he hadn't then the project would have been cancelled. They had won the international bidding war and Harvey's career was at stake. So he turned to Ben.

"None of the other team members has leadership skills," said the Director. "My backup refused to go because of the physical risk. We're all in deep shit. I need you, Ben."

"I know," Harvey had said, in that impossibly warm voice, "that I'm asking something I shouldn't ask even my worst enemy. I can't take Mann out of the expedition. He's a mess as leader, but he's a genius and we need his brain at the far end. Time travel is largely untested. We've not sent people back before. We can't do the big project without him and everything is secondary to that project. I can't argue with his choice of second-in-command because he's technically in charge. All I can do is add good people. That means you. The French Government demands a representative, and you have the language and the interests and the background. Hell, you were an ENAque! Trained by the French government, groomed for leadership and service. If anyone can keep the expedition from imploding, it's Ben Konig."

That was Ben's real job. He did his research, but for every hour he spent on science, he spent two hours thinking through events and happenings and personalities and trying to find the best way of keeping everything in line.

Ben didn't mind the lies heck, he lived with lies. Had lived with lies since his childhood. What he hated was being headmaster without the authority. Konig wasn't blind. He could see that Geoff Murray was polite around him and that Cormac Smith took forever to meet any of his requests. He could tell that without his looks he wouldn't have Sylvia and Pauline onside.

Artemisia was a bit of a saving grace. She was so isolated that she was willing to talk to anyone. He used her isolationpushed at it and stretched itbecause it meant that he had a place in the crowd. And he needed that place to do his job.

He hated himself. Every time he saw her excluded from the jokes and chat, he hated himself. Every time she disappeared to her room, he hated himself.

He would hate Harvey, too, if he could, for the Director had said, glibly, that an old friend of his had agreed to be the replacement historian. "She needs the money," he'd said; "suits everyone." Then Artemisia Wormwood had appeared, with those big vulnerable eyes and that vast self-awareness and he saw echoes of his own hurt inside her. He hated being the person to turn the knife. And yet…he couldn't find another way. Harvey was not a good friend.

Ben developed the habit of quietly slipping out of the caves when he hurt too much. He would take work with him if he could, but if he couldn't, he would simply lie. He had as many excuses as he had stories about his ancestors, and his stock of imaginary tales about invented ancestors was vast.

He did work when he was out. Even if he didn't plan to, he worked. He identified species distribution and looked at the water and the landscape and how people fitted themselves into that landscape. Ben Konig was a driven man.

Before Ben worked, however, he breathed the air and felt the season. He understood the wind and how it slipped through the hills. He knew the Cévennes and the littoral and he loved this region between them. As his eyes slipped over the garrigue and took in the stunted kermes oaks and the twisted bushes, he would smile. He named everything in French and he thought in French when he was out, for that was the contour of this land in his mind. He tasted the South in every breath he took and it grounded him.

This land made it possible for him to endure the impossible. His deep dream was to one day have a vineyard in a place like this. One far removed from politics and lies.

Ben didn't know if he was blessed or cursed. Blessed because he had intelligence and looks and skill with people. Cursed because of his background. Also cursed because that intelligence and those looks and that skill with people always meant he was given work that drove him further and further from where he wanted to be. And he took that work because he had guilt to expiate. Personal guilt. Family guilt. So very much guilt.

* * *

Guilhem-the-smith was very happy that he wasn't a consul at this moment in time. Berta's husband, in his ineffable way, had really made an awful mess. It was for someone else to handle. Someone else could work with all the interested parties (on behalf of the abbot, of course) to clean the section of the Verdus that was distinctly odorous and to find some sort of solution. How had the cobbler done it? It looked as if more than rubbish was dumped: it was excrescence.

The artisan looked at the clear water above the mess and the way it worked slowly to remove the foulness and he made a decision, as he had done many, many times. If there were something like this, where everyone disclaimed culpability and liability, and if he were named arbiter, he would hand it back to the abbey. His reasoning was that if Abbot Bernard didn't give them full power over their lives, then the worthy abbot should be the one to handle all the disgusting cases. Guilhem never said this aloud, however, precisely as he never answered back when someone (usually Sibilla) asked when he would marry. There were some things one did not say aloud.

In the meantime, he avoided that section of the stream (as he had for two weeks) and, crossing at the stones, he walked the broad path to the main street, where he watched the village go by.

Peire had been striding in his big way. He was about to walk into someone. He took a swift step sideways. His beads clattered and his stylus fell to the ground and his wax boards refused stubbornly to catch the sun. Peire had mentioned this several times, how the wax was too thin, how parchment was better, how the heat melted the wax unexpectedly and how he never knew what notes he had made for himself. As the priest bent down to reach for his stylus, his tablet also crashed onto the ground, its leather thong too short. Guilhem-the-smith wondered if the tablet had split in half, but it was too far to see.

It was getting dark. The smith didn't move. He stood there, in the growing shadow, watching. There was nothing to go home for and his cold meal could wait a little longer. He wanted to watch Berta walk through the streets cautiously, on her way to see someone. She was carrying a little oil lantern in her right palm, very gently. The glow lit her face and made it softer than usual. Her prosaic sharp features looked angular and mysterious. Nevertheless, Berta was still not tempting.

Guilhem-the-smith knew precisely why he could not get married. It was something that didn't even reach the confessional. Or maybe, he thought to himself, it was something that he particularly couldn't talk about in the confessional, if Peire were the confessor. He might burn in Hell for it, but at least he would retain dignity while he was on this fair earth.

"Come here!" Pauline's lamp was less secure as she reached to grab a child. Ah, her children were loose again. Guilhem was relieved that he had spoken up for the girl and found her an apprenticeship. Despite the comb just now being run through Bona's hair and the scolding her mother was giving, that family was not a good place to be a child. Not enough training and not enough attention.

The smith yearned for a child of his own far more than he yearned for marriage. It was one of his deepest wishes to be able to scold and say, as Berta was saying at this moment, with all that love and all that mock dismay, "You are such a mess!"

Berta gave Bona a quick hug then the wild child was allowed on her way again.

The ironworker decided that maybe, after all, it was time to eat. He closed the big door to his workshop, went through the little one, up the stairs, to his home. He closed the shutters firmly, making himself safe from the fears of the night and the lives he would never lead.

Chapter Twelve: *"I need a friend"*

"**M**cGyver," shouted Luke, striding through the kitchen and through a conversation. "Mac! I need another white board marker. Now!"

Sylvia and Pauline ignored him and continued their conversation. Technically, it was about shops and shoes. In reality, it was carefully delineating the circles they mixed in and ensuring they were on the same wavelength. Sylvia knew this, but Pauline simply participated. If they had been closer in age, and from America, *Sex and the City* would be part of the conversation about now, Artemisia reflected, as she wandered through the kitchen. She wished she could email Lucia this insight. Lucia would frown at her: "Not *Sex and the City* again," she would complain. "What's wrong with it? Why do you always pick on it?"

Gradually, over the course of a couple of hours and more than a couple of cups of coffee, Pauline and Sylvia cemented their relationship. Pauline was the strong one. Self-sacrificing. Could deal with anything.

Sylvia was more than happy to be the needy one. She launched into a little litany of illness to cement that role and Pauline commented on her courage.

"If you get one of those migraines here," she said, "Come straight to me. I'll take care of you."

Once that was settled, they talked about their work and their workmates.

"Not everything fits, does it?" Sylvia asked wryly.

"It's not fair that you have to make it fit. The others should do their stuff."

"They should, but I can't see them doing it. They don't see the big picture. And Tony! Tony doesn't see anything."

"Artemisia keeps complaining."

"Oh, I *know*. All the time. Hasn't got this book or that piece of paper."

"Hasn't got real coffee. Two types of instant, we have."

"She really doesn't belong here."

"But we have to make do with what we've got." The two women smiled across at each other smugly. Everything was now in its place. Which as just as well, because Luke had found his pen and walked through the kitchen again, "Meeting. Common room. Now."

Meetings were depressing. Artemisia knew this before she slumped in her chair and she certainly knew it by the time she had slumped so far she couldn't get up again. Couldn't get up. Wouldn't get up. Getting up meant walking past the huddle of scientists Sylvia had determined needed their own meeting after the general one. It meant Ben Konig looking down his long nose at her and nodding the way he had twenty minutes earlier when Sylvia Smith had categorised her work as 'easy' and 'only semi-skilled, really'.

This had a context. Of course it had a context. Sylvia was explaining how very hard she herself would have to work, doing both her science and administration, and had used Artemisia as a comparison.

And that bloody doctor had agreed. She had nodded at Dr Sylvia Smith's analysis and said, quite smugly, "Some of us are here through personal sacrifice and for the good of others, not because we're going to change the world with science." Artemisia felt that comment as a sharp knife that scraped off her protection and left her hurts bare. She thought of her sister the way she had seen her the day before departure, barely out of her first set of hospital visits from the new treatment, skin covered with pustules and pain. Lucia had been determined that Artemisia wouldn't lose out.

"Lose out? How can I?" Artemisia lied. "Harvey's offered me a brave new world and that brave new world has such people in it. Shakespeare says so it must be true." And Lucia's sad short hair stuck up and every strand of it pulled at her sensitised skin and even smiling back at Artemisia's joke hurt so much that Artemisia could see it in the way she held herself and the way she courageously looked across at her sister. Artemisia's heart broke in that moment, for she knew that when she came back in nine months, Lucia might be gone. But still…still… Lucia had to have the chance of life. Money gave her that. And here Artemisia was, slumped in the chair, a person of no importance, hidden in a cave beyond the end of the world.

She stayed slumped until she could control the tears. She would not give Dr Smith the satisfaction, or let Dr Adamson think that she was a lamb for the slaughter.

When she was composed, Dr Wormwood pulled herself as inwardly as she could, walked right through the gauntlet, not looking right or left or up or down. When she reached the safety of her room, she allowed herself to cry.

Back in the huddle of scientists, Sylvia said to Ben, "Not very friendly, is she?"

* * *

Guilhem's token from Jerusalem was one of his certainties. He had done his pilgrimage. He was forgiven his heinous crime. The scallop shells that Berta and Father Peire had in the village were nothing, everything else was lead pendants from their nearer walks. Lead badges, lead pendants, they were everywhere. But Guilhem had his token from Jerusalem and he was not scared any longer.

The outcast lordling was alone in Saint-Guilhem. He had left his valet back in the house, since that boy could never get anything right. He felt debonair. As he walked slowly down the street, he gave his greetings to each and every soul and noted that the men doffed their caps and he himself bowed his head just enough. He felt very satisfied being himself and knowing what to say to each and every person. It was a craft.

Like every craft, it required dedicated work. It wasn't that Guilhem wasn't interested in idle chat. In fact, Guilhem wanted to talk, but all seemed very uphill when he only had artisans to talk to. He knew the villagers were talkative because he heard them, all day, every single waking hour. The bells silenced them, but otherwise Saint-Guilhem's conversations flowed like the Verdus, gentle and constant. Guilhem knew that the folk held political views and views on religion and views on the crops and the weather and the idiocy of those people down in Aniane, because he had heard this, too. They didn't talk about these things with him. They didn't talk about anything with him. He continued to grimly work at being polite.

He was so determined that he almost missed it when Guilhem-the-smith invited him for a drink. "I'm sorry," he said. "I'm on my way home."

"I need a friend," he said to himself as he walked back through his door to scold his lazy page yet again. He had accepted the sentence to exile because he knew this place was fortified. Fortifications, in his experience, contained people like him. He had made a mistake. Those who lived in the castle were nothing like him. His sort passed through, but didn't stay. Only the Templars at Pézenas understood him and his life, only his secret friends in Montpellier understood his other interests (and if he went there often, his aunt would find out). Here and now, in this place made of rocks and hardness, he was alone. Miserably so.

Inside the rocks and hardness, in the places Guilhem didn't understand, there was green. Courtyards glowed with it, there were flowers tended carefully and woodfires providing warmth and flickering colour. This was the month of warmth and friendliness, where the land was less demanding and there was time to talk, to sit, to do the small works of hands. It was when the people of the town turned inwards, to their private spaces, and gained some small happiness. Or not. It was the time when some members of the town felt vulnerable, for the small familiarity of souls would never be theirs.

Chapter Thirteen: Dead Saints and Their Amazing Adventures

Briefing: The papacy (file from Artemisia Wormwood)
The papacy is currently in interesting times. This is the year that started the train of events that led to the Great Schism. Three popes at once. Not yet, though. This is the beginning of that time. Right now we're finishing an interregnum a year with no pope at all. There will be a papal coronation in November, and after that the Papacy moves from Rome to Avignon. Not far from here. Also a universe away. Just so very different from our cave and the small town with its abbey and pilgrims. Avignon is bigger and more important and wealthier and full of life. It's surrounded by giant walls. It has a bridge where people dance (a joke!).

The papacy has just finished a small implosion and will be at the beck and call of the king of France for a bit, and then it will implode bigtime. What this means is we have to be extra specially careful on matters religious, as I keep saying.

We're past the Albigensian Crusade, thankfully, so no big groups get burned as heretics until the Templars, which isn't going to happen while we're here. In fact, 1305 is probably not a bad time to be here, religiously. No expulsions until next year. No mass murders at all. Also no major plagues. Sorry, Ben (*à propos* your comment to Sylvia, yesterday, if that comment was supposed to be *sotto voce*, then I'm sorry I overheard it) and sorry, Luke, we're not in the middle of a Connie Willis novel. This is the fourth reference I've heard to Willis and there have been six to Michael Crichton. I hope you all get tired of these jokes very soon. Until then, I'll keep counting them.

You need to know a bit more about the background. Who was whom and when. It will make sense of where we are. Let me start with a chronology of the possible saints. Sorry, slip of the tongue. I meant the popes. One was a saint. All the rest were mere mortals. No papal infallibility round now, nor much in the way of common sense. Also a ten month interregnum. Although I did say that.

Being a pope right now is not a recipe for happy ever after, though one pope from sort of around now was married, once. This is a really transitional period in Church history. Married priests are a dying breed. Almost gone entirely, I think, though I recall some oddities found in France in a tour of an archdiocese around the fifteenth century.

Chastity is growing. The Marian cult is growing. Church lands are growing. Papal politics are becoming very, very interesting. I can brief you on all these things if you want. Maybe not on the concubines of priests from the fifteenth century that was from a class I took during my B.A. and I have a half-memory only and no notes. There's nothing in our e-library about it.

The only thing you can assume is that the Church is not unified or modern. It's highly political and very interested in making earthly affairs heavenly and vice-versa. (Why hagiography is so very cool, of course, but I get the message quite clearly that no-one wants briefings on hagiography. You don't know what you're missing. Dead saints and their amazing adventures!)

Here's a brief chronology (approximate only):

Boniface XI was pope from 1303-1304. His original name was Nicola Boccasini. Didn't get on well with Philippe the stunningly gorgeous statue (King of France, current). His predecessor was beaten up by Philippe's men. Died (in his sixties, thrashed, sad but probably inevitable death). Dante didn't like him either, and placed him in Hell in the Divina Commedia. Or was that one of his predecessors?

Dante is alive as I type, but his Beatrice (one of the Great Loves of History) is dead. I have no idea where Dante lives right now, but it's unlikely to be in Saint-Guilhem-le-Désert. If you meet someone on the street and they claim to be Dante, I expect they're lying. Petrarch lived around here, though, if you count Vaucluse as around here, which it isn't. This isn't one of those SF novels where all the great people of history just happen to walk by. (The SF comments really get to me for some reason.)

Anyhow, Boniface XI is dead after a very short rule (he died possibly of poisoning that fits: one beaten, one poisoned just keep getting rid of them until you find a pope you like) and, as I said earlier, there is an interregnum. That means there's no pope, although there will be one quite soon.

Bonefficace's (a joke on his name! if you got the joke it means you're actually reading this briefing hi, Cormac) successor is Clement and he gets on far too well with the King of France. That's another briefing, though. He should be crowned while we're here one of the big political events of our time.

I've attached a thousand years of medieval popes in case you want to know who ruled when. The modern papacy is quite different to the Middle Ages, so what you were told as a child (I can't be the only once-a-Catholic) was probably wrong for this time and place.

* * *

Guilhem sat on his front doorstep, unable to see down to the main street. Someone was playing a cornemuse badly. Guilhem wondered where anyone had obtained a cornemuse he wasn't surprised that they couldn't play it.

Sibilla winked as she walked past him, coming out of his neighbour's house, her clothing slightly awry. Guilhem frowned. If she weren't careful, she might get a bit of a reputation. He gave up on the steps and walked into the main street. Maybe the smith would be taking a break from his forge. The smith was a man who spoke intelligently.

There was a little cluster of people in the street. Guilhem-the-smith was walking towards them. The two men fell in together.

"I can't get anything to work today," the smith said conversationally. "I leave the iron in the heat too long and it becomes brittle. I should know better than that. I need a break."

"I need an intelligent conversation," admitted Guilhem.

"You're in luck," his companion answered. "Listen."

The cluster of townsfolk were talking loudly about papal politics.

Guilhem listened with great intent for a while, moved to put in a word from time to time. When the subject shifted to the Gascon Wars, however, his face lost its openness. When the subject didn't look as if it would change again any time soon, Guilhem spun on his heels and left, abruptly.

"He really doesn't like us," said Peire, frowning.

* * *

Sylvia was rugged up very solidly against the cold. It was night, and dark, and Sylvia's favourite time. It had always been her special time. She always had a solitary place where she could sort out her day and her mind. She started with her regular observations of angle and position. Then she would drift into her quiet time. Sometimes she would do craftwork, sometimes she would dream, sometimes she would sing.

Here, in this cloistered cave, she needed the space particularly. There were too many irritants. Too much to be aware of. Too much that she was responsible for. And Luke was hopeless. He didn't make decisions and he only backed her sometimes. She needed that quiet time.

Sylvia had worked out a path to the hilltop above the caves. It was flat, that hilltop, and she could see vast distances. When the weather was fine, the Languedoc nights were clear and bright and she could climb up Mac's little ladder to the top then walk to the nearest decent rock for sitting, and she could be alone.

She didn't care that the others noticed her going up the ladder and into the darkness. She had a cast-iron excuse. She was always going up there to work, even if she intended to do no such thing.

"Double trouble boil and bubble," opined Mac.

"That's not how it goes," said Geoff. "At least, I don't think it is."

They looked to the others for answers, but the others weren't paying any attention. Neither Ben nor Artemisia had enjoyed Sylvia's little display of need, and were hiding behind their computer screens. Ben was working. Artemisia was thinking about zombies again.

* * *

"Throw some words at me." Theo was at his most expansive. His gestures were big and his voice ruled the room. "I want to fill that whiteboard with our work. Words, not concepts. We need to see the shape of the expedition now that we've been here long enough to get a feel for it. Be on the same page."

It was a very big page. Four normal whiteboards cobbled together and flattening the uneven wall behind it. Turning the cavern into an office. Turning everything dull. Artemisia was thinking rebellious thoughts about dullness mainly because she knew that she wouldn't be allowed to throw words at that whiteboard. She and Mac and Pauline were at the meeting only to see what the page looked like, not to actually contribute to it.

"How technical should we be?" asked Sylvia, all seriousness and scientific intent.

"Not too technical. Allow the non-specialists a bit of leeway."

"Plant collection," suggested Tony.

"Testing predictability," added Theo and wrote them both up. What were they testing the predictability of, wondered Artemisia, but remained obediently silent.

"Ozone layer density, carbon dioxide levels," was Geoff's contribution.

"Diversity of species," added Ben.

"Temperature measurement," Geoff added in a rush, "And rain. Modelling changes on my lovely new computer."

"Slower," said Theo.

"I think in spurts," explained Geoff.

"Then think in smaller spurts," suggested Artemisia. Pauline and Sylvia turned and glared at her, in unison, like well-trained monkeys. Artemisia glared back, half-heartedly. Then she smiled. "Fuel use, land use," she volunteered. This was easy. All the information fell into neat packages. She could probably fill the whiteboard on her own, without knowing the science at all. All she had to do was think about how her new friends approached their work and how they talked about it.

"Good, good," said Theo, and the monkeys subsided.

"Local species identification." Ben again.

"Changes between medieval and modern species." That was Tony.

"Dead stuff!" Mac shouted. When Theo looked across he explained "Extinction. Aren't we looking at extinction?"

"Ben?" asked Theo.

"Yes," said Ben, "that comes under species diversity."

"Dead stuff," said Theo and wrote it on the whiteboard.

"Astronomical observations," said Sylvia.

"Make that stargazing," suggested Mac. Sylvia looked around at him and he smiled back at her, beatifically.

"Biomass measurement," suggested Ben.

"Adaptation of the ecological system following the Medieval Warm Period."

"Shorter words, Tony, and fewer," said Theo, scribbling madly.

Artemisia wondered that silent Tony was being told to speak less. This group was living in irony. They were making new discoveries using old paradigms, she realised. It was how they constructed their science, in fact, congratulating themselves on newness while not questioning where their basic approaches came from.

"Biological indicators of climate change," added Ben, defiantly. When Theo raised an eyebrow he explained, "It's what we do. They're all aspects of understanding biodiversity."

Theo looked across at Ben, as if he were analysing the comment for hidden sarcasm. "Biodiversity," he said, eventually, and wrote it on the whiteboard.

"Erosion analysis," said Sylvia.

"Vulnerability of forest," said Ben.

"Medieval warm period ending," said Geoff. "And if there's water stress." Artemisia thought that stressed water probably needed counselling.

"Nature of the managed ecosystem," Ben volunteered, into silence. Artemisia's thoughts turned to why it was fine for Ben to use five words at a time and not for Tony. She suspected they were all so used to his silences that even three words would sound voluble. This feeling was reinforced when Ben added, "Impact of climate change on pathogens and phytophages" and Theo quietly wrote it down.

"Temperature and rainfall measurements," said Geoff.

"Haven't we had that?" asked Sylvia.

"Then put down atmospheric pollution." Theo did.

"Modelling the impact of climate change, studying the effects of change at the local level."

"How does that work?" asked Artemisia.

"We have modern studies," explained Geoff.

"This is one of the most studied regions of France," added Ben. "It's why we're here." To chase answers that they'd already half-formulated, Artemisia added to herself.

The explanation gave Theo a moment to catch up, but before he could turn away from the board, Geoff added "The human factor in climate change."

"I hate you," Ben told him, informatively. "That was mine."

"You can do all the work," Geoff reassured him. "I just want the whiteboard credit."

"Delta T," Sylvia said, defiantly. "Refining it."

"You're a very refined person," Geoff volunteered.

"Thanks for that," Sylvia retorted.

"CO_2 measurement — titre molaine," Geoff answered. Theo sighed and kept writing.

"Plant genome study," said Tony.

"Geology," said Sylvia.

"What about your project?" Pauline spoke up. "Theo, there's nothing of yours up there."

"Later," he said. "My hand is tired."

"Well, then," said Sylvia, "Can we talk about briefings?"

"Good idea," said Ben.

Theo nodded and took a seat.

"I think that Dr Wormwood's last briefing was far too long and discursive and wasted a great deal of our valuable time." Artemisia waited for someone to defend her, but no-one spoke. "Perhaps they could be short, in future, and only deal with essentials?"

"Good idea," said Theo, obviously exhausted by the inordinate strain of writing using words. "Also, Sylvia, have you given Artemisia a picture yet?"

"Done. Two days ago. No results."

"I may be able to help a bit," said Geoff. "I've noticed he keeps an eye on the back paths to the village."

"You've seen him," said Sylvia.

"Three times, but by the time I found Artemisia, he was gone."

"You could return the book," Sylvia said.

"Yes, Sylvia, I could, and I could apologise, but he wouldn't understand a word I say. I would be arrested for stealing."

"Huh," was Sylvia's considered response.

"Anyhow, I know more about him. For instance, he's not a forester. At least, I don't think he is?"

"What do you mean?"

"Or maybe he works for someone who's not a forester?"

"Maybe if you start at the beginning?"

"What a fine idea," Geoff grinned. His grin was very much like a child's, direct, confiding and perhaps a little bit cheeky. "I saw him with someone in a uniform and the guy checking the paths was very respectful to the guy in uniform."

"What kind of uniform? Maybe it was some kind of livery?"

"White. Long red cross. He carried a sword, but then the other guy does, too."

"Templar," was all Artemisia said. It was all she had to say. She was surprised that none of them had read up on the Templars back in Melbourne, given the team's destination. She wasn't quite as surprised that one had appeared here, on a pilgrim route.

This made things complicated. Artemisia had to return the book to someone who was involved with one of the long, dangerous arms of the Church. Maybe they would be lucky and maybe their forester/farmer/knight-about-town had been hailed to ask the way.

* * *

Guilhem's next visit to Pézenas accomplished nothing, which was Guilhem's aim precisely. When Bernat wanted to talk about his Order, Guilhem let the man babble. He was so proud of the organisation, with the groups of subordinate locations and the central commanderies all over the Christian world. Guilhem was surprised to discover that France was the jewel. After seeing Jerusalem, Guilhem himself was expecting to hear that all Christendom was at the edge of the world.

"The pilgrim routes," explained Bernat. "Pilgrims pass through France."

"You protect pilgrims, of course." Guilhem nodded as he expressed his understanding, but his mind drew a picture of the routes and their Templar protectors and his mind did not like the chart it visualised. He had seen the brother-knights in action.

For all their immense courage and military skill, they had failed at the single most important command: they had lost the Holy Land. They should have dissolved their Order in 1291. Now they were living on borrowed time, usurers in so many ways. They should give up their money-changing and their loans and their network of command and either they should reconquer Jerusalem or they should petition the Pope to forgive their oaths and excuse their failings. In the shade of the limestone big wall, Guilhem thought the position of the Templars was very simple and very ugly.

From that moment, he walked through the Commanderie with his eyes open to what it was.

He saw the complex of buildings outside Pézenas as somewhat more than a monastery, with its squat and powerful buildings and its position of control. He wanted to hate the complex, but realised that, really, it was the Templars about whom he was ambivalent. He was comfortable with their lifestyle. Too comfortable. *I need to consider this thought next time I visit.*

* * *

Luke called Artemisia into his office. The walls were faced with temporary whiteboard, covered with equations and words and diagrams and arrows and squiggles. Luke worked in as many dimensions as he could colonise and the boards moved and the equation shifted and each time Artemisia entered his office she wanted to look at the new patterns they made. She wanted to ask what it all meant, but she had done that the first time. He had dismissed her. "Basic university mathematics is going to be tough for someone like you: this is going to be impossible." She ached to ask, *But what questions are you posing? What is your framework?*

"What's it for, then?" she timidly pushed a little, instead.

"I'm shifting our paradigms here," and he waved at the tall wall, where he must be standing on a chair to reach the top and scrawl those sums. That tall wall had been jerry-built from other whiteboards. Under Theo's writing, 'titre molaine' was still faintly discernible. "Over here I'm processing the data from our transit. I believe I can reduce the likelihood of certain potential errors. And all the rest" his arm took in the remainder of the office "is what we couldn't even think of until we had travelled here and produced the data here," he patted his computer fondly. "It will change our reality."

"How?" Something that changes the questions that people asked, something that gave inconceivably new answers. This was big. This was exciting.

"Later, later," he said, "It's still early days. It's why we're all here. Why us and not that American mob. Early days." His voice drifted into some other realm for a moment, then he pulled at his beard, sat down and he got down to business, checking permissions and making sure that he and Artemisia agreed on what would keep the team's environmental impact low.

The next time he had refused to explain at all. It was obvious by the rearranged boards that he had been working mainly on changing reality. Artemisia took this to mean that he didn't want to talk about how he intended to change reality. Maybe he intended to surprise everyone when they woke up one morning and the sky was purple and the sea was ink-black?

This time she didn't push. She merely admired the pretty pictures the equations made and then she sat down.

"You haven't given back that book," Luke said, without preamble.

"I haven't found the person to give it to. I know where the shepherds run their sheep. Goats and I scare each other and the goats run away a lot. I've learned the times that farmers are likely to be out and about. Oh, and I've worked out that those packs on animals that head up the cliff from time to time are bringing supplies to the castle."

"The others have seen him." He didn't quite sound accusing, but his tone certainly made Artemisia seem negligent.

"I've noted where they saw him. I'll keep trying. I'll keep documenting everything else while I try. It's important to know land use patterns and lifestyles and what farmers actually do and when."

"Write a paper about it for when you get back. Maybe it will be published one day," Luke's tone was dismissive. Artemisia looked across at his 'changing reality' equations. Maybe Luke didn't realise his attitude condemned?

"Did the others tell you the man was seen with a Templar?" Artemisia was determined to make sure that the team understood their locality and its ramifications. She would push the history until they damned well accepted that the world outside the caves was no theoretical study, but actual people leading real lives. What was wrong with all Luke's notations all over his office is that they left out the people and the consequences that people always brought. There was something missing in his emotional makeup…his next statement confirmed this thought.

"No," Luke was only half interested. He wanted his information packaged according to his needs. *How on earth does that work, anyway, when he's trying to change realities?*

"It could be important. The Templars were"

"Write me a briefing about it," said Luke. "Just get that book back to its owner before Sylvia reclaims it."

"Yes, sir," answered Artemisia, sarcastically. Luke nodded and turned his face towards his computer.

Luke might have something missing in his makeup, but he

understood Sylvia.

"If you can't find that man, the book is mine," she announced over dinner two days later.

"What?" Artemisia was totally flummoxed.

"I found it. It's mine."

"Sylvia," said Ben, gently, "it's not yours unless the Director decides, when we return home."

"I'll find the owner," Artemisia said. "I'll return it."

"Hah," said Sylvia, her face showing her thoughts with window-like clarity. She had Harvey twisted around her little finger, as she had Luke. The book was hers.

* * *

Guilhem was sitting on the hillside, sunning himself. He fell asleep. It was that kind of day and he was in that kind of mood.

A noise woke him up. He thought "Hillfolk" and kept his eyes shut. He wasn't sure he wanted to see strange beings that day. Then he heard laughter. He knew that laugh.

He opened his eyes a slit and saw a hand moving away from the pommel of his dagger. His own hand reached out very quickly and grasped that other hand. A piece of chalk dropped out of it.

Fiz said, "I wasn't doing anything."

Guilhem opened his eyes fully and said, "We'll see about that."

He looked at his dagger. Its beautiful flat pommel was now decorated with a very silly and rude picture.

Fiz twisted his wrist and freed himself, and then scrambled down the hillside. Fiz was remarkably good at negotiating impossibly steep slopes in a great hurry, Guilhem thought. He himself was not half mountain goat. So he stood there, arms crossed, looking dour.

When Fiz was out of sight, the boy looked back at where the knight was invisible and smiled, a big, goofy smile. That was a good moment, when he saw his drawing on the dagger. His drawings of knights with huge male parts were the best of anyone's, he thought. Fiz frowned. Bona was scrambling up the slope, anxious to join him.

"Go away," he said. "I don't want you."

She still came, obdurate, but a bit careful. Fiz used that care and went down the hill in the other direction, faster than she could catch. He could climb these hills better than anyone!

Bona had another hindrance. In the distance, she could hear her brother crying. He had followed her. He had skinned his knee. Bona gave up her attempt to be adventurous and glumly made her way down to the wounded one. Fiz, as usual, would have his adventures without her.

* * *

Artemisia was determined to write about William. Not the short briefings that she was told she had to write, and not academic papers, but the stories. She wanted to engage the time team and make them understand that the outside was real and that the figures they saw in the landscape were human beings with lives. Whose possessions mattered. Whose futures mattered. Consequences she wanted to get the rest of the team *feeling* that there were consequences.

This was still the country of heroes, even if the time team was the opposite of heroic. Maybe heroes would do the trick. They wouldn't read it now, but if they read it later, maybe it would work. When boredom struck, she might be able to make her strike. Maybe when someone was ready to realise that the world outside was real, her briefings would be there, ready to lead them into an understanding of it. Maybe.

"Historical briefing (file from Artemisia Wormwood). William was a great hero..." she began. It made her happy to state the obvious right up front.

* * *

William was a great hero. He was Charlemagne's kin. It was thanks to him that the invaders were driven back beyond the Pyrenees and also thanks to him that Charles' son, Louis, ascended the throne after Charles' death. He won himself a pagan bride and many pagan cities. In fact, he won bride and city and the name he is known by all at once, when he entered the city of Orange.

In real life, he was known by many names. William of Gellone, the second Count of Toulouse the different names and titles reflected the man himself. He was larger than life, but at the same time he was a real person. He was Guillaume al corb nez; he was Fierebrace; he was the most famous Guilhem from the South. He was one of France's greatest heroes.

He lived from sometime in the eighth century and died early in the ninth. While he was Charlemagne's cousin, he was also one of his trusted leaders. He fought many battles and was key to Charlemagne's expansionist policies. In 803, he took Barcelona from its Moslem rulers and cemented himself in the popular mind as the hero who fought for Christian Europe.

In 804 he founded our monastery, at a place called Gellone. This is where he retired and this is where he died, on 28 May. It is he who the tourists visit, his bones and a piece of the One True Cross that he brought here. In the modern monastery, both his bones and the cross are backlit and glow in the dark. I have pictures, if you want to see them. I doubt they are backlit right now.

* * *

Additional historical briefing (file from Artemisia Wormwood)

You asked for one fact about William, since a complete briefing takes many hours for scientists to read and scientists are lacking in hours. Your one fact is "The story of his cousin's mother's life was a famous romance. Charlemagne's mother was known as Bertha Big Foot and her husband was Pippin the Short."

The team read this briefing. Artemisia knew this when she heard Ben referring to Charlemagne's father as 'the hobbit emperor who married the abominable snowwoman'. Not even Sylvia had questioned Ben's description.

She also sent Luke the first part of a briefing on the Templars. He thanked her for it, but didn't notice that it was only part one. She wondered if he had read it at all. *The Templars are here,* she thought. *In this place. Knights militant; knights dangerous. This cannot be good.*

Then she scolded herself for exaggeration. One Templar didn't make a tempest. Or even a crusade. As long as the team kept avoiding the locals, it would all be fine. No-one would even know they were there. No-one except the owner of that book.

Tomorrow I'll try at dawn. Maybe he's an early bird.

While Artemisia flagellated herself over not knowing if it was Templar singular or if there was a group of them or if they were even a concern, while she looked vainly through her antiquated reference library, trying to answer her own questions, one of the other team members demonstrated a different way of looking at things.

"Templars," Pauline said, to Sylvia, when they shared a coffee break. "I know about them."

"You do?" Sylvia was willing to listen, though not to be

impressed. Pauline's qualifications were in medicine, after all. Still, she was a nicer human being than Artemisia, and she always gave Sylvia the best coffee and she always had an interesting take on things.

"You know the *Da Vinci Code, Holy Blood, Holy Grail?*"

"Oh!" Sylvia's face lit up. "Those were the Templars?"

"They were. Framed and tortured and murdered. They had the biggest hidden treasure in Europe."

"That's why that book was so nice?"

"That's what I think."

"We should keep an eye out."

"We can glean stuff. That path those pilgrims travel? I bet there are more Templar treasures."

"Are we allowed?" Pauline sounded as if she was just waiting for permission.

"If we're careful, I don't see that there's a problem."

"And you're in charge of day-to-day stuff."

"Everything except scheduling." Sylvia looked as if she had swallowed precisely enough cream.

"Templars," breathed Pauline, her face dreamy.

"Templars." Sylvia nodded, in complete agreement.

* * *

This is how the team discovered the End of the World and its precarious paths. There was a flat track where people could be found and there were the safer goat trails and the sheep trails and the hill ways which were hard to discern and even harder to walk. Around and under all the paths were the many shades of white and cream and brown that comprised the limestone, whether cliff or rock face or simple slope. And around and wedged into that, always, was verdant green.

They didn't find Templar treasure at the end of the world, but they found bits and bobs from time to time and they were well clear of the town, so Artemisia couldn't complain. Gleanings were slow, however, and usually meagre and every now and again Sylvia or Pauline would look around impatiently. Wanting more. Expecting better.

One or other of them would bring the subject of gleanings up at mealtimes, sounding Artemisia out on the value of this or that.

Sometimes it was obvious that they were making things up, inventing from an insufficient knowledge of the place or time (Artemisia's personal favourite was the faceted diamond necklace Pauline apparently coveted, at a period when there was no way of faceting diamonds). At other times, Artemisia would look across the table sharply, wondering if they had found something and left it, or had hidden it somewhere in the caves, or had simply seen a covetable object in a traveller's possession.

She talked about the importance of the everyday and ordinary in the process of discovery. If the team understood that, maybe they would be less tempted by the sort of stuff that would get everyone into trouble. They were scientists, after all, and surely understood knowledge and its acquisition. Leavings of used-up old clothing and broken combs were less dangerous on so many levels.

Not that there were vast amounts of anything, really. People saved up their findings to show them off, all at once, in visits to the bin because, really, despite the big talk, they were not common. Not a lot of litterbugs in this place and time. Which didn't stop the time team members talking as if stuff of value was lying around everywhere.

While asking Artemisia for her advice, Sylvia would turn attention back to herself at every opportunity. The discoveries were about her. The work was her work. The knowledge was the knowledge she needed. Artemisia wondered how Pauline tolerated this. Even Tony was unperturbed by Sylvia having turned up one day to help with his digging. Artemisia was puzzled, not only by Sylvia herself, but by everyone else's acceptance of her behaviour.

* * *

Sibilla and Berta were sitting on the lowest wall of the vineyards just outside town. It was terracing to protect the vineyards, nothing more, but that carefully constructed drystone artefact was the perfect place for two women to kick their heels, hidden by shrubbery.

Berta noticed that one of the hillfolk was an older woman. She disliked her on sight. That woman had greedy eyes and a grasping right hand. She was trawling the path, *their* path, for lost objects. Also, she walked as if this land were hers. Which it wasn't. Every morsel of land for miles either had clear ownership or was undertaking dispute resolution. There was no space for strangers. If that woman, with her white hair and her taking ways, would remain under the hill, then Berta wouldn't feel so aggravated, but here she was, causing waves. Yes, Berta hated her.

Sibilla's voice communicated to Berta constantly. It informed Berta of exactly what she was seeing and why her gaze was not upon the strange gleaners.

"He's rather nice," she whispered, her right hand fiddling with her belt clasp. Her eyes were firmly fixed on Guilhem, training on that spot where the main path met the stream. The combination of path and stream and edge of field gave the knight more space and less stone underfoot than anywhere else.

"He's rather young," answered Berta, absent-minded, her gaze still on Pauline. Pauline and Sylvia had seen the knight, however, and were soon out of sight.

Guilhem himself was trying to gentle the edge of his unhappiness with much physical effort. It wasn't real training, but it was better than the work he had put in with those at the castle the day before. They didn't know and they didn't care.

Guilhem had given up on his driving need to survey the route from the Cevennes. *The town can defend itself*, he admitted, bitterly. *I have no function here.*

* * *

"However did his girlfriend let him go? Why is he even here?" Sylvia whispered to Pauline, as they watched Geoff walk past half-naked. Every day he did this. Walked from the showers to his bedroom to get changed. The others either dressed in the showers or wore some sort of covering back to their rooms. Geoff never bothered. He was cold (the coolness of the caverns froze his blood, he claimed) but he still walked back near-naked to his cubicle after his shower, slapping himself to stay warm. He was quite beautiful now that his hair was growing back, and entirely unconcerned about nakedness or possible audience.

"She was a stupid girl," said Pauline, her gentle dusky voice making the words condemnatory.

* * *

Tony had persuaded Mac into creating better soil using a whole new method. Mac hadn't taken much convincing. All Tony had to do was look helpless and use the magic word.

"Better soil through explosions," Mac rubbed his hands, gleefully. "I didn't know it was possible. ANF will do it. Let me find you some ammonium nitrate and fuel." Tony had no idea, himself. He wanted something, however, and obviously stealing good soil from the farming land below was not going to get Luke's approval.

Tony was careless of his physical self and Mac was far too keen to make big bangs. Mac caught Tony sitting on the sack of ammonium nitrate, simply because it was the right height.

"You're sitting on an explosive substance," he said. Tony stood up in a great hurry. "Just kidding. It's your fertiliser until I add the diesel."

They both had a fine time and made a great deal of noise.

Luke called the culprits into a meeting with Sylvia and with Ben. He read them all the riot act noise and the locals were the substance of it. Keeping their imprint small. Not being idiots. Mac was too happy and Tony was considering how to use the side product of the explosion to change his soil in two of his plots and neither of them paid much attention. Sylvia, of course, disowned it all. "If they can't use proper procedure" and Ben was strangely silent. His eyes slatted nearly shut as he thought about the explosive. When Luke's temper was all blown out, Ben went to Tony's garden and assessed the situation.

* * *

Artemisia and Geoff were alone in the office area. Everyone else had found excuses to leave the claustrophobia behind. Artemisia found herself choosing between the caves with Geoff or the possibility of running into Sylvia in the very limited outdoors they had available that day.

"You ought to have sad eyes, you know," she murmured to Geoff, surprising herself.

"Why?" His gaze connected suddenly, viscerally. It was as if he had seen her before, but not noticed. That gaze was amused, interested, complicated anything but unhappy.

"Those big brown eyes. Tragic."

"You've got big brown eyes, too."

"Mine are Italian. We left tragedy behind a generation and a half ago, in a little Italian village with nothing to its name except saints and good cooking."

"I'm Islander," Geoff volunteered. "I'm supposed to be joyous. Stereotypes tell me so."

"And sing hymns."

"Only if you're desperate."

* * *

6 May, Ascension Day

Sibilla was in the mood to be virtuous. Her church of choice was Saint-Barthelmy, boldly, to celebrate, wearing purity like a badge. She was watched the whole time not even the hymns could hide the looks she was given. Symbolism upon symbolism. A moment out of time.

Chapter Fourteen: Colonising

Mac was showing Geoff some of his stuff. They were using the common room with the chairs pushed right over the edge of the wire mesh. The chairs tilted dangerously. Each man held a wooden sword.

"These are practice weapons," Mac explained.

"So I don't get to kill you yet?"

"Later," promised Mac. "Though I'm pretty sure I could kill you, even with these, if I really wanted to."

"Then don't really want to," said Geoff. "I'm far too pretty to die. Now tell me what I'm doing with this."

"You're learning the basic sword guards. There are four."

"And remind me why we're avoiding the good doctor-historian?"

"Because the manual my group uses is German and later and Artemisia would tell me that. In detail. And I know it already."

"You mean it hasn't been written yet? That's just wrong."

"Shut up."

Before Geoff could say another word, a cry came from the kitchen.

"Weevils! In the flour!!"

This sounded promising, so Mac collected the swords and the four basic guards were postponed until another occasion. The weevils were in the flour and Artemisia was sitting at the kitchen table, watching Pauline squirm as she stared in horror as the flour gently shifted before her eyes.

"Get rid of it," Pauline said to Mac. "I shall make the food we have last the distance," she promised, valiantly, her eyes still disturbed by the crawling flour.

"D'you want me to clean the tub and stuff, too?" he asked.

"Yes."

Mac did that first in his workroom, then went to get fresh flour. Geoff tagged along for the ride.

"So much stuff!" he said.

"Don't tell Doc," Cormac confided, "But we didn't use much

flour when we set up. No time for cooking. Made pancakes twice."

"So those weevils are your fault."

"Absolutely."

"And there isn't a food problem."

"No.

"And we're not going to tell Doc?"

"Too right."

Geoff looked around at the impossibly crowded storeroom. "Of course, she could walk in here and see for herself."

"She won't."

"What's this hole last night's dinner?"

"It leads where I keep the dangerous stuff. Stay out of there. It's also my secret escape to freedom and the outside world. Where I lose myself when Theo hollers."

Geoff sighed in envy. Theo was very demanding for someone so apparently abstracted. When Mac couldn't be found, he was the one roped in to find things and fix things and say "There, there." Harvey had warned him that Theo was needy "Won't make sexual advances," he had been told. "He has a partner. Also, he's careful about not exploiting power differentials — aware, professional. But he might try to get your attention from time to time."

Artemisia saw them lose themselves in the storeroom and repressed a sigh. She had been excluded from the kitchen until the crisis was over and was feeling unnoticed and rebellious and rather childish. Sylvia kept walking back and forth, fluffed with her own importance. Sylvia made her feel childish, just by walking past.

Artemisia had found some erasable crayons in one of Cormac's stashes and had been using them on one of the portable whiteboards they helped her think she had always done her outlining on paper and had been missing it. Her writing had been missing it, too, she realised. At least, they helped her think until Sylvia looked down on what she was doing and sniffed.

Sylvia had brought enough makeup so that she could look beautiful and charming every single day of the two hundred and seventy odd they would all be together. Artemisia hadn't brought any makeup at all. Not even a lipstick. Sylvia walked with her own aplomb, even with her haircut growing out. Artemisia slumped into her chair and wondered if it was too late to learn deportment. It was:

far too late. She slumped out of her chair and decided to go for a walk.

She meandered around the caves, admiring the rocks and the shadows and the cold that underlay it all. When she found herself next to a particularly favourable blank stalactite, large and curved and hardly rippled at all, she realised she still had the erasable crayon in her hand. She wanted to draw a funny face. She wanted to dream about how it would be interpreted over the centuries. The blue crayon came closer and closer to the rock as she formulated theories about how the drawing would be thought of devil worship, an odd manifestation of ancient belief, early graffiti?

Unfortunately for her, Ben Konig had returned from checking in his latest batch samples. They were safely in cold storage and he felt satisfied enough to give Artemisia an evil look. Being excluded from weevils didn't worry him at all.

She pulled her crayon back as if she were a schoolgirl. *Still* a schoolgirl. Ben looked at her, disapprovingly.

"Do you know how many people we've upset by coming here?" Artemisia was determined to spill her emotions on Ben Konig, the species diversity expert. That's how she always thought of him "Ben Konig, the species diversity expert." It was her little way of not trusting, not letting him and his smile and his lies get close.

At that moment in his very long day, Ben Konig would have chatted with a cave bear if one had existed and if that cave bear been willing to talk. The night before, Ben had argued very loudly with Luke about having a copy of the interim results to check to see if anything more could be done to meet the French Government's list of outcomes. This had the salutary effect of reminding the other scientists that he had entirely the wrong loyalties.

This is why Ben leaned against that oversized stalactite with its pale purple face and he listened to Artemisia, regardless of the fact that Artemisia had just nearly defaced future French Government property. Also regardless of the fact that Artemisia had been nominated Evil Historian Who Did Not Do her Job in a Timely Fashion.

First Sylvia, now Ben. This was life underground. She sighed. Ben laughed. Her mood turned from schoolgirl to confessional. She sat on the nearest rock ledge (more a lump than a ledge, she reflected, hard and cold and almost comfortable) and talked at him.

"Who in particular would you upset by drawing on this stalagmite?" Ben asked.

"The cave people. The rock people. The people who hate us for cleaning out the wildlife and the rubble."

"So we're studying everything except what we destroy?"

"Oh, the set-up party took notes and pictures before they built us this little home-away-from-home. Mac said. He couldn't make up his mind if it was fine, or a pain because they had so few amenities until it was done."

"Still."

"What?" His voice was offended, but there was something in his face that suggested a willingness to be persuaded.

"It's so very nineteenth century."

"I don't get it." Ben had a very nice voice, Artemisia realised again. Almost baritone. She let herself be persuaded to explain further.

"We're the Great Explorers. We're the people who know so much that we're allowed to destroy things."

"We have our rules," his defence was mild. In fact, his tone was not at all defensive. Almost as if he was agreeing with her.

"And for the things they cover, those rules are good. Except..."

"What?" This was a softer, milder, more curious question. Artemisia had suddenly become a whole person in Ben's eyes. Why was this happening with the men her age, and why now? Artemisia decided to reserve her opinion as to whether this was a good thing.

"They're like the rules of anthropology in the early days. Just being here changes and contaminates."

"We're careful. No grandfather paradox for us. Not a single local has seen us. Except Sylvia, that once. And you, as soon as you deliver that book."

"And yet we've changed this whole section of the cave system, just by living here. Maybe it was dull stuff when it was explored back when"

"Future when."

"Back in the future, then," Artemisia grimaced. The jokes got old very quickly. "Maybe it was dull because we killed it. Caves are living."

"We know that," Ben's voice was softer and gentler still. "We ignore it, but we know it."

"Then why all the talk about being clever at avoiding paradoxes? Why take any risks at all?"

"Because most of us are very good at compartmentalising," finally the real Ben Konig emerged. These words came out with the slight hurry of words that have been waiting to be said, waiting for a very long time. *And yet*, thought Artemisia *he's not saying much. What is it with Konig?* "The damage is done with our habitat. Not with anything else."

"Compartmentalising."

"You do it with your history," Ben said. "You keep saying 'I only know about saints.'"

"I was so the wrong person to bring on this trip."

"Maybe. But maybe it's because you weren't vetted and your mind rejects all the hype and self-justification that we need you."

"So you agree that we're nineteenth-century explorers, changing everything we touch."

"Yes. Yes, I do."

Chapter Fifteen: Data

Berta was smug. The abbot had sent one of his men to order a special piece. That would show those idiot weavers in Aniane just who made the best cloth.

* * *

It was the ninth of May and Sylvia had commandeered the observation area. She had forgotten to book it, but she didn't care. It was the perfect night for watching. Uranus, Mars and Saturn created a gentle curve pointing downwards, towards the rising moon. Neptune was there, too, invisible to the naked eye, but completing the curve and making it whole. When it aligned with their curve, the lunar eclipse would be over.

Sylvia's angel-bow lips pursed lightly in concentration as she pondered recording secular acceleration. If she could refine delta T then she could expand the time travel envelope back two thousand more years. It wouldn't be safe, but safety wasn't her task. She was here to observe a lunar eclipse. And she loved lunar eclipses. She was using old-fashioned observation — extra-galactic radio sources weren't available to the time team.

Geoff emerged in the dark and started to set up his equipment.

"Not tonight." Sylvia's voice was obdurate.

"I booked with Ben — I'm sharing my space with you, and you have half my equipment."

"Tough," said Dr Smith, "this eclipse is mine. All mine. Go watch it from downstairs."

"With that light contamination? With the sky half-obscured by cliff?"

"Not my problem."

* * *

Sylvia and Luke were putting together the second datastream. The first datastream had been basic. This one was more ambitious. Everything the future needed to know about the past, to be blipped forward in the shortest possible time and taking the least possible space. Sylvia was designing forms and methods and Luke was working on the physics.

Luke was challenging his changing universe. This datastream was the first test of the first part of his theories. The data would go through twice, once under the old system and once using his new one. He was quiet about it, but everyone knew it was big stuff.

"It's a symbiotic relationship," Artemisia said to Pauline, as she went for much-needed cuppa. Luke had stopped in the middle of walking from place to place, his steps doing his thinking. He was writing down a thought. Sylvia would come along shortly and fit it into his main material.

"It is," agreed Pauline, almost conversationally. "They work well together."

This made her a little sad. Luke had already determined that the universe was black and white and he wanted to know how much black there was and how much white. But what if it were purple? Luke's big ideas still rested within current scientific constructs. Scientists weren't superhuman.

* * *

The village was divided, mostly along the usual lines. Saint-Laurent versus Saint-Barthelmy. Too many possessions left outside the walls had vanished. It had become a common pastime for a half dozen parishioners from Saint-Barthelmy (plus Berta and Sibilla) to lurk behind bushes and watch the gleaners. This group kept their silence, however. Guilhem-the Smith made sure of that. He thought that things could get very ugly very quickly if blame fell on these outsiders, however much they stole.

* * *

"Grapes," said Ben. "The leaf shape. With fine dentata. I think we have a new variety."

"An old variety," Luke corrected. "With teeth." He showed his own bright white teeth a bit wolfishly as he smiled at his own mild pun.

"Something that will make our future employers very happy," Ben promised. "Not just one that was lost with the phylloxera one that went a long time before then." He was lying again. If he gathered enough samples, however, one would be a genuine unknown.

"Will it make good wine?"

Ben was impatient. "That's something you can't tell from a bloody leaf shape, Luke, you know that. The big thing is it's a variety that these people make wine from, and that we don't know it."

"You want space when we exchange for supplies.

"For a living plant preferably several."

"Cut the slips now, then. Be careful that no-one sees you. Ask Tony to grow them for you. I'm not going to be responsible for magic disappearances in someone's vineyard when we're short of time."

Ben nodded once and almost ran out the door.

Luke smiled at Ben's back. No matter what else he thought of the man, Konig was a damned good scientist and loved his work. More than anything else, this was what mattered.

* * *

"We can hear the bells inside," said Sylvia.

"My handyman's secret," Cormac grinned. "It only works at this spot in the workroom."

"Like that little passage. Where you sneak in and out." Sylvia's voice held faint condemnation.

"I like it when you're rumpled." Cormac's grin grew, and Sylvia turned round and went back to her desk.

There she worked assiduously until dinnertime.

* * *

Both town and hill collected clutter. On this day, the clutter included: a coffee mug, half full of weak instant coffee, diluted with powdered milk, a clump of yellow powder floating near one edge; a pair of fluffy green slippers, with eyes; one small computer, chugging away in near silence; a blue biro, heavily chewed; a chocolate wrapper; a frayed towel, woven in 1296; one portable brazier, containing charcoal; one cooking fork; the relic of a miscellaneous saint, wrapped in soft leather and label illegible on a scrap of parchment, waiting for its reliquary to be cleaned; a staff; a pilgrim's scrip; a cockleshell, once from Santiago de Compostella, now broken where someone misstepped; a pruning hook.

* * *

The air was dense and moist in the non-colonised parts of the cave system.

"We're people of the light," joked Luke, "and so we live near the light where the air is dry."

Chapter Sixteen: The Look of Things

Guilhem couldn't rid himself of the memory. He recalled seeing a woman, indecorous, entirely unknown, reaching down and picking up his book. He saw the look of glee on her face and the defiance she flung at him when he called out. He remembered how very fast she moved. How she disappeared. How he had not seen his book since. Every time he walked near this spot, he remembered, and his bitterness grew.

Now here he was, back in the same spot, looking in vain for the woman with hair like gold thread with her pretty face and her greedy hands. There was a new woman waiting for him, taller, with big eyes and dark hair. Dressed decorously. Of his own rank. And in her hands was his book. She was holding it out to him. It was all he could do not to snatch it and run home, where he could put it in its leather book bag, out of harm's way.

He reached out and took it. Guilhem took a deep breath.

The lady said nothing.

The lady was too busy thinking, *Thank God, he has the book. Thank God. And he's young. Early twenties. Mid twenties at most. And he's so bloody young! And he has his book and he's been missing it. Look at how his fingers run over it and his eyes, how nothing else matters.*

When Guilhem had assured himself that his great treasure was in good condition, and that there was his private joke in the main illumination for March to prove it was his, that he and no other had commissioned this book from one of the best workshops in Paris. When he had finished, he looked at this second woman and thought *From good stock comes good fruit but from what stock does this woman descend? She is strange to me.*

"Permit me. Please. Excuse me," Artemisia stumbled. "I must speak with you. I am Artemisia. I am called Artemisia."

"Guilhem," the knight said, briefly, and discourteously. He regretted his brevity and said, reluctantly, "My name is Guilhem."

108

"Guilhem is a good name," said Artemisia cautiously. 'Bon nom' was pretty safe, in old, new or any other French.

"I don't speak that language," Guilhem replied, understanding Artemisia perfectly well. Why should he speak that Northern tongue? What had the North done for him? It had given him his uncle. And his cousins. And a lifetime of guilt. He would not speak that tongue.

The woman excused herself slowly and haltingly. She had not understood his denial. He looked at her braided hair and small veil, not quite demure, nor yet immodest. He looked at her dress. Imported cloth, from its fineness, but with none of the decoration that would show him her class, her taste, her wealth. He didn't want to talk to her.

Eventually her apologies overcame his temper and he finally spoke to her in the French of France, slowly and with many allowances for her little brain. *Renart has stolen my mind,* he thought, *for all I am doing is full of mischief and this lady is in distress.*

Artemisia didn't let her face show that she realised that he spoke the French of France perfectly well. She also tried not to let herself show how very afraid she was. She wanted to pick up her long skirts and run away. This was too impossible. Her talking to someone educated from 1305. Her talking to anyone from 1305.

All his words were careful, as if he listened for their intent before he could speak them aloud. They emerged in short phrases; one word, five words, never more. A micropause after each phrase, or maybe before the next. It wasn't lack of self-confidence, Artemisia decided, but it might be awareness of consequences. Either way, the delays gave her time to deduce what he was saying, most of the time.

She apologised again and explained that she had been looking for him, to return the book, that it had been a mistake.

He thanked her with real gratitude *This book is his,* she realised. *Important to him.*

The young man then said, "Ill-gained goods never lead to profit."

"A saying?" she ventured. She thought she recognised it. She hoped her pronunciation was not too improbable did one say the 'c' in 'dict' aloud? Was 'dict' an earlier word? A later one?

It didn't matter: Guilhem understood her.

"Yes, and a good one."

"I am happy I could return it to you."

She explained that they were a group living in the hill until after Christmas. "We will try to be…" She looked in her mind and found only English.

"You wish to be secret."

"No. Yes. To not…"

"I think I understand. You wish to be little seen. This is why it has taken you a long time to find me."

"Yes, that is it. My people are not clever in this. They know this. They have asked…"

"For help?"

"For forgiveness. But we need help. We know so little."

Her language was halting and it was hard to find words. *That will improve,* she thought. *It's hard to move from reading a language to speaking it.* It took a long time, but in the end Artemisia thought they understood each other.

They had a place, and a signal. If she tied a ribbon to a bush he would look for her there the next day, and if he tied a different coloured ribbon to that same bush, then she would do likewise. If they couldn't come, then they would leave more ribbons.

"Fairies have ribbons?" asked Guilhem, half-seriously.

"We are not fairies, although we do live under the hill, but we have ribbons. The very best ribbons."

Artemisia smiled. She had no idea why there were ribbons in Cormac's stash, but she would sequester the colours, and hope the signal system would work. She remembered looking through the box of long soft silk in many shades, wondering if she could plait her hair in a better way, more in accordance with twelfth century fashion perhaps, ribbons winding through, glamorously.

She and Luke had spoken for a long time about the need for a contact in the town. This young knight looked as if he had goodwill and enthusiasm, despite the initial contretemps. It was especially important since Luke still refused to allow language lessons. Her halting Middle French was the only Middle French they had.

Mind you, she thought it was Old French still. Her brain analysed the use of cases and his syntax and his pronunciation, even as she struggled to make herself understood. Hardly Middle French at all. Thank goodness he spoke some northern dialect. That was the big thing. Not that she wasn't sure about declensions or conjugations, but that he spoke the language she could read and for which she had Godefroy's huge and unreliable nineteenth century dictionary.

She asked Guilhem about the local language and said she didn't know it, and she thought he had offered to be a kind of go-between. Which meant he lived here but wasn't a local? Or was staying here? Or lived in the castle? He had a sword and dagger and his clothes were nice and he had no tonsure and he owned a bloody expensive book that meant that he was no peasant and no priest. At least, she didn't think so. *A knight,* she decided again. *I already thought that. Except what's an ordinary knight doing with a Book of Hours? It's an expensive calendar to be carrying around in 1305. Maybe he's a time traveller from the 1450s? Or maybe he's dirt-rich and in love with art and calendars, like the duc de Berry?*

Too much knowledge and not enough understanding, that was her trouble. This was going to be slow and difficult. She only hoped she got it right. There really wasn't any margin for error.

* * *

Templar time again. Guilhem almost looked forward to his visit. As he followed the broad path to Pézenas (smooth, like the road to hell) he contemplated the money Master Bernat would hand over and calculated his finances over and again. That was the reason for this visit. No avuncular oversighting and no examination of the state of his soul. Some of his income had arrived from his aunt's careful stewardship, in the north where lay the French of France and civilisation. Also far too many relatives, all full of opinions about him and his doings. Still, the money was a good thing.

Guilhem calculated. He had already allowed himself 10 sous for the year. Maybe he could stretch that to 12 if he really needed it. The original figure reflected his new lifestyle, and didn't reflect his actual income. It didn't permit him to show his worth and to give the way a noble should, to his dependants and others around him. It was money for his personal use. A bit more would permit him to show his quality.

Guilhem measured each of his estates in his mind and wondered how much his aunt would send him. She would no doubt keep a significant portion for herself, but she would also keep aside money for taxes and to put back into his land. He hated her, but she was a good steward.

There would not be much coin, he realised. He would still go. He would collect it to prove to his aunt that he would jump when she asked him to, so that Bernat could send another report home. His real income came from elsewhere. Far away from his aunt.

As he got closer to Pézenas, he became more and more nervous. Had Bernat's previous report been good enough so that she would reward him with enough money so that he could live according to his rank and worth? Or would she send him a pittance along with a message, as she had in Gascony? What would he do if she found an excuse to keep a larger proportion of his income? Would he be forced to pretend to live off the tiny parcels of non-contiguous land that were his holdings near Saint-Guilhem? Would he be forced to manage that land himself and squeeze an income from it? Would he have to solve the three outstanding legal claims?

Would she invoke his uncle's name?

That was the worst possibility of all. For all his cousin's vast power, it was his uncle of whom Guilhem was terrified. He wished the journey were over and he was in Pézenas and knew what his relatives thought. He knew his fear was wrong. He was an adult and a knight. But the memories of childhood lay more heavily on him than the memories of war.

* * *

The day glowered. While the cave was oppressive with the sky low and dark and the air thick, outside it was worse.

Mac dealt with the weather by becoming more practical. Their in-house handyman decided it was time to call each and every expedition member into the kitchen and to work out their needs, over coffee and cake. Artemisia wondered if this was Mac's way of ensuring that Pauline baked and that he obtained the lion's share of the baking. She wouldn't put it beyond him.

It was all straightforward. Mac made two lists one for collection after breakfast the next day and another for requisition through the next datastream. It was straightforward. He had to be doing it for the cake. Not that it didn't have to be done, but to take most of the day, in the kitchen? She noticed that all the cake-eaters of the group took much longer to sort their needs out. She noticed this because she, herself, was bored to tears. *You'd think one became used to boredom,* she thought.

The next day was as bad. Artemisia listened, with fascination, to Mac's breakfast announcement.

"Today I want everything you have that's broken. Bring stuff to the stores area as soon as you can. This morning. No excuses." Mac was enjoying bossing his bosses.

Later in the day, Luke paid a visit to Mac's workshop. "Hard at work, McGyver? If you wouldn't mind taking a moment and mending one of my whiteboards…"

"You broke a whiteboard?" Cormac was polite to Luke's face, but inwardly he was swearing full revenge. He hated that nickname. Hated it.

"Some indentations. I was a bit emotional."

"Indentations?" despite himself, Cormac was fascinated.

"Holes, then."

"Give me a few minutes and I'll see what I can do."

* * *

Friends kiss, Artemisia knew. Modern Australians didn't. Not unless forced. And even then, it was awkward. What was more awkward is that Old French texts were full of references to making salutations then kissing. But how did one kiss and why and would kissing make Guilhem move from stranger to friend to something more worrying? She was jumpy about men.

She took the easy way out.

"It is normal among your people to welcome and kiss. I have read this. My people have a different courtoisie. We do not touch, except the hands and maybe a touch, so," she tapped her own shoulder in explanation. "Do we observe your courtoisie or mine?"

The approach worked. Guilhem stopped in his tracks and assessed her alienness. Artemisia hoped that admitting literacy would help.

"How do you touch hands?" he asked.

Artemisia held out her hand and when Guilhem held his out, she shook it. Guilhem laughed. "This shall we do. It amuses me."

"Thank you for being amused," said Artemisia dryly.

Guilhem laughed again. "Now you must learn something of my world."

"I would like…"Artemisia paused, suddenly concerned. Guilhem nodded, so she continued, "To learn the language of the people who live in the town. Just a little."

"Not more French?"

"Also French. We will speak French, and I will learn when we speak. Will I not?"

"Some words only. You do not need anything but French." Artemisia wondered why his caution. Who was this young man? He didn't talk about himself.

In the end, the words and phrases he gave were few. They included *detras lo castel* below the castle; *for a lo portail* outside the entrance she computerised them when she returned to the caves, knowing she had added precisely nothing to the sum of human knowledge in the twenty-first century. She had also discovered, as Guilhem relaxed a little, that the people of this region were regarded as unreliable, full of vice and traitors.

"I would we were drunk as Gascon knights," he said. "It is better than being of the line of Charlemagne with the character of Ganelon."

Artemisia wrote 'drunk as Gascon knights' down too. It was a very good phrase. Guilhem had more than a little of the drama queen about him. He also liked his historical references. And his sayings.

He was no peasant. Not in any way. She wondered why it was so important to her that he not be a knight. She kept looking for other possibilities. Something about him? Something about her expectation of knighthood? Or maybe he was a wealthy landowner who happened to carry a sword. Not everyone was a knight and this was the country, swords couldn't be that uncommon. Or could they? She needed to check this up in the reference library. She didn't know much about arms or about the rules for carrying them.

As she left Guilhem, she used a carefully prepared phrase, straight from the *Song of Roland*: Go with Jesus' leave and with mine. She didn't know if it was right, but it did the job. Well, her new-discovered knight didn't come charging at her with that sword.

When she walked into the coolness of the cave, with its steady artificial light, she found it strange, as if she had moved from a large movie set to a confined and crammed and cabined reality. It had been easier to make the transition when there were no people outside.

It didn't help that she walked right into a jazz track. The track she walked into was the one she and Cormac had labelled 'summer insanity'. At least it wasn't the opium effect or bebop waah. She was certain that Geoff's six hours of music were played by amateur bands and one day she would ask who so that she could avoid hearing them ever again. Today however, it made everything seem tight and modern and too, too small.

Artemisia hid herself behind a briefing note on the languages of 1305 and how they worked to structure cultural constructs until it was time for the meeting.

* * *

The main feature of the meeting that evening was supposed to be Artemisia's report on the meeting with Guilhem. Sylvia reported her results first, then Tony complained about the poor soil. By the time they got to Artemisia, she had two minutes before dinner. Artemisia wanted to feel aggrieved but really, she was relieved.

Sylvia was polite but dismissive, and that was what got Artemisia's goat: she'd got Sylvia out of a hole and Sylvia should have at least listened. Obviously Artemisia was a person of no importance. Well, she'd been that before. And it was only for nine months. Less, now.

She didn't have to like it, merely to endure.

Chapter Seventeen: Interpretations

"The parishioners from Saint-Laurent are idiots," Guilhem-the-blacksmith said, largely to fill in the time. He was having a quiet afternoon and the priest was bored to tears and gossip was a useful diversion.

"I thought you went to Saint-Laurent yourself? I see you there, all the time. In fact, I was entirely certain that you were one of my parishioners."

Guilhem busied his hands for a moment, making sure that he didn't catch Peire's eyes. When his hands were more fully occupied with his work he said, "Oh, yes, but I don't take sides. There are a few of us who remain even-handed."

"Because horses from both parishes still need shoeing? Because pots need mending and tines need sharpening?"

"Precisely."

"So what have your non-parishioners done?"

"They won't stop talking. They say stupid things."

"Like what?"

"One of the monks at the abbey had a waking vision."

"I bet I know which monk."

"We all know which monk."

"He's not very bright."

"But he thinks he's very holy."

The two men bowed their heads in quiet agreement.

"What did he see?" Peire finally asked.

"I don't know," admitted Guilhem-the-other. "I only know what everyone said he saw."

"What did everyone say he saw, then?"

"One of the people who live under the hill, clad in white garments, walking alone."

"As if they were dead."

"Precisely."

"Who has been suggesting violence?"

"You know who. The usuals. From the castle. They'd beat up pilgrims, if they dared. They gave Brother Benedict a headache and many bruises just last week."

"Indeed. Then I believe this vision is real. It simply needs a bit of interpretation."

"What interpretation do you offer?"

"That if those strangers were to die at the hands of the louts of Saint-Laurent or the castle or even by the fools of Saint-Barthelmy, the dead would roam the hills," and he gestured up and out and across, covering the mountains and the valleys and the fair stream Verdus and the great river below, "and would haunt us forever."

"Especially if the death were violent?"

"Especially if the death were violent."

"It's well known," said the blacksmith, "That sudden and violent and premature deaths are the most important cause of hauntings."

"And it would be a terrible thing if our beautiful country were haunted."

The smith and the priest bowed their heads in quiet agreement again.

Meanwhile, Bona was explaining to her brother that she was trying to be as good as her name suggested, really, but that it was impossible and she couldn't breathe and they needed to leave Saint-Guilhem.

"Everyone wants me to grow up," she complained. "I shall be grown up in Montpellier. I shall be an apprentice and learn my craft and not run barefoot on the hills."

"We can run barefoot now?" suggested her brother, hopefully. "Find the funny people and look at them for a bit?"

"Yes! Or we could look for the cat."

"Our cat never stays where it should. Just like you."

"I'm good," said Bona, stubbornly. "Just not...not..."

"I have my pipe," her brother said, with a rush. "We can play music under an olive tree and call the cat." His fingers clutched possessively around the tiny bone flute with its three finger holes.

"Yes! Let's go!"

* * *

Guilhem wasn't very good at public observance. Being seen to be obedient made him grudging and he hated being grudging. It didn't fit with his view of himself or with his view of his family.

This unhappiness with public display of belief didn't stop him from doing his Matins and Prime readings from his book of hours every day when he awakened. He could do it from memory, but he loved to read it from his book and treasured holding it again. He wondered, idly, if the book were his missing soul. If he had been saved by its appearance.

His unhappiness didn't stop him from reciting the Office of the Dead every single day. He had started halfway to Jerusalem and none of his experiences since then had encouraged him to stop. Guilhem felt his mortality every moment of every day. He would be judged and his heart and soul would both be found wanting. This he knew.

When Artemisia walked past and he was reading the Office, however, he shared it with her. Then they talked about *Ora pro nobis*. There were things Artemisia knew like death and shame. She knew, like him, the need for God's help.

Guilhem was looking at Artemisia's bare foot, sticking out from under her dress. Artemisia looked at her toes peeking out and wondered what the right sitting position would be on a rock for someone of good upbringing. This sort of thing never made it into modern studies. This was probably because the only source for it was watching real people, and the only real person any of them could watch was this young knight. She sighed in frustration.

"You have no shoes," Guilhem said.

Was that all? "They brought shoes for me, but they do not fit. I chose to wear no shoes."

"Ah," he said. "Better bare feet than pain. You have no cordwainer?"

"Not with us. No shoes for me until I go home."

Guilhem frowned.

* * *

"OK," Sylvia said to the assembled masses, without preamble. "I've decided that the best way of doing the first report is if you all give me your data and I process it."

"It's a lot of work," said Geoff, surprised.

"I'm happy to do it," Sylvia said, firmly.

Sylvia Smith had been taught by her mentor that it was very important to have control of reporting. That the way one was seen in the distant future was through reports. One could be caught out or misrepresented so easily and it could make a big difference to access to funding and advancement of projects. It could mean staffing and publication. It could mean the difference between an untenured teaching job in a two-year U.S. community college, and a career. Sylvia therefore called for reports, as Luke had vaguely asked, and she put them together herself, adding explanations and contexts wherever necessary.

She couldn't control what went into each person's personal input, but the group report was hers. Luke had to approve it, but as long as she didn't contradict anything he thought he knew, she would be fine. Sylvia didn't see this as unprofessional: she had been taught, in fact, that it was part of the job.

It was Sylvia, therefore, who documented Artemisia's meeting with Guilhem. She reported that Artemisia had to return a valuable item to a villager. She did not indicate how the valuable item had been separated from the villager in the first place. It wasn't that she was trying to hide her culpability; it was of no relevance to the twenty-first century.

Artemisia had to write her section of the report, but there was nothing new to write about. She explained the book's return from her viewpoint, and then analysed Guilhem's language and gave examples.

She suspected that people were still squirreling material under their beds. She had no idea why, when the technical folk would see it all and measure it all at the other end. One would have to have extraordinary reasons and a great deal of assistance from other team members to avoid scrutiny. Or maybe limit the smuggling to one's backpack. She went through the specimen tub with a fierce frown, trying to find something useful to say. In the end, her note to herself said "The stuff of daily life remains remarkably constant: dishes and towels. Clothes and accessories. Equipment for animals and for farming. It's the stuff of the afterlife that has changed." She wrote this up so that it took twenty pages, lavishly illustrated with examples from the samples.

What a waste of time, she thought. *An archaeologist would have got so much more out of these stolen goods than I did.* But no, the expedition didn't run to archaeologists. She wondered, nastily, if

Harvey would even know what an archaeologist was if one bit him on the behind.

Most of the reporting and the putting in shape was straightforward, as Sylvia explained at length. When Sylvia took a break to speak, it was as if the world took a breath with her. Words emerged with a sense of excitement, of something special happening. Thus the most ordinary aspects of daily life were infused with the sense of something extraordinary, and most of the team accepted that Sylvia herself was worth their attention, simply because of the way she spoke. She used this possibly unwittingly, definitely unashamedly to get work done.

She described that she had had trouble getting research material from Tony because somehow he never quite realised she was demanding material from him. This time she said, "I need this by tomorrow," and he asked, "What do you need?" and she spelled it out and he provided it on the spot — he had been doing his documentation as he worked and it was all ready. She made a note, however, that he required specific and direct instructions. That talking to the group and explaining something meant that his brain said "Not for me." She found this annoying because it meant that Tony's reports weren't in quite as early and the whole package wouldn't be quite perfect. It was important that it be perfect. This, too, her mentor had taught her. Looks count.

In the interest of looks, she set up the reports to make it quite clear that she had put everything together. This was despite the fact that the others all input their own information and Artemisia and Geoff had helped her set up her systems and massage the material into shape. Again, it was not something she processed it was simply a part of her work habits. If Guilhem were there, he would have used a proverb, "No-one can serve two lords." One of Sylvia's lords was herself and the other was Luke.

Guilhem could equally have said that about Ben Konig. At this moment, the needs of Ben's two lords dovetailed. Luke was happy with Ben and Ben's report to the French Government was going nicely. They were both anticipating ticks on their records when their own respective lords read the report, back in the twenty-first century. They weren't that worried about reporting, in fact, given that the databurst wouldn't contain anything problematic.

"The records are depressing," Ben said to Sylvia. It was his way of apologising for not having finished his background work. Unlike Tony, he had heard. He had simply not finished.

"Why?"

"There's a bad decade from 1310. Lots of suffering."

"Like the Plague?" Sylvia was intent on being helpful.

"The land suffered. Plants and animals hurt."

"You weren't talking about people. My bad."

"It's good we didn't get here a few years later." Konig was determinedly morose. "Heat from 1310. Floods in 1315. Crop failure 1316. The worst decade in 150 years. The indices are simply fabulous."

"And after 1350 it was all bad," Artemisia added helpfully.

"You've read the records." For a moment Ben saw a kindred soul and there was a spark as he looked at Artemisia.

"No," said Artemisia. "I know the politics. Politics reflect the way the land hurts."

Ben's little spark turned into a flame. "Show me!" And Sylvia's report was forgotten.

There were two results from this little moment. The first was that Sylvia's somewhat negative neutrality about Artemisia turned into active dislike. The second was that Ben enlisted Mac and Artemisia as fieldworkers to help document species diversity. He wanted to test Artemisia's statement about politics reflecting the state of the natural environment. He wanted to widen his information base.

The immediate consequence, however, was that Sylvia pulled all the workthreads back towards her. She called meeting after meeting to explain the records and go through the records and make sure that they would be ready to go in time. *In time,* Artemisia thought, sourly as she sat through more useless agonising. *A joke! Just like these meetings.* She was sour because her work didn't count in Sylvia's eyes and yet she was still forced to sit and to listen.

* * *

Once upon a time, the castle on the hill was called Géant. Not in the Middle Ages (Artemisia would have explained, if anyone had been listening) but later. The castle was called Géant because it was inhabited by the evil giant Gellone. Giants were all evil in those days, remnants of the offspring of men and demons from the time before the Flood. Artemisia thought about the story and about William and about the Giant who lived in the castle called Giant and she looked back through her database until she found a reference to it. Then she wrote a briefing. She kept the briefing short, as instructed.

The story goes that there was a fight between Gellone the giant and William and William won. It says so in the Guide pittoresque from 1837. I can email you the details if you want.

Sylvia had obviously read the briefing almost the moment Artemisia had posted it, for there she was, standing behind Artemisia, a smidgeon too close, her index finger pointing accusingly at the screen.

"Very helpful," said Sylvia, with sarcasm. "You've already told us."

"I'm glad to hear it," said Artemisia politely, taking the wind right out of Sylvia's sails.

"I'm not putting it in the report home." The scientist made one of her pretty pouts, pivoted and went back to her own desk. Artemisia wondered what other information she could repeat, just to annoy Sylvia. Everyone needed a hobby.

* * *

"I thought…" Artemisia didn't know how to say it. The ribbon had been gone unexpectedly and she had hung around to see what would happen, mostly out of boredom.

Guilhem laughed and explained slowly that his horse had cast a shoe. He had come to check in case Artemisia had visited, and was on his way out. About an hour, then, Artemisia estimated. She had no idea how to ask. Clocks had been invented, but did that mean Guilhem counted time in hours, or not? "When do you leave?" was what came out of her mouth. She wanted to bite her tongue.

"In a little," said Guilhem, amused. "Perhaps I could ask some questions this time?"

"Of course," said Artemisia, uncertainly.

"I shall speak slowly."

"Good."

"The tall man with dark hair and copper skin…"

"Yes?"

"He is an Ethiop?"

Artemisia's day was suddenly merrier. She was entertained by the thought of Geoff as an Ethiop.

"No," she admitted, regretfully. "He is from a lot further away. Terra Australis."

"Ah," said Guilhem, "the Antipodes."

"Indeed. His skin is dark from the Languedocien sun."

"And he has made no pact with the Devil?"

"None of our people have anything to do with the Devil. We're from a very long distance. Our ways are not your ways, but we are good Christians." Some of us were, once, she corrected herself, mentally, hoping that her lies wouldn't haunt her.

"Not even Cathar," Guilhem sounded disappointed.

"I thought there were no more Cathars." Artemisia was excited. Was there a popular understanding of Cathar survival? Would this lead into the Inquisition's efforts a few years from now?

"I believe so," Guilhem dismissed Artemisia's hope with a wave of his hand. "I merely asked."

"I have never met a Cathar," admitted Artemisia, wistfully.

"Nor have I. I have met the worshippers of Mohammed, and I have met many, many Jews, but the Cathars are gone."

"Sad."

"Maybe." The sun shone down on the two of them, as it would shine no longer on the Cathars. Eventually Guilhem volunteered, "There are Jews in Lodève and in Béziers and in Pézenas and in Montpellier. They look ordinary. I threw stones at one, one Easter, but it drew blood and I stopped." What an odd little confession.

"There are no Jews here?"

"Not in William's town. Only good Catholics here, since the very beginning."

"The bones keep them away?"

"Or the abbot." Artemisia was surprised at Guilhem's cynicism.

A thought struck her. "Geoff," she said, "the tall one. He is like Rainouart."

"Who became a good Christian. A hero. Not skilled at arms. Not very clever."

(Artemisia repeated this to Geoff later and he found it very amusing. "Grandma would love to know I'm a good Christian," he said. "She already knows I'm not very bright.")

"I'm told that the Devil leads all non-Christians," Guilhem said, still conversational, still keeping his speech slow.

"Who tells you this?"

"The priest at Saint-Barthelmy, Father Louis."

"Ah," said Artemisia. "He sent you to ask." She was relieved that she had lied. The sunlight occupied the space between their speech.

"And so I have done. You may ask me something now," Guilhem filled in that space.

"Processionals," Artemisia heard the word emerge from her lips and smiled. She needed to know, even if the rest of the team didn't even know what one was and how they might affect everyone's work. "I would like to know the days and the paths they travel."

"You wish to attend?" Guilhem didn't like this thought.

"I wish I could," said Artemisia, with honesty. "What I wish to do is keep my friends away from them."

"You would know the days," his voice was stiff.

"My year is not your year. We celebrate different saints. Allow me to help us respect this place and these people."

After this Guilhem explained to Artemisia only that he would be away for a little. "I will not have your shoes this time. I am sorry for the delay — nothing happens the way I plan it. When I return, you will know." He gestured to the bush. "Until then," Guilhem suggested, "you should stay away from the village. Try to keep your friends from misbehaving?"

"Try?"

"Yes, I can try."

The two laughed, united in sarcasm.

Chapter Eighteen: Ethics

Ben was teaching Cormac how to observe. They had wedged themselves comfortably into a limestone cleft, looking down over the hills with their groves and their deep runnels from water and their pale houses. The lower they looked, the more green it was. Up high, it was windswept and exposed and bare rock.

"This is a shaped landscape," he explained. "Olives, grapes and the crops over the river. Sheep and goats and charcoal."

"The briefing said that. It's the Middle Ages." Cormac was being intentionally dense. Ben was playing the carry-on-regardless game.

"I know. But *already*. We should have come two thousand years ago. Or ten thousand. Before forest was turned into garrigue."

"Medieval Warm Period," said Luke, passing. "Very important for climate research. You said so."

"Shut up," Ben whispered. He picked himself up very quickly, but Cormac sported a big grin.

"I won't tell anyone you said that," he promised.

"If you don't, I'll write you a list of things to watch for. On paper." Ben knew that Cormac was in love with lists, and had been left out when the paper rations were allocated.

"I never knew I'd be so bloody happy to see a piece of paper."

"What will you do with the blank parts?" Artemisia walked by at that moment and couldn't help but ask.

"Write rude limericks."

The three smiled. Konig felt that a crisis had been averted. Smith wasn't the sort of man who'd care much about disrespect. He was, in fact, more the type who would deliver it. He attached some blank sheets to his list, however, as a bit of a thank-you. He had paper, after all, and Mac had none.

* * *

Tony had become firm friends with an elegant ginger cat that had found his hidden garden. The cat mostly slept under a bushy plant near the south edge of Tony's patch. He would tickle it under the chin on his way past, and rub a leaf or two of the herb. When it bloomed, the flowers would look like clusters of thin tubes with a little bell at the end. He pictured it in his mind's eye. *Badasse frutescens*, he murmured every time. It smelled like a very faintly acrid sweetpea, delicate and interesting.

One day, he realised he was naming the cat as well as the plant. He never thought to tell the others that the little ginger cat shared his work, or that it was called Badass, although it slipped out once when Cormac was helping him.

They had a very amicable relationship, the cat and the scientist. Tony liked the babble of voices in the background he just didn't like words so Badass's loquacity suited him perfectly. As well as talking, Badass would investigate. Tony was his and Tony's garden was his and Tony's garden equipment was his and it all needed inspecting.

It was when Badass introduced his friend to Tony that things became more interesting. The goat was a dirty cream, slender and shaggy and muscular, with an inquisitive face and a hungry mien. Tony was not expecting a goat to stick his nose into the garden. It was eating something. That something was definitely not plant material.

Flustered, Tony chased the animal. He chased it from his level horticultural zone to the rocky slope. The goat jumped a small jump to get over a rock and so did Tony. The goat nimbly landed on the uneven ground below and looked back. Tony slid down the rough slope and fell on his trowel. He cut himself. He looked down at his leg and wondered why it wasn't bleeding more. He wasn't worried about it. He was worried about the goat.

Tony saw that his ball of twine was next to the trowel. He grabbed it and chased the goat again. He caught the wiry animal and tied some of the string around its neck. He dragged the goat to the caves and presented it to Pauline.

"I have a problem," he said.

Pauline was full of organised calm. "Let's get that goat out and I'll take care of your damage. Geoff! Goat! Now!"

"No," said Tony, quiet and very stubborn. "The goat needs help. Might have eaten something."

"Goats always eat things," said Geoff. "My cousin breeds them and they win ribbons and then eat their own ribbons."

"You need to look at it," Tony was becoming upset.

"Give me the string," said Geoff. "I'll take it outside and check it and we'll wait for you there. How does that sound?"

Tony nodded. Geoff coaxed the animal through the caverns, trying to prevent it from investigating and eating and getting into more trouble. How Tony had brought it this far was a mystery.

When the goat was out of sight, Tony sat down and held out his leg for Pauline to look at. She shook her head at him, but brought her supplies into the kitchen and cleaned and stitched and bandaged. She didn't scold him. She never tut-tutted. She simply dealt with the wound, patted Tony on the head and sent him outside to check the goat.

Geoff was persuading it to trim the grass near the front door and they were both happy as larks.

Back in the kitchen, Pauline hardly had time to clean the last of the mess when Luke arrived, needing clean white surface, coffee, and someone who was willing to listen to him mutter. She and Luke had become good friends, and she was happy to be there for him. She felt safe, and treasured. Pauline brought out chocolate biscuits and put one next to Luke's cup. He didn't notice, but he ate it anyway.

Luke was certain that he was the centre of whatever in-group the caverns aspired to. Pauline felt likewise, because she fed people, because she was implicit in the private conversations and the politics, and because of Sylvia. They were both very well self-satisfied, which showed in their interactions, all the time, how Luke accepted treats and how Pauline ensured he was given them. She also ensured that Sylvia was treated well. When that scientist came into the kitchen in search of Luke, Pauline was ready with coffee and a biscuit.

Artemisia, on the other hand, was so used to a lukewarm reception that she walked in, saw who was there, and walked out again. Ben, a few minutes later, simply put his notepad on the table, sat down and got on with his work. He saw the exclusion zone, but he intended to destroy it. After a few minutes he set to work.

"Excuse me, Luke, Sylvia, I've got a couple of questions."

Before she could answer, Mac marched from the direction of his workroom, his hands full of items he was working on and he, in turn, interrupted Ben who had interrupted Sylvia. Mac only had a moment before Tony drifted out of his usual reverie with a cogent question for their leader. Luke was looking harassed.

Pauline leapt into protect her people.

"Stop this, at once!" she said. "Sylvia and Luke were talking about something important."

Luke, freed from all of them while Pauline started a good scold, picked himself up, took himself to his office, and put up a *Do Not Disturb* sign.

* * *

Guilhem and Peire looked steadfastly at the carving of Christ docent. Peire loved that carving, while Guilhem loved the craft within it. Neither of them loved being here, in the abbey, waiting for an opinion from on high, or from Abbot Bernard, depending on whether God or Bernard felt like giving an opinion that day.

No-one knew what the abbot thought about the denizens of underground. They weren't even sure that today's pronouncement would be about the hill-dwellers. Guilhem wondered if he would be given another set of penalties — he had taken to assuming that, since life dished him out so very many. For Peire, the fact of the pronouncement was crucial: each decision the abbot made kept the village a village. A little more independence and Saint-Guilhem-le-Désert would become a town. A town in the abbey's shadow, always, but a town. And so the two studied Christ as if his long face were all they needed in their lives.

Long men with bony faces were carved into the abbey. Their grace and strength perpetually reminded dumpy monks of what they never could be. The carvings for heretics were a perpetual reminder to the monks of what they never should be. The interior abbey was a place of great beauty that served to perpetually humiliate its inhabitants and make them small in the eyes of God and of those long-boned carvings with their flowing robes.

Bernard emulated these statues and said nothing of import that day, but he said it gracefully. The villagers and country people are full of wild beliefs, he said, and needed to be reminded of God.

A while later, Peire found himself sitting at the edge of the Verdus with Guilhem-the-smith, the stone beneath them warmed by the sun, the tumbling water downstream almost swallowed by the moss and the sheet that had somehow escaped the hold of one of the women, washing nearby. They were sharing wine (almost the last of the previous year's vintage — a fine drop) and talking slowly.

"The Saint-Barthelmy folk have been talking to me," said the smith, eventually.

"What is it this time?" Peire tried to not to sound long-suffering.

"The strangers. Father Louis gives them no guidance, they tell me."

"And they don't want to be seen near Saint-Laurent so they come to you to ask me. It must be serious."

"No more serious than your parishioners announcing yet again that it's Saint-Barthelmy's problem."

"Because of course they are closer to the strangers."

"Of course. Saint-Laurent protects us from travellers from Aniane, after all." The smith was being ironic. Aniane was full of cousins and friends. Just like the tall walls that sheltered this spot in the centre of the town.

"I think it might be the castle's problem," suggested Peire, tentatively.

"I've already tried that. The abbot told the castle that we were telling stories and embroidering the landscape — there are no strangers under that hill."

"How did he come to that conclusion?"

"No evidence of transgression," Guilhem-the-smith was obviously quoting. "No-one that the monks have seen."

"They don't really transgress," said Peire, with his habitual mildness. "The missing items were dropped by the path or lost in the fields. And no-one has ever died from the looks of curious strangers."

"Indeed, the knight says that his contact tells them to refrain from coming too close. She has returned valuable items."

"Nevertheless, we possibly should think about action."

"Possibly." The three women looked up from their washing and the boys looked across from their game of chance. For a moment, the only sound was that of the stream. "But not yet."

"We will tell the knight, I think."

"These strangers cannot be expected to know our law when those idiots gambling around the corner do not."

"We are not idiots!" Fiz called out.

* * *

"Our ethics are fucked." Ben gave up on convincing anyone and shoved his keyboard away. Filling in all the regulation forms suddenly felt futile. Artemisia had a way of saying things that changed realities if you listened for too long.

"Come on. Surely all these protocols are for something," Mac wore his I-can-get-a-rise-if-I-look-serious-enough face. He was missing people. Over the last three days, his tasks had taken him everywhere but the common workplace. Also, he had spent three hours fishing various dropped items out from under the wire mesh. Mac had therefore descended on the office area to see what trouble he could make. It was fair return.

"I love these protocols," Ben declared. "I would marry them if they only had a heart. But our ethics are still fucked."

"Why?" Sylvia peeked her head out from behind her computer to show she was part of the conversation. Cormac took one look at her pretty head and decided that there was no more stirring. He took himself off: there was always maintenance to be done, especially since every single one of the scientist buggers was careless as hell. Except Tony, who was a good bloke.

Sylvia kept working away on cleaning up her data as she was listening. Tomorrow she would be on-site, and she didn't want to return to the mess. Buried underneath the rational reason for tidying was Artemisia in the dormitory, 'sorting out a couple of zombies' which had propelled Sylvia into finding something of her own to sort.

Sylvia hated it when the historian said something strange and tantalising and left everyone wanting more. She did it on purpose, too. Artemisia was just greedy for attention. Zombies! Sylvia deleted a whole batch of dud files with a huff of release.

"We cleaned out these caves. Pre-modern and all the surveys were perfunctory."

"We had permission. I've read the permission slips myself."

"Sure. The French Government in Paris in the twenty-first century has given us permission to muck round with something in Languedoc in the fourteenth and told me to check that we're good little people and don't change things too much. That's like the Yankees giving permission for someone to exploit the South during Restoration."

"What's Restoration?"

"Bloody Aussies."

"You're from the South, aren't you?" Sylvia was only half-curious. Konig's accent was TV America.

"University of Texas. Austin. Also Paris. Paris, Texas and Paris, France. I get around."

"So what are you trying to say?"

"That the south in France is a bit of a second-class citizen in Paris. We're here pretty soon after the genocide, too."

"Genocide?" Sylvia looked concerned.

"Ask Artemisia."

"She'll get grumpy and write me one of those briefings. It'll either be too short to tell us anything, or it will be twenty pages long or it will threaten us with death and doom and damnation. Artemisia is predictable. And boring."

"Can't blame her."

"So you've shifted. You're seeing things from her view."

"More from my view."

"As a Texan."

"Actually," and Ben gave Sylvia a very sweet smile, "I was born in South Carolina. And I can't see that we should have made the decision to destroy this habitat."

"We need to live somewhere."

"That race to get back in time was a mistake. All the hype compromised us. Luke's secret project is still a pipedream. We're fucked."

"Do me a favour — don't talk like that to the others."

"I won't. Destabilising people in a difficult situation is not something I do. I'm just saying, to you, that we made a big mistake. The others know it. Did you know that Tony has taken to wandering the long way to his horticulture zone?"

"What long way?"

"The very long way. Via the Cirque de Soleil."

"I don't know the Cirque de Soleil. Damn these names." Sylvia looked for her map.

"The End of the World. He checks out the path leading from the castle. He picks up lost items like the rest of us. Keeps them under his bed. Doesn't put them in the bin for home."

"We should report it."

"If we do, will we have problems? If I tell everyone we're compromised, will we have problems?"

"It'll make Artemisia look like a prophet." Sylvia's mouth was tight around these words.

"And we wouldn't want that." Ben's tone was harsh. "The ring-in seeing the whole thing clearly."

"We all care too much."

"Except Artemisia."

"Except bloody Artemisia. Say, if we rename her Mary, then we could call her bloody Mary."

"And she could come after us with an axe."

"Or we could do what Pauline suggests."

"What?"

"Next month, send a message saying they need to collect her."

"That there, sending her home, would cost more than you and I will be worth in our whole lives, by ten. We're with her for the duration. Briefings and all."

Chapter Nineteen: Plain Sight

Historical Briefing — wimples (file from Artemisia Wormwood)

Murray, you remember when we hid to avoid those women and their basket-things? You asked me about the baskets and they're that shape so that they can sling over the shoulder/back. If we had seen the women on their return journey then we would know what they were gathering, but my guess is they were out for a bit of wild harvesting.

Anyway, that's not the subject of this brief. The subject of this brief is your comment when we saw the three women.

"Bloody heck, the Moslem invasion," you said. There actually was a Moslem invasion of this region, but that was around 800 and Charlemagne and his forces repelled it and won back cities and stuff like that. One of Charlemagne's great leaders and counsellors was a guy called William — he's the one whose bones are in the abbey. It's why we're trapped indoors due to medieval tourists this week.

He is, to use one of Cormac's favourite phrases, "An awesome dude." Although he's been dead hundreds of years even now (and way over a thousand years in our time) he has that special status between life and death because he's a saint. He can intervene with God for humans. Hence the pilgrims and the very Christian nature of this town compared with others in the region.

He died here and his bones are the ones we would see on display if we were allowed to move publicly. There's no way we can see those bones — they're very valuable and that whole abbey has been built to house them and a piece of the True Cross.

The reason I say this so adamantly is because I know that Cormac will want to visit his awesome dude because William of Gellone who is also Saint William and William of Toulouse is also William of Orange, an epic hero. I can't remember if I've briefed you about this yet, apart from the giant legend. I have something detailed on file, should you want it. He's important and legendary and complicated. It's filed under "William stories about."

So what were these women with head coverings if not Moslem?

Almost anything. In this region they could be generic Western Christian (what we think of as Catholic) or Jewish. I don't know if any Cathars escaped the Crusade here (Guilhem says not, but he's not the kind of person who would tempt anyone to self-identify as a heretic), but if they did, adult Cathar women would probably cover their hair, too. It's the respectable thing to do. Given the proximity of a major abbey (built by William — he's doomed to haunt me) my bet is on generic Christian. Not nuns, just everyday women doing everyday tasks. Adult women wear head coverings in this time and place. Social norms and all that.

* * *

Guilhem didn't have much time, so he hurried Artemisia along. He also spoke too quickly. She had to ask him three times before she understood what they were doing.

They were, apparently, walking the village boundaries and the boundaries of the important landowners outside Saint-Guilhem, so that she and her people would understand the markers and stay outside them. To reassure the townsfolk that Artemisia and her friends knew to stay away. This worried her — it meant people knew of the time team. She would have to talk to Luke again, and maybe Sylvia. She so didn't want to have a conversation about boundaries with Sylvia.

Away from the boundary markers, Guilhem was more relaxed, although still hurried. He showed her where the charcoal burners worked and told her it would be a good idea to stay clear. The blacksmith controlled the charcoal production, it appeared and he was someone to be reckoned with. Also, Guilhem made it clear, someone Guilhem respected. A man who was not reluctant, Artemisia worked out (her brain was working overtime, even as her lungs and legs found Guilhem's pace tough) to talk to men of rank. In other words, the rest of the town left Guilhem very much alone. Interesting.

* * *

Artemisia was being excluded again, so she noticed small things. For instance, when Geoff wasn't concentrated and focused, the area around his eyes relaxed. Then he smiled and his eyes became brown and merry and all his Islander ancestry glowed through them.

She wondered what else he had in his genes. Nothing he talked about, or that worried him. She liked this about him there was deep joy, rather than deep anxiety. Konig was all anxiety and fraught beauty. Mac was half anger and half clown. Tony was in a world of his own, watching the team as if it comprised an alien species. Luke was…Luke. Geoff was a regular nice guy. He wasn't uncomplicated, but he was…easy to get on with? Comfortable? Funny?

She wasn't the only one who liked Geoff Murray. Artemisia suspected that every woman in the expedition was secretly in love with him in those moments when that puppy-bounce and that exuberance made his eyes glow warm. Or when he walked around near-naked, complaining about the cold. Or when he threw Pauline out of the kitchen saying, "You're on holiday I have a recipe within me and it needs to express itself before I explode."

* * *

The scientists were not being stretched enough. They were ticking items off their laundry lists and working solidly on the day-to-day of data collection, but they were not excited about their work, Artemisia realised. The culture of science had its limitations. Or maybe these scientists, in this situation had their limits.

Luke called them together for a meeting. He had left the lid off his whiteboard marker and his pocket sported a black stain. Geoff's eyes kept returning to it. If Luke didn't carry those markers everywhere and write on every whiteboarded surface, he might not look so stained. Or maybe that was the Great Scientist in his Natural Habitat. Right now, it was disconcerting. It was like seeing the Theodore Luke Mann of the meetings back home, splendid and somewhat like an ancient prophet, emerging from the body of a tired old ragman.

"We can add a study of the effects of increased population density on a rural areas, I think," he radiated assurance. "Without straining our resources or losing time on any of our real work."

"Cool," said Geoff. It was the only way to react to such splendour.

Artemisia wasn't part of the meeting, but her workplace was their workplace and she couldn't help overhearing.

"What increasing density of population are you referring to?" she was honestly bewildered. "Montpellier would be good, but it's a long way away. I can't see"

"Here," interrupted Sylvia. "He means the village down below."

"Oh," said Artemisia. She was unable to suppress sarcasm. "The town that has a stable population except during tourist season and has been that way for hundreds of years? The one in a place with such low population in general that its general location is known as 'The Desert'. That place? Pilgrim Central? That place?"

"That place," said Geoff, not even trying to hide his grin.

"When did these tourist seasons begin?" asked Luke, in an attempt to rescue his dignity.

"Four centuries ago. Maybe five."

"Could you brief us on the tourist stuff? Why they come? What they do here?"

"Sure thing," said Artemisia, bright as a burnished penny. She had already written the briefing and circulated it. When they were trapped in the caves by the first pilgrim onslaught she had done it and sent a note round telling everyone. Maybe this time they would read it. Maybe this time Tony would take heed and avoid the tourist trails and the track the castle used for provisioning.

"Then we'll think about this again when we have perhaps a bit more context." And the meeting was over. The matter was never raised again. The next day, Luke buried Artemisia's brief on the religious tourism unread and unmourned. Again.

Chapter Twenty: Introducing Zombie Ancestry

When Artemisia went to her room and said she was working on zombies, she was really trying to regain a little balance and perspective. She was reminding herself of the impossibility of most people as regards their past.

The zombies were real. A real theory. When she had started teaching, she had started to collect opinions about the Middle Ages and, indeed about other times and places. She explained it to Lucia as "A kind of Darwin Award where the stupid die off. Only they don't just die off, they become zombies and beget zombie children who believe in the stupidities because their ancestors did. The original Flat Earthers."

"I don't understand," Lucia had confessed, her golden-brown head shaken to emphasise her bewilderment.

"You know how people keep telling me that in the Middle Ages meat was rotten and disguised by spices?"

"Yes?"

"Well, the people who ate the rotting meat obviously died and their zombie descendants are the ones who are so very stupid."

"You know, you should stop being rude about my best friend." The sisters smiled at each other conspiratorially, as was their way. Artemisia remembered that smile one day and whispered her theory to Geoff. She didn't expect him to listen, of course. She was seeking the memory of her sister, lost with cancer in a future too far away.

Artemisia found her sanity in her zombie notes and thoughts whenever the time team lost their brain. Cormac pressed her for explanations of those zombies and she put him off each time. She gave no excuses or reasons.

Inside herself she knew exactly why she wouldn't tell. *If they paid attention to my briefings and respected me as a member of the team, then I'll tell them about my private research. Until then, it's none of their concern.* So she teased the team with her mention of zombies.

She didn't know she was tantalising. For her, it was the work she wanted to do, her long-term project that would one day lead to a book. *Zombie Ancestry from the Middle Ages,* she would call it, and it would give her a bit more than the tales of saints and nineteenth century accounts of Languedoc to write about.

She used the expedition library for her work on Languedoc, of course, and those nineteenth century accounts. She had some favourite descriptions of Philippe le bel already. In fact, she was full of colourful descriptions of Philip the Very Pretty. Notorious kings lend themselves to such things. Philippe could be turned into briefings if the others required it.

Zombies were private.

* * *

"We need to monitor how we affect the water supply," Ben told Luke.

"I thought we did that already?"

"Mac does some tests, but they're ineffective."

"Tell Murray. He can handle it."

"Thanks, boss."

Mac and Geoff then spent a glorious afternoon puzzling over diagrams and maps.

"We know where the water goes," said Mac. "Can we check it now?"

They ran a light dye "Amino G acid," said Cormac, proudly through the system and took samples from the places it emerged and checked those samples. All very neat. All very effective. They had checked to see if there was damage from the cave dwellers, if the time team were damaging seepage or springs.

"All clear," Geoff reported. "We found traces of clay sediment and organic acids but that was all."

"Good," said Luke. "Check again in three months or so."

"Next time," Mac asked Geoff when they were keying in the results, "can we use something that will turn the waters red?"

"No," said Geoff. Mac gave him an I'll-convince-you look, but left it there. "You know," Geoff continued, apparently unworried, "This is almost entirely against protocol."

"Sylvia and Tony break protocol all the time. And besides, it's not *really* so bad. Only a bit of colour."

"And only very locally. Out of sight of the villagers." Geoff nodded. "Not breaching protocol really, just stretching it."

"Carefully."

Very carefully."

In the meantime, Sylvia decided to brave her headache. It wasn't as if walking from her bedroom to the office area was a great problem. It was just that she hurt.

Dr Smith forgot about the uneven floor. She had been negotiating it so automatically for just long enough that forgetting to look could have consequences. The chief consequence was that her arm was in a sling for a week and Geoff Murray gleefully appropriated her time on the viewing flat above their cave.

* * *

The priests handled the villagers' concern over the blue waters. It was nothing, said Peire. It was nothing, said Louis. Abbot Bernard didn't say anything, for no-one told him. It would not be nothing if he had to intervene. *It's a practical joke*, said Peire, many times. *A practical joke*, echoed Louis. *Remember the green baby*, they said. *Humans did this. It's not the work of the Devil.*

"Is it the fairies?" Guilhem-the-smith asked Guilhem-the-knight.

"They don't have holy powers."

"Unholy, then?"

"Neither. They're human."

"And yet the water is blue in seven places."

"Very strange."

"Very strange."

Chapter Twenty-One: Communications of a Kind

Ben had taken the afternoon off. No-one knew, because he was technically out making observations. He had his little notebook and his camera and his backpack. He had climbed up a slope and fallen down it again, slipping on scree. He had laughed at himself both for slipping and for even considering whether it was scree or lumps of rock, because the day was hot and the weather was steady. It was the perfect weather for self-mockery.

He sat down on the nearest fixed lump and looked around. No-one could see him from here. Not the people from the village, not the people from under the hill. He took out his water bottle and swigged. Then he put his backpack on the ground, stretched out next to it, and watched the sky flow past.

If anyone had asked, he would have claimed to be collecting data. He listened to birds and the noises in the brush. He kept a weather eye on the kermes oak whose spiky branches floated at the edge of his vision. He would have told anyone this, if they had asked. No-one asked and so he lay there, eyes half-shut, at peace with the world.

Ants crawled across him on their way to work. Birds twittered and cooed and called. Ben stopped naming the birds and thinking about the ecosystem. He let everything flow over him.

Eventually, his nemesis arrived. His nemesis took the form of boots stamping through the undergrowth. Soft boots. Medieval boots. Still, the stamping was heavy.

It was Mac.

"Stop following me!" Mac's voice caught on the kermes oak as he turned to face behind him.

What Mac was doing out here and who followed him was a mystery. Why he had boots was less of a mystery. Mac had brought all his own equipment. He hadn't trusted the expedition to outfit him.

Ben was tempted by much of Mac's specialist equipment, being the same size. Mac was the only member of the party who had boots. Ben carefully put this thought and Mac's boots far from his conscious mind. Bad enough that Mac was disturbing his equilibrium.

Ben didn't have to find a hiding place, however he could stay where he was. He pulled out his notebook and pretended to be hard at work.

"Hi, Ben," Mac's voice was definitely in his direction this time. Damn. "Mind if I join you?"

"I'm working," Ben said, pointedly.

"Yeah, I know. But I need to talk with you..."

"Let's go back, then."

Mac shook his head and sat down. "Won't take a mo. Just gotta warn you about Pauline. She keeps sticking her nose in my workshop. Wants stuff."

"So stop her."

"I will, mate, but I'm giving you fair warning. Like I gave them kids."

"Kids?" Ben had trouble keeping up with Cormac's leaps sometimes.

"Let's babble for a tick. You'll see for yourself."

"Fine, let me tell you what I was doing," and Ben invented a rather fine tissue of lies that had nothing to do with the landscape anywhere within a hundred miles. He even waved a hand mildly at "that eucalyptus over there" and found Cormac nodding enthusiastically. "Mac," he started to say, "This is France, it's the Middle Ages. There are no gum"

Mac leaped up from his piece of ground, made beast-hands and shouted "Boo!" at a bush. The bush giggled. Mac slid on the same surface that had defeated Ben and fell in a heap. The bush giggled some more, and then two children ran out of it, heading for the village.

"That sorted them," Mac said. He picked himself up, brushed himself off, waved goodbye and started back toward the cave.

Ben shook himself off and wandered into the hills. Now that Mac had seen him, he might as well work.

This led to Luke making an announcement.

"Ben has found something that may or may not be wolf scat.

It has hair and bone chips. No going into the hills alone." Mostly, Luke's announcement was ignored and the samples were consigned to the sample bin. Wolves were rare in modern times, even in the garrigue.

"Aren't you worried?" Pauline asked Ben.

"They might come down during winter," he said, "If they're hungry. I can't see any problems coming into summer."

* * *

The day was hot and still. A woman sat on a steep step, folding and twisting supple willow into a basket, her clothes loosened and her body angled to catch the least breeze.

That woman was Sibilla, luxuriating in the heat. When she noticed Guilhem watching, she gave him her secret smile, the one that caused him to walk over and to stand close. He would not have done this if he had known that Sibilla was responsible for the rest of the village keeping its distance.

"The people under the hill?" she had said, the day before, the week before, whenever she had an ear, "They're ghosts." This meant that Guilhem, as intermediary, had special secret knowledge. And that knowledge meant that Guilhem, in his turn, heard the swish of cloth as people turned away. He thought that this was a sign of respect, but the way that the procurators and syndics were treated wasn't as distant.

He stood near Sibilla, leaning into her warmth.

Guilhem-the-Smith had been roped-in by the syndic named to handle Louis. The good priest had interfered with forage rights and stopped Sibilla from gathering willows for basket-making. Louis was a repeat offender, having recently denied the smith himself water access for their animals. The priest ought to be someone who worked for the common good. He didn't. And the villagers never quite said this aloud, ever, just as the subject of the monastic lands never came up and were never the subject of a dispute even when the dispute was tearing families in pieces.

"I can't do anything," Guilhem-the-smith pointed out. "I'm not free of bias in this matter. Besides, it's the priest. Isn't this why we have a public notary?"

The public notary also worked for the abbey. The combination of a written decision on rights and of the abbot knowing that Louis was causing a fuss again would quieten things down for a bit. And so the matter was settled even before the sun had moved enough to force Sibilla inside. Or the matter was not settled (merely postponed), the way that the access to the deep clefts and their water and good soil was never settled. The way villagers even without a claim in the world sought to pretend ownership of land at Saint-Jean-de-Fos, because everyone knew that the grapes tasted better down there.

* * *

Ben moved between all groups. Mac and Geoff were buddies, and Ben sometimes joined them. Tony was alone. Pauline, it seemed, understood Sylvia's loneliness. In return, Pauline defended Sylvia against all comers and all potential threats. They made a little coterie of two. Artemisia wanted to draw a diagram.

There were no other women and Artemisia wasn't used to chatting casually with men. That let's-not-forget-home-values upbringing. She'd forgotten how lonely life could be without a girlfriend. Or a sister. At that moment she would have sold her soul to find out what was happening with her sister.

Meanwhile, Sylvia had problems bigger than Pauline's shoulder could bear.

* * *

"Sylvia has a headache," Mac observed. "Don't go in."

"Sylvia *is* a headache," Geoff observed. "All I want is a glass of water."

"If I stay out, will that be OK?" Appeasement was uppermost in Artemisia's thoughts.

"You wanted a cuppa," objected Geoff.

"I can manage." Artemisia was not going to be the one who set Sylvia off.

"What's going on?" Prince Valiant's voice sounded.

"Ben! Our man!"

"Mac, what are you up to?"

Cormac looked entirely innocent. "Not me. Just a small problem."

"Sylvia has another headache," explained Geoff.

"In the kitchen," explained Artemisia.

"And everyone who goes in there is intruding upon her pain?" Ben was not amused. "This is the third time. Is it going to be a regular occurrence?"

"Not if you find a solution," said Mac, brightly.

"A gentle solution," added Artemisia.

"Leave it to me." His jaws firmly clenched, Ben went straight to Luke's office. Artemisia swore she could almost hear the sound of raised voices. A few minutes later, he was out of there, looking harrowed. "You all owe me," he said, briefly, and then went into the kitchen.

He and Pauline came out, nursing the ailing Sylvia. They whisked her through the workroom and into the lounge. A moment later he came out, looking very tired.

"The kitchen is ours. Now I need a cup of something, too. Sylvia has Luke's chair and some very strong painkillers and the whole of Doc's attention."

"And next time?" Geoff's voice was not its usual warm self.

"Next time she can go straight into the common room. We can do without that more than we can do without the kitchen."

"The rest of us have beds to be sick in"

"Leave it, Mac," Artemisia wasn't interested in more fuss. "Limestone echoes strangely the bedroom may be too much for someone in pain. I wouldn't wish a migraine on my worst enemy." She walked towards the kitchen, wondering if she could steal the good coffee and enrich it with something stronger.

Geoff walked beside her, whispering in her ear, "Even if your worst enemy is a bitch?"

Artemisia stopped suddenly and looked up at him in surprise.

* * *

The ribbon-laden bush looked festive and fluttering as the wind merrily blew the silk. Artemisia watched this and remained very quiet. Thus she found herself the surprised recipient of Guilhem's confidence.

"I am lonely," he said.

Everyone in the little rift between the hills spoke romans, he said. He spoke romans, but also good French — he didn't belong. Knights were excluded from the village doings because the castle looked to the abbey and he was excluded from the castle because it was a nothing-place. It was managed by the abbey and linked to the town and had little of the castle management he knew and the men there were unfriendly. His status was too great for him to be called on legally and he did what he could to protect the back roads, but it wasn't his role and he knew it. He would rather pay taxes than be so alone in the village.

Guilhem's mood shifted. "I miss those of my kind," he admitted. "I miss training with my gens."

"You sound like Richard I," Artemisia admitted.

"How is that?"

"You share the mood of his rotrouenge."

Guilhem said "I do not know this rotrouenge."

Artemisia sang him the first verse of Richard's *Ja nus on pris*. She loved the song even as she thought the words were of someone fundamentally unlikeable. Maybe Sylvia was Richard's reincarnation?

Never has one captured explained his situation
clearly unless he has spoken with sadness;
But for comfort he can make a song.
I have many friends, but their gifts are poor;
Shamed they are, if through lack of ransom
I am two winters imprisoned.

Artemisia gave herself a mental pat on the back for remembering the words and the music and for singing precisely on key. Dr Murray would be so proud of her. Or maybe he would laugh. Either way, he'd be happy. Her voice was its usual small faded self. It was better than her sister's voice. Lucia sounded very much like Tweety Bird when she tried to sing. Tweety Bird on dope.

Guilhem listened with great courtesy and then sighed and said, "Just like that. My duties have been paid in coin by those who want to keep me distant. My family and my peers do not come to my aid. I am alone."

While she sang, Artemisia reflected that Guilhem was somewhat of a loner by nature, and that this was a time and place where being alone was a bad, bad thing. His personality might not help. He wanted the support, but he really didn't act like a team player. He and Sylvia should swap places, she thought, meanly. This is when she realised that she still disliked Sylvia. *How many more months do I have to put up with her? And, fairly, how many more months does she have to put up with me?*

"At least," she said, tentatively, "at least you have time. If you are alone, you have time to find friends; if you are without your people then it is only time before you are with them again. You have time."

"Only time," echoed Guilhem. "Yes, I have time."

After the song, after the agreement, after Artemisia's wise words, came a silence. Artemisia was still lost in her thoughts.

"One moment." Guilhem held up his hand to emphasise this. "If you would please sit down on that rock?"

Artemisia sat. Guilhem produced some coarse parchment and a lead. He made her hold her feet out, one at a time. He would not brook refusal. His hands were intrusive as he drew the line of her feet on the parchment and made measurements and, apparently in error, gently stroked her ankle.

Guilhem explained the measurements by saying, "One good deed deserves another. You restored my book to me, and your feet are too soft for this hard land." She had never felt so unsettled by a shoe measurement in her life.

Artemisia was saved from finding a reply by a hail from a hill.

"Not a good thing," said Guilhem. "That stretch of ground is visible from the village."

"I'll warn them," said Artemisia, and made what she thought of as her *courtoisies* and then her escape.

She didn't know what to think of being measured for shoes. It was very intimate. It was one thing to pontificate on what people did from the safety of the twenty-first century. It was another thing to risk being thought of as a woman of low repute by a man who might or might not be dangerous.

She would wear a wimple from now on. The veil had been based on her careful reading of the clothes the fairies wore in all the Arthurian romances. She had quite a few Arthurian romances in her strange library, and she had examined them very closely. They might have used sweet veils and those same light veils might be perfect for this climate, but she wasn't sure if that was right, even for a woman of rank. Sensibility above comfort. She would miss her pretty veil. She would miss the wind in her hair. She would sweat. But she wouldn't have to worry about Guilhem's hands lightly tantalising her ankle.

"Join us," said Ben. "We're mapping straight onto the handhelds and could use your help."

"Guilhem says not to stand on that hill. You can be seen from town."

"All this creeping around," said Mac.

"I know," Artemisia was torn between twinkling at him and being sympathetic. "It's positively unheroic."

"We need to move on anyway. The goal for today is to map two hundred metres over there," Ben's arm waved vaguely. "That should take us out of line of sight."

"What are we mapping and why two hundred metres? And isn't it all impossibly steep over there?"

Ben ignored the latter question. "I want to illustrate the transition between garrigue and forest. Make close comparisons with the modern treeline."

"Three hands are better than one, then."

"Indeed. I brought you your very own hand-held. We've got a fair way to walk, so we'd better get moving. I'll tell you what to look for as we march."

"Quick MARCH!" shouted Mac, joyously and ironically, as the three clambered slowly away from the town.

* * *

That night, Artemisia did a quick and somewhat dirty translation of Richard's rotrouenge and posted it to the bulletin board. Maybe it would tempt the others into actually learning one of the languages of the country they were visiting? It didn't matter that Richard had been dead for a hundred and six years and that the language had moved on. The song haunted her.

And, of course, she was rather worried that she was the only one of the team able to talk to the people of the region. She was being honest with herself, even she could only really talk to the well-born, and her language was faulty and slow. It wasn't safe. There was no backup should something happen to her.

Still, Richard's song was beautiful, and his words showed that he was a self-centred whinger. Translating the rhyme was earning her keep. Sort of. And if her fellow team-members couldn't handle concepts like a 'raison' then they could ask. Maybe learn something. That'd be a change.

Never has one captured explained his situation
clearly unless he has spoken with sadness;
But for comfort he can make a song.
I have many friends, but their gifts are poor;
Shamed they are, if through lack of ransom
I am two winters imprisoned.

They know well, my men and my barons,
English, Norman, Poitevin and Gascon,
that I have never had such a poor companion
Who I would ever leave in prison due to lack of money.
I do not say this with any reproach;
But I am still imprisoned.

Now I know well and with certainty
That the dead and the imprisoned has neither friend nor family,
This gives me sorrow for myself, but even more for my people,
Who after my death will have so much reproach,
If I am imprisoned long.

It is no wonder that I have a sad heart,
When my lord makes my land suffer.
If he would remember our oath
That we made together,
I know well in truth that for such a long time
I would not be imprisoned.

They know well, the Angevins and the Touraines,
Those knights who are rich and well
That I am burdened far from them in the hands of another.
They loved me greatly, but now, not at all.
They do not see grand feats of arms on the land
While I am imprisoned.

My companions whom I have loved and whom I love,
Of Caheu, and of Percherain,
Tell me, song, why they are not true:
Never has my heart been false or fitful towards them.

If they go to war against me, they will be truly lowly/villainous
While I am imprisoned.

Countess sister, your great renown
Be defended and protected by those to whom I complain
And for whom I am imprisoned.
I do not speak of that one from Chartrain,
The mother of Louis.

Chapter Twenty-Two: Badass and Baggage

Sylvia was communing with a cat. She had taken the camera out with intent to commit topographical analysis. Her rock sampling was finished, despite the idiot rules Theo had instituted that restricted her movements. She could demonstrate what was happening through pictures, through simple tests and through rock samples. She had cleared the places she wanted to go and asked for proper permission. She was ready for anything. Including and especially a cat.

It was a little ginger tom, full of inquisitiveness and charm and just a little bit demanding. It introduced itself to her gently, inserting its presence into her pictures and, when she sat on a rock to do some workings, rubbing itself around her legs, then jumping on her shoulder and giving her affectionate kisses.

For a moment she wondered if there was any evil cat disease that belonged in the past that scientists had cured before she was born. Only for a moment. She loved the feel of affection. The sun and the cat and the bees buzzing and the perfection of her research made the day perfect.

Her eyes were alert when she came back to the caves. It took them a couple of minutes to adjust to the artificial light, but when she did, the first person she saw was Geoff Murray. He disguised how hard he worked beneath a veneer of laziness. Sylvia thought of that cat, arduously winning her affections, and she thought of the cat's colouring consistent and elegant — and she thought of the lines the cat's body made, lithe and sinuous. All this she saw in Geoff as he lounged, his work negligently distributed around him.

She told him about the cat.

* * *

Guilhem needed to stretch his legs. He also needed to let the village know that he was around. He might have been put aside and his judicial skills ignored, but he was no nonentity. He may never be given the role of consul: he was a knight, not a doctor or a notary. Still, he would make the village accept him. To that end, today, he would be seen. He would walk the long street and the curved one. He would walk from the tower at the top past the church and past the last house and right down to the Devil's Bridge. Then he would turn right round and walk up again. He would be seen.

While he was being seen, Guilhem noticed small things. He noticed Berta sweeping up garbage, her big keys clattering ostentatiously with every movement. Obviously there had been an accident. Guilhem walked around it, careful of his shoes. He didn't know and didn't care that the accident was Sibilla throwing her best green jug at her latest amour…and missing. The jug now sported a bold crack.

The cooper's doors were wide open and the light flooded in, showing him busy with barrels. Always barrels. This place would not exist without a constant supply of barrels. Wine and oil and prayer lined the street and kept Saint-Guilhem from falling into the clutches of greedy Aniane. It had saved them from the Cathars and the Inquisition. The barrels the cooper crafted kept the dark from this small town, trapped between mountains and shore. Guilhem didn't know that the cooper was the cousin of Guilhem-the-smith and that the reason he was working so furiously was because he was the one who had discovered Sibilla with her latest amour and that Sibilla was (because of the affair) hanging onto his wife's ring, instead of redeeming it for coin. His wife was due back from Aniane. Guilhem's cousin had taken the ring back and failed to pay. Life at this moment revolved around a fractured jug.

He left the cooper behind and passed Fiz. The first person whose name he knew, and whose personality reached out to his own.

"Another Guilhem," he had said, ironically. "An unusual name."

"That's why everyone calls me Fiz," explained the boy.

"Your father was also Guilhem?"

"Maybe."

Fiz was working, for a change, sawing wood on a portable rack. There was always building to be done around here. Why were they always busy, always building, always making things? What was it all for?

The knight went into Saint-Barthelmy's for protection. He made his courtoisie and said a prayer. When he left, he turned right. Looking up and back, on the right was the castle. Below it lay the square tower that always made him think of Pézenas. Towers in Saint-Guilhem weren't as squat and heavy and demanding.

If he left the village at this point and walked through the last of the fortifications, he would reach the hillside in mere moments. Paces away. And then, the path led near Artemisia. It was tempting. It was always tempting.

Today, however, he had an aim. He needed to be seen.

The best way to be seen, his cousin always said, was to stand with one's feet a little apart, to raise one's head a trifle, and to stare. He chose to stare at the castle and its structure. This, also, his cousin had taught him. Know your enemies, but also know your friends. Know their strengths and weaknesses. Know their walls and their doors and their gates and their men. Watch for their moment of vulnerability.

Philippe the king had said this once, when he was suffering a rare moment of communication. Guilhem's last conversation with him had been quite different. More typical. Silent. The tall one had stood with his feet a little apart and stared at his cousin until Guilhem's thoughts tangled and he shifted his feet uncomfortably. Today, his feet were firm and his thoughts were clear. He wondered, as he looked up at the building on the peak, if Philippe had visited this town when he had visited this region, over a year ago. Had he analysed the defence and the people? Had he noticed how Fiz joked with the woman who swept, how each and every member of the town informed each other continually, of what was going on? Glances and gestures as often as words, but the flow of information was constant. What did this mean?

He ran out of walking, suddenly, and sat down there, in the shadow of the castle, without regard to anyone around him. He opened his flat-bottomed leather purse and withdrew his signet ring. One day, it would matter. One day, he would matter.

Guilhem went back to his house and spent the rest of the day working with his man on his equipment. The town was for now and Artemisia was his entertainment. In his equipment was his future. His armour and his horses were his path to that future.

Meanwhile, Saint-Guilhem and its bones and its abbey and its people went about its business, regardless of Guilhem's small posturing. Those bones were the key to their calm. The objects of their worship and the cause of their security in so many ways.

Bones of the past. Memories of the dead. The means by which the first Guilhem could talk to them, be with them, protect them from ill. If Guilhem's walk had taken him into the abbey, he might have remembered this.

* * *

Mac had finally mastered drawing on a hand-held. He was on a slope at the End of the World, looking up at the high path that led to the castle, attending only to what lay before him. Artemisia caught him by surprise and tickled him.

"What are you doing?" she asked, when he had recovered from the attack.

He showed her. "You historians probably know all this already. I grok it when I draw it. My stylus helps me understand, but." He had sketched a pack mule. "I'm trying to get the baggage right how pilgrims strap it, and how knights use it for their equipment and how supplies are carried to the castle. It's not all the same. Look at how this smaller set of bags are strapped right around the mule, and how this big set, on this other mule," he scrolled across with his further finger, "uses the bags to take the work out of the balancing."

"That's an excellent idea," Artemisia sat on the ground, out of sight of the line of pack ponies and mules that was making its way laboriously up the ridge. "Also, the only evidence I've seen for the fourteenth century is one painting at Uffizi."

"That's all?"

"That's all I've *seen*," Artemisia corrected. "This sort of thing is hardly my area. Paintings and sketches only show us a small amount of it, even so. Here we're looking at material goods in a different context, without the eye of a painter intervening. What you're doing, sketching the everyday and all the variations you find, will expand our knowledge."

"I could photograph it as well, if I had use of the camera," Mac suggested.

"You could. I'll ask Luke. No, on second thoughts, I'll ask Ben."

"Shouldn't we be doing this with absolutely everything? Documenting it? Even if we can't go too close?"

"In theory, yes. In practise, this isn't an historical expedition. I'm here to advise, really, not to research. I asked about the camera, and about recording the conversations with Guilhem, but Luke said no, not really."

"It must be killing you inside." Artemisia didn't say anything, but it was nice that Mac understood. "When I signed up, I thought, because we're going to the past..."

"It's all about the science," those words weighed heavily on both of them. "The environmental stuff and Sylvia's delta T and the Big Secret Formulae Luke spends his time on. That, and making money when we get back. Luke will OK anything that has a potential income stream attached. History is not important." She was proud that she said this with resigned realism.

She hated it. Hated being in the Middle Ages and people not CARING. She wanted to shout that last word. Instead, she bit her tongue. No use making waves.

"Surely big movies will want the history?"

"No, not really. Lots of words, not much actual history, in movies. Do you know what medievalists call *Braveheart*?"

"Tell me?" Mac seemed eager for secret knowledge. Artemisia almost regretted what she was going to say.

"'The film that shall not be named.' Most film history is total garbage. Most documentary history is primary-school stuff. There's no money in it for the expedition."

"But you think Konig will let me have the camera?"

"Not ahead of anyone else," Artemisia warned. "He doesn't privilege the history side, but he does have a sense of it being a part of what we're here for. Have you noticed, too, that he likes it when we all do interesting work?"

"He's fucked up," said Mac. "But he wants it to work. Sylvia is fucked up and only cares about her own skin. Our Great Leader is just fucked up."

"But his science is intense and amazing. It has to be."

Chapter Twenty-Three: In Case of Trouble

They were heading for the three month deadline. Underground, everyone held their breath. A third of their stay was nearly up.

Then the race began. It was almost time for a big report. For every single aspect of their lives to be documented and sent back to the future. Even Mac was involved. Sylvia hadn't quite set things up for Mac to be involved. She did Pauline's reports and requisitions, but Mac had to do his own. He insisted. He loomed over Sylvia as he insisted.

"Oh, very well," she was peeved. "You can work on Artemisia's machine. Use her password."

"Thanks, Mac," Artemisia said, as she logged him on. "Exactly what I needed."

Artemisia had been bored before even she started. She had her requisitions all prepared. Old French material, Old Occitan material, recent research covering the region, work on Templars, on knighthood, on medieval masculinities, all the main journals. It was very straightforward. She was requisitioning the electronic library she had expected to find when she arrived. Language training. Just as essential as it had been when they arrived, just as far away.

Mac gave her his goofiest smile, and took over her machine. Artemisia worked on zombies in her room for a little but she had no new thoughts and became bored very quickly. Then she tried reading nineteenth century histories on a hand-held. After a bit, she gave up entirely. Artemisia went outside and slept in the southern sunshine until she was called.

Mac was longer than anyone except Geoff expected. This was because Geoff kept 'borrowing' him. It was not easy to file reports: there were hyperlinks and categories and code numbers.

"Secret passwords," said Geoff, gloomily.

"We can't just send our work, we have to turn it into arcana first." Mac was no better than Geoff at decoding the systems, but they refused to ask the systems' designer and they refused to be defeated.

Early on, Sylvia provided entertainment.

"There's a beetle in my bed!" her voice was shrill and she entered the office area running.

"Careful," Geoff advised. "You'll trip."

"What sort of beetle?" asked Tony.

"What were you doing in bed at this time of day?" Ben gave himself a wry smile as he regretted what he had said. "Here, let me sort the beetle out for you."

Three minutes later, Dr Konig triumphantly bore the beetle aloft, in a specimen jar.

"It's a cave beetle," he pronounced. "Not Mac playing a joke on you."

"I don't care if it's a dung beetle," Sylvia was not in a forgiving mood. "I want it gone."

And that was it. For hours, it was dull and beyond dull.

Eventually, Mac and Geoff settled down at Geoff's machine, leaving Artemisia free to work again. Mac woke her up and brought her back into the cold. "About bloody time," she said. "I thought I wasn't going to get to my reports until next year."

"Bugger off," said Cormac, very cheerfully. "This is complicated."

"Besides, yours is easier. You don't need as much time as us educated folks," Geoff claimed. "You write everything as you go. And look at what you're doing at this precise second, you're just copying and pasting text you wrote for the Bulletin Board. Lazy git."

"Admit it," said Artemisia. "History is more fun than science."

"You have a wild imagination," and Geoff mussed her hair as he walked past.

Artemisia couldn't help but run her eye down Mac's requisition list as she added her own. Some of the items were obvious. More of the chemical that made the toilets function so interestingly, jelly beans, ammonium nitrate, a set of tools to replace the ones that had gone missing (probably fallen down cracks in the mesh) and detonators. She wondered about the detonator caps. For Artemisia, to wonder was to ask.

"I have the training, if that's what you're on about." Cormac was curiously defensive.

"No, it's why. I'm curious, is all. Explosives."

"Ben asked me. In case of things going wrong. We can hide everything from the natives if we blow things up and run."

"He thinks there'll be trouble?"

"He's someone who prepares for trouble," said Mac, darkly, and finished with the formatting and files and gave Geoff back his computer.

When Artemisia reported to Sylvia that her files and requisition orders were in, Sylvia's response was a disheartening, "Oh, I didn't know you had any."

Artemisia responded to the comment by logging back into the requisition form and adding a request for a hard copy of Padel's Old Occitan manual to her exceptionally carefully designed library request. If she could leave it lying around, maybe someone would pick it up.

She then compressed her files before she sent them to Sylvia. She didn't trust Sylvia not to look and edit. In fact, after that comment, she didn't even like Sylvia. She had been trying to, she told herself. Really trying.

Artemisia handled her dislike of Sylvia far more professionally than Sylvia handled her dislike of Artemisia. Sylvia decompressed the files, looked through everything, designated the library request as 'low priority' and added her confidential assessment of Artemisia.

Luke noted this in his covering remarks. Neither jeopardised the viability of the expedition, Luke also noted, but left Sylvia's assessment of the library's need standing. There were no crises the current system couldn't handle.

When it was all done, it sat for days, waiting for the window for upload. When Botty flicked on there would be new provisions and all the samples would go and there would be fresh food. Everything was ready, waiting. Sylvia was delegated to start the data zipping across the years, the microsecond Botty's platform went live.

Sylvia dwelt on her comments, however, while she waited, ready to press that magic button. She had acted on her justified feelings, but they would hear nothing back for a full month, and even then, there would only be a limited datastream, so she might not get a full response. Only data, from this lot of requisitions. All the non-electronic items would be processed in the final material exchange, in three more months. The others would criticise her, but it was none of her doing. Foreordained is foreordained. She felt aggrieved.

Mainly, Sylvia was annoyed by the length of the bibliography Artemisia had requested. It intimated that Sylvia's decisions regarding the library could have been better handled, and it was wrong of Artemisia to suggest this. She should have simply found another way around the problem. If there was a problem at all.

Sylvia didn't have long to ponder on the misdeeds that comprised Artemisia. Timebot's light blinked on.

Sylvia sent the datastream. The rest of the team watched the physical material flick out and replacement material flick in. The moment the designated section of Botty's platform was full, they rolled full fridges off and the old just as full ones on. They hefted boxes and crates and tubs and did everything within the bare half hour of the wormhole. Botty's light changed to red five seconds before incoming, which led to one mad scramble and a hurried dive for the floor when Cormac and Geoff were too busy hauling to notice the colour shift.

"Nearly went back," Cormac grinned at Geoff. Geoff wasn't paying attention. Instead, he was looking at the last load to appear, the one that had nearly displaced him into the wormhole.

One of the fridges was a slump of metal. Its rollers were weirdly intact.

"Freaky," said Cormac, admiringly.

"Worrying," said Geoff.

I hope I don't end up like that, on the way home, thought Artemisia.

Luke looked unconcerned.

"We'll do the sampling from that container again," Luke told Sylvia, "Just in case it didn't get back in order. The data can be retransmitted with the next monthly report, just to be certain it arrives intact. I'll redo our calculations, too. See if anything needs recalibrating. Sylviacheck the supplies. We should have enough redundancy, but I want detail of what's gone."

The big question Luke didn't address was Artemisia's thought what this meant for them. *What if the failure had melted a person, not a piece of equipment?*

"We knew there was a risk," Ben said. "We signed our waivers."

"What waivers?" asked Artemisia.

Every single person looked at her. Ben raced to his computer and checked his HR material. The whole team was excluded from the lounge area the rest of the afternoon while Ben shouted at Luke and Luke shouted at Ben and Sylvia spoke in a small self-justificatory voice.

"What happened?" Geoff asked Ben, when he finally emerged.

"Luke won. The bastard."

Chapter Twenty-Four: The Noise of the Middle Ages

There were two special processions in Saint-Guilhem. There were two where everyone brought out their veils and best sleeves and visitors appeared with their devices and their banners and the whole village shone with solemnity and joy. The first of them had been on 3 May, for the Invention of the Cross, and the local people still talked about it, now, during Ascension, weeks later. The day the True Cross made its journey around the village, protecting it, letting its people know that the abbey wasn't a stranger in their midst, but their protector. It was a noisy procession, and a happy one.

The time travellers heard it from their vantage point.

"This is the noise of the Middle Ages," Geoff said.

"Or just the noise of Catholicism," suggested Artemisia. "I wish I could be there." She was taking assiduous notes and recording when she had access to equipment, but it still felt like doing a tenth of what she should.

"Don't even think it," snapped Sylvia. Artemisia was willing to bet that the tone of voice meant that Sylvia possessed that same precise thought.

The procession took the Cross past the two churches, and each congregation clustered with their own. They were full of hospitality, for this was the day when everyone talked to each other and when friends and relatives took the walk from Aniane and worshipped with their smaller counterpart across the river. Aniane's folk forgot their greater prosperity and their assumption of immense knowledge and the fact that they were founded first and that William had followed his friend in creating an abbey. It was when all the residents of the outlying hamlets came in and admired the bigger town. The piece of the True Cross unified the region.

Just for a short time, Saint-Guilhem felt smug and superior and, after the Cross had been returned to its niche in the wall of the abbey church, all the residents of the region gossiped and played games and ate good food together. The children kicked balls around the streets and, in the evening, everyone shared fables and stories. Inevitably the ghosts came into the tales.

Or the demons. Or the fairies. In different parts of the village, different tales were told.

* * *

Geoff was reading. His problem was that he had only brought a very few books. He was a slow reader and he had little space and he had thought that he would be fine. Like sailors and their months at sea. He had assumed that the time somehow filled. He hadn't thought to requisition more until it was too late. So he read and reread the same three paperbacks.

He wasn't at all fine with just three volumes. He realised this as he started *The Golem, Dancing* for the fifth time.

"Is it a good book?" Artemisia's voice was wistful.

"It was the first two times through. Now I'm sick of it. You didn't bring an e-reader, did you?"

"I use the computer," Artemisia admitted. "I wasn't that organised. I'm not short of books, though, if you know how to transfer them."

"How can you not be short of books?"

Artemisia's golden laughter filled the common room. Geoffrey Murray liked that laugh and realised he hadn't heard it much. He resolved to provoke it frequently.

Unaware of Geoff's thoughts, Artemisia carefully explained, "Whoever put together my database didn't know fiction from non-fiction. They lumped a great deal of fiction in with my history. I can sort it if you like. Put it in a new file?"

"That's fine I'll access it as it is. Reading! Do you want to borrow my book?"

"I'd love to. I love the feel of turning pages."

* * *

Guilhem would not go to Pézenas as Bernat had demanded. This was because he didn't want to. Peremptory orders from someone not his equal did not match his mood. He sent Bernat's messenger home with polite words explaining that he was particularly busy. The business that consumed his time so much that he was unable to travel was pique. He would not let Bernat think, even for a moment, that he, Guilhem, was the Templars' to command.

* * *

8 June, full moon

Artemisia had the hilltop observation to herself. It was a bad viewing night and it was one of those periods when everyone avoided her. She spent a pleasant hour watching the moon rise in the east and bring a soft glow to the barren hillside. Fragments of thoughts drifted. Where did the scientific inquiries originate? What assumptions preceded the scientists' questions? Did her colleagues ever push back the veil that hid their initial impulses? Did they ever question their direction?

Inside, the others chatted in the kitchen.

"Why do we get these damned emails about saints all the time?"

"You forget. Artemisia is an expert in the lives of saints."

"Artemisia has explained it at least three times," Luke intervened. "I wish you would pay attention. We need to understand the religious calendar because of the abbey. Processions. Events. Avoidance thereof. What's the use in bringing a damned specialist back hundreds of years if everyone treats her as a lightweight?"

"You're a Catholic, just like Artemisia," said Sylvia, suspiciously.

"Guilty as charged. Also lapsed, just like Artemisia," Luke's tone was mocking. He didn't have the time for Sylvia that he once had. "That doesn't make her work any less essential to our well-being."

Sylvia picked up on Luke's sarcasm. It would have been hard not to. Artemisia noticed this (it would have been hard not to, given she had just walked in for a hot drink) and also wrote in her journal that Sylvia was Dr Sylvia Smith again.

'Dr Sylvia Smith' was Artemisia's shorthand for a woman who demanded that her own results be processed first, that her pain was higher than everyone else's, and that she was a special petal. These words were not what Artemisia typed. Not ever. 'Dr Sylvia Smith' was the best she could do. She knew what she meant.

Artemisia could tolerate Sylvia if she had to, but when Dr Sylvia Smith walked into a room, the historian became a mouse and hid, mostly at a computer terminal. Sylvia's manner of demanding respect for her own work was not conducive to Artemisia's contentment.

* * *

One morning, about an hour after the saint of the day had been posted on the intranet, Ben found that someone had replied to the post. He read it and chuckled and set up an alert. Cormac had written an entirely false biography for the saint in question over the top of Artemisia's work. Cormac was the first. He was by no means the only. Artemisia did her best to ignore the others. She was upset, however.

No-one mocks Sylvia's rocks or Ben's plants or Cormac's fixes or Pauline's cooking. Only my work is the subject of deletion.

Or ignored.

I want to go home.

Except she couldn't. Not until 31 December. Less than six months. Artemisia kept telling herself. Less than six months.

* * *

Guilhem was disaffected. Guilhem's valet was even more disaffected. The boy was impossible, but Guilhem observed the niceties in his vicinity. Everyone else knew that this was mere show, but Sibilla thought of his youth and his attractiveness and his wealth. She exploited his mood by getting him into bed with her. Guilhem wasn't upset by this. Guilhem's page was, however, and expressed his personal dissatisfaction by taking a knife to Sibilla's second best dress, which Sibilla had left carelessly on the page's personal chest, and by shredding to the sounds of their lovemaking. It was not his best moment.

* * *

"Ah, Raindrops on the Computer," Luke observed as he walked past Geoff's desk. "Nice music."

"I'm sorry?" Geoff had been in a dream world, half listening to his jazz track and half thinking through the weather patterns. They fitted with Artemisia's data that suggested it wasn't a good year, and he was comparing them with modern data. Artemisia's information had been minimal, after all, just a notation of poor years in Western Europe.

"Lucky to have that data," Konig had commented as he passed it on. "This came from her thumbdrive. She downloaded it from the net before she left England. Our library doesn't have a thing worth looking at."

"You checked."

"Damn right I checked. Every tedious document. I don't know how she lives with that library."

So Luke's comment about raindrops half-fitted with what he was thinking, but really didn't make sense.

"What the guys call that track," Luke gestured with his thumb at Geoff's speakers. "Your music. As I said." He let it be seen that he was being patient with Geoff's slowness.

Suddenly, light dawned. Luke was in a social mood. Geoff gave up puzzling the weather patterns and grabbed the nearest chair. Luke could be very good company when he chose. It was incumbent upon Geoff to take advantage of it while he could.

* * *

The rain fell gently, in big drops. It ran over the countryside and down the streets in rushes and torrents. It swelled the river for a very brief time and it left the people of Saint-Guilhem wet to their ankles. Then it stopped.

* * *

Most of the team was in the storeroom, sorting their samples and finds from the last fortnight. Artemisia looked at the 'historical' samples she had been given and wondered just how far team members wandered to find these things. It looked suspiciously as if someone had ventured near a building site or a workshop. There was worked iron, and there was a piece of glass and something that rather looked like a cotton rag. She picked it up and examined it closely.

"Mac," she called out looking towards his workroom.

"Yup!" he replied, from directly behind her, making her jump. She had no idea how he had got there. His workroom didn't have any exits to outside, so going out and coming back in using the main entrance wasn't a possibility. Or was it?

"Did this used to be a piece of clothing? Has it been used for polishing something and then washed? Look at that seam and the way this section is all shiny."

"I think you're right." Cormac's pronouncement caused the others to gather around the collections bin. Now Cormac had an audience. "I found it, you know." He sounded pleased with himself.

"Then label it," Artemisia snapped. "Provenance, too. We need to know where you found it. Even time of day." She was going to use Mac's audience to make a point. "It's essential data for analysis when we get home."

Cormac was entirely unperturbed by Artemisia's tone. "I nearly got cat hair today," he volunteered.

"Fur," corrected Sylvia.

"If the damned cat hadn't escaped I could have given you the whole skin and you could call it what you like. I'm sure someone will want to study cat DNA, sometime."

"It's probably not a priority," Geoff's mouth betrayed his amusement. "But let me give you the list of parts of animal that we collect, just in case." For a moment, Artemisia and Mac both believed him.

"There once were two cats of Kilkenny" Mac began, as he started to label the rest of his finds.

"We're going to run out of space." Sylvia's face was dour.

"You're just worried because we're re-doing your rocks."

"I'm worried for the good of the expedition," she snapped.

"Children," Luke appeared from nowhere, "Behave. Cormac, I need you to fix my bed."

"What's wrong with it?"

"It fell apart."

"It's napping during the day," Geoff confided once Luke was out of earshot. "Does it to everyone. I never had to nap when I was in my twenties. Although it's distantly possible that the collapse of Luke's bed might be related to the fact that person or persons unknown were using said bed to explain how our beds are made."

"You didn't?" Sylvia looked up on horror.

"No," and Geoff was truly regretful. "Tony wanted to know, and he doesn't stop when he has a question. Not ever. I found him with Mac when they were putting the bed back together."

"Why Luke's?"

"I don't think Tony asked whose bed it was. Artemisia found the pattern for them in one of her books, said they were used by the British army in India and that they fitted into a calico bag, so Tony had to see. Mac was happy to help him. He even produced the bag it came in. It was quite a small bag."

Sylvia played with her samples for a moment. "Are you really in your thirties?"

"Yep," said Geoff, more interested in the notion of collapsing beds than his advanced age. He himself had checked everyone's age on the staff profiles, back in the twenty-first century. He had known since the beginning, for instance, that Sylvia not only lied about her age but had changed the records on their 1305 system.

"You look younger."

Geoff shrugged and took his completed and labelled specimens over to Konig for official deposit in the current official sample-holding unit for samples that needed cold conservation. It had recently been full of meat.

"Watch out," Konig said. "You're now officially a target. No longer too young."

Sylvia heard him. "Oh, shut up," she said, and left her specimens half sorted.

"Like a pouting teen," Konig said, admiringly.

"Just your type," commented Geoff, and took himself back to his desk. There he typed on the Bulletin Board, anonymously:

There was a young person from Wight
Who travelled much faster than light.
She departed one day
In a relative way
And arrived on the previous night.

If this time travel is going to drive us all crazy, he thought, *we might as well enjoy it. Artemisia's got the right idea. Mac too.*

Sylvia was obviously not enjoying things. She called a planning meeting the moment she was back at her desk. When Artemisia turned up for it, she was sent summarily away. "You're not needed for planning," she told Artemisia. "You're support staff."

Sylvia didn't see Geoff Murray's open and pleasant face turn into a mirror of Tony's inward and shuttered visage. He watched her, absorbing every nuance of those words. At that moment, Geoff and Tony might have been cousins.

Chapter Twenty-Five: A Dialogue of Silence

Sibilla finally admitted that she had taken some dye from Berta's workshop and given it to Fiz. Fiz was faced with the accusation of having polluted the font at Saint-Barthelmy. He was entirely unperturbed. When Guilhem-the-Smith asked him, very puzzled, why Sibilla had not told anyone before this, Fiz explained, still unworried, that "I threatened to tell all her secrets."

"We all know her secrets anyway. We've all had goods in pawn to her, too," someone said. Fiz was happily unrepentant, but said, "I didn't turn all that other water blue. That wasn't me. I wish I knew how. We just changed the holy water."

* * *

Back in the caves, by a happy coincidence, the team suffered a briefing session about the local water systems. The chart of the blue dye and its reaches was shown. Artemisia found the chart to be beyond her simple brain, but no-one stopped to explain. Underground water was a puzzle to her.

"Cormac's an idiot," said Geoff conversationally. "Ben should have known better. All those chemicals will be in cave sediments for us to discover in the twenty-first century."

"We change things anyway," said Artemisia mildly. She had been silenced too often on technicalities and found herself unable to ask the questions she ought to ask. She didn't want to say *We change things*; she wanted to ask how the water worked, what changes the dye made, what changes the cavedwellers made and why the hell they had all stopped caring. Maybe they hadn't all stoped caring. Maybe they'd developed a dialogue of silence.

"I don't like to think about that too much," admitted Geoff, his eyes softening ruefully.

* * *

June 22, St Alban

Harvest would start soon. Sometime. No-one knew when. Without harvest, the town was poor, so everyone watched the earliest fields, anxiously. Grapes and olives were the lifeblood of the region. They kept everyone alive when the pilgrims could not. The quality was the pride of Saint-Guilhem. Even Bona and her brother watched the grapes and olives anxiously.

* * *

Ben Konig's past was never what he claimed. It was more exotic. More undependable. More worrying. He told lies to hide it.

The more someone pushed, the more dramatic those lies became. Sylvia pushed the hardest of anyone, so he told her many different stories. His personal favourite was that he was descended from an exotic dancer who had once performed before the Czar of all the Russias. He hadn't even needed to suggest that he had a genuine claim to the Russian Empire. Sylvia wanted him to be born to glory. Ben just wished that his past was different, any way different. That his grandfather had been almost anyone other than who he was. A war hero. Of the wrong religion. On the wrong side. The lies helped, a bit. It didn't delete three generations of guilt, but it applied a mild salve.

Ben's extravagant words were in exact contrast to his modest personal habits. Unlike Geoff, he never paraded half -naked. Unlike Geoff, he never, ever complained about the cold. Also unlike Geoff, he didn't push himself past Artemisia's boundaries until she snapped. Konig played things safe, exactly as his grandfather had. This was his single biggest problem, exactly as it had been for his grandfather.

While he was contemplating his own sad history and half-dreaming about the next tale he would spin to the very attractive Dr Smith, he half-listened to Artemisia Wormwood read Geoff Murray the riot act.

It had started with a Pronouncement from Murray.

"I can't hang round the office when I have work to do," he had said, breezily. "I don't want to wait and read your briefings when they emerge, a bit each day. Just send me to the best general history you have in your database and I'll free up some time."

"Do real work?" Artemisia's look was mild, but her voice glared.

"I can figure things out. From books. I'm literate. All I need is a good general work and I'll be fine."

"How good is your nineteenth century French?"

"Pardon?"

"The best general book we have on the Middle Ages in this region is volume seven of the general history of Languedoc, published in the middle of the nineteenth century. The only modern material we have is the Catholic Encyclopedia and five megabytes of material on my own personal thumb drive."

"I wasn't kidding."

And this is where it became interesting enough for Konig to forget dreaming up new pasts and to pay proper attention. He hadn't realised until now what a fine grasp of scatological language Dr Wormwood possessed.

What he noticed particularly was how Murray's body language had shifted. Murray was looking at Wormwood. With far too much interest. Again. He probably asked for that book on purpose, from the intent way he was enjoying watching her very thoroughly lose her temper.

This would bear keeping an eye on, Konig thought. Just when the power play had settled down and the hierarchy established, Murray was going to turn things upside down. Ben Konig wondered how he could use it.

* * *

June 24, St John the Baptist

"It's midsummer," said Artemisia brightly. It was hard to be bright over breakfast normally, but today was special. "All sorts of frolics and fun."

"Frolics and fun?" Cormac, of course, was instantly fascinated.

"I don't know any details," admitted Artemisia.

"Didn't you ask what's-his-name?"

"Guilhem. He doesn't know either. His mother is from Langudeoc, it seems, but not his father and he was brought up by entirely different people in any case and he really doesn't like the thought of midsummer here. I do adore regionalism." Artemisia beamed.

"So you don't know what will happen today?" Luke looked worried.

"Not really. Except that I hope it will include dancing. We don't have much evidence for dancing this early."

"People didn't dance?" Geoff was fascinated.

"We don't have dance steps. Or many of them. Just music. And I don't even know if we have music from this region. Our library has de Grocheo, but he documents Paris."

"As usual," said Sylvia, "That was less than helpful."

Artemisia sighed. As usual, Sylvia was less than supportive.

During that space, Luke had pondered.

"Right," he said. "We're all confined to the cave until joy has ceased." He smiled at his little joke.

"But why?" Several voices spoke at once.

"Because we don't know if there'll be action out here. Orgies on the hillside and whatnot."

"Oh surely," said Ben.

"No." Luke wasn't interested. "Indoors, all of us, until I say otherwise."

Confinement only lasted two days. Sylvia blamed Artemisia anyway. "Confinement impedes our work," she proclaimed, loudly.

On the second night, Luke surprised everyone.

During dinner, he tapped on his glass with his spoon. Ben wondered why he didn't just use that booming voice of his and demand to be heard. Luke had his ways, however, and they were a never-ending source of entertainment to his drones. Konig thought 'drones' and his thought was coloured with resigned contemptuousness. He also wondered why everyone else still believed they were part of a magnificent team. Except maybe Pauline, who thought she was here as a sacrificial lamb and maybe Artemisia who knew full well that the whole damned thing was a mistake.

And here's the announcement, Ben thought. Luke loved his bit of drama. Taking his time between one action and the next, so that every person present would hang on every word he uttered.

When even Ben Konig was watching him fully, Luke tapped his glass one last time.

"Well," he started, "Now I have your attention…" he smiled around the table until he was certain everyone got his joke. No-one laughed, although Pauline smiled slightly. "A half hour after dinner, there will be music in the recreation room. I expect you all to attend. Murray, I expect a strong performance from you in particular."

He nodded in confirmation, got up and left.

"I resent that assumption," Geoff's voice said, mildly, "and think I have come down with a mild case of laryngitis."

"Don't look at me," Pauline stated firmly. "I'm not going to lie on your behalf."

"You can sing, Geoff, I hear you in the shower," said Sylvia, earnestly. "Your voice is quite nice."

"What are you doing paying attention to me when I'm in the shower?" asked Geoff, mostly amused. "The shower partitions are nearly transparent, you know."

"She does know," said Mac. "That's why she pays attention."

"I shall sing," said Tony. "I can't sing, but I shall sing anyway." The moment he had finished his unexpected pronouncement, he stood up, took his plate and spoon to the sink, and left.

"Excuse me," said Artemisia, her voice barely under control. She, too, took her plate and spoon, but rather more hurriedly. Geoff found her in her bedroom, her hands hiding her face. She looked up at his knock.

"I think I'm having hysterics," she said, as he came into her room.

"Knock it off," was Geoff's reply. "It wasn't that funny."

"I've heard Tony sing."

"I haven't."

"Obviously," Artemisia regained some control of her voice. "Quite obviously. Because if you had heard him sing, you would also be having hysterics."

"He's that bad?" Geoff sat on the bed, close.

"He has a nice voice, actually. But he's so right. He can't sing."

"Tone deaf?" Geoff moved just a little closer.

"Very. But at least he has a voice. And stop that. Now. I need to calm down before our singathon. Quit stirring."

Geoff laughed and moved a fraction of an inch away. "It's going to be fun."

"I forgot," Artemisia said gloomily. "You're an expert in amateur musical evenings."

"Enjoying them is a fine art," Geoff assured her. "And one at which I have a vast repertoire of skills."

"Just pinch me if I start laughing at any stage. Please?"

The evening wasn't too bad. Luke's giant day-voice turned out to be small and a bit pitchy when put to a tune. Ben Konig sang a ballad, almost respectably. Geoff Murray could, of course, sing, and did so with much charm. If Pauline's looks had been weapons, however, Geoff Murray would have exploded into fragments every single time he sang the chorus of his ditty. He had chosen *Shaddup you face*, effectively saving himself from ever having to perform in the caverns again.

Tony sang on two notes, his face solemn.

Sylvia, to everyone's surprise, sang divinely. Her voice was high and hard and bright.

The next time Sylvia drifted to the hilltop, the rest of the group paid attention. This was the sort of place that one sang, if one wasn't a shower singer "Or a grouch," said Artemisia to Geoff, "like you."

Sure enough, Sylvia sang to herself, up there above the caverns, when she was supposed to be working. Cormac engineered it so that her previous most comfortable place had developed the wrong kind of rocks. Sylvia wasn't the sort of person who tolerated discomfort.

She thought she was singing solitaire to the stars every few nights, but her new spot was close to the opening above the lounge area. And she didn't realise that she could be heard below. Or that the stone had been placed there very carefully by Cormac.

It became a group activity to sit in the cavern, the lights dimmed, in the comfortable chairs, listening to Sylvia run through her favourite melodies. The acoustics were oddly excellent. Cormac, being incorrigible, recorded her echoing soprano and made a compilation of his top ten tunes. He made a second compilation of Sylvia's goofs, which he saved to play back at her when she condescended towards him once too often.

Chapter Twenty-Six: Soul Sorting

June 25 Saint Guilhem's day

There was nothing to report from the cave that day. They were all still hunkered down. The only thing of unusual interest in the town was Guilhem getting drunk after church. Everyone watched it with great interest and laid bets on how composed he would be.

Fiz won the bet. Guilhem was calm and courteous throughout. "It's his temper you want to watch," he warned, "Not the wine."

* * *

"Watch out for wolves," Ben reminded them. He said it once a week, like clockwork. He also said that they were highly unlikely to appear before winter. It was mid-summer. And Sylvia was sick and tired of being shut up in those caves. When she got back there would be data to process. Never-ending data. She had to get out.

She came back looking amused.

"I saw the wolf and the wolf saw me. It looked at me. It turned around and it went the other way. Fuss about nothing, if you ask me."

"Lucky," said Geoff, envious.

"It wasn't hungry, I guess," said Sylvia.

Artemisia tried to help. "Sylvia, that's not what Geoff—"

"Forget it," interrupted Ben.

Later Ben tried to extract details of the wolf and the sighting and all he got was, "It was grey. Looked like a big dog." Sylvia was very cagey about the location.

While Ben was doing his best at improvised inquisition, Geoff was telling Mac about the episode.

"How long would it have taken for the wolf to kill Sylvia, if she had spooked it?"

Mac contemplated this important question. "About five seconds," he finally concluded.

"And then, what do you think? Indigestion?"

"Bad, bad indigestion."

* * *

The most recent data download from the twenty-first century had finally been sorted and Luke was looking harassed. It appeared that the twenty-first century was concerned with paperwork and that not enough had been completed. It also appeared that it had taken twenty-first century administration all this time to discover the insufficiencies. Most of it Luke was able to fill in himself, but every now and again he descended upon the office and stood against the open sky, his shadowed figure dramatically demanding answers to stupid questions.

"Who here isn't WASP?" Luke asked. Pauline had brought in cupcakes, making the atmosphere party-like. He still stood at the gap to the outside world, Languedoc's landscape framing him. There wasn't enough display space in a cavern for Professor Theodore Lucas Mann.

Artemisia, from the cover of her computer, called out "Why?"

"Not a single bloody one of you put your ethnicity on your personnel forms and some idiot back home picked up last month that I had filled them all in as WASP. Except mine, of course. Obviously. Since I'm not WASP." *That's right, he said he was a lapsed Catholic,* Artemisia thought. *Funny. I was sure he was Jewish. Harvey said there was someone Jewish in the team. 'Can't have no Jewish scientists. Need our stereotypes.' Harvey must've been wrong.* Harvey's golden voice held so much wrongness that one more bit was neither here nor there.

Most of the team looked down again at this next statement. Luke was shadowed but he could see each of their faces perfectly (except Artemisia's which was safe behind her computer screen.) and not a single one of them wanted to meet his eye when he said "I'm just asking to make sure I was right. Obviously."

"Obviously," said Geoff. "Except that I'm not white, not Anglo-Saxon and I am a fully-functioning atheist." The white start and head-dress in the middle of his pin-badge stuck defiantly out from Geoff's lapel.

"Me neither," said Artemisia. "Except that I'm white and once was Catholic. Every other molecule of me is Italian."

"Wormwood isn't an Italian surname," said Geoff, his face swivelling in her direction, almost detaching itself from his head. *How does he do that,* Artemisia wondered.

"Artemisia is an Italian Christian name, however. Wormwood is what I chose to be called when I divorced my parents."

No-one knew what to say to that. Artemisia felt proud of herself.

"I'm white, Saxon and almost Protestant, so you could call me WASPish, perhaps?" Ben offered.

"WASP to the core, that's us," said Pauline, nodding to include Sylvia.

"Tony?" Luke asked.

"What?"

"What's your ancestry?"

"My ancestry." It was a statement, not a question. Finally, he pulled the thought out from deep within himself. "I'm Australian."

"Where did your family come from, before Australia?"

"My mother is Australian. From the Northern Territory." Tony said. "My father was brought up in France. He was French."

"And his mother?" Sylvia was fascinated.

"She was from Vietnam."

Artemisia followed the puzzle further, "What about your mother's parents? Where were they from?"

"They were from Malacca. They were Hakka."

"They were Malaysian Chinese?" Artemisia was fascinated. Malaysian Chinese fitted with a Northern Territory background, too. She just hadn't thought it through.

"They were from Malaya."

"Before it became Malaysia?"

"Yes." Tony folded his arms and looked down. He had said all he was going to say.

"My God," said Sylvia, "It took a historian to work out what sort of Asian he is."

"Geoff, when did your family come out?" asked Artemisia, who wondered why Sylvia didn't think of the rather Ocker Tony as Australian. "Or did it come out? Is it Kanaka, Islander what?"

"I don't want Luke putting it on his bloody form. I'll tell you later."

"You'll keep, Murray," Luke had filled in one set of boxes and wanted to move to the next. "How about we check through all of your educations? There are a couple of holes. And Mr Smith appears to have acquired three doctorates. One of them is in the close study of reversing polarities I assume that refers to *Star Trek* or Whovian analysis and is a creative doctorate." Luke's voice was heavy with sarcasm.

"I'll go get Mac for you," volunteered Geoff, helpfully. Thus Geoff escaped.

It was the season for small annoyance. The farmers were out doing whatever it was farmers did in late June. Whenever a team member tried to work outdoors, they were driven indoors by whistling peasants and shepherds and other locals. There seemed an inordinate number of them for a desert of souls. It was very hard to work around.

The locals were abroad very late, because of the full moon. The whole team was confined to quarters, only allowed outside for essential matters. The viewings and measurements from above the cave went on as usual, but everything else slowed down. Outside the weather was perfect. Inside, the temperature was even and the atmosphere cold. Artemisia found herself wondering what would happen if one of them committed murder. Then she found herself wondering who would be murdered. *Probably me. That'd solve stuff, for certain.*

"Too much," said Geoff.

"Too much that I can't observe," said Ben.

"Too much I'm not bloody allowed to document," Artemisia whispered to herself, and crossed her arms, grumpily. Then she looked at the time and realised she had an escape route.

Artemisia attired herself most anciently and went to meet with Guilhem, in the usual place. Guilhem warned Artemisia, "The men have been remarked upon again. Also a woman." From his tone, Artemisia knew that Guilhem was referring to Sylvia. She wasn't even 'that woman'. She was unworthy of any more than minimal notice. Guilhem was not the forgiving type.

"I shall tell them," Artemisia promised.

This was the last straw. Not for Sylvia, who shrugged her shoulders at the warning. Not for Tony, who ignored everything, as usual, and went about his own business, in his own world. It was the two free-spirited souls (as they liked to describe themselves) who felt caged.

"Trapped," Cormac said to Geoff.

"We're going to develop cabin fever," Geoff confided in return.

"Turn into mass murderers," agreed Cormac. Obviously, thought Artemisia, the thought was getting around.

"We need to do something about it."

"Too right!"

That night, they walked out the main door nonchalantly, walked up to where the path met the steep hillside, and they shouted slogans to the air.

"A bas les restrictions!" cried Mac, in his best faux French.

"Let us live in freedom or let us die," shouted Geoff.

This shouting lasted for about five minutes. The two then sat on rocks, still in the dark, and chatted quietly.

"What's up?" Ben asked Sylvia.

"Ask Luke," Sylvia's voice sounded prim. "He gave them permission."

After a little while the slogans returned. Then the duo trooped happily indoors.

"You could have broken your necks," said Sylvia.

All she received in return were looks of consummate smugness.

Chapter Twenty-Seven: Lure of the Fair Folk

Guilhem hid his fury well. The bishop of Vivarais had just accepted Philippe's sovereignty. His friend, the other Philippe, had sent him a message confirming this. He felt betrayed. Guilhem had stood by his principles and ruined his future and the bishop had not. He wanted to slash at someone, and he could not.

* * *

Geoff Murray was working. Since there was no-one around, he allowed his air of laziness to disappear. He was intent on his gauges. He was sure that they were inaccurate. Either that, or the summer was cool and the rainfall atypical. While this was a possibility, his first reaction was to check his equipment. This took close attention.

Geoff didn't notice that he was being followed everywhere by a small shadow. After a while, he was also being followed by a larger shadow that stopped every now and again to scold the small shadow.

The children were still arguing about whether Geoff was a fairy. His skin wasn't that dark, they agreed, but it was certainly the wrong colour.

"And his nose is a bit squashed," the boy said, firmly. "He's a fairy."

"Only a little bit," his sister argued.

The argument then turned to the rest of the party. If he's a fairy, were the others fairies? The very pale woman looked like a fairy, they agreed. The hair like spun gold, the white and pink skin, the clear eyes. A grumpy fairy.

"Maybe she's a demon," suggested Bona. "Or maybe she lives underground, like those green children."

"What green children? You mean like the baby who turned green?"

"That pilgrim told us. The tall skinny one who told us lots of stories of relics. Just before Advent. Don't you remember? He was very boring until he started songs and stories. His singing was very bad, but his stories were good. Don't you remember?"

"No. You're telling lies. That's bad. You'll have to confess."

"Stop talking about things like that. I don't want to hear. Anyhow, the pretty one isn't green. She must be a fairy."

"She never looks happy. Fairies are happy, aren't they?"

"I like her when she sings."

"Me too," his sister confessed. "She's a lot better than the tall man."

"I remember him! He had red hair! And tall as that tree! He was funny! If we trick him again, can we get him to scare us again? Do you think?"

This led to the two children sneaking out at night. Sylvia's singing was one lure. The lights from the caves were another, and the interesting noises and strange language. It was otherworld and wonderful.

* * *

"Watch out for fur," said Ben.

"Seriously?"

"Seriously. If Sylvia's wolf is local, there might be some round."

"Reconstructing ancient wolves from their DNA and then they kill us all?"

"Hardly. We'll know a little more, is all. The paths that dogs and their ancestors have travelled, for instance. Breeds, distribution, extinction, genetic variation."

"You don't sound hopeful."

"I'm not. I'm not expecting to see any more until winter. They'll be hungry then, and probably more dangerous."

Artemisia chose this moment to upset both Ben and Geoff. "Wolves were killed off quite intentionally in England in the thirteenth century. They're probably rare as hen's teeth here and now. Except in the mountains. Sylvia is endangering a dying population." After that nice bit of work, the second half of which she had made up on the spot, Artemisia visited Mac.

Artemisia was admiring her new boots. She was a bit reluctant in the admiration, just as she had been a little diffident when Guilhem triumphantly handed them over.

The boots came up to the bottom of her calves, laced at the side with flat leather straps. The lacing started at the ankle. The toes were closed in fact, the whole boot was closed and slightly pointed.

Artemisia took them to Cormac to show off, since he knew costume. She wanted someone to appreciate them. They were strange and alien and wonderful, boots from an actual medieval cordwainer, made just for her. She wanted to be intimidated. Cormac would share the wonder and help her forget the strangeness.

"Very nice workmanship," commented Cormac. "Very nice indeed."

"They're a bit like leather ugg-boots." Artemisia was dubious. If she had been a textiles expert or an archaeologist she might be able to think more useful thoughts. Ugg-boots were not her area of expertise.

"Comfortable. Keeps you warm and dry. Very practical. Look at those calfskin uppers. Very nice."

"I guess. I feel bad about them."

"At least you won't have to rub that stuff Doc likes on all your bruises."

"'Tis true my bruises will be entirely different in shape and colour and she will find entirely new stuff for me to rub on."

* * *

It was a beautiful day. Hot and languorous and the sort of day when bees buzz and the scent of lavender makes the rosemary and thyme faint with envy. Ben had covered his turf and collected specimens that needed collecting (one) and recorded everything that needed recording and he wasn't ready to return.

He checked that he was out of sight of everything and everyone. He put his knapsack full of equipment under his head, and lay his head on its knobbledness. There would be one of those flash storms later in the day, and he wanted to breathe the air while it was still lazy. As the warmth unravelled the tension from his muscles, his right hand let a half-eaten scavenged fruit slide to the ground. Wild harvesting was second nature to him. So was drowsing in the sun.

He woke up just when the wind shifted, and returned to the caves before the storm hit.

Chapter Twenty-Eight: The System is Dynamic

The town was divided. The abbey had demanded that Fiz and his friends stop their depredations of their garden. The abbot had said that the two boys should enter the monastery, start the path to monkdom, and learn discipline.

Sibilla and Berta were especially divided. Sibilla thought it was a bad idea, while Berta championed the safety of her dyes. Neither of them, however, wanted to support the abbot, so they aired their differences with each other and didn't talk for three days.

In the end, Fiz's accomplice in crime was sent to Aniane then to one of Aniane's satellite villages. Not even Saint-Jean de-Fos.

Fiz was alone.

* * *

"Better dead than living defeated," Guilhem was explaining to Artemisia. He was trying to make it clear why he was the only person she should have dealings with and why her people should avoid the village. She had no problems with this and decided to make a joke. One about zombies and rock bands, about which Guilhem would not know. It amused her.

"You are the Living Dead," she opined.

"It's true," he reflected, sadly.

Artemisia felt guilty at her sorry little attempt at a joke. Guilhem misunderstood her silence and tried to explain further.

She didn't really understand everything he had iterated, but it was pretty certain he was talking about life choices. If he had joined the king's household as he had been offered (which king? Why would any king want him?) then he would have a good future working with supplies and organisation. He would develop…something. Honourably. Or he would develop honour. It was not clear. But he was not good at these things. His mind was too simple. Yet he was good at fighting and at war.

He was angry (this she was certain about) because he was not given honours or notice for the work he did. Only castigated for the single wrong he had done.

Just like a knight in a tale of King Arthur and his court, Artemisia had said.

"Yes," Guilhem had vehemently agreed. Then Artemisia had regretted making the link in Guilhem's mind, because the knight in the Arthurian tale inevitably found his richness and honour with the help of a fairy. She had tried to divert his thoughts.

"What will help you regain honour?" she asked.

"The king wants me to agree with him. My uncle supports him," Guilhem was more than angry about this. With his anger his speech sped up and Artemisia understood no more. Guilhem was listing and describing at a rattling pace. Some words shone: war, peers, command. Most she missed entirely. Still, what she had gleaned was important. Guilhem wasn't local. He was here for a kind of thinking time. And a king was involved.

If there was a king involved then Guilhem might be far too close to the centre of events for comfort. Not a solitary do-nothing on the outer edges of society. Artemisia was worried. She needed to find out more.

* * *

Guilhem found himself the unhappy accepter of yet another letter from the Commanderie. A gros it cost him, each time Bernat wrote. The knight had better things to do with his money than read Bernat's thoughts, turned elegant by Bernat's assistant.

The letter was, for a miracle, full of good news. More of Guilhem's rents had made it safely into the Templar coffers. He planned a spending spree, instantly. He couldn't leave to collect the money for a few days, but those monies would spend well whenever they were received.

* * *

Guilhem had cached himself and Artemisia out of sight and they watched pilgrims. The young man was teaching his new friend how to identify the rank of a person by their horse.

It was a slow explanation on a slow day and was peppered by silences and by noises from the valley below and by small confidences that Guilhem made, almost out of nowhere. Artemisia had trouble understanding the comments that came out of the blue, but she tried to follow.

She understood that he missed his horses. Guilhem could see that understanding on Artemisia's expressive face.

"I only have the one riding animal with me," he said. "And even that horse is small and low to the ground."

He missed the view and the sense of being above the world that his big battle steed gave. As he explained this, he saw that Artemisia didn't understand. He didn't care. It was safe to tell her. Safe to regret. Safe to miss his horses.

Even the horse with him was chosen for its capacity to be ridden hard, not because it was a pleasure to ride, but because it could cross mountain passes if it had to. He said this slowly, but with an almost-comical despite, as if he hated himself for his horses. Then his tone lightened and Artemisia could hear love in his voice.

"When I was young, I had a black horse. A horse as black as ink."

Artemisia thought about his words. 'Enfances' didn't mean young, really, but possibly his teens, or when he was a young knight. Guilhem sometimes used very ambiguous language.

She caught herself and picked up on the last part of a story of a trick that Guilhem had played with this black horse, using his friends' association of black horses with the devil. She wanted to ask him to tell the story again so that she knew she understood it, but she was overcome by shyness and couldn't. There was something intimate about being half-hidden on the hillside with this knight.

Fortunately, Guilhem didn't notice the intimacy or Artemisia's hesitancy. He told her about his Great Horse and how he had left it behind in his exile but that it cost the same as the keep for two of his local household, even though it was so far away and he couldn't so much as exercise it.

* * *

Artemisia needed more paper. To her annoyance, Mac told her she needed permission.

"We're not running out," he said apologetically, "but Luke wants to cut down what gets carried back, so he says that no-one can get paper without permission. If we don't use it, it can be burned, he says. We spent half yesterday working out how to diminish the quantity of material to be returned home, then the other half on checks to make sure nothing's left behind. Me and Geoff and Sylvia and Pauline we're the rubbish collectors."

More and more, the systems and processes ground Artemisia down. Everyone was feeling something from the closeness. Jokes that Mac and Geoff shared shredded Sylvia's nerves. Pauline's self-righteous sniffs sent Ben marching outside in search of air. Little things frazzled.

Little things also reassured, Artemisia realised, when she found Sylvia (source of her permission to write) giggling over a silly joke. Pauline was obviously the one who had told the silly joke and it was obviously about men because of the teenage air the two wore. Artemisia smiled at both of them.

She obtained her permission and was about to ask if she could join them for a cup of tea. Luke came in at that point, bearlike and magisterial and so Artemisia beat a hasty retreat. She never knew how to handle the bizarre silences caused by Luke drawing on the table and pretending to be human. She admired Pauline for taking it in her stride, but she returned to Mac.

"One notepad I'm allowed you enter it in under B5 on the stationery allocations, Sylvia said, then I show her my goods so that she knows you gave me the right thing."

"Those words are honey to my ears," said Mac, "especially the trust the honourable Dr Smith dedicates to us," and gave her the paper.

The kitchen remained clear of more than Artemisia. Of the team, only Geoff came in, got what he needed, and paid no attention to the select group at the table. He probably ignored the cool kids at high school, too, Artemisia thought, enviously, returned to show the paper to Sylvia.

Pauline was making conversation.

"I calculate," Theo said, patiently, "to minimise uncertainty."

"And since you can't eradicate it, we signed our waivers." Pauline gave her best try-hard smile.

"Time evolution is in continuous transformation. We currently don't know any way of eliminating that uncertainty entirely. It's that dynamism that makes everything so very exciting. The system is dynamic. It changes constantly. In that change lies our future."

"Your big project?"

"Absolutely. Beyond the singularity. It would have been easier if we had gone further back in time, of course. We're only getting marginal information."

"Why didn't we? I never understood why we came here."

Theo nodded, "You just came. A good soldier."

"I've always been that," said Pauline softly.

"We can't go further back yet. We need better data for delta T."

"Sylvia's observations?"

"Sylvia's observations and modelling. From here, we will be able to convert Terrestrial Dynamic Time to Universal Time. Our work opens many doors." Theo's explanation was only taking a small amount of his attention. All the while he spoke, his right hand drew on the table, sketching and thinking and rubbing out and rethinking. His deep brain changed reality even as he gave the doctor an impromptu lecture. He missed his students.

"Why here, then? Why the middle of nowhere in the south of France?"

"The sex factor," said Theo, unexpectedly. "France, the Middle Ages. Templars, Holy Grails. And because the French Government has studied this region, so we can collect parallel data and our minor projects have more staying power. Plus the French Government has underwritten a part of our journey. The sex factor of being Australian. You know" he said, struck by a thought. He would never complete his thought, for the kitchen was invaded by Ben and Tony. Not only they were an unlikely duo, but their enthusiasm filled the room and crowded Theo's formulae out of existence.

"We collected too many specimens," said Tony, unapologetically.

"That wasn't quite how it happened," said Ben, and put piles of plants on the table, crowding Theo's formulae even more. "But it's as good an explanation as any."

Tony smiled. "Wild rocket," his deep voice enumerated, with love, "And wild cress and three varieties of wild chicory and salsify and purslane. Kitchen plants."

"I don't know how to cook them," said Pauline helplessly.

"We asked Artemisia on the way through. She says she has a Languedoc cookbook on her thumb drive. She had it with her when she was recruited." Tony looked so radiant that Pauline made salads and sandwiches and a salsify fry-up, just to keep the look on his face. *It's good for our health,* she justified her unaccustomedly gourmet cuisine.

* * *

The summer was one of fire. The summer was one of a thousand insects.

Finally, the fire cleared sufficiently and observations were better. The scent of the smoke was all wrong, thought Artemisia — no Australia in this air. Where was the sharpness of the eucalyptus burning?

"Can I borrow you tonight?" Geoff had asked her.

"I beg your pardon," was her elegant reply.

"I need to do some measurements. Sylvia doesn't have any observations due and isn't going to play with her full moon photography stuff until later, and a second set of hands would help."

"Sure. Just tell me a time and help me up the ladder."

The measurements weren't complicated. Nor did they take that long. Artemisia suspected Geoff invented the need, especially when she found herself sitting down on a comfortable rock, very close to him. She wanted to say to Lucia, "Possibly need a chaperone." But Lucia wasn't there. She banished that thought. Lucia was alive: she had to be.

"This isn't Sylvia's favourite spot, is it?" she asked suspiciously.

"That would be that big boulder over there," Geoff pointed to a dark silhouette. The stars were very bright. "No-one can hear us from here."

"You checked," mocked Artemisia.

"Mac checked, when we fixed things for Sylvia."

Artemisia found herself caught up in a flurry of giggles. Geoff waited quietly until she calmed down. "You two are so bad," she finally said.

For a while they just shared the stars.

"Tell me about these stars," Artemisia commanded.

Geoff pointed to Hercules directly above and to Andromeda near the horizon to the north. The planets were bunched awkwardly in the southwest, and in the south proper was the moon. The air was full of movement and made the space seem friendly and gentle.

It was Geoff who broke the silence the second time. "I wish I understood what you did and why it's so important to you."

"You know," answered Artemisia, in the tone that suggested that she didn't expect to be listened to. "We're looking at the sky differently to the people down in the valley."

"They think it's a flat earth?"

"That's a furphy." Artemisia sighed. "I spend half my teaching life telling students that what they think they know about the Middle Ages is wrong. Then I spend half of the other half helping them find the right questions so that they know what to ask. And then I come here and spend half my life being told by scientists that the people in the Middle Ages are irrelevant."

Geoff stretched out and stood up. "Let's look at the sky and you tell me about the cosmos."

"I'm suspicious, you know," Artemisia advised him.

"Don't be suspicious tonight."

"I'll save it til next time." They lay down on the crumbly and rocky ground, shifting stones and wiggling until they could lie flat.

"What am I looking at?" Geoff didn't ask. He commanded.

"We're inside, looking out at God," Artemisia said.

There was a silence, filled only by the wind.

"That's beautiful," Geoff finally said.

"It's pretty much what people thought. Between us and God are all the planets and all the stars and the Moon and the Sun, but we're in the middle of a giant, giant sphere, and God is everything outside that sphere."

"They believed in a big universe, then."

"Don't sound surprised."

"But I am. I may have to do some more reading."

"I can find you something," Artemisia promised and rolled over, ready to stand up for her descent into the caves again.

"No. Don't," and Geoff's long arm snaked out and stopped her. "Tell me about zombies. Instead."

Artemisia laughed. "You mean you lured me here to find out my Big Zombie Secret."

"Yup," Geoff said, complacently. "I also want to know about saints."

"Now you're just trying to butter me up." He didn't say anything. "OK, what do you want to know about saints?"

"You keep comparing them to zombies and ghosts. I can't see it."

"Look at that sky again," she said, softly. "Look right out there. Look at how far God is."

Geoff looked at the deep expanse above him. He felt that he could smell the stars, cold beneath the summer fires. "A long, long way."

"Yes. So the people here, the people now, think that God will hear them better if there's someone who can traverse that great distance."

"Saints."

"And Mary. You know, it's like us. We can hear the Middle Ages better from here. Much better than in the twenty-first century. Even with all the limitations Luke has put on me, I've learned more in this little time than I could in a lifetime back home."

"Why are you so upset, then?"

"There's so much more I could be learning. So much evidence I could be collecting. I'm not even allowed to record Guilhem's speech, for goodness' sake."

"And yet you're hearing the Middle Ages better than if you were in the twenty-first century."

"It's all a matter of data. Of evidence. Of how much we can know and how reliable the information is. Guilhem isn't interpreting himself according to my cultural norms, but according to his own. The boots I wear aren't a reconstruction, they're the way he knows boots look."

"I get that. I don't get zombies."

"Zombies will have to wait. You told Sylvia she could have the viewing area in an hour. She should be climbing the ladder any minute."

"Damn Sylvia," grumbled Geoff. He stood up and then held a hand to Artemisia. "Let's meet her halfway down the ladder and cause a traffic jam."

"You miss traffic jams?"

"Hoy!" Mac's unmistakable voice came from the ladder. He poked his head up. "We have a small crisis in the kitchen. A matter of some smoke and a tiny explosion. It may or may not be due to certain unexpected chemicals that found their way into Doc's big saucepan. Luke says to tell you two to stay up here until it's clear."

And his head disappeared again, the lid put on it like a jack-in-the-box.

"Certain unexpected chemicals?" Geoff looked down at Artemisia.

"Mac remembered he had them. I wondered why he was so enthusiastic. He said he would get even with Pauline blowing up her sanctum must've been his revenge. That young man likes explosions far too much. Let's find our rocks again."

"You're avoiding telling me about zombies."

"Didn't I tell you about my Zombie Ancestry Theory of History?"

"People eating rotting food."

"Yes, that. Doc's ancestors were zombies and mine were human."

"I'll pay. Why?"

"Because Doc believes that when the peasants in this region are starving, they will disguise the flavour of the rotting meat with spices. I heard her telling Sylvia that, with much conviction. It's a furphy."

"Why is it a furphy?" Geoff was enchanted.

"Because the spices come from Java and other places far distant. Anyone who can afford enough to disguise that much flavour"

"Can afford fresh meat."

"Or cheese, or to hunt a few sparrows."

"What do you do with this theory?"

"I hunt down examples of them and I put them in my little blue book."

"Your little blue book of zombie history. Can I see it?"

"When we're allowed back into the Underworld, of course you can. I'll lend it to you for light bedtime reading, if you like. I'm certain the sadly moral tale of how a dinner party in England ended in many lives lost because the cook left the pan out overnight will give you appropriate dreams."

"Why did that kill them?"

"It was a copper pan and the tin had worn thin. You can do the science, seeing as you're a scientist."

"I shall look into it," he promised.

"Then I shall lend you my precious zombie research."

Very romantic, especially the zombie history, Geoff thought. He was about to point this out when a small dark furry creature jumped onto Artemisia's lap.

"It's a cat!" she said, and scratched it under the neck. It purred and rubbed against her.

"That's Badass," Geoff explained. "He has adopted us."

"Badass."

"Tony named it."

"Tony named a cat 'Badass'? That seems very out of character."

"That's why I love it," and Geoff's generous chuckle rose into the night.

The two then sat, silently, and spoiled the cat and let the wind whistle past until Mac gave them the all clear to return. The whole cave system smelled slightly of brimstone.

Chapter Twenty-Nine: Affiliations

Fiz was in the cloisters, running a message. He hopped from foot to foot, restless. He stared at the long boned carvings with their flowing robes and wished they would flow just a little more, like water, and join the Verdus. Better that than staring at him like a piece of ordure. He did not belong here, and he knew it. The statues and carvings and curved walls all rubbed it in. The paintings over the archway were better, but not much. All reds and browns. He had no idea what they were for, but suspected hellfire. He hoped no-one was going to tell him to become a monk again: he wasn't cut out for it. Next time, someone else could run the message to the abbot.

* * *

September was the month for bird migration and that month was nearly past. The whole team was outdoors, observing what was possibly the last of it.

The whole team being outdoors at once meant that Luke and Ben and Sylvia had sorted out a whole new series of permissions. These took several members of the team into plain sight of the village. Artemisia's objections were registered, but not acted upon. Artemisia worried, but, given that all her views had been meticulously recorded before being ignored, there was nothing much she could do except fret. And it was hard to fret in the sunshine, lazily watching the sky.

Sylvia was surprisingly good. She stayed within her allocated space. In her mind, she was recalling the golden eyes of that wolf.

When Artemisia had done her required time in observation, her lonely figure slowly made its way down the slope and went to her regular meeting place. She was early. Rather than rejoin the others, she waited by the bush. *Badasse frutescens*, Tony would have told her. She stripped it of its accumulated ribbons. The activity helped fill her empty brain and drive away thoughts of Lucia, dying. The long stalks that carried them were battered and bent.

Also while she was waiting, Artemisia carefully filled her head with her favourite William and how he handled loneliness. He had been out-manoeuvred after his retirement and sent on a shopping trip. His fellow monks had expected that it would be fatal. He had taken an ass and spent the money and returned to Saint-Guilhem-le-Désert through an isolated mountain pass.

Robbers had descended from the hills. Robbers loved the woody and lonely country that bordered on the Cevennes.

William had no weapon so he (according to Medieval story) ripped a leg from his ass. Using it as a weapon, he attacked the bandits until, one by one, they fell into the ravine beneath. Then he calmly returned the hind leg to the ass and went on his way.

When he was back at the monastery, several monks were missing.

"How was the journey?" the remaining monks asked.

"Uneventful," said the saint.

When Guilhem arrived, Artemisia reminded him of the story of his namesake and the bandits. Guihem smiled, a bit distractedly, and warned the historian.

"The townsfolk talk," he said. "Walls breed idle chatter. Tell your friends to take care what they do and where they go."

Artemisia felt a little humiliated by the reminder. It was worse because she knew Guilhem was right. All of the cave-dwellers were guilty of bad science and bad manners and all kinds of bad things each and every time their lives impacted on the locals.

From there the conversation turned to horses. Guilhem explained that he had only one real riding horse with him. There were good horses at the castle and even at the abbey, but he couldn't use them. His best horse had been hired out from under him twice now. The people who took care of his animals had no compunctions about such behaviour. Also, each and every time he wanted to travel, he had to retrieve his animals. If they were there. He wished the high town walls enclosed more space for beasts. He missed the closeness between man and his horse.

Before Artemisia could respond, Guilhem changed the topic.

"You need to talk to your people again." He changed the topic abruptly. "Ask them to stop taking things."

"They want to collect small things to take home, for understanding."

"Tell me what small things?"

"Linen, pots, charcoal, wine, bread — anything."

"I will bring you linen and pots and charcoal and wine and bread and anything. In return, your people will stay clear of mine."

"I will ask our lord to order it. I promise."

"Riens n'est qui vaille bon ami," said Guilhem, with careless affection. This silenced Artemisia very effectively for three minutes as she tried to work out what the proverb meant. She thought he was simply valuing her friendship, but there had been a look to his eyes as he darted a glance across. His moods were vagrant.

She stood up too quickly and tripped and fell over him. Guilhem laughed, but Artemisia felt a sharp stabbing pain in her leg. She rolled over onto the ground and found that her dress was stained with red.

"My spurs," said Guilhem, all contrition. "Let me help."

"No, we have a doctor. I can be home quickly."

She made her leave hurriedly, and staggered a bit getting back to the cave, Pauline patched her up quickly enough, and gave her a tetanus boost for good measure. She also took pictures of the wound, and measurements. "A spur, you say? This can be my scientific data for our next report."

* * *

Guilhem had been wearing his favourite new spurs because he was on his way to Pézenas just as soon as he left Artemisia. He was going to spend a day or so there, contemplating becoming a brother-knight. He wanted to show off and let the brother knights recognise the new spur design and wonder at his equipment. No-one else knew a thing, not even his triple-idiot page.

A very useful bit of information had appeared, concerning the town of Pézenas and Guilhem had decided to test it after he had finished with his duty. It might take his mind off the lady from under the hill and the sweetness of her smell. Like a saint, he thought, and smiled as he remembered how soft she was when she had tumbled and how very delicate her scent.

Then he turned his mind to Bernat and his order. Each time Guilhem reported to the Templars, the abbey and castle both sought to find out what the Templars were up to. They wanted Guilhem's information, but not his affiliations. Reporting, therefore, was becoming very uncomfortable. This visit would be no better than the last.

He admitted to himself that he liked the lifestyle. Thirteen paternosters at Matins, without fail. Every morning. All the Hours in prayer, every day, without question or interruption. It was immensely consoling. It also meant that he could stop thinking and worrying . He could live in a perpetual present of prayer.

Wine and bread and the rest of it. That was what the Templars would give him. Both the physical sustenance and the religious. The sacraments, the healing, the everyday, laid out neatly for him with no effort. His aunt was a clever woman and knew just how tempting this would be.

The reality was less tempting. No-one, for instance, remarked upon his spurs.

Guilhem ate at the Commander's table. This night was uncomfortable. One of the brother-knights was in disgrace for treating his horse badly. He was being punished in the usual way, eating from the floor, not permitted to push away the dogs sniffing after his meal. Guilhem found the humiliation uncomfortable. Maybe the life at Pézenas wasn't for him. If the Church was the rock of Peter, then the Templars were not made of solid rock, nor was this fortress they held truly sacred ground.

None of them gave a toss about Guilhem's decision or what he did with his life. Ultimately, they would rather he were gone.

They could turn, Guilhem realised, *just as my family did*. There is no loyalty in this world. This reinforced the resolve he had made on his way to Pézenas. He found the town brothel and re-made the acquaintance of one Raynalda, who owned it. He said, "Whores here should always be called Raynalda — such a pleasant name." She slapped him very lightly and he gave her extra money.

* * *

"You should take the pilgrim's road. It will be good for your soul and give you a rest from the interminable problems of this place," said Peire.

"And who would shoe horses while I am gone?"

They watched Guilhem walk his horse slowly down the street. Stupid he would have to walk it back out again, once he had unloaded. Why didn't he just ask for help?

* * *

Guilhem was finally back from his journey. Artemisia was surprised to find that she had missed him. She had also missed her travels outside the caves. Those Gaudi walls could become very claustrophobic after a few days. Artemisia always dealt best with Sylvia and Pauline after she'd been outside.

Today there was no breeze. The sun fell on the garrigue, turning the rocks and shrub and herbs each into heat traps that reflected the molten scents of summer.

He looked pleased with himself. An I-have-a-secret kind of pleased. After a few minutes of small talk, he opened a little cloth parcel and showed Artemisia its contents.

"My little cousin sent me this it was waiting for me at the Commanderie."

"What is it?"

"She bought it at the Great Fair of Champagne. I have no use for it. Here. Take it." Guilhem handed over a long piece of silk braid, brocaded with silver thread. "It glitters," he said, helpfully.

"I thought," said Artemisia, "that you were a monk. Or a Knight Templar. Chastity. Eschewing worldly goods."

"I think about taking the oaths, but, truly, I have not taken orders yet. Not even an acolyte."

"And this?" She flourished the elegant braid.

Guilhem smiled. Artemisia shook her head vehemently. She did not want consequences.

"Nothing, I promise," said Guilhem.

"No more gifts. I was brought up to avoid the deadly sins. No greed. No lust. None of them." Artemisia hoped that firmness would sort this out. Also the wimple she was wearing. Wimples didn't look at all sexy, she hoped. Especially not ones that went wonky. She wondered if she could give back that braid without issues, but suspected not. She tried to look motherly. Guilhem smiled again.

* * *

On her return, Artemisia logged the braid and deposited it. She also logged her continuing concerns about Guilhem and marked the note for Luke's attention.

* * *

Vintage was still not arrived and it was the dying days of September. The village complained to Guilhem about the delay. Other years they would complain to the abbot, blaming God or the monks' poor behaviour. This year, however, they blamed the folks under the hill. Guilhem pointed out it had been a cool summer and the representatives of the two parishes went away, partly placated.

* * *

"Ben, can I borrow you for a second?" Luke sounded as if his life was full of burdens.

"Those forms again?" Ben guessed. Luke nodded.

"A discrepancy. Harvey wrote you down as Jewish on another set of forms. I want to get them right this time."

"I'm only Jewish according to some definitions," Ben explained, sitting down on Luke's guest chair. He tried for a relaxed look, but he was nervous. "Harvey only put it down for the historians, in case there were issues."

"Either you're Jewish or you're not Jewish." Luke was adamant.

"My family is Jewish, but most of it comes from Germany," Ben was wondering how soon he could escape.

"So you're not practising?"

"Not at all. My mother wanted us to, but it was too difficult."

"How difficult could it be? You're a Yank. Lots of Yids there. I studied with them, I should know. Good people, too. Some fine scientists."

Oh God, thought Ben. *Not that kind of bias. Please, God, not someone who has a best friend who is Jewish but doesn't actually know a thing about Judaism. Not someone who knows the Jews who he has worked with, but knows sod-all about Jewish history.*

"Luke," he said, trying to speak slowly and remain collected, "My family was German Jewish. Half of it escaped before the war, and the other half"

"Was in concentration camp. I get that. It's not easy for the children and grandchildren. My father…"

Ben wished he could lie. He wished all the lies that flowed so easily would pour out of him like honey. But he couldn't. Not about this. He had never been able to. The impossibility of it, the impossibility of lying about it had poisoned Judaism for him made it the great temptation, just beyond reach. He had grown up in an area with Holocaust survivors. Every time he looked at them he thought of his grandparents and he ran away. He couldn't pretend his family had suffered like theirs. That would be the ultimate betrayal. He took a deep breath.

"No concentration camp."

"What, then," Luke was impatient. He liked his information to be neat and this was getting messy.

There was an empty silence. "My grandfather was quite senior in the army. He married someone who converted to Judaism. So he was allowed to stay. They were all allowed to stay. Some of them had mischling stamps and all of them had special permission. They were hounded, but not sent away."

The silence became emptier and then it became angry. And then…

"I don't believe you," Luke said, abruptly. "No German Jew would fight for Hitler."

"He wasn't fighting for Hitler. He was fighting for Germany. Besides, there was no way out. None. Every country closed its borders to Jews. God knows my family tried. So they stayed alive and fought for Germany." Konig was bitter. He had been bitter about it all his life. Bitter and ashamed.

"Well, I don't believe you. Your family is lying. Or this is one of your inventions."

"Maybe." Ben was tired. If Luke wanted to believe this was a lie, then he would let him. This was a battle Ben could only lose. "Put whatever you like on your damned form."

* * *

Ben dressed in his medieval costume and went for a walk. He took no equipment with him. He needed to get away from Luke and from his own past, and the only way he could do that was to go further into the past. He noticed a farmer silently working in a vineyard, alone. First grapes of the season. That was something that needed company. An event.

Ben swung himself up three levels of terracing, grabbed a spare basket, took out his knife and started picking grapes. The man looked across and checked that Ben knew what he was doing, and then he nodded. The farmer was silent. Ben was silent. It helped.

* * *

30 September, St Jerome

The grape harvest had finally begun, Artemisia noticed, and told Ben. "Early grapes only," Ben noted in his diary. It wasn't simply a bad year. It was a very bad year.

Bad years had consequences.

There was a rumble right along the bent street that led from the wall to the Hérault. The rumble was that the blue water had been an omen. That the wine would be sour and that people would go hungry. It wasn't just those who grew vines. Guilhem-the Smith would have to tighten his belt until there was more money. Berta's husband would have to sell her cloth farther afield and seek higher prices. Even Fathers Peire and Louis were affected by lower tithes. Omens were in order.

Bad temper was also in order. That temper caught the mood of those who were too busy working at bringing in the poor harvest and producing possibly the worst vintage on record. Sour grapes were everyone's lot.

Guilhem took on the mood of the town and so did his page. Not publicly. But words were said and blows were given.

"There is a price for laziness," Guilhem informed his protégé.

"Oh yeah," said the young man, uncaring. He just wanted to leave this place. Leave Guilhem. And he was tied. His whole family was tied by the brilliant opportunity that had arisen when Guilhem was shamed, but he was the one paying.

"You will stay here, in this miserable stone village, while I do some errands in Montpellier. You will demonstrate to me you're not as lazy as you look and then you will demonstrate to me that you're not as disrespectful as you sound. If you do this, I may talk to a friend about taking you on. We're obviously not suited." His page hated Guilhem for his honesty and for his generosity and for the fact that he himself now had no reason not to work.

This argument was why Fiz found himself sitting in a high stone hall a very long way from home, outside a decorated wooden door, while, below, someone was practising on a stringed instrument. At first it was delightful and exotic — the sound was given a plaintive lilt by the stone and it reduced the size and grandeur of the place to something more comfortable. Even the wide stone stairs (worked stone, smooth and polished) seemed almost like the softer stone of home. It started to annoy, as she played the same riff over and over. Fiz wondered what the penalty was for murdering musicians in Montpellier.

* * *

The text sat on the computer screen, glaring in dark red.

Jimmy, thinking life a bore, drank some H_2SO_4.

His father a GP gave him $CaCO_3$.

Now Jimmy's neutralised, it's true; but he's full of CO_2!

"It wasn't me," Geoff said.

"You look too innocent." And indeed he did. He was all hair and big dark eyes at this moment. Artemisia looked up into those eyes, trying to work out if they hid a lie. Ben didn't look into Geoff's eyes. Instead, he argued.

"It's been you other times."

"Yes, it's been me. And Mac. And once it was Sylvia. Twice it was Pauline. You can blame all of us, if you want." He was entirely unconcerned.

"You started it." This was sounding like the playground.

"Actually," said Artemisia, a little timidly, "I think I did."

"Sorry?" Ben's startlement was painfully clear.

"I put a second version of the saints' lives under a hyperlink. We all used to do it in my old department, and I was bored."

"Let me show you," said Geoff, far too enthusiastically.

Ben clicked and read and clicked and read, then he swivelled on the chair and look at the errant duo. "This has been here, all along?" Konig gave up. He shook his head, then laughed. "You two deserve each other," was all he said.

Chapter Thirty: Places in Time

Guilhem was always astonished by Notre Dame des Tables. It was halfway between the shapes of the Christian lands he knew best and the lands of the Moslem world. It dominated the square, not just through its size, but through its strange mixture of round and square and columned, and because people thronged around it in a very precise manner. They ebbed and flowed like the tide. Pilgrims went in one door, those with business flowed around them. If one watched, one could see the world happen.

"I'm hungry," said a voice at his elbow.

Guilhem looked at Fiz and wondered why he had brought him. This boy was nothing but complaints. "Stay close inside the church," was all he said.

They avoided the pilgrims and the nave, crossing only where they had to. Guilhem headed straight for where he needed to be — the statue of the Black Virgin. He made his courtoisies, and then went directly to the moneychanging tables outside and to business.

There were definite advantages to a city famous for its decadence. One of those advantages was that business was neat and fast and no-one asked one's background. Word of his business here would not reach the north. This was one of his reasons for accepting such an exile Saint-Guilhem-le-Désert looked to Montpellier, so no-one thought it surprising that Guilhem should visit. In fact, it was expected, and he carried messages from the town to the city. Almost as if he belonged. Almost.

Guilhem ensured the silence of his young man using a very simple but effective technique. He warned Fiz about the taverns and hostels frequented by the pilgrims.

"They're not as holy after they've been to the church," he said. "And Montpellier is decadent. Not a sensible place for a young man to go by himself."

Of course Fiz went. Guilhem had to haul him out of a ditch by the elbow and he did so without grace and without gentleness. Yes,

Fiz would be silent, for if word of that ditch and his doings near it had got back to his family, he would be in trouble. There were advantages in borrowing a young man from a small place to be one's servant.

Fiz found Montpellier big and desperately exciting. The streets were different and there were some houses that were impossibly huge and there were so many, so many trades and talkings and people. Whenever he found himself overwhelmed, he would reach out and touch the stone and orient himself and remind himself of his native town. People walked differently and talked differently and spoke strange languages and used strange money. Not his people.

He wondered how Bona would handle her apprenticeship in this foreign city — he was pleased he had no-one to push him forward for such a thing. Even so, he eyed the shops of the silversmiths enviously. He would never be able to buy anything from them if he inherited those small patches of land and remained his mother's son. And yet... Fiz stomped the stones underneath his feet and felt himself, rooted to the rock, safe in what he knew and who he was.

There was a summer thunderstorm. Such a wet summer, everyone was saying to each other as they flowed past him, going about their strange city lives. The aftermath of the shower changed the stones beneath Fiz's feet and made them less secure.

All sorts of scents emerged from beneath the heavy streets. Some were charming: some were foul. At one moment it seemed that every dog and every horse in the whole city had shat at once and that the ordure had settled beneath the rock and developed in rankness and that the rain had brought all that smell forth.

In Saint-Guilhem, the water always ran and such smells weren't given time to develop. Even when he and his friends had tried to create them, the rain mostly washed them downstream and downstream again. Maybe that was what he was smelling here? Himself from a month ago? Bah. He didn't know. All he knew was that, despite the odours after the storm (or maybe because of it, as the sweet smell of mint and then lavender chased the dung away) he was glad to be here, in one of the biggest cities in the world. Still, he was happier at home. He didn't want to live here.

In reflecting on his future, Fiz had decided something important. If he was not coming back here, he needed to see the place properly.

He ignored Guilhem's instructions a second time. While Guilhem was dining in elegance with his friends, he paid a visit to the places the pilgrims stayed, taking just enough coin to get a little drunk. He emerged bruised and cut and impressed.

Fiz took care of his bruises and cuts before Guilhem woke up and arranged his sleeves carefully to cover the worst of them. His care was wasted he kept drawing back his sleeve to check the very best one. Such well-earned pain! Guilhem found him watching bruises grow and darken while he was waiting for Guilhem to emerge from yet another message in yet another shop, next morning.

"It doesn't really hurt," he explained.

"That's not the point," said Guilhem, "The point is that you're a fool." Fiz gave a big grin, happy in his foolery.

Guilhem's mind was only half on Fiz. He had personal business. For the last few months his mind had revolved around it, wavering between Lodève (possible) and Nîmes (preferable). Finally, he had decided to sort himself out at Montpellier, because it was possible to remain anonymous here and because there were more available prostitutes. Pézenas, of course, had been the easiest, but he wasn't ready to annoy the good brother-knights again, so he would save that possibility. His need would grow again, no doubt.

Guilhem had finally found the details of a safe and clean establishment while he did business that day. His mind tossed around how much worry it had concerned him, deciding where he would find a woman and how that worry was nearly past.

The next day he spent some of his new money. Upon emerging, and upon grabbing Fiz by the collar and marching him away from trouble, his mind dwelled on chastity again. Did he want to become a priest? Did he want to follow one of the many wishes his family had for him and become a templar or perhaps a Hospitaller? He doubted he was suited to priesthood, for his chastity was rare and hard-won. Maybe, however, a militant order? Still, priest or knight militant both held appeal.

Two possible paths. Guilhem laughed aloud at the thought at himself as a bishop. He didn't want to go that route (couldn't go that route) because his legitimate half-brother was already one and the family believed in not keeping all their eggs in one basket. And other orders were not possible either, for similar reasons. And here he was re-inventing the wheel, when this had all been discussed in tedious detail before he was sent south. All that was left was returning to the fold or joining the Knights Templar. As his aunt had convinced his uncle. Those reasons were all tired, but still they returned and returned and wove threads of annoyance into cloth of dissatisfaction. It had all been easier when he had been Fiz's age.

Guilhem visited the guild of goldsmiths and delivered a promise that Bona would be there next season. He carried a long message back for her family, entrusting it to Fiz, who rehearsed it over and again as they walked the distance back to the moneychangers. He tried to remember the child or her parents but couldn't. The request itself had come from Guilhem-the-smith.

After sorting out his money for a second time, ready to spend some of it on objects of need and desire, Guilhem found himself admiring the gros. It was not a coin from the north. Such a big coin. So much buying power. Also, the king of Aragon instead of the king of France. An improvement on familiar coinage in almost every way.

Final messages and tasks and then he would return home. If one could call a cream and cream stone village in the middle of nowhere 'home.'

One of the links on the guard chain for his helm looked very insecure. It might be a long time before he used it, but he wanted it to be fixed. He left it with the specialist and went to do the remaining messages, now that he knew how much money he had left. He eyed off lanceheads made with Bordeaux steel — if he bought weapons now, however, he would send the wrong message to his family. He dreamed of a lance with such a head. He dreamed of it piercing plate, driving through aventail and killing his opponent. His mind dwelled on the image, of the lance pushing through the neck and his enemy awash with blood.

He shook his own neck to clear his head. He had business to attend to. More business.

The most pressing business was financial. He had miscalculated the amount of money he needed. He paid a quick return visit to Notre-Dame-des-Tables to find a moneychanger. After that, he walked lightly. The coins his aunt had sent, so hard to spend, were all instantly disposable whenever he wanted. And he had done this in Montpellier. Outside France. Where his cousin had no jurisdiction.

Where the coins were stronger and the government very much not that of Paris. Guilhem felt faintly wicked, like a child who had done something forbidden. He would soon do more that his cousin would dislike. He wanted luxury goods, from the Levant in particular. He wanted the stuff of his own exotic past, where he had the special freedom of a noble pilgrim.

* * *

"It's a horseshoe," Artemisia said, a bit blank. "What do you want me to do with it?"

"Tell me about it," said Pauline.

Sylvia wasn't near. Artemisia sighed inside. She wasn't going to get into squabbles about how Pauline managed to get a horseshoe, nor about who should be where. Nor was she going to hide anything. She would do this by the book.

"I'll have to ask Guilhem. He knows horses. Horses are to these people what computers are to us. Make the world go round. So I need to ask someone who knows."

This she did, at the very first opportunity.

"Old," he said, squinting in the golden sun. "Shoes today do not have this," and he pointed to the wavy rim. He had learned not to use too much technical language in talking to Artemisia. Artemisia understood most things except when Guilhem forgot and simply spoke, at great length. "Also," he added, "it's light. Very old. Dropped long ago." He handed the shoe back.

The two walked until Guilhem said, "We can hear the bells from here." They sat down and waited for those bells.

Guilhem's head tilted towards the abbey, "This place has a good mass. So does the church near the Hérault."

Artemisia knew mass, but, "A good mass?"

"They pay proper attention to the dates and the correct prayers."

"Where I come from all masses are good."

"Such a perfect place," Guilhem mocked.

"No, just a place with well-instructed priests."

"Not all places are fortunate."

"You have encountered some that are less blessed? On your travels?"

Guilhem paused to remember. "Sometimes," he said, "Sometimes I wish that I were a Cathar. Or a pagan. Did you know..." and his voice tailed off before he turned to her, enthusiastically. "Did you know that pagans do not really worship Tervagant or Apollon?"

"You asked?"

"I did."

"How wonderful and strange is the world," remarked Artemisia and the two sat there in peace, the scent of lavender and rosemary and the hum of bees making it pastoral and carefree. The mood was spoiled by two children peeping out from behind a kermes oak.

"It doesn't hide you," Guilhem called out, cheerfully.

"Not them. The other one is better," the girl told the boy, and they ran away giggling.

* * *

Since vintage brought the townsfolk into the hills and the time team had no idea how to handle it, most of the team was underground until harvest was done. The exceptions to this were Ben and Artemisia.

For Artemisia, Guilhem brought a sample of the new wine from Fr Peire, to thank the holedwellers for staying out of the way. "It's very earthy, but not bad," Ben said, and didn't let on that he'd already sampled it.

Ben tested some of the wine, put some away for return home, and spent an evening writing it up. While his notes were theoretically triggered by Fr Peire's gift, in reality they were from his experiences in the field and what his farmer-friend had taught him. He was determined to make it possible for the wine to be produced from the descendant grapes, upon their return to the twenty-first century.

* * *

Geoff Murray had been sprung. He had gone out illegally, as he had many times before. This time, however, he was unable to hide his venture into the open. He had been kicked in a delicate place by a sheep and had needed Pauline's gentle attentions.

Pauline asked "What were you doing to it?"

Naturally, this led to a spate of smutty jokes at Geoff's expense. "How could it not?" Artemisia said to him, unsympathetically and privately.

"You're cruel," Geoff said. "Very cruel. I don't like you anymore."

"Tough," Artemisia replied, and kissed him.

Chapter Thirty-One: Very Big Children

The whole team had become stir crazy (again) so Luke gave them permission for limited movement. They all crept out of hiding (except Geoff, who was still suffering punishment) and were watching a traffic jam of pack files in the narrow back path leading to the castle. The children were watching them watching the traffic jam, and soon all attention was on the two little figures, looking across the valley so very seriously.

"Why are they there?" wondered Sylvia.

"They're looking at us so intently," muttered Pauline.

"They're monsters," invented Mac, cheerfully, "disguised as children. They will murder us in our beds. Only Geoff and Luke are safe."

"Why are Geoff and Luke?" Artemisia asked.

"Because they're not here. Their molecules haven't been memorised by that still and intent gaze."

They spent an hour happily telling each other stories about the children. As the hour progressed, the group wriggled out of hiding and ended up in the open. Only Artemisia remained sheltered. As the hour progressed, Sylvia managed to exclude Artemisia more and more from the telling. As the hour progressed, Ben became more and more confident. Storytelling gave him back some sense of his legitimacy.

At the end of the hour, the group was scattered by Guilhem, striding angrily into their little cluster of tales and waving his sword. Artemisia hung back a little when he caught her eye and motioned her to stay.

"They are children, all," he said.

"Some very big children, indeed," she agreed.

* * *

Guilhem suffered from a small land dispute. It was only a tiny one, but it made him feel very lacking in authority. No matter whom he asked, he was unable to find anyone willing to represent him. Not only did this mean that the dispute was impossible to resolve but, more importantly, he felt that this was a strong indication that he still didn't belong.

He hated not having a place in the local community. He went to the abbey church for solace and found himself standing next to Guilhem-the-smith.

When Guilhem-the-smith stood in front of the reliquary in prayer, his hands were clasped worshipfully. This was the big man's pretence at gazing at the saint in reverence and joy. In truth, all he wanted was peace and quiet. Reverence and joy could come later. Next to him, Guilhem displayed almost the same gestures, but his emotions were perfect. These were the bones of his saint. His distant kin. This was Guilhem's place. This was Guilhem's moment. He was in awe.

* * *

Despite his German name, Luke had Irish eyes (from his mother's side of the family, Artemisia presumed). They were hooded and expressive, sometimes laughing, sometimes sympathetic and sometimes damned condescending. Right now those patronising eyes were looking down his long nose and speckled beard and contriving to make Artemisia feel like dirt.

Mac was in trouble again. Except that it was not Mac who was in trouble. Mac had set up a rather complicated practical joke to entertain those children, using Badass and Tony's goat. Luke was standing over Artemisia, who was huddled in one of the cane chairs. Luke was methodically listing all the sins Artemisia had committed in letting Mac do what Mac always did. He gave her no chance to speak. He simply perorated and, when he was finished, he turned on his heel and went back to his office.

Ben sat paralysed behind his computer throughout the whole episode. He watched Luke treat Artemisia as if she was a waste of space and was unable to do anything. He had played the historian off the others one time too many, and now Artemisia was fixed in the role of scapegoat.

For the next few days, Luke's lowering look when Artemisia passed was supposed to indicate to the historian that she was at fault. She didn't discourage the children enough and she was the one with the local language. The fact that she had the wrong language was something Luke was too uptight to consider: besides, he needed a scapegoat. This was the same reasoning that led to him delegating all database maintenance to Sylvia. Luke had ideas and expected the world would conform.

Ben saw this play and replay and he noticed how, each time, Artemisia took more weight on her shoulders. Her big eyes started to look always shadowed. He thought of his own behaviour ever since they had arrived in 1305 and felt that this recent hurt was his fault. He had set Artemisia up for it.

Ben cracked. He asked to see Luke, privately.

There was another of those explosive arguments that led to the rest of the team being excluded from the workspace. Instead of leading nowhere this time, however, it led to another confrontation concerning Ben's Jewishness. Ben felt like dirt by the end of it, just like Artemisia.

Ben responded by walking out of the cave system and into the sunlight. He went down to a terraced vineyard where his farmer-friend was working alone and he helped harvest. The two didn't talk at all. They just worked their way down the vines, neatly plucking and basketting and preparing for vintage. He had to use a small knife, while his co-worker used a special hook, but apart from that they worked in harmony, parallel along the rows of vines.

* * *

Mac was trying to tell Artemisia how to dress properly. Artemisia was trying to be patient. Finally she said, "I appreciate that this is how your friends dress but it's not how the townsfolk here wear the clothes."

"I don't know how the townsfolk here wear the clothes," Mac's tone was vicious and mocking. "You never go over there when we're outside."

"Oh, for goodness sake!" Artemisia was used to Mac as an ally and was losing patience. He had said three times that he knew more than she and now he wanted to do her job. Maybe he didn't. Maybe he was just tired of being cooped up.

"I'm beginning to think that Sylvia was right you don't know what you're doing."

"I'm hamstrung," Artemisia said. "But if you want to help with my research, I'll do what I can. You've got a good eye." *And no real understanding of the period and place at all*, Artemisia wanted to add. He could learn that, though. She could meet his needs and still do her job.

* * *

Ben had stolen some time to help his farming friend. He loved the silence and the work and the sun and the company. Ben was set to repairing a small patch of unstable drywall. At first the farmer watched and helped, but when it was obvious Ben had learned enough, he went back to his other work.

They had worked quietly for a while when Ben heard a cry. He dropped the rock he was about to place and leaped over the wall. Guilhem-the-silent had cut himself while sharpening a knife. It was a deep cut, so Ben bound it quickly, stopping the bleeding. He then carried the farmer home before he cleaned the wound properly and bound it again. As far as he was concerned, the incident was over, especially when, a few days later, he saw his friend in the field again. Obviously the cut was healing cleanly.

Not a word was spoken between Ben and the local at any stage, leading Ben to say, misleadingly, at a later date when another visit to the town wall by Pauline had led to yet another inquisition by Luke, "I have never spoken to someone from this time zone." No-one believed him, because he had lied so often about other things. Ben had the self-satisfaction, however, of being a truth-teller while hiding a very dangerous reality.

* * *

"Artemisia!"

The woman in question looked up. "You don't need to shout, I'm right here."

"The others are outside."

"I know. It's one of Sylvia's things. I don't know what. It's just the scientists, though. Sylvia's explaining her magic breakthrough that means other people can travel further back in time."

"Not me! I wasn't there," Geoff had a very big grin.

"I bet you crawled up a cliff-face to avoid them, too."

"Too right. Even Luke was clustered on that bloody hillside, and no-one looked happy."

"So you knew I was alone in here when you walked through that big entrance, shouting?"

"My powers of deduction are beyond awesome."

"So are mine," said Artemisia, sarcastically. "What do you want?"

Geoff laughed. "A book. I want a book."

"I thought you could find them yourself?"

"You're in a mood today."

"I'm stuck inside, doing Sylvia's paperwork, while she's taking everyone on an excursion to a place that's within sight of the village to explain her discovery of wonder. And Luke scolded me as if I were five bloody years old when I explained this to them. It gives him the tools to change reality and he wants to celebrate."

"Poor Cassandra," Geoff's words mocked, but his tone was sympathetic.

"You want something special to read, or just anything?"

"Something special."

"I'll email you a link," she promised. "And I'd better get on with this data entry, because otherwise I'll not get to do anything interesting all day."

"You're a mate."

"And you're an idiot but a nice one."

In view of his nice idiocy, she emailed him the link to *Tristram Shandy*.

* * *

There was an informal meeting in the square outside the abbey. The strangers were causing distress again. They had not taken any valuables or done any harm, but four of them looked at the good folk of Saint-Guilhem as if they were objects, not saying anything, and not even nodding. They had eyed them up and down as if they were objects.

It was disturbing.

Guilhem-the-smith pointed to the conversations the knight had with one woman who spoke their tongue. The others, he said, were probably stupid. And there was the matter of Guilhem-the-silent, he pointed out. A wound was healing very nicely when he might, if the stranger had not been there, have bled to death in his own field.

Nevertheless, said the assembled crowd. This meant that Guilhem was designated to deliver another scolding. He put a ribbon on the bush and returned the next day, as usual.

Artemisia was glad that Mac was there (*for research purposes*, he had claimed, when he had agreed to accompany her) when she saw the look on Guilhem's face. She suspected that the rest of the team had been doing things they should not. She was right to be unsettled, for Guilhem was short at first. They soon got that over with and Artemisia promised to relay the scolding. Their shoulders relaxed and they smiled at each other.

Now that the crisis was past, Cormac wanted to exert the rights he now perceived himself as having and to talk with Guilhem himself.

Cormac demanded, "Tell him to tell me all about fighting and battles."

Artemisia patiently translated. "He asks if you would tell him about wars, about battle, about fighting."

Guilhem's reply was straightforward "I will not. It is not his concern or yours."

Artemisia admitted, "They like it if I know, but I'd rather know the stories of saints and tales of heroes."

"What are you saying?" Mac shot the words into the silence, before Artemisia could switch from one language to another.

"I can't hold a bloody three way conversation in two languages, one of which is dead," Artemisia turned to him, exasperated.

"Then I might as well go," said Cormac.

And this is how Artemisia came to meet with Guilhem with no chaperone again. Mac wasn't interested anymore. He had never really thought it as his job he had been along for the history and the clothing and the exoticism.

Artemisia felt as if she had asked too much and not given enough. *Just like my family. Everyone does this, eventually*, she thought, *except Lucia. At least we solved the flirtation stuff before I lost my chaperone.*

Indeed Guilhem was behaving like a perfect gentleman, every time they met. Even today's conversation was reassuring.

"The poems say much about women." He looked at Artemisia and laughed and wondered how she would interpret this. He liked pushing at Artemisia, seeing how she reacted. He still wasn't certain if he read her correctly and if he understood where she belonged. She wasn't of his people and he thought that, if he tried hard enough, he could place her, know who she was and how she fitted in his world. He had done this on his travels and it worked it took time and patience, but eventually station and family showed themselves. Everyone had a place in the world, after all.

"I prefer saints' lives," Artemisia answered with huffy dignity. She had taken the meaning he had intended and she did not like it, not one bit.

"I thought you might," he said, smugly.

"Why?"

"You hold your skirts in such a way."

Artemisia looked down at the way her hands gripped her long dress for security. She was still not comfortable wearing it. How many months would it be before she could walk these hills in this garb and not feel as if she were part of a costume drama? Then her mind flitted and she wondered for a moment's moment what it would be like to sleep with someone so very long dead. She knew she never would. Some parts of one's upbringing stuck, even if one's family didn't believe it.

Chapter Thirty-Two: They Had Buildings in the Middle Ages

Mac was looking at the calendar.

"Murray," he called out across the workspace, "Come over here."

Geoff obliged.

"What is it?"

"Time to do the water-flow thing. Need to check our footprint again."

"A bit past time, isn't it? I'll clear it with Luke and Sylvia."

"Can we use red dye this time?"

"No. I'll check with Artemisia, too, to be safe."

"Check with Sylvia first. She might not want Artemisia involved."

Geoff sighed. "I wish you hadn't said that."

"Reduces the number of permissions," Cormac was, as ever, unrepentant. "Can't complain about that."

The water ran red and Mac was jubilant. Geoff realised too late that Mac had switched the dye. He blamed himself for not supervising Mac more closely.

"At least only we know about it," he reassured himself, half-heartedly.

Artemisia heard about it from a very scared Guilhem. He had been walked around seven different spots, along with the two priests, the abbot and Guilhem-the-smith. "Tell me it is your people, and not a curse," he said.

Artemisia found out about the dye and received the crash course in maps and the paths of underground water she had missed earlier and pointed out the places that Guilhem had seen the water.

No-one was happy.

* * *

"What about the novel?"

"I liked it," he said.

"Don't sound surprised," Artemisia twinkled, although she tried to hide it.

"I wasn't expecting it to be funny," he defended himself bravely against her twinkle.

"I like the curse best," said Artemisia. "It's when the Middle Ages meets Sterne and Sterne wins."

"Of course you like that," nodded Geoff.

"You don't remember the section!"

Geoff laughed. "I do. In fact, I bookmarked it." And he opened the file and went straight to the section and proceeded to read the whole thing aloud.

'By the authority of God Almighty, the Father, Son, and Holy Ghost, and of the undefiled Virgin Mary, mother and patroness of our Saviour, and of all the celestial virtues, angels, archangels, thrones, dominions, powers, cherubins and seraphins, and of all the holy patriarchs, prophets, and of all the apostles and evangelists, and of the holy innocents, who in the sight of the Holy Lamb, are found worthy to sing the new song of the holy martyrs and holy confessors, and of the holy virgins, and of all the saints together, with the holy and elect of God, — May he' (Obadiah) 'be damn'd' (for tying these knots) —'

It went on for pages. When Geoff read out uncle Toby's interpolations, his voice took on a particular relish. "Our armies swore terribly in Flanders, cried my uncle Toby," he said, "but nothing to this. For my own part I could not have a heart to curse my dog so."

It was a very long curse, and a very effective one. At the end of it they looked at each other, satisfied with the reading and with the curse and with each other.

* * *

4 October, St Francis

The green and cream and brown and rushing water were stained with colour. The broom and cyclamen were both blooming. Only a few souls of Saint-Guilhem noticed the brightness on the hills. The eyes of the others were turned to the skies. The birds were still migrating.

"So late," worried Peire to Guilhem-the-smith.

"Why are they still doing that?" Berta said to Sibilla.

The flocks overhead added to the town's disquiet. They weren't, however, the source of it.

* * *

Sylvia loved being near the curtain wall that divided the pilgrim path from the main street of Saint-Guilhem. She originally explained it to herself as it being outside the town, but she had ceased explaining it to anyone. She walked past houses and past gardens and past the cemetery to get there. She would sit down by the wall and watch the goings on. It was like a play, enacted in a strange language, just for her benefit.

Her steady gaze and her refusal to engage in conversation (not even a greeting or a nod) annoyed the townsfolk more than anything else the hillfolk had done. The woman sat there, head indecently uncovered, arms crossed, looking at them as if they were…they didn't know. All they knew was that they hated it.

"It makes my skin crawl," said Sibilla.

"We could kill her," suggested Fiz, hopefully.

"Don't be stupid," said Guilhem-the-smith. He called upon Guilhem-the-knight.

"I'm meeting with the one who speaks our language today," he said. So that strong young man took Sylvia by the arm and pulled her from her comfortable seat. He pushed and shoved her until she was half running and half stumbling ahead of him. He didn't treat her kindly, but he herded her to the ribbon-covered bush. There he handed her over to Artemisia, with an explanation.

"She simply doesn't pay attention to the instructions of others," Geoff told Luke, later.

"Only with small things," Luke argued. "She's there where it counts."

* * *

"I have more than one string for my bow."

Guilhem's mind was not participating in this conversation at all. Armour. That's what really concerned him. Guilhem was thinking of a new suit and calculating how to gather together 25 livres tournois. Wishing he had spent less in Montpellier.

With new armour, he could sell his soul and become a mercenary. The opposite of a Templar. Only temporary oaths. Only temporary obedience. No chastity.

It was tempting. He didn't need new armour, but he knew that he would do better if he had equipment. Some of his stuff was fine, but bits had been battered and bent in the war and would never be the same. And he had sold all he had captured, in order to ransom Philippe. Damn friends. Without that ransom, he would have had more choices. Why did Philippe get away with everything and Guilhem, with nothing?

If I were a minstrel, I would sing of William, for he will be my hero. If I were a troubadour, I would sing of love and war. Here am I, Guilhem, sitting under a tree beyond the end of the world, singing a small song. I sing to a woman who is here no longer, for if she were still present, she would know that I know that she comes from a place far beyond our knowledge.

* * *

Pauline was chatty at dinner that night. "I saw a couple of builders today, when I went for my walk. They had a plumb level and were checking a wall they were building. I didn't know they had plumb levels back now."

"Back now?" Geoff smiled lazily across the trestle table.

"Here now? Then?" Sylvia suggested possibilities.

"And a plumbline, hanging from a bloody rope?"

Mac was puzzled. "Didn't you know they had buildings in the Middle Ages?"

"Baths, too," said Artemisia.

Pauline ignored them both. "Their lines were dead straight. Different plumbline, but the same bloody technique my late husband used when he built our extension."

Artemisia looked down at her plate. Explanations weren't going to help. Pauline would just look like an idiot. Was it ethical to not brief people, when she was the person who had been brought back all these years just to brief people, though?

She was saved by Luke.

"Pauline, what were you doing in town?"

"I wasn't in town," Pauline justified. "Not really."

"And your jobs as cook and doctor took you there?"

"Actually," Sylvia challenged, "I took her there. No-one should stay underground forever. And you did say that I could keep an eye on things."

Ben's head whipped up. He looked at Sylvia, gauging what

she had just admitted. He looked at Luke, gauging what he might actually have permitted.

"Luke," he said, very calmly, "Can I have a word with you after dinner?"

"Must you?" Luke sounded long-suffering.

"So you've been expecting it?" Ben's voice was low, almost threatening.

"Oh," said Luke, "I always expect talks from you."

* * *

As the pressure of season eased, the villagers had time to compare their recent experiences. There was that woman from under the hill who sat by the wall so very often, staring at them. There was the water that had run red. There was the bad harvest. There was the late bird migration. There were deaths and portents and small accidents. They all added up to the whole town (with the possible exceptions of Fr Peire, Guilhem-the-smith and young Fiz) being spooked. Something had to be done.

Guilhem had his own concerns. Bernat had decided that he should join the Templars and had told his aunt and uncle. He refused to go to Pézanas. He paid no attention to village concerns. In fact, he had his hands over his ears and a blindfold over his eyes and he noticed nothing, by choice.

Chapter Thirty-Three: Wild Harvesting

Back in Melbourne, the scientists had laid a very clear foundation for the time team's work. It was a brilliant team of scientists, and, like all brilliant teams of scientists in the field of modern physics, they worked with statistical certainty and with an utter acceptance of the implications of the Heisenberg uncertainty principle. Luke, of course, was one of them. He defined uncertainty as security in a way that only a few advanced thinkers were capable of.

It was Artemisia who discovered what this meant in terms of their own lives. She had been trying to find out more about the waiver she hadn't signed, and why it perturbed Ben so much. In fact, she was trying to find out why Ben was so worried and why Luke was so insouciant. Nothing added up.

She found the original team on file. Bill who Tony had replaced, the two historians who she had replaced. Pauline's daughter. The original doctor. They had all been recruited a while earlier. Up to two years, in fact. This made sense in terms of coming to such a strange place. It didn't make sense of the library, but it made sense of the clothes and the supplies and why there were no shoes that fitted Artemisia. Shoe measurements had been done very early.

Tony and Pauline and Artemisia herself were wearing outdoors clothes that fitted by happenstance they just happened to be the same size as people they replaced. Tony was the same size as Pauline's daughter, who was larger than Lucia even, if Artemisia read the clothing sizes correctly Pauline's daughter was Amazonian Artemisia found this ineffably funny. She had assumed that the other Dr Adamson was tiny and delicate. This was because of the way Pauline protected the tiny and delicate Dr Smith. Pauline was the same size and sex as one of the missing historians.

This was interesting, but didn't answer the need for the waiver. Nor why everyone had dropped out. Artemisia asked Geoff. It was he who finally explained.

"The likelihood of us surviving is quite high," he explained, "but you can't take all the doubt out of it. Coming back in time or going forward in time is risky."

"How risky?"

"Dead risky," he joked, but his eyes were serious.

"So why is Luke so bloody unconcerned?"

"Partly because for him the science is bigger than anyone. Partly because he's super-Luke. He cannot die."

"And Ben? If he knows it all and doesn't like it, why did he come?"

"Harvey twisted his arm, I believe. Made it hard for him to refuse. He said something to that effect in the briefings."

"Ben did? How odd."

"Not Ben, Harvey."

"Remind me not to ever date Harvey again," Artemisia said, not quite bitterly.

"You dated Harvey?" Geoff was incredulous.

"How do you think I got here?" And now Artemisia was indeed bitter. Because she had to come. Because she would have come to get her sister that medicine, even if she had known that she was risking her life. But she wished, oh how she wished, that the choice had been hers. "I'm going to call Harvey 'Saruman' in future."

"Why?"

"Beautiful voice. Working towards evil."

Geoff laughed and said, "You need coffee."

"I'm a tea drinker now," Artemisia confessed.

"What?" Geoff was astonished.

"I can't take instant coffee anymore. If only we had beans!"

* * *

Geoff brought in fresh fish.

"No," said Luke.

"Naughty boy," said Sylvia.

"No-one saw me," Geoff wasn't bothered by their comments, so this was more as reassurance than excuse. "Should I put them back?"

Luke sighed.

"Take them in to Pauline," he said. "But don't do this again. We don't despoil our environment."

When Geoff was finished with his delivery, he had another to make. He had a found item.

"This smells fishy," Artemisia said.

"Fish for dinner." Geoff was still cheerful.

"You need to quit stirring."

"Never. Now tell me what my found object is. At once!"

"You're totally daft," was Artemisia's response. "Totally."

"It's an agnus dei," she said, a few minutes later. "An amulet. Women and children carry them, I think. I'll look it up for you. In the meantime, if you could get rid of that smell…"

Geoff leaned close to her. "You don't love me, then?"

"I don't love anything that smells so very much like a fish."

Geoff laughed and went to clean himself and the amulet.

* * *

The time team celebrated Halloween with sweets and with a bang-up meal. Luke wanted the others to try fancy dress, but they refused. Instead everyone watched an old football game and microwaved the last of the popcorn. Three times that night Luke made slighting references to Ben about his Jewishness and the festival being foreign to him. Pauline snickered each time. Ben found himself edging out of the group a bit more with each comment and he finally gave up and sat on the ledge outside the front door, looking at the dark hills and the stars and remembering the Halloweens of his childhood. Australians knew nothing of Halloween and Luke knew nothing of Ben. He consoled himself with these thoughts, but they didn't really help.

The moon and Aries were kissing in the sky, while Taurus was edging below the horizon. Tony also sat there in the dark, listening to the merriment below, the cat on his knee, thinking that to loneliness there is an end.

* * *

"Now they're making planks by the cartload," reported Pauline. "Bloody good industry it is. Every plank identical."

"Just like real wood. For real carpentry." Artemisia was unable to refrain from being sarcastic. *Honestly*, she thought, *I am my worst enemy. I should accuse Pauline outright of having zombie ancestry.*

Pauline ignored her anyway. "And I saw two blokes with a whacking great saw between them, making the planks. Or maybe not planks. Something with wood, any old how."

"And what," Luke's smooth voice interrupted her tale "were you doing there? Again?"

"Taking a walk." Pauline's face was without guile.

"You have no work that takes you to the village. You are doctor and you are cook not historian and not scientist. I repeat, what were you doing there?"

Pauline was stubborn. "Taking a walk. I was in costume. No harm done. And I was outside the village." *And besides*, her face said, *you let me do it before.*

"You are confined to quarters for the next two weeks. After that, you may walk only within two hundred metres of this hillock we live under."

"Boss, that's unfair."

"No. You're endangering our lives because you can't fucking follow instructions *that's* unfair."

"Dr Wormwood goes there."

"Not to the village. She doesn't go within 300 metres of the fucking village."

"She talks to locals."

"To one local. Who is our official intermediary. And Dr Wormwood has nine years of university training to equip her for that conversation. Remind me how much history you have studied?"

"It wasn't bloody dangerous." Pauline was recalcitrant.

"So why didn't you ask permission?"

Everyone was silent. Pauline looked at Sylvia. Obviously she *had* asked permission. Sylvia, was, however, busy being silent.

"I see," said Luke. "Everyone except Artemisia and Tony and Geoff is confined to within a three minute walk of one of our entrances. You three will only go where you have to no new contacts. Understood."

"Yes, sir." They all chorused, like good schoolchildren.

Cormac and Sylvia glared at Pauline, as if it were all her fault. It wasn't. Pauline was just being honest about the amount of transgression everyone except Artemisia was regularly visiting the outskirts of town, despite Sylvia's run-in with the villagers and despite the children nibbling at the edges. It was tempting, to see how close to the big towers one could creep without being seen.

Artemisia had warned them and warned them and she knew what the next step was going to be. Everyone who was grounded refused to speak to her.

There was no virtue in being right.

Chapter Thirty-Four: Cues

2 November, All Saints.

The team was assembled outside at dawn, by Theo's command. Sylvia and Geoff were observing the last of the lunar eclipse. With the moon in shadow, Aries and Taurus shone very brightly.

Theo stood on the rocky plateau above the caves, enchanted by the feel of the air and the audience. He launched into a lecture, talking about the nature of narrative in the universe. "Observe the moments of clash and change," he declared, "those are the points that will give us our new understanding. We yearn for the elegance that emerges from dynamism, not the dull patterns than emerge from a simple, static state. Our presence here, today, will give us the power over the narratives of time, of space, of dimensions we're only now learning to measure."

"What shapes our thought?" Mac asked, as if it hadn't occurred to him before.

"Maths," said Sylvia, finished with her observations, sucking up to Theo.

"English lies," added Ben.

"You know what I've been thinking," said Artemisia almost defiantly, "I've been thinking about the cultural limitations of scientific processes. You get what you set out to find. Your language and your preconceptions govern that."

The others looked at her as if she had sprouted horns.

* * *

Tony was remarkably chatty at dinner that night. No-one knew how to respond. This didn't perturb him. He simply addressed his remarks to whoever was sitting opposite.

"I don't understand," he commented to Ben. "I don't understand how people behave. I was watching you all today and it's like you follow secret cues. Like my plants. They have biological cues waiting and when something small happens, when the temperature changes or the air becomes moist, they follow those cues and it looks as if they magically grow or blossom. I know how cold this season was by how my plants behave. I don't know any of your cues. I don't know why any of you behave the way they do. Humans are strange."

He went silent and shuttered while he thought it out. When he emerged from his thoughts, it was Sylvia sitting opposite.

"I don't know why you behave so strangely," he announced, again, as if it were a new thought. "You must have those secret cues. Reacting to environment, perhaps. I don't know if they're genetic. I want to know. When I get home I shall study it. I shall keep notes on it now, however. I need more data."

Sylvia's mouth was agape, but Tony didn't notice. He turned back to his meal and finished eating, slowly and methodically.

Ben had taken his dinner outside. It wasn't comfortable outside. The wind made his teeth ache. Still, outside was better than inside. Grounding meant being surrounded by politics every minute of the day. Grounding meant that he could never take a break from being nice.

Not that he wasn't guilty, he reflected. He himself had been a little more daring than the others and had walked quietly up to the big old wall of one of the churches and had laid a hand on it, wondering. He'd faded into the background quickly when he saw a group of people, arguing. They weren't arguing amicably, but they weren't passionate, either. Neither side was paying much attention to the other. A word here and there was understandable they were speaking a kind of French, for certain. Ben's political brain interpreted them as factions, perhaps, or having a long-standing difference. If Artemisia had been there, she would have told him that they were arguing about. Or she would have told him to get out.

What Ben Konig didn't know was that the argument linked to the precise wall he had so tenderly admired. The parishioners were arguing the old arguments, about the roles of the two parishes and the needs of the two parishes and how the folk from under the hill were getting in everyone's way.

"We need to send a priest in," the cordwainer had said. "That knight does no good."

"Which priest?" That was the question and that was what had started the discussion. It had moved on to boundaries, however, and old unresolved disputes. It was that stage that Ben overheard.

Sylvia hurt, however, more than anyone. She took Tony's comments personally. He was watching her, and she didn't deal well with anyone analysing her or criticising her. She took this to Luke, who had championed her so much in the early days.

"Grow up, Sylvia."

Luke was tired. Everyone was still grounded. What hit harder than the loss of personal freedom this time was the loss of research.

The workstations become silent hubs of pained effort as the effects of the grounding hit. Artemisia wondered who would explode first. Guilhem was away, so she was grounded too. It didn't worry her.

When Guilhem returned, the unease from under the hill invaded everything they talked about. Guilhem shared the mood.

He had been in Pézenas, this time at his aunt's instruction. Bernat had again told him he should join the Templars. That his family would appreciate the holiness of it all. And Guilhem knew that Bernat was lying. All he wanted was another link into yet another ruling family. He lost his temper at the hypocrisy of this man. Finally, he and Bernat had fought openly. There would be consequences. Guilhem did not want to face them.

"The desert surrounds us," he said, pensively, kicking at a stone. "It's like forest. It hides dangers."

"Dangers?"

"Borders." The word he used was military 'marches' it had become in modern English. Artemisia had reached the stage where she annotated Guilhem's speech almost automatically, barely missing a word.

Tactical boundaries ones that needed defending. Artemisia needed to check if he really meant that. "Like where you have battles?" she asked.

"Where you prepare constantly for attack. Where you have less control."

"And this is why people believe we are…"

"Yes. Truly. Yes."

Artemisia tried another of her farewells on him and then left. He smiled at the formality of her words. "May God who made everything according to his will save you and all your people." She never understood what to say and when. It was endearing.

Later, after Artemisia had gone, Guilhem reminded himself. "Deserts aren't places to be alone. They are places where a man is tested by God."

Forest and desert places for penitence, places for adventure, places where he, Guilhem, did not belong. He would still hold out, he thought, against taking those Templar oaths. Against Bernat's blandishments. Against his temper. Even against his aunt.

He would plant seeds concerning the wealth and danger of the Templars in the minds of certain of his cousins. That would reach back to the king, even if Philippe were not speaking to his unimportant and embarrassing and somewhat illegitimate junior relative. It would find a place to lodge in Philippe's ever fertile brain.

He was settled. He could escape the Templars. He just needed to slow down and to think it through. His heart required more time.

* * *

Artemisia had to show Guilhem a found item. It was a very pretty white plate decorated with a picture of a blue-green girl dancing amongst roses. The border was blue. The edging was decorated to look a bit like a door. The rest of the team was greedy to keep it. Artemisia wasn't looking forward to reporting back on this meeting. Most meetings no-one wanted to hear a thing. This one, she would lay odds, they would want every word.

There weren't many words. Guilhem was in a hurry. He was leaving the next day for Montpellier.

"Keep it," he said, dismissively.

"But it's someone's?"

"They left Saint-Guilhem yesterday. They will be past Aniane already." He had more important things to tell her. The town had told him precisely what to say.

* * *

Artemisia had a rare chance to brief the whole team. She told them, without fuss, what Guilhem had told her, that the group was perceived to be not human.

"This is why Sylvia got into trouble. We're OK if we stay away from people, but if we look as if we're poking our nose in their business, it could get dangerous. This is not just a colourful landscape. These people are real and these people are angry and these people have given us boundaries. We've been put on notice."

* * *

"Have you sorted out the seasons yet?" Tony was pressuring both Geoff and Ben. "I need to know. If this is a bad summer and a bad autumn, I need to know. I think it's a bad one. I think the summer was too cold. I think the fruit is all late. But I need to know."

"Studies of harvest dates don't quite get back this far." Ben explained what Artemisia had told him, and showed her composite data from more general European information. "We think this is a bad year."

"We're creating the data," explained Geoff. "That's one of the things I'm working on."

"For this locality only," Ben said. He was right. The whole of Europe over the Middle Ages was not able to be depictured by the weather in one tiny region, caught between the coast and the mountains, in one single year.

"That's how science works one step at a time."

"I don't care about anything except here," Tony's words were mild, but his tone was surprisingly passionate. "I need what you have that affects my crops."

"I'll do you up something," promised Geoff.

"Thank you," said Tony, and disappeared.

"He said 'Thank you'," Geoff mouthed at Ben.

"Today is a day of miracles," intoned Ben. "Our saint's life of the day says this."

"Which version did you read?"

"What do you mean, which version?"

It was as if Artemisia's sprite self was an entity that could be forgotten.

Chapter Thirty-Five: Explosions and Desolations

It was a morning for discoveries.

"It's all William," Geoff declared. "The town, the holy saint in the abbey, the local stories." He was stunned.

"Even the locals are all named after him," observed Ben. "Artemisia said this ages ago."

"I don't think I was paying attention," confessed Geoff.

"Admiring her legs?"

"Not her legs, no," Geoff demurred and refused to be drawn further.

Sylvia had given Pauline access to the personnel files. It was theoretically so that she could treat everyone, should something go wrong, but in reality it was because Pauline was bored and was not good at either self-entertainment or at being a research assistant.

"You're Jewish," she said to Ben, accusingly.

"Only technically." Ben wondered if life would have been easier if he had the upbringing as well as the ancestry. He didn't, however, and it was no use repining. Time to face the music. "And not even that, really. Just my ancestors."

"So your family isn't German at all."

"Oh, my family is very German. My grandfather fought in the war."

"Your Jewish grandfather fought for the Nazis." Artemisia was fascinated, rather than repelled.

"Since both my grandfathers were Jewish, this must be true." He turned back to his computer and tried to pretend this conversation wasn't happening.

"Look at me when I'm talking to you," Pauline was furious. "Your grandfather murdered millions."

"No, my grandfather was a patriot. A fucking war hero."

"On the wrong side," the deep angry voice speaking so softly was Luke.

"And what can I do about it? Choose not to be born?"

"My father," said Luke, still with that dangerous voice, "Nearly died in a concentration camp. He had the wrong politics. Your grandfather had the wrong fucking religion and fought for Hitler. He should never have had children. His children should never have had children."

* * *

Guilhem was dreaming about joining the Catalan Grand Company and fighting for Roger of Flor.

"I know these Aragonese warriors — they'll fight anywhere and be damned. They'll not bother with courtesy or cleaning up. They'll have money." He would have to convince himself before he took that route. He needed to make some decision, however, soon. One day his time at the end of the world would be up, and if he made no choices, then he would have his family make them for him. All this was old, but the Catalan Grand Company was polished and new and brought all his previous notions back into contention. Templars. Family. Montpellier. The Aragonese. The world was getting bigger.

* * *

Artemisia read the words 'le mistral, qui désole' and couldn't get it out of her mind. It summed up what happened inside her whenever a particular breeze blew. She didn't know if that breeze was the mistral or something else, but it made her desolate. Maybe it was that look on Ben's face the other day. She had never seen anyone so alone. The truth had stripped his soul.

"God, he must have been lonely as a kid," she thought. "No wonder he protects himself with lies." But he had no more lies. No refuge. The wind had torn it all away. Carrying that desolation, she left the caves earlier than usual and took the long route to meet Guilhem.

Artemisia was witness to a fight. She only saw it at a distance, but it hurt. She was in the usual spot, waiting for Guilhem and two men had come to blows. Those blows touched something deep and very bad inside and Guilhem found her with her head in her hands.

"It's an argument," Guilhem was dismissive. "The villagers will name their representatives. The disputants will make peace."

"I just hate violence," Artemisia said. "Goes back to my

childhood. I have no defence against it."

"Ah," said Guilhem, as if he understood. He told the villagers they should continue avoiding the people under the hill. That he would continue to keep the people under the hill from the village. That no harm would be done by anyone or to anyone.

The villagers argued about it, even now that they had finally agreed that the strangers were probably not demons. They agreed they were fairies, fragile and strange. And they agreed, as they had agreed three times before, four times before, a thousand times before, to keep this from both the abbey and the churches. They assumed the castle knew, through Guilhem, and Guilhem didn't tell them differently. There were so few men at the castle, and none of them talked to Guilhem, even when he was included on a small hunt or in training.

"They will have gone soon," said Guilhem.

"So much the better," was the final agreement.

Guilhem never told Artemisia that the fight she had witnessed was over the status of the folk under the hill. He had settled it she had no need to know.

Chapter Thirty-Six: Hearing the Music of the Spheres

When Luke had sung on the karaoke night, he had produced a tolerable tune. When he sang to himself, however, he was blithely tone deaf. As tone deaf as Tony.

Geoff challenged him about it, as Luke did one of his occasional 'I am supervising my staff' walks past all their desks. He did this when he remembered. Most of the time he ignored what they were doing, and simply walked the walk while his brain went about its own business. This time he was humming tunelessly along to Geoff's sound track. Geoff was amused.

"You're not on key," he informed his boss, with a commendable lack of tact.

"You mistake," Luke said loftily. "I'm not singing to anything you can hear. I listen to the music of the spheres."

He knows the damnedest things, thought Artemisia. *He doesn't notice anything and then he notices everything, also. Odd man.*

* * *

Berta wanted to be surly. The mood had taken her again. She had worked too long both before and after the holy day and her husband had not done anything. Not even housework. Instead of annoying her neighbours with her attitudes, however, she was sitting on the hillside.

Fr Peire had caught her and correctly interpreted her mood. "Find a quiet place," he had advised, "and listen for the music of the spheres."

Just out of Beta's earshot, two others sat on the same hillside.

"Tell me a story, then." Artemisia found it very hard to get anything useful out of Guilhem. The young man was either mooning or sulking and he reminded her of one of the more annoying of her undergraduates.

"I shall tell you the story of how the great William won as his bride the pagan Oriabel and how she converted to Christianity and became Guiborc."

"I know that story." That wasn't the only reason for moving him gently away from that particular narrative. Artemisia suspected Guilhem of thinking that she was his Guiborc. This disturbed her.

* * *

Mac told Artemisia over and over that Guilhem wore ravel spurs. "I want to hold one and examine it so very much," he said. He also said that these were new technology and infinitely exciting. Artemisia failed to see why she should be interested. She was missing her saints' lives. More, she was missing her sister.

While Mac had been yearning for spurs, Luke had cut himself. He turned up to the kitchen, looking like a lost sheepdog. Pauline ushered him into her little clinic, and she latched him up. When she finished, however, they started talking.

"You never seem happy," observed Luke.

Pauline didn't seem to mind his lack of tact. "I see no reason to be happy. I'm going to die, after all."

"Didn't you have the health check before you came?" Luke scratched his beard in puzzlement.

"I read those clauses three times over, you know. The ones that explained the risks. I read them twice in my daughter's contract and once in my own."

"I remember. I thought it was very funny. Adamson and Adamson. Smith and Smith. You're not going to die, however. Those bits were put in there by the French Government. They were being difficult. They also shoved Konig down our throats. Not reasonable at all."

"We're travelling into death." Pauline said this calmly, as if she was deeply accustomed to the idea and had articulated it many times to herself.

"Why did you come then?"

"My daughter also applied," she was scornful. Pauline Adamson hated belabouring the obvious. "When she was called in for an interview, I had no choice. I saved her. You needed a doctor/cook more than you needed another scientist."

* * *

Berta and Bona had listened to Fr Peire and had decided to live good lives and prepare for heaven. Since Berta had heard nothing on the hillside, she worried about the state of her soul.

"Why," Guilhem-the-smith asked his friend, "do they listen to you now?"

"Berta is certain she will burn. She practises charity, prayer and much, much penitence to secure her place in heaven."

"I'm happy to hear that," Guilhem-the-smith barely suppressed a smile.

Bona was part of the austerity drive reluctantly. Her mother, however, gave her no choice. Bona missed the hills and her adventures. She became restless.

Berta solved her problems by persuading Sibilla to sell her a relic. When she came home, she wouldn't meet Bona's eyes. She felt so guilty at spending the money on it that she told no-one, in fact. She thought she had taken Bona's money from her apprenticeship stash.

Bona noticed the missing coins from the household's tax collection money, but had developed a cynicism towards her mother. She had not, for instance, informed her parent that her apprenticeship funds were somewhere safe because she did not trust her mother not to do something stupid like, for instance, buy a relic. Her father knew the important money was safe. Her father might not be very reliable in most things, but he was trustworthy where it counted.

Sylvia refused to tell anyone details of her work. Ben wanted those details for his reports for the French Government. He took up Sylvia's recalcitrance with Luke.

His request for information failed. In fact, it backfired. Not only did Luke deny Ben access to Sylvia's result, he cut back space for Ben's own samples. He and Luke were again not speaking.

Chapter Thirty-Seven: A Dream of Travel and Time

"Geoff, I need you," Artemisia said. "I need to get away from it all." Her gaze swept over Ben, who was hunched over his computer unhappily through to the silence that was Luke's office.

"I can see that," Geoff replied. "Your eyes look tired. Why not ask Cormac?"

"If you want me to ask Cormac, I can. Or Sylvia."

"I'm joking," Geoff hastened to reassure her.

"Not in the mood for jokes."

"You so need to get away from it all."

"I said so." Artemisia felt grumpy. She thought she looked grumpy. "And I don't feel it's sensible to go out alone."

"So you don't want my wonderful company?" Geoff looked down, teasingly.

"Not if you're in a mood. Forget it. I'll go to my room." She started to move off.

"No," he said and reached for her hand. "I promise I'll behave."

And he did. Fifteen minutes later they were ensconced on a quiet piece of rocky ground; no plants, no people. Ten minutes after that, Artemisia had unwound and they were chatting away.

"I can't believe you and Mac both said 'Scotty, beam me up', Geoff."

"Well, we were teleported. Or beamed up." He was smug. The sun shone on his smugness. Artemisia felt a small rush of happiness.

"Oh, I wish I had thought of that."

Geoff grinned. "You would have said it too." His child-grin made Artemisia happy again. Little wavelets of contentment.

"I would have at least have thought it. What a wasted opportunity."

"Would you like a copy of my music, as atonement?"

"Your huge jazz track?"

"Six hours. All by my family."

"That explains it."

"There is much love in those six hours. The trumpet that's so loud? That's my second nephew in his high school band. And the track that's distorted, the very modern one? That's an illegal recording done at a very alcoholic event."

"Half your family are musicians?"

"And the other half think they are."

"How does that fit the Islander stereotype?"

"Easy. The music comes from the idiot Aussie side."

"Idiot Aussie?"

"Official family nomenclature."

"Why you didn't own up to the Anglo-Saxon side of things to Luke for his forms?"

"He wrote us all down as WASP I was making a point."

"We all did, I think. I loved how very ruffled he looked."

"Yeah. Especially when Tony explained his people. Classic."

"Poor Ben," said Artemisia.

"Yeah. Pauline's a bigot and Luke wants Ben to pay for what happened to his father."

"I didn't realise Pauline was a bigot."

"Yep. She's careful around me mostly, and she stopped picking on Tony when he started writing notes about it, but since Luke lost it with Ben, she's not so careful around him. Little things slip. It's gotta hurt."

"Poor Ben."

"Yep."

* * *

Guilhem was dreaming aloud to Artemisia.

"If I join the Templars as Bernat suggests, I would have horses again with no effort on my part. They have rules about brothers and their horses."

"How many horses can you keep?"

"One."

"That's what you have now?"

"I had. It died, remember. Now I have none. Here. In Saint-Guilhem. Only pack animals. The great Guilhem rode a pack animal after he retired here, but I am not of his age nor his stature and I will not ride one of them. I have many horses elsewhere, with my warhorse eating its head off and not doing any work."

"And you really want to give up all those horses to have one now?"

"It sounds foolish when you say it like that."

"I wouldn't join the Templars just for a horse."

"You're a woman, you may not join the Templars."

"What are your other choices?"

Guilhem became stubborn and refused to say. After Artemisia had gone, however, he started calculating. He walked round and round the group of rocks, wearing a path. Finally he decided to calculate how much he'd need if he wanted to upset his family in style and sell his services to the highest bidder.

Food soldier 3 sous per day, squire 10 sous per day, attendants 2 ½ sous per day. He decided to call in some of his money, in case. He said to himself as his feet did his thinking (it had all been easier when he could ride whenever he needed to consider), "As they say, without money, one has no friends. Fortunately, even with my lands being controlled by my cousin and my mother, I have still some money. I can do this."

* * *

Guilhem was feeling sorry for himself. He sat alone on the hillside and tried to rhyme his unhappiness. He failed miserably. He was not a poet.

"I am not a king, not a duke, not a count. I am not a bishop, not a monk, nor a clerk. My family has given me the scraps from their table, made me a knight and expected me to be as grateful as if they had given me everything. When I expressed just feeling and anger at what was happening in my own country and to the people I love, when I joined the Bishop of Palmiers in righteous indignation and not the King of France in bad rule, I was sent first on pilgrimage and then to war. When I behaved in war as a soldier will, I was sent here, to Saint-Guilhem-Beyond-the-Edge-of-the-World."

This was Guilhem preparing, for the thousandth time, to make a decision, any decision, that would allow him to leave.

"I could take orders," he said. "Major orders. My family would honour me for this step. I could become a priest. Or I could marry. My family has a girl for me," he reminded himself, failing to remind himself that he and she hated each other. "She has land and a powerful family," which is why he had been unable to just walk away without putting himself out of her reach entirely, using religion. "If I married, it would consolidate my lands and give me back some of my power. It would also hamstring me I would never be able to say again what I said about the king. I would still be a knight and forever be treated like a page. I should leave it all behind, all my scattered bits of land and all my family and all my sorrow and I could go as a paid soldier. Take my wealth on my back, break my duty to my new lord and not have to see the despite in his face again. I could leave behind my rank and make use of my training and carve out a new life with people who do not know France."

He went round in circles. Round and round and round. So many choices. All simple. All with big consequences.

Artemisia stopped his thoughts by simply walking up to him. Guilhem smiled wanly, hoping he looked fraught. Artemisia noticed.

After shaking hands and an informal salute (her greetings were never formal enough and her farewells always those of a stranger) she asked him what the problem was.

"There is a dispute in the village," Guilhem chose to say, avoiding the deeper issues.

"Yes?" Artemisia wasn't surprised.

"I was not called," Guilhem felt he had to explain.

Artemisia, bless her, understood. "You are a knight. You can read and write. You should be able to help settle disputes."

"Yes," Guilhem answered.

"No," Guihem answered.

"Perhaps," he said, finally. "In this town they nominate a prud'homme or maybe two to represent disputants and to make the peace. I am not of them, perhaps because I am a knight, perhaps because I have no kin here. I am not of them. I may belong one day. I do not belong now. I am excluded from justice."

Artemisia didn't know how to answer this, so she sat quietly, hoping that her silence would be interpreted as companionable.

"Would you like to see something?" Guilhem asked, his mood changing. He took an object out of his purse and he handed it over to Artemisia.

"It's an astrolabe," she said. "When I was younger I wanted to learn how to use one of these. They're beautiful."

"When I was younger, I dreamed of Jerusalem. When Jerusalem was no longer a dream but a hard-won reality, I bought myself a dream of travel and time to replace it."

"A dream of travel and time," Artemisia repeated as she held the dainty object.

* * *

Guilhem was spending more time with his supposed peers. Every time there were visitors who needed a little extra dignity, he was called upon, like a page, to be polite and to make those feel important. This was supposed to result in larger donations by the visitors to the abbey. Every time he did this, the village remembered who his cousins were and resiled from their reluctant half-acceptance. It was becoming increasingly obvious that he would never be seen as belonging.

All this frothed up and choked him when, one day, he sat quietly on the middle step leading up to his house and his neighbours walked past the alley, talking loudly.

"And he consorts with demons."

"You mean they're not ghosts?"

"Demons."

Chapter Thirty-Eight: Family Matters

Finally Guilhem had his horse. It was true, Montpellier had everything. Even fine Andalusian palfreys. His contacts delivered his new pride and joy, as promised when he had handed over that money in Montpellier.

He managed to hang on to his horse for exactly two weeks.

After two weeks, his cousin passed through, pretending to be a pilgrim. He had nothing to give her. He tried to get her to accept his French translation of Vegetius. Isabella refused it in the charming way only a precious child can.

"I love you without gifts," she proclaimed, and spoiled it all by saying "Besides, you're stuck here, beyond civilisation. You need everything you can get." Then she took his horse.

It was the fault of the pilgrims. Guilhem wondered why he had ever mentioned the Templars as desirable. Pilgrims were plaguey and demon-possessed. Especially his little cousin Isabella, who had taken his horse with her when she left. Repeating that she had taken his horse felt good. She took his horse.

"What good is a horse like that in these hills," she had scoffed. "You need a mule, like Guillaume d'Orange."

"You want me to tear off its hind leg and defend myself against robbers," he teased.

"You could do that." She was serious.

He loved this little girl, with all her passion and all her intensity and all her lack of humour. He loved her even when she insisted on taking his beautiful new palfrey north. "One of my men will ride the beast and train the beast and the beast will be ready for you."

"The beast," Guilhem said. Isabella did not know horses very well yet. Or men. It was just as well he found her very easy to love.

He was explaining the whole debacle to Artemisia.

"My cousin Isabella wants to marry me."

"Didn't you mention her age? I thought she was a child."

"She is ten. Most certainly a child."

"No," said Artemisia. "Completely no."

Guilhem laughed.

"Betin Cassinel likes me," Guilhem said, with pretend enthusiasm.

"I'm delighted to know that," Artemisia said, with more than a trace of sarcasm. "Who is Betin Cassinel?"

"My cousin's master of money. Isabella's father's master of money, to be precise. In charge of the coinage of the realm."

"How useful is this to you?"

"Not much."

Artemisia went straight back to the cave and looked up Betin Cassinel and tried to link the name to an Isabella. There was a Betin Cassinel or Bettino Cassinelli who was a moneyer in charge of the French monies from 1287 to 1312. This would make Guilhem's cousin Isabella the daughter of Philippe the Very Pretty, King of France. It also meant she knew a lot more about Isabella than Guilhem did. Isabella would grow up in unexpected ways. About the only thing she didn't do was marry a cousin called Guilhem. Anyway, if Guilhem was related to the king, what the hell was he doing pretending to be a poor knight in the middle of nowhere?

She had to tell Luke. Thank God the little cousin was gone. Guilhem, however, was still their chief contact. They could be changing history.

* * *

Every member of the time team was going about their business. Luke hadn't altered a thing.

"Check it," Luke had said. "Make sure you're right." He would not adjust operations unless Artemisia proved that there were real problems. Not the imaginary problems she was apparently devising out of pure hellish boredom.

There was only one way of fixing this. Artemisia asked Guilhem directly.

"Who is your cousin?" she asked, next time they saw each other.

"Which one? My family is numerous as the stars in the heavens."

"Your cousin whose master of money likes you."

Guilhem took a coin out and flipped it. On one side was the pascal lamb.

"Do all your cousins look like that?" Guilhem laughed and

flipped it over. On the reverse was a king, seated in majesty on a throne. Artemisia's heart sank. She knew that coin. She read the inscription anyway. *Francorum rex*, it said.

"My cousin the forger," Guilhem said.

"You were exiled, then?"

"For telling the truth about the king." Guilhem shrugged his shoulders shamefacedly.

"Was this in the debates in 1302?"

"Yes."

"Why didn't you tell me?"

"I am a knight," said Guilhem, with offended dignity, "And the son of a knight. This is important. Not my cousins. My lineage is a good lineage."

But were your parents married? wondered Artemisia. *Or was it your grandparents who didn't get married. And what did you say about the king that got you into so much hot water? You called him a forger, for certain you've admitted that. But other people called him that. What did you say or do at the meetings? Or maybe since then. How have you actually spent the last three years?*

Artemisia went back to her chronology of the period before talking with Luke again. He said tiredly, "I need a briefing."

* * *

Briefing King vs Pope

Phil the Exceptionally Gorgeous argued with the Pope over who owed whom what. It was a long argument and way acrimonious. Lots of people were drawn into it. I have attached a chronology. Phil wanted a nation state, is what I was taught, and the Pope wanted a Catholic universe. Boniface especially didn't want the clergy to pay taxes. When he acted on this wish, Phil blocked supply. Not really, he just blocked income (same difference no money and one can't govern).

This led to ongoing skirmishes and battles. The best of them was probably in 1302, when Phil's mates actually burned a Papal bull. The French Estates-General were formed (first time ever!) and wrote angry messages to the Pope supporting the king. The Pope responded with another bull (*'Unam sanctam'* remember that name it's totally important historically) saying that the Church was more important than the State. Phil's chief minister said that the Pope was a criminal. It was all amazingly cool and I don't even begin to understand it. The debates got everyone sparking mad, though, and people in this region became heavily involved. Our knight apparently disgraced himself and didn't support the king-his-cousin.

And I've run out of words. If you want to understand it, you'll have to ask that my briefings be allowed to get big again.

Chapter Thirty-Nine: Companionship

Tony was alone in his garden. He had nothing really to do, but he enjoyed pottering. It helped him think. It also meant he could avoid being scolded. He really didn't enjoy that. He also didn't understand what the problem was. If people knew he didn't remember things, they should stop expecting it of him. Eventually they would realise and all would be well. That's what happened, every time.

After a while, he found the children pottering alongside him. He dug something, they dug the same thing. He used the unexpected help to extend his bed a little. Not a word was exchanged, but he and the children were happy.

After a while the children left. Badass then came to investigate all the new happenings. Tony nearly trod on the animal three times as it wove through his legs, purring. Eventually he resigned himself to the inevitable and picked the cat up. Badass was delighted with this and sat on Tony's lap, demanding attention.

Tony's thoughts expressed themselves fully on his face. The team members, who still mostly thought he was somewhat inscrutable, would have been surprised. The truth was that he had a social face. He never brought it to work, however, because if he did, people stopped and chatted and he hated that. It spoiled his concentration. He hated large groups and he hated anything that interfered with what he did. His face was his barrier, his privacy. With the children and the cat, he didn't need words, and besides, he wasn't really working. His face showed this. It glowed with gentle happiness.

The sound of a goat came from a few metres away. Badass jumped off Tony's lap and went to investigate his other friend.

Tony looked around. His plot of land was hemmed in by space where he didn't belong. For the first time since he came to 1305 he felt lonely.

* * *

Guilhem's house was actually his own, through an odd quirk of inheritance. He supported it with lands nearby, for it had none itself through an even odder quirk. It was ironic, he contemplated, that for him the end of the world was being sent to his own house in disgrace.

He finally realised that this very fact had opened up another choice for his future. If he wanted, he could become accepted as a prud'homme and a villager. All that was missing was time. It wouldn't take that much effort to be accepted. To belong. He could give up all dreams of greatness and settle down as a small landowner in the middle of nowhere. He contemplated this a bit longer. Then he remembered that he'd already decided to do that, and it had failed. And yet the town had given him a task.

He thought of other decisions he could take, ones his relatives had not considered.

"Guillaume won his pagan lady," said Guilhem to Artemisia.

Artemisia correctly interpreted where this was going. "I'm too old for you," she pointed out. "I'm from a different world. We are not suited in any way. Do not ask. Do not even think of taking this path."

"You smell as sweet as a saint," Guilhem said, leaning closer.

Artemisia curtsied in the most saintly fashion she knew and she fled. Alone in the dark, in her bed, she had nightmares. The least of them had her laughing hysterically. A thousand virgin martyrs. She focussed on this one, not on the return of the ones from her teenage years. She was well past all of that.

Chapter Forty: Relationships

In his fit of enthusiasm for changes and in discovering that he had more income than he had thought, Guilhem ordered stuff from Narbonne. Cloth from Arras and Bruges. The vermilion cloth coloured with the local kermes dye he gave to Artemisia.

Artemisia tried to refuse it but couldn't handle it when Guilhem begged her, very sweetly. He pointed out that the kermes dye was made in Saint-Guilhem. Guilhem knew that she would want it if he said that. He knew this woman very well, he thought, smugly.

Artemisia hated being so transparent. He knew that, too.

He was very pleased that she responded to pretend tears so very well. He knew what he wanted and this was one step closer to it. Guiborc wasn't willing at first, either, he told himself. And all he was doing was wooing her there was no force involved.

The cloth from Narbonne went to his household they required no persuasion. Vintenas and canvas were useful. He also bought linen from Champagne and Rheims to be made into clothes for himself, and fustian from Lombardy. There was a load of mixed furs and sheepskin. He didn't forget other household items: wax, loaf sugar, spices, soft and hard soap. He was scolded by his people for buying some things they already made, but in a happy way, because he was learning to take care of his own.

He saved one item, a paternoster made of crushed rose petals. He had meant to give this to Artemisia now and the cloth later, but he had been so pleased with the cloth, he had forgotten. It would wait.

Later that day, Artemisia and Geoff were wasting time. They had taken themselves as far from the caves as they reasonably could. The atmosphere was poisoned and, as Geoff said, they needed fresh air and sanity.

Geoff taught her all his favourite hymns (the ones that he had told the others didn't exist).

"Why?" asked Artemisia. "Why must I learn them?"

"You need them. You lost too much when you lost your family

and your religion. Hymns are a good replacement."

"I don't believe anymore," Artemisia warned him.

"Nor do I." Geoff was unrepentant. "It's the music. Never lose the music."

So they sang hymns on that hillside, until it was time to return to the caves for dinner.

* * *

A week later, Artemisia sat on the hillside, listening as demurely as she could. Guilhem was trying to explain how he was seen by his peers back home.

"By my words in 1302, I announced I wasn't one of the family," he explained.

"I don't understand," said Artemisia, willing to try, given that Guilhem was no longer ranting about how happy he was to see his friends dead.

"I rebelled."

"1302," said Artemisia.

"There are other ways of telling the year," Guilhem said, mildly.

"I like this one."

"The following year, I was sent to Gascony to redeem myself. This was not good for anyone. To atone, I went to Jerusalem. My family was, I believe, happy about my pilgrimage, even when they complained. When I returned I was angry. Jerusalem is no longer God's kingdom. The Templars suggested I join them and help make it so, and I listened for a moment, and they have now an interest in me. My family has asked that I stay away until I cease…"

"Losing your temper."

"Acting in a way that they deem lacks honour."

And yet Guilhem had never shown her any violence. Nothing but calm and patience and much talk about his dreams and ambitions. He was a bit of a mystery, in fact. She decided that maybe his words were bigger than his deeds and he just didn't get on with his family. That would explain it. *It had better explain it. I'm stuck with him until 31 December.*

"I would like to know more about 1302 and 1303. Are you willing to talk about those years?"

"What should I tell you? When the prince and the pope argued, my responses did not please the prince?"

"You came of age?" Artemisia guessed.

"In some ways." Guilhem's wry smile was more for himself than for Artemisia.

"I don't understand why, in answer to the king, you talk to the Templars. I thought he didn't like the Templars."

"He hasn't noticed them yet. When he sees them, then he will dislike them. That is how Philippe's mind works."

"But why do you want to join them?"

"I am not sure yet if I want to. When I was young I wanted order and duty and the return of Jerusalem and the Templars promise that." Artemisia wanted to say *Don't think about the Templars. They'll all be gone in two years, many tortured. You won't like it.* She couldn't, however. She didn't know what it would do. No-one really knew about their effects on the timeline. That's what Luke said, though he hid it beneath ten thousand words, most of them pompous. Guilhem didn't guess her thoughts. "Now I am less certain," he continued. "I am exploring possibilities."

"Staying out of the way?"

"With the master of the Commanderie at Pézenas keeping a close eye on me."

"Ah, the way out has become part of the prison."

"Sometimes you see too much."

When she got home and wrote up her notes on the conversation, Artemisia smiled to herself. She saw Guilhem in her mind's eye, far too young, standing in front of those portentous councils that changed the relationship between monarch and pope forever, thinking that the right of the case ought to prevail, standing up for the Christians who were caught in between two rulers. She saw him expostulate and shout and finally turn a desk over and leave the chamber.

Guilhem had told her all this, by the end of the hour. He had not told her the names he had called his cousin the king or the vilification and violence. Even without this, Artemisia thought that this was not the way to win the support of Philippe IV, who was known down history for his coldness. Or maybe not even the way to have a career as a knight or a Templar. Or anything.

If he were in the twenty-first century, he would be given counselling for his temper. In the fourteenth, he had probably been given all kinds of advice as well. Guilhem was not the sort to listen to kind advice.

What a moment that must have been, telling everyone what he thought over the French king's bid for power against the papacy.

Oh, what a way to murder one's future prospects.

* * *

Fiz was in a fine mood. He passed Fr Louis and Sibilla on the street. He assessed the way the priest's head tilted in Sibilla's direction, and said, "You should marry her."

Louis' face became red and he tilted that head towards the boy. He reached out and landed him a great whack around the ear. So heavy was his blow that Fiz fell to the stone pavement. When he didn't get up, the priest just looked down, arms crossed, unperturbed.

Sibilla regarded Louis and screamed, "This is how you treat your son, you unholy bastard, and you complain that I won't come to your bed."

Chapter Forty-One: Bitter Truths

There was no weather. There never would be weather again. Time travel had done it. Made all the weather go away.

Of course, there was weather if one walked through the door to outside. "Can't do that." She wished. Luke, however, had finally responded to the briefing and a follow-up discussion by confining them all. In her mind, she took twenty steps forward, five left and then ran the rest of the way and yanked the invisible doors open in a grand heroic gesture and then stood in the bright mountain sunshine.

That was an alternative universe. In this one, she was locked up until they could work out how many lives would be risked if she were sent home. Artemisia was taking up more than her share of the precious space. Making everyone even more crowded, even more cranky and, in some cases, even more scared. Not everyone thought she was wrong. And if she was right, they were all in trouble.

Maybe she was being melodramatic. Maybe it wasn't all so bad. But if that were the case, why on earth had Sylvia thrown such a tantrum? She hoped Luke would solve it. That Ben would step in and calm things down.

She hadn't realised how much she missed the outside and how small the caves were until now. She hadn't realised how much she hurt when there was no news from Lucia. She knew there wouldn't be anything (for Lucia didn't have clearance, she'd been told, quite severely, two days before she left), but she still wanted an email, even three words, as long as those three words said, "Treatment a success." At this moment she despaired. Lucia was a cat caught in a box, neither dead nor alive.

Artemisia wanted to go home.

* * *

Guilhem was in church. He was often in church, but this time he was noticing that it was a holy place. Normally it was the time he emptied his mind and dwelled not on his worries. Maybe this was the higher matters the priest assumed, and maybe not.

Today he was in Fr Peire's church, celebrating the eighth Sunday after Pentecost. Halfway through *Deus in loco sancto* he found himself wondering if the hills around Saint Guilhem were holy. If they were, what did that say about the folk under the hill? Should he talk to a priest? Or to the Templar fool? Or would that put Artemisia in danger?

He would leave it to God to decide if the place were holy and if the people were holy. It was a subject for theologians who were not present or for God, not for the power-hungry abbot or the stupid parish priests. All these men of God and they hadn't been able to assist on simple matters he could not trust them on something as subtle as Artemisia's soul. If the Bishop of Pamiers made his stand against the king again, Guilhem would not argue against his condemnation. He might not support Philippe, but he no longer saw the clergy as true men of God. He puzzled on this, reaching no good conclusion, right until the *Ita missa est*.

* * *

Peire was being calm. Despite everything. He stood in the middle of the street, radiating calmness with all his might. If he did not, then that fool woman who sat at the foot of the wall, watching as if they were a group of travelling entertainers performing for her benefit, that woman would be murdered.

Berta wasn't helping. Nor was Fr Louis. In fact, Louis was scolding Berta and when anyone tried to intervene, he would say "The heathens must go" and return to the scolding.

Calmness was all Peire could manage, and he was having trouble even with that.

Louis changed his tune.

"You whore," he said to Sibilla. "You usurer. You shame our town."

"That's rude," said Fiz, approvingly. "You should hit her the way you hit me."

Louis swatted vainly towards Fiz's head. This time the boy was prepared and ducked out of the way. He hit Sibilla instead.

Louis started calling the boy names. Inevitably, he called Fiz a bastard. "Bastard, son of a bastard," he said. "Son of a prostitute."

"Everyone knows that." Fiz was trying to be encouraging.

Sibilla had been nursing her ear; Louis had hit her hard.

"Not everyone knows that the bastard who fathered you is the priest who is calling you names," she said.

Calm descended. Also silence. This time the whole village had heard.

Chapter Forty-Two: Being Debonnaire

"I want," said Guilhem, out of nowhere, "I want next Eastertide with my family." Except that the word wasn't family, it was gens family/peers/kin. Artemisia was glad not to have to translate. "I want a new sword from Toledo, and a helmet. I want a shield that is cloven half way through. I want to look down upon the field of battle and feel alive. I want to live again."

Artemisia felt sick. It was one thing to know that Guilhem lived in a warrior culture. It was another thing entirely to hear it as a wish list for a happy Christmas. *Dear Santa, I want to murder ten people and get a model train and a giant lollipop.*

"Why can't you have that Eastertide?" Artemisia asked, tying to steer the conversation in the safer direction.

Guilhem's eyes shuttered and he looked inside himself. "I killed all the prisoners after a siege. Everyone expected it. It was Gascony. I did not show good judgement. I didn't spare those who could pay ransom. I didn't spare those who were related or who had arrangements. I killed them all myself, in anger. I am here because of the anger."

"You killed" Artemisia began.

"That's not all," Guilhem's eyes unshuttered and his face looked whimsical. "I also told my cousin that he looked like a tanner. That alone brought me here rather than to a more comfortable place to mend my ways."

"Calling your cousin a tanner was worse than murder?"

"Not worse. Different. Courtoisie and being debonnaire," Guilhem said, and shrugged. "There are places when insults are worse and places when insults can be laughed away. War is about honour and livelihood. I impugned his honour and lost many their ransoms."

Murder didn't even come into it. *I should have known this,* thought Artemisia. *I did know this. This is the sub-text of the saints' lives and the epics. I didn't know...* she thought and her thoughts stumbled...*I didn't know it was people. Or I didn't know what it meant that it was people, that it's real, that it has emotional human truths behind it. Books are safer. Stories are safer. This man sitting next to me, he's not at all safe. None of them are, who carry swords.* She felt sick to her stomach.

Guilhem didn't feel sick. In his head echoed "Patience is the virtue of kings" as he announced his kind and generous response to Philippe's action. Guilhem hated his cousin the king with all his soul. Guilhem knew then and knew even more now that death was preferable to exclusion.

Despite his promises to the town, Guilhem felt isolated. No-one wanted him to be a part of their community. He played with his seal as if tossing it and turning it could create a legal document it could then be used on. He wondered if it were the people from under the hill who created this barrier. If they could somehow be explained, be brought into the real world, maybe he himself would be less isolated.

He still had choices: knight-errant, Templar, or obedient marriage and acceptance of his family as his lords. He wanted none of those. None. He also didn't want to become a small prud'homme in a place deserted by everyone except God.

Intimate conversations inevitably led to more intimate conversations. How could Artemisia have forgotten this?

"Your skin is too dark for beauty," said Guilhem, running a finger along her jaw.

"Stop that," Artemisia said, and took a step back. She stumbled on the sloping hillside and Guilhem held her steady by her elbow, smiling indulgently. As if he were claiming ownership.

That evening ran parallel to the afternoon.

"I love your Italian skin," said Geoff. "So beautiful."

He bent down and kissed her gently in the moonlight, first on her mouth then gradually over her whole face.

* * *

17 November

The partial solar eclipse started at 7.30 pm. Luke wanted everyone up on the hilltop, observing.

"Bonding," he said. "Final haul. Prepare emotionally for the last weeks."

The whole team was stubbing toes on stones and tripping on

tussocks and getting in Sylvia's way and in Geoff's way. It felt a lot better than it had. Being confined had frayed too many nerves.

Maybe we're finally all seeing the same picture, from the same direction. Maybe it is *bonding,* thought Artemisia, *after a kind.*

* * *

Guilhem was haunted by *Dicit Dominus* throughout November. Every time he went to church, it seemed he heard it. He couldn't puzzle out its meaning. What was God saying? Or was it God? Was the Church laying down messages for his soul?

Last time he had read messages from the echoes of liturgy, he had agreed to take himself to Jerusalem, in penance. His soul had been very healthy as a result, but he had been deprived of a significant amount of land. His family considered him unstable, extravagant rather than generous, unreliable in temper, and told him, even now, that he put himself above family needs.

"You choose not to belong," his cousin had said. "We choose to let you, this time." His own choices made. One day he made one choice. Another day he made another.

If he chose the Templars he would owe a duty to the Patriarch in Jerusalem. He would live in the world but be sworn to poverty and to chastity and to obedience. The Patriarch was a temptation it would free him from many of his conflicts. To be able to tell his cousin "I am sworn elsewhere" would be a delight. The rest, however, required thinking. Especially that part of the rest that was a mob of soldiers, everywhere. He needed to talk to his 'friend' at the Commanderie again.

The talk was explosive. The two men nearly came to blows.

Guilhem walked furious out of the Templar fortifications.

Guilhem was tired of losing his temper. This time he didn't confess. He refused to accept that his loss of control and judgement was a bad thing.

"At certain times I am on the field of battle and I know, inside, that the poets are right. There is glory inside me. At other times I see the field and on it are my friends. I will not see them again in this world. Their wives, their children, their mothers, their friends, will not know them."

* * *

Artemisia noticed that someone had been accessing the Godefroy.

She traced back the access to find who it was Ben Konig. Good. She left it alone. Ben spoke modern French better than she did: Old French was not such a stretch if one had a good base. And it meant she would have backup, perhaps, if the constant worries became tangible reality. She didn't tell Luke. Luke was currently pretending that the rest of the team followed protocol. Artemisia was tired of Luke's lies. Ben's lies were lesser creatures.

Tony cut himself on the hillside. It was a deep cut and, after a bit of a struggle, Tony realised he couldn't do anything. He called out for a little, then gave up. He lay there, his blood seeping into the soil. Bona found him while her brother was stalking the cat. Bona knew what to do. She applied pressure to slow the bleeding and she sent her brother off to get help.

Within minutes, Geoff felt a tug on his right sleeve.

"Fairy, we need you. Come. Come!" Geoff didn't understand, but followed the insistent pull on his sleeve.

Sitting around the dining table that night, it dawned on Tony's workmates that those children had saved Tony's life. The chatter hushed, gradually, and was replaced by silence. The silence was replaced by a very special tension. Every member of the time team started a vehement discussion about the cat. It was better than thinking of the alternatives. The whole group was divided over the damn cat and its interference. It distracted them from the matters they would not face.

* * *

Guilhem and Artemisia were talking about language. Specifically, they were discussing the phrase "bread, wine and the rest". This simply meant 'food'. Artemisia loved it.

"I say this," said Guilhem, "and I know I am of the Languedoc, despite my father and his family. Despite my brothers and my language I speak good French, the French of France, of Paris, but I know I am not of France because when I want to eat, I think of bread, wine and the rest."

"I bake bread sometimes," said Artemisia. "Not here, of course. At home. It's very sweet? No, not sweet. Calming." She was so involved in trying to find an Old French word for 'soothing' that she failed to notice that Guilhem's face had frozen over at her mention of baking.

He continued the conversation perfectly affably. Artemisia didn't realise that she had just committed a serious error.

Guilhem was entirely taken aback by her comment. He wondered if he had misinterpreted her other-ness. "Maybe she is not noble but strange? Maybe she is a peasant, with education? In her world many things can happen she says so. The devil never sleeps how can I be certain of her good character?"

Artemisia baked bread. Guilhem couldn't get it out of his mind. She talked and acted as if she was of good family. Her hands were fine. Her manners were learned. She read and she spoke the same French of France as he himself did. But she was not from France and he had excused her oddities as due to that, and that alone. What if they were because they were not noble? Was she then more available? He found himself dreaming of her. He did not dismiss those dreams.

* * *

Guilhem was still thinking of William and Guiborc. Guilhem didn't know if he dreamed of that option himself transforming into a great hero and Artemisia becoming a hero wife and a good Christian. If Artemisia were converted, that would be a good solution. One's past was washed away with baptism, even if that past included work not suited to a wife of Guilhem. In his mind, Geoff was Marsile, Guiborc's husband, who deserved to die.

Guilhem found his hand clenching into a fist as he thought of the way the man's eye looked at Artemisia and how he walked the hills as if he knew all the boundaries and owned the very rocks beneath. If any of the team were a devil or a fairy or a pagan king, it was the tall brown man. Then his mind slipped to another story of Charlemagne, one of Roland's tales, not William's. He remembered the hour of Roland's death as they told it in Aragon, where the Sarrasin Falceron gave him comfort. Roland had been Guilhem's distant kin. Was one of Artemisia's friends his Falceron? Certainly his friends were not his Falceron, Bertrand and Philippe and the others were all good Christians.

* * *

Artemisia was concerned about her safety. She brought it up at a meeting, since Luke was forever agonising and asking for briefings and making no decisions.

"Later, Artemisia," said Ben. Sylvia backed him up. Artemisia's concerns were silenced to benefit Ben's political needs. He wanted back into the group, despite Luke.

Artemisia took it back to Luke again. "Guilhem now tutoyes me but hasn't given me permission to do the same back. He didn't get my permission either. He just switched when we spoke, with no warning. I don't know why and it worries me."

Luke said, "It's probably nothing you're his friend."

"We don't have the historical database to test that theory against. We have no way of knowing apart from my evaluation. I feel very unsure about why he changed. It could mean friendship, but it could mean something else and I don't know what," argued Artemisia.

"Extrapolate."

"I did," Artemisia pointed out, logically. "That's why I'm here."

Luke extravagantly ruffled his hair, stymied, then ran his hand through his beard to assert his authority. "Collect more data. Analyse it. Until then, take precautions."

"Precautions?"

"Take Cormac or Geoff with you when you go out. They're big blokes. Mac is probably better only does support work and has some martial arts training. We can spare him for this. Murray has a cooler head, though. If you take both, he's in charge."

It was a great theory.

Two times out of three, however, Mac had found more important work. "Luke said I had to do this," he would say, and leave Artemisia to walk alone.

Chapter Forty-Three: The Hunt

There was hunting in early October. There was earlier hunting than this and other hunting than this but it was in early October that Guilhem thought of the hill folk and realised they would be a problem.

Guilhem helped the team block out the most likely places to avoid and suggested they stay underhill as much as possible, then he took himself away to hunt. It was only a little hunting, but it whetted his appetite.

He saw himself as a dreamer and a murderer and recognised his deep belief. The Temple was tempting still (and tempting to dismiss yet again), but he realised he needed more guidance.

The whole valley was dealing with the aftermath of a violent storm. Trees were down and plants had been uprooted by the tumbling water.

Guilhem's housekeeper blamed it on a demon. He heard the voices of the town in that blame. He almost didn't warn Artemisia, but then he felt he should. He found a morsel of soften linen paper he had found in his big travelling chest and quite forgotten about and wrote a note and gave it to Tony. Tony put it in his backpack and forgot about it.

* * *

"Prostitutes trade outside town walls," Guilhem said, à propos of nothing.

"This town has only partial walls," replied Artemisia, tartly, "And I am no prostitute." She left her courtoisie behind her and she ran to get away, leaving him bewildered behind her and Mac hurrying after her.

From then on, she took both Cormac and Geoff for meetings. Guilhem made no more references to prostitution or sex. He didn't run his finger along her jaw or talk about her skin. He did however, still continued to tutoye her.

He also said, "My friends arrived this morning." He warned

Artemisia that her people should stay out of trouble and he went with his friends. It was time to hunt.

* * *

At hunt, Guilhem's friends and their friends all talked interminably about fights (serious and less so) from which Guilhem had been banned. He didn't mind. The hunt filled some of the need he had felt for jousting and a good melée.

They hunted for boar, for it was still the season. Boar was one of the best preys it was more dangerous and also more challenging than most other prey. It was malign.

The sense of the day was disorganised, frantic, triumphant. Men, nets, dogs, hounds, beaters, horn. Lots of success. Lots of excitement.

Philippe was impressed with Guilhem's speed. "You came down that slope as lightly as any deer," he said.

The sows could and would savage a fallen man with their teeth, but boars, boars were the game of men. Wolves were even more so, but the last time Guilhem had seen a wolf, he had seen a whole pack. It was following the armies in Gascony and eating the dead. He hated wolves with all his being. "Hunger chases the wolf from the wood," he thought, but what does that mean? "That famine brings the wolf to the field, of course, but also that we need certain things to control the wolf within us. How do I control my wolf?

There was one chien baut that made Guilhem think of Artemisia and her quest for understanding — beautiful, fluid in movement, intelligent. Was Artemisia as obedient as a good dog? Guilhem began to wonder, then dismissed the thought. There were more urgent matters at hand.

A boar, Bertrand said. "We have one."

It was a good boar. It challenged everyone. Its challenge to Bertrand was irrefutable. It had spit him on its tusks and followed that by killing a horse. Then the boar itself fell.

Guilhem found something visceral and almost sensual in the way Bertrand dipped up and down as the tusks gored through him, despite the fact that his friend was dying. The rhythm was like sex, he thought.

At the end of the day they settled into their village of tents. The dogs were given the intestines, stomach, spleen, liver and testicle mixed with bread soaked in blood and toasted on the embers of the fire. It was the post-hunt ritual that brought everyone together and consolidated the day. The heads of the kill were already severed and the blood put aside. While the fire burned strong, the bristles were burned off the boar and then the butchery was done. After that, it was time to eat and drink.

There were always available women at hunts like this. Men needed women at times like this. Guilhem ate; he drank; he laughed; he had sex. He honed his memory of violence. His friends saw that this hadn't left him and they were careful with their offers. Before the hunt they had promised much.

His place in the hierarchy depended on esteem, given his birth. He wanted it back. He craved it. That memory had also returned, of being someone with a future. With privilege. Normally he'd leave his boasts behind after the hunt. This is what he had learned. This time he carried his sense of what was owed him: he fanned the flames of his grievances. His friends had not helped him they had made everything worse.

The group gave gifts of deer and boar carcasses to the landowners and local bishop and then separated to make their way home.

On his way back to Saint-Guilhem-le-Désert, the knight had time to think. He couldn't imagine Artemisia hunting, not even elegantly, with a fine bird. He started to think of what he could imagine her doing. The heat of the chase ran through his veins. That moment when the boar gored Bertrand returned to his mind again and again. He imagined Artemisia naked beneath him. He smiled to himself.

Despite the intense joy he had felt while hunting and despite his fine companions, Guilhem returned full of honour and darkness. He left with hope and trust in friendship, he reminded himself, over and over, but his friends offered him nothing except empty promises. Once they had left, he had nothing except the memory. There was no offer of employ, no pretty sister who needed a husband, no ointment for his pain.

* * *

Ben loved this season. Every excuse he could find, he left Luke and his opinions behind and he worked outdoors. He loved the sharp smell to the air and the dusky breeze. He worked long hours in the caves to process data and extrapolate and draft his analysis this was the payment he made for his pleasure.

* * *

Guilhem noticed that Artemisia laughed with her mouth open, like a lewd woman. He started to notice other signs of lewdness and remember still more: the way she walked, the way she tilted her head to examine a flower. Every move Artemisia made and had ever made was suddenly infused with sexual significance.

He realised his fault. He took himself away to report to Bernat in the hopes that he would think chaste thoughts. At the Commanderie he felt suddenly comfortable he was among his own kind again. As one does, he talked about what he had recently enjoyed. He started describing the hunt.

"Templars don't hunt," his advisor said.

Guilhem didn't do him the courtesy of calling him Sire Bernat and Bernat returned the lack of courtesy. They tolerated each other, merely.

"Not at all?" Guilhem was dismayed. Did this order take all the dutiful joys from life and replace them with duty that contained no pleasure?

"Lions," said Bernat. "We hunt lions."

Guilhem had never seen a lion, not even on his travels. He only half believed they existed. They were not boars, or even deer. They were not what he thought of as a good hunt.

I do not want to be a Templar, he thought. *I never wanted to be a Templar. It was simply an escape my family would have accepted.*

On the way out of the Commanderie, he saw it with an evaluative gaze. He remembered remarking on it like this once before. Fortification in a place where none ought exist. Knights with no hunting to release their tension, and no women. Knights who owed no allegiance to the king, who were trained in battle and lived in the king's land as if they owned it.

Chapter Forty-Four: Judgements

Artemisia had been to meet Guilhem, but he wasn't there. She waited and waited, but he didn't come. She decided to go home the long way. Anything to keep her out of the caves a little longer. She walked the very long way home, past the end of the world, past the small hell, almost as far as the other cave system. The small caves. The ones about which Luke had said, "Just as well we didn't settle there," with such joviality.

Eventually she was ready to turn back. She was tired and had run out of goat-trail. There was nothing to return for, but the only option was to climb the hills and her legs were too tired. Emotional fatigue lost to physical and she pushed herself to gain the pilgrim path. When she reached it, she was not alone. Walking in her direction were three townsfolk.

The townsfolk looked at her. She looked at them.

She stepped politely aside to let them past. One of them, a woman, said "We don't want you. We don't want any of you."

Berta decided it would be a good idea to make the message clear. She walked towards Artemisia. She meant no harm. Only to make things clear. Berta raised her fist. She re-thought the closed fist and, opening it, landed a thwack on Artemisia's right cheek.

Her husband raised his hand. All Artemisia saw was a big man, ready to strike. She ran.

She didn't look behind. She turned back the way she had come, though she had no idea she was doing so. She ran as fast as her skirts allowed, hoping that the three weren't following. As Artemisia stumbled uphill, the sky lost its light. She tripped and fell in the dark, lost. The rain started to pelt down. The wind blared through her.

Eventually, she was hailed, by name. It was Guilhem.

"I'm lost," she said, hopelessly.

"There are caves. We should shelter." He supported her that final distance and soon they were out of the rain and out of the wind and Artemisia felt safe. Her cheek stung and she was cold through and through, but she was safe.

"You're cold," he said. Guilhem reverted to his mother's tongue. "Vilaria o domna. Virtuous woman or prostitute," he translated, trapping Artemisia. "I have considered all else and these are the only two choices. You are no fairy. You are no saint."

Artemisia tried to collect her wits. "I am myself. My people are not yours and my ways are not yours. I will not sleep with you. Let me go!"

What happened next was awful. It was Artemisia's teenage nightmare all over again. At home she would have had mace. A tough handbag. A whistle around her neck. All kinds of protections.

Here, in 1305, she had nothing.

* * *

Artemisia refused to let herself think about what precisely had happened in that cave. She couldn't forget some things: the knee in her stomach, the groping hands, the humiliation. She tried to balance that with the bruises Guilhem would have, and the bites, and the scratches. For Artemisia had refused to give in. She had fought to the best of her ability the whole time. The best of her ability was never enough. Never enough.

When Artemisia crept back into the time team's own caves at dawn, no-one noticed. No-one noticed when she used ten times her shower allowance. Only Geoff saw that she went back to bed straight after that shower. Only Geoff saw that she cried.

Geoff hung outside her door, worried. He peeked in and realised that he couldn't help her. She needed to stay in bed.

The moment she emerged, however, he was there, pretending to be casual, but watching and making sure that she had hot drinks, that her chair was right, that she wasn't squinting into the sun when she worked. Watching for when he could help, not being too intrusive. Worried beyond belief.

He had not realised how much it would hurt him when Artemisia felt pain. His heart was breaking that she was suffering. But interfere he would not.

Not until she was ready.

Chapter Forty-Five: In Town

Guilhem didn't sleep that night. Instead, he talked to himself.

"This is the country," Guilhem was full of self-reassurance. "Artemisia is not of us. I do not even need to confess this."

Finally he compromised. He confessed to sleeping with a fairy, to Fr Peire.

After confession he hung around the village for a bit, not wanting to go home. He became vastly drunk and told every man present that he had slept with a woman from under the hill. He talked about it as a form of exorcism. He had exorcised them, as if they were demons, by sleeping with her. Alcohol was as effective as bell, book and candle, he told Sibilla and Berta. Fairies aren't men, he told Guilhem-the-smith.

* * *

18 December

Luke was overseeing first aid, his shoulder and his beard expressing sympathy, his hand upraised.

Down in the village, Peire stopped to see who had hurt themselves. His right shoulder leaned slightly forward. Peire's hand moved automatically to the healing gesture he knew so very well. He saw it in carvings all the time, whenever he visited the abbey. Whether it helped or not rested with God, but his parishioners undoubtedly found it comforting.

The town had arrived at the view that the people under the hill were not fairies, despite Guilhem's drunken claims, but were demons. This conclusion was largely the work of Fr Louis, aided and abetted by Sibilla. Sibilla might have been influenced by the fact that Guilhem had slept with a hill woman but had stopped sleeping with her.

The town knew it had a problem. Guilhem had not told what he knew that the strange folk from under the hill were only with them for two more weeks. When the townsfolk talked it through, they realised that Guilhem had given them surprisingly little information.

Every time someone asked, he gave them different dates, though Lady Day had come up most often.

Lady Day was insupportable. Lady Day was months away. And maybe Guilhem had invented it.

"We know more from the children, "said Berta, "than we know from that knight."

Her husband added, "And from Sibilla's inventions. In fact, we don't know anything."

"We should be concerned," Guilhem-the-smith finally agreed.

* * *

It was the nineteenth of December, the fourth Sunday of Advent. Even church hammered Guilhem's sins into him hard and unrelenting. *Memento nostri, Domine, in bene placito populi tui. Visita nos in salutari tuo.* He needed that salvation. He thought he had been tormented before, but now, he could not face himself. He could not confess. He could not take back what he had done.

His mind went back to his thoughts on death and exclusion. Now was the time to choose to not be excluded. He didn't consider that death and exclusion shared a border and that, with his actions, he was moving other people closer to that border. Other people had never been a big concern of Guilhem's, in any case.

He drew his seal out and looked at it. He turned it over and back. Suddenly he tossed it in the air and then he smiled. If the people under the hill could be exorcised, surely Guilhem's actions would be right. He had been tempted and he had subdued demons. Exorcism would prove this.

He went to talk to the priest at Saint-Laurent. Each time, a different priest. Each time, another sector of the local population. Guilhem didn't analyse his own actions. He worked himself up and then confessed his sins, as he always had. He knew that it was this behaviour that had got him into trouble in the first place, but he couldn't stop it. He didn't want to stop it.

Chapter Forty-Six: Consequences

Artemisia decided that she would bear this nausea no longer. If it was a virus, then it was a virus that had gone on for too long. She went to see Pauline.

"You're pregnant," Pauline said, without any drama. "Birth control works for most women, but you're obviously an exception. You can look forward to a big family." She paused a moment. "Or you could have a hysterectomy." She paused another moment. "I wouldn't have picked you," she said. "You've been very circumspect. Which one is it? Tony? Ben?"

She ignored Pauline's prompts. "I'd better tell the father."

Artemisia worried. It could be Geoff, after all. She really hoped it was Geoff.

"Or you could lose it. Although the fewer procedures we do at this late stage in our journey, the better."

"I'll think about it." Where had Pauline missed that Artemisia was Catholic? Abortion was not an option. In a way, she was relieved the birth control hadn't worked. In another way, she really wished that it had. This pregnancy was one mess too many. She wanted to forget everything from the last month. The last year. She wished for the privacy of modern times, where she could have walked into the chemist and simply found out. She wished she had never got lost that bitter night. She wished she could go to bed and curl up under her doona and weep.

That, at least, she could do.

* * *

Guilhem thought of his hero namesake. He remembered that, when William had gone away on his battles, his warrior-lady had barred the gates and would not let him return.

"How can I know you're my husband," she had said, "When I do not recognise your face?"

* * *

"One in four women are raped," she pronounced, proud of her

266

control. Geoff was not so calm, but he kept his reaction to the news of both rape and pregnancy very firmly inside himself. "Some of us are raped twice. Some of us are disowned by our families because rape is a girl's fault for wearing tight jeans and talking to the wrong boys."

Geoff didn't say anything, but his long fingers were stroking her hair, very gently.

"I can't tell the others what Guilhem did. Pauline knows I'm pregnant, but if she knew I'd been raped she would make one of her dinnertable pronouncements and Sylvia will instantly be deeply emotionally distressed. Luke won't know what to do and will issue all kinds of orders to hide that. There will be fallout. I had too much fallout last time I can't take it this."

Geoff said, "There will be no fallout. The baby is mine. Regardless of biology."

"Thank you," said Artemisia. "You don't have to, though."

"I do. This isn't up for argument. The baby is ours. And you get to decide who knows about the rape. If you prefer, no-one need to know, not ever." And then there was a silence. Less fraught than the earlier, but still a silence. Sylvia's bright song was the only noise.

"I keep thinking," she tried to explain things, before Geoff lost that silence and felt he had to make more impossible offers, "that if we were part of this time I could take this to court and maybe Guilhem would be punished. Death, maybe, or castration. The records have both as punishment for rape. The likelihood is, however, that he'd get off free. Or maybe he'd be fined. A few sous."

"Do you need to confront him?"

"I think I do. I don't want to, but I think…it may be all I can do."

"It's for yourself."

"Yes, for me."

"You can't be alone."

"I think I can trust Mac. I can't tell him, though. I don't want to explain and I don't want to argue and I don't want to see any look that makes me feel as if I am a slut and beyond redemption."

"I can talk to Mac. He won't lay anything on you."

Artemisia felt very bold in reaching out and holding Geoff's hand. Geoff held hers back. It was a redemptive moment. After the first rape she had been shunned. She'd had to divorce her own family to find herself again. This time, she had Geoff.

"It might take me a while to get through this," she whispered.

"I'm here. I can wait."

Artemisia sat there in the darkness, Geoff's hand in hers, her cheeks wet with tears. It was as if all the evil that life had given her was able to be turned around, as long as Geoffrey Murray was here, with her, holding her hand.

* * *

Guilhem knew the men with Artemisia didn't understand him. He proceeded to accuse her and make her complicit in his guilt. As the accusations became stronger, his tone remained dulce and gentle.

She said, "My body is sore and abused. Your guilt is not mine. I will not live with your guilt." Artemisia let the silence grow. "Make amends," she said.

"You were not a virgin."

Artemisia pulled Geoff forward. "Meet my betrothed." *I will tell him we're going to get married act as if it's real,* Artemisia had explained to Geoff. *The Church doesn't like it when couples sleep together before they get married, but they do it all the time.* Geoff did his best to loom possessively.

This took Guilhem completely off-balance. "I do not know what to do."

"None of us do, for I am pregnant. The baby could be yours."

Guilhem sat down on the ground, his face in his hands. "I must think," he finally said. "I must confess this again. I am still unclean. My hands need washing. My soul needs to be cleansed."

"You confessed, but you haven't said that you are sorry. You committed this violence against me and you don't regret it. Your soul is black as ink. You are foul as Ganelon."

"I am," he admitted, still not looking at her.

Artemisia looked at Geoff and at Mac. She shook her head.

"We should leave," Geoff said.

"Good idea," said Artemisia. As they walked home, they kept talking. It was as if they were scared about what silence would bring.

"I wish…" Cormac stumbled in saying it, "I wish I could of done something. Could have done something."

"We all bloody wish that," said Geoff. "Let's go and not a word of this to the others."

"Why?"

"They'll make it into Artemisia's fault and it isn't. It's all of ours, for letting her carry so much for so long. If we'd all been professional and if we'd all listened and paid attention, none of the women would have been out without protection."

"This is a violent society," Artemisia said.

"You told us, over and over. We didn't believe it."

"It got so that I didn't believe it, to be honest. It felt safe enough."

"And that's our fault too," said Geoff.

"I need to think," Mac said, then blushed deep red. "The Middle Ages isn't what I thought."

Later that day, Artemisia asked Geoff and Mac if she could borrow them for a moment.

"They have got real work to do, you know," said Sylvia.

"This won't take long," Artemisia said.

When they were out of earshot, Artemisia said. "I need to do something. I need to stop Guilhem doing that again. And I need to explode."

"You can't explode," said Geoff, peaceably. "It would be a bugger of a mess to clean up. All those innards."

"I have to do something. Make a point. Something."

"But what?" Cormac was frustrated. He also needed a point made.

"That's why I wanted both of you. I think we can make Guilhem feel bad for the rest of his life. And I think we can do it in a way that will make us feel better. But I need to be safe. He needs to be held down or something."

"You want to castrate him?" Mac's eyes glittered. "Didn't you say it was a punishment for stuff in the Middle Ages?"

"I do not," Artemisia was emphatic. "You're right, though. It's a punishment for rape."

"If we held him down, he'd think we were going to castrate him," Geoff pointed out. "Give him a well-deserved shock, even if we didn't do a thing."

"I have a better idea than that. I want us to do a spiritual castration. I want us to devise a curse and I want to deliver it. In Latin. To his face."

"My God," said Geoff. "That's bloody perfect. A curse like the one in *Tristram Shandy*."

"I thought we could use that exact curse. My Latin's not good enough to write one from scratch. Besides, Sterne got the form right. He took a real Medieval curse. Guilhem will be listening for certain parts if he hears them, he'll believe it's real. It's got to reflect the liturgy. The *Tristram Shandy* curse does that."

"What's the curse in *Tristram Shandy*?" Cormac was puzzled.

"Come on, mate, I'll find it for you."

"Feel free to make suggestions," Artemisia called after them.

"Oh, we will," and the intensity of Geoff's eagerness was almost savage.

Chapter Forty-Seven: Catharsis

The smithy was full of people, talking about the hillfolk. Speculating particularly on Artemisia, given Guilhem's revelation. Sibilla was particularly accusatory. Guilhem-the-smith had finally had enough. He calmly listed the men she, Sibilla, had been sleeping with.

"Slut," she was called, openly. Everyone had known it, but now they said it.

The next day, Sibilla turned the whole of Saint-Guilhem upside down. She named Fr Louis again as the father of one of her children, as the father of Fiz and his two friends. This time she named him formally, in public. The abbot was forced to act. Louis was deprived of his parish pending investigation. There was no priest at Saint-Barthelmy.

The townsfolk were more worried about the leadership of the Saint-Barthelmy congregation and what this meant in terms of the hillfolk than about the state of Fr Louis' morals. They started to compare notes about bad things happening again, from storms, to poor harvest, to coloured water, to one of Louis' other sons drowning in a feat of derring-do. There was no way in which this was a good thing.

* * *

Three days later, Artemisia and her escort were waiting for Guilhem at their meeting place. Guilhem looked a bit down, and wouldn't meet Artemisia's eyes.

"You wanted to talk to me," he said, not bothering with politeness.

Artemisia had prepared very carefully for this. Geoff and Mac were standing by, ready to step in when they heard their cues.

"I thought you were *courtois*," Artemisia answered, "But I find that you are *villain*. In my language we have no words that say this and yet it is you who have transgressed. In your world, there is little I can do. I have a power, however, that you forgot. You will now remember it. You will never hurt another woman," and Mac and

Geoff took Guilhem by his elbows and his shoulders and forced him to his knees, holding him there.

Artemisia slowly unfolded the piece of paper on which she had written the revised curse. She read the Latin:

"By the authority of God Almighty, the Father, the Son, and Holy Ghost, and of the undefiled Virgin Mary, mother and patroness of our Saviour, and of all the celestial virtues, angels, archangels, thrones, dominions, powers, cherubim and seraphim, and of all the holy patriarchs, prophets, and of all the apostles and evangelists, and of the holy innocents, who in the sight of the Holy Lamb, are found worthy to sing the new song of the holy martyrs and holy confessors, and of the holy virgins, and of all the saints together, with the holy and elect of God, may Guilhem be damned."

She paused for a moment and looked across at Geoff. He nodded to go on.

"I deliver him with Dathan and Abiram, and with those who say unto the Lord God, *Depart from us, we desire none of thy ways.* And as fire is quenched with water, so let the light of him be put out for evermore, unless it shall repent. Amen."

"Amen," repeated Geoff and Mac, holding Guilhem down, tightly. Guilhem stopped struggling and went silent, his face white.

"May the Father who created man, curse Guilhem. May the Son who suffered for us curse Guilhem. May the Holy Ghost, who was given to us in baptism, curse Guilhem."

Artemisia flung the word 'curse' into the empty space between them, making it stronger and more powerful than all the other words.

"May the holy cross which Christ, for our salvation triumphing over his enemies, ascended, curse Guilhem. May the holy and eternal Virgin Mary, mother of God, curse Guilhem. May St Michael, the advocate of holy souls, curse Guilhem. May all the angels and archangels, principalities and powers, and all the heavenly armies, curse Guilhem."

Everything was silent except for Artemisia. Not even the birds chattered in the golden light of late afternoon. Each time Artemisia said 'Guilhem' her voice was hard and unhappy, and each time his name reached Guilhem himself that unhappiness was transferred. Each time, Artemisia felt lighter and less burdened until her soul started to free itself from what Guilhem had done.

"May St John the Praecursor, and St John the Baptist, and St Peter and St Paul, and St Andrew, and all other Christ's apostles, together curse Guilhem. And may the rest of his disciples and four evangelists, who by their preaching converted the universal world, and may the holy and wonderful company of martyrs and confessors who by their holy works are found pleasing to God Almighty, curse Guilhem."

Her voice strengthened as she moved on.

"May the holy choir of the holy virgins, who for the honour of Christ have despised the things of the world, damn Guilhem. May all the saints, who from the beginning of the world to everlasting ages are found to be beloved of God, damn Guilhem. May the heavens and earth, and all the holy things remaining therein, damn Guilhem."

Artemisia realised that with Guilhem she was damning her family and with that damnation she was freeing herself from a burden she hadn't known she still carried.

"May Guilhem be damned wherever he be, whether in the house or the stables, the garden or the field, or the highway, or in the path, or in the wood, or in the water, or in the church. May he be cursed in living, in dying. May he be cursed in eating and drinking, in being hungry, in being thirsty, in fasting, in sleeping, in slumbering, in walking, in standing, in sitting, in lying, in working, in resting, in pissing, in shitting, and in blood-letting. May he be cursed in all the faculties of his body."

Artemisia frowned at Cormac, who was stifling a laugh. She threw the words out of her mouth as if the world would end the instant she finished reading.

"May he be cursed inwardly and outwardly. May he be cursed in the hair of his head. May he be cursed in his brains, and in his temples, in his forehead, in his ears, in his eye-brows, in his cheeks, in his jaw-bones, in his nostrils, in his fore-teeth and grinders, in his lips, in his throat, in his shoulders, in his wrists, in his arms, in his hands, in his fingers. May he be damned in his mouth, in his breast and in his heart.

"May the son of the living God, with all the glory of his Majesty curse him and may heaven, with all the powers which move therein, rise up against him, curse and damn Guilhem unless he repent and make satisfaction! Amen. So be it, so be it. Amen."

"Amen," chorused Geoffrey Murray and Cormac Smith. They stood up and let Guilhem go. He looked distressed, but he held his ground. Slowly he stood up. He was about to say something, and then he decided against it. He pivoted and he walked away, not quite stable.

It was Mac who peered down the slope after him. "He's running," Cormac said. "If he's not careful, he'll hurt himself."

"No shit," said Geoff, turning to look, then, a moment later, "I was wrong. There is shit."

He and Mac found this very funny. Artemisia, however, was drained of all emotion. There was no space in her for humour. She sat down on the ground and hid her head. She found two arms around her, Geoff on one side and Mac on the other.

"He won't hurt you again," said Geoff.

"He crapped himself," added Cormac. His irreverence broke Artemisia's emptiness and she started crying long slow sobs with no tears. The men stayed with her until she was done and then they helped her home.

They found the kitchen empty and helped themselves to coffee.

"He really believes he's cursed. I can't take this reality. I want to go home," said Cormac. It had taken longer to reach him than it had the others, but now he was in familiar circumstances with much-sweetened coffee in front of him, he was faced with the same truth the other two had seen, on that hillslope, when Artemisia had finished the curse.

"Only a few more weeks," reassured Geoff.

"A few long weeks," said Artemisia.

Chapter Forty-Eight: Webs

Guilhem turned back towards the town. It provided nothing. He was scared and the scared need the sacred. He wanted protection from the curse and protection from the torments of hell. He wanted protection from himself. He trekked to Pézenas.

Guilhem told Bernat graphically about the rape. Bernat's reaction was to have him confess again and to make due atonement.

Confession helped, for a little, this time. After that little, Guilhem realised that he had made his peace with God, but that this was not sufficient. He had raped Artemisia. She had cursed him. Justly.

Until this moment he hadn't considered it, but Artemisia had been his friend. He remembered her confusion and how quickly she learned about his people and his language and his ways. He remembered her smile, and her friendly laugh, and her odd accent. He tried not to remember the sweetness of her scent and of her unruly dark hair. He remembered complaining about the colour of his skin, when he was really thinking, "She could be one of my mother's kin. She could come from the Languedoc, or from Rome. She is of the Mediterranean, not those cold northern countries."

He was only a few miles outside Pézenas so he turned right round and went back to the Commanderie and talked to his mentor again. Bernat dismissed his concerns. "You have made amends with God. The woman is unimportant."

Guilhem looked around at the Commanderie in its defended glory. In his mind's eye he saw again a network of Templar outposts throughout France. He saw the Templars no longer as an army of God. He saw them as spiders, spinning a web to catch noblemen, make them forget their human obligations.

When I leave the South, he thought, *I must pay my courtesy visit to Philippe. My aunt has said. I shall tell him what I have seen, of the wealth of the Templars and of their spidery willingness to take over France. I won't tell him of their heartlessness, for he himself has no heart. He will want to know, however, that they owe him no loyalty*

*and that they are so well armed and that they span the length and
breadth of his territory.*

Guilhem didn't know what to do about Artemisia, whether to
atone, to make amends or to leave her alone to recover from what he
had done. He certainly knew what he would do with Bernat and his
unmanly thoughts. Why wait to see Philippe? Guilhem took a detour
of several days and reported to Philippe's nearest representative.

"I had not considered these knights in this way," the seneschal's
sprig said, gravely. "I shall make a proper report. It must be verbal,
I think."

"The Templar knights come from good families," Guilhem
agreed, "There is always the danger of false loyalties."

And so it happened.

It was slow. First the report had to be made to the seneschal and
then it had to go to Paris and then to the king himself, but the lure of
the Temple money and the threat of the Temple's arms throughout
France both fitted Philippe's way of thinking. This Guilhem had
known.

Philippe, however, could not simply act: the Templars had their
Order. Even with the Pope under his thumb, Philippe needed more
than visible threat. In the report from the Seneschal, Guilhem's
circumstances had been noted (although Guilhem himself was not
named). *'Consorting with demons'* was excuse enough to check for
Templar irregularities. If the knights were guilty of heresy and of
making a mockery of the Church, it would be simple enough to bring
the new pope to heel. And Bernat, if Guilhem were lucky, would be
burned as a heretic.

Having set this all in train, Guilhem returned to Saint-Guilhem.
He still felt bad, but at least he had done something.

* * *

"We need a clearer understanding of boundaries," said Luke,
earnestly.

"How can I help?" Artemisia's question was sincere. It was so
unusual for her to be called into Luke's office for something that
was not a scolding that she felt a particular desire to assist. Maybe
she could belong to the team, still, even after all the water under
the bridge. After all, it was simply water. And Sylvia was simply
Sylvia. Artemisia wondered if this was about the good doctor and

her tendency to drag Pauline into places they should not be.

"I want you to annotate the map in the office."

"The big one?"

"The big one," Luke nodded. "I want it very clear where members of the team will be seen from the town. I want to see where the locals work and where the pilgrims walk."

"You want us all to walk in safety?"

"Precisely." Luke looked rather smug. He had a solution to all problems.

Maybe not all problems, thought Artemisia, as she worked on that map. Or maybe if he realised that not all problems waited for his lordly attention. Ben had been called into Luke's office after her. She heard the names Luke called Ben and they were not good. There was one she didn't know: mischling. Luke called Ben "Son of a mischling. Grandson of a traitor mischling." The anger in his voice was more terrifying than the words.

Artemisia realised that she had no idea why Luke thought it was an exceptional insult. She was worried for Ben. It seemed to be about what he was, not about anything he had done.

Artemisia looked up *mischling* and her worries were confirmed. It was a German word for mongrel, someone who was part Aryan. All she could do was be nice to Ben when he got out. His ancestry was not something he could change. She wished that there was someone she could take this to, but there was only Sylvia, and she knew exactly what would happen if she took the issue to Sylvia.

Artemisia was completely correct in her estimate of the good Dr Smith. Sylvia made certain that she heard her response to the annotated map. She took Pauline out on an excursion to the town wall and debriefed the doctor in the main office area, pointing things out on the map the whole while. Her reasoning (expressed loudly) was that anything Artemisia did had to be redone anyhow, so they might as well check things out.

Luke refused to help. The map was there, of course everyone would use it. Artemisia wondered if his personal grief was the fact that Ben had disappeared.

Two days later, Ben reappeared, perfectly cheerful. It was as if nothing had happened.

* * *

There was a big difference between being unchaste with protectors and being unchaste without. Sibilla was discovering this difference the hard way. Three times she had ventured out and three times she had been beaten. Berta did her shopping for her and tended Sibilla's garden and helped with the housework, but this would not work in the long term. In the long term, Sibilla's life was at risk if she remained in Saint-Guilhem.

Fr Peire and Guilhem-the-smith talked about it and decided that something must be done. Both of them handled the matter of the local conscience. Every day they stirred the pot and made people feel more and more aware of their role in Sibilla's broken arm and her bruised body. Additionally, Fr Peire found some money from the church coffers and set things up so that Sibilla could move to Montpellier.

"No-one knows you there," he argued, "You can start afresh."

"I don't want to leave. This is home."

"I know," said Fr Peire, gently, "but it's an unhappy home. You're not safe."

Sibilla gave her best belt to Berta, the one with the removable letters. Sibilla mostly used those letters to spell as it currently did words like 'amor,' to quietly boast about her latest conquest. "You can spell prayers," she told her friend, "Look, see. That shows why I got the belt. My first husband gave it to me as a part of my relic collection."

"It's not a relic, though," Berta objected.

"No, but it can be used in the same way. If you spell out a prayer then it will act as a charm and keep you safe. If I'd worn it, I'd never have been beaten up."

"Thank you," said Berta. "I shall miss you."

"You can visit me when you go to Montpellier to sell your cloth."

"I never go to Montpellier to sell my cloth."

"It's about time you did. Think of the prices!"

"Maybe I'll visit you and see." Berta put on her new belt, admiring the metal letters.

Sibilla handed over the bag with extra letters. "Ask the priest for help that way you get a better prayer."

Once Sibilla was gone, she ceased to be a target. Once she ceased to be a target, those who had looked to beating her up as a solution for their problems had to find new solutions.

They started to blame the folk under the hill again. The parishioners of Saint-Barthelmy, in particular, jostled and talk about action.

"It's our parish that is threatened."

No-one said this in the presence of Fr Peire or Guilhem-the-smith, of course. What they said to Guilhem-the-smith, was that he should talk to Guilhem-the knight and that Guilhem-the-knight should persuade the strangers to leave.

Guilhem was in a quandary. He knew already, from Artemisia, that the team would leave at the end of the year. He also knew that he didn't want to see Artemisia or talk to her ever again. He didn't want to leave ribbons on the bush. He didn't want to see her walk towards him, her long skirts making the steep slope almost impassable. He didn't, and yet he did. He yearned after her in a most uncomfortable way. He hated her and he loved her and he missed her and he wished he could undo what he had done.

He wandered the pilgrim's path, alone, trying to sort his thoughts and his feelings. When he reached the End of the World, he made his decision. He would leave.

In preparation for his departure, he wrote Artemisia a letter. With the letter were many of his treasured objects, carefully placed inside a solid and large messenger's satchel. In giving them up, maybe he could forget her and forget the guilt and, maybe, avert the curse. At the last minute, he placed the rose paternoster on top of the satchel and on top of the note.

He packed his travel chest and he took himself and his valet to Montpellier.

* * *

Artemisia didn't expect to find Guilhem at the meeting place, but went there anyway. If there were no new ribbons, she could take the old ones back and either pack them or burn them, as early preparation for departure. Everything now was about whether something could be burned or whether it should be packed. And the curse was not a farewell. She needed to farewell the good as well as the bad. So she found herself at the clump of badasse frutescens, looking for freedom.

There were no ribbons. Bona had helped herself to them, as she had other times. There was, however, a lump of strange matter next to the plant. Artemisia went close to investigate. She lifted up the paternoster and smelled it, the rose scent clinging to her memory. Then she looked at the folded parchment with its seal. The seal of a knight, she noted, with its man on horseback.

She didn't want to open the note. She took the bag and the paternoster and the parchment back to her room.

"Geoff," she called, gently, into the main office space, "Can I borrow you a minute, please?"

"Sure," said Geoff, alert.

They walked to her room, Artemisia ahead. The corridor had seemed wide all those months ago, but it wasn't broad enough for the two to walk together. Artemisia reached back for Geoff's hand anyway. They reached Artemisia's room and shut the door behind them.

"What's this?" Geoff looked at the bed.

"I think it might be from Guilhem," Artemisia said, "But I didn't want to open it alone."

"I'm here," Geoff said, and they sat together, the satchel and parchment between them, the paternoster on the chest of drawers.

I am sorry, the note said. *I cannot explain what I did. You should not forgive what I did. Please take these gifts. They are not atonement, for I must atone before God. They are simply a gift, to a much-loved friend whom I have wronged. There is nothing on this earth that does not have an end, but this end is not the one I would have wished. May you travel safely to your far home. My thoughts will be with you. May you walk in the grace of God, always.*

One of Guilhem's phrases resonated: "There is nothing on this earth that does not have an end."

The soft scent of the crushed dried roses softened her mood just a fraction. She realised, "If the child is his, then it needs something from the father. His father will be seven hundred years dead when we return. There will be no record. Nothing. The baby needs something this is not about me."

"That sounds fair," said Geoff. "We'll have to smuggle all this home in our backpacks."

"You'll help me?" Artemisia didn't know why she was surprised.

"Of course."

* * *

Ben was alone, quietly working with his friend the farmer. His silent companion never caused him the grief that the people from his own world did. They understood the land and its needs, the two of them. They understood the vintage and the joy of treading grapes. They understood wine.

This was his farewell to his silent friend and to the vines he so loved. He gave the farmer Cormac's boots they were close enough in size he justified that the boots would perish in this dry climate and would cause no rift in time.

It was a good gift.

Chapter Forty-Nine: Waiting

"Time's up!" Luke clapped loudly to reinforce his point. "We're going home!"

From that moment on, things were frantic. Sylvia and Ben had to massage the final data and get it ready for upload. All the other scientists supported them and also helped Mac. Cormac was instructed to burn everything that could possibly be burned and that wasn't essential for reporting home on top of the hill. Ben was sent to do the rounds, by himself, and to check they had left nothing behind, anywhere.

"We don't have any indications of problems from the town, do we?" Luke looked across at Artemisia.

"Nothing I've been told," she said. She couldn't admit that there was no-one to do the telling.

"Good. We'll start the fires at once. It's going to take days to deal with all this stuff."

"Anything that can be burned we should get rid of, so we don't need to take it home. We won't have much of anything in the last couple of days, so you may want to prioritise. Don't wait to collect and document specimens I want all collection and all data entry regarding it finished by 23 December. I want all the refrigerators and machines on that platform on 24 December so we can start piling stuff on top of them. From Christmas Day, we're roughing it. We will have 25 minutes to get everything and all of ourselves back at midnight on 31 December and I don't want to lose a second of it. This means the final stages start now."

Artemisia was delegated to do the schedule for the final hour, in consultation with Mac, who knew what could go and how quickly it could be shifted. Mac was responsible for making sure everything was shifted and also to double-check Ben's final check. Nothing could be left behind. Sylvia and Pauline were responsible for outside checks. Artemisia and Geoff and Ben were to assist Mac whenever other duties permitted.

Luke said, "It should all work nicely."

The first thing Artemisia did was put most of what Guilhem had given her in her satchel and backpack, ready for 31 December. Geoff took the rest. She dumped some of her clothes into the bonfire, to make space. Her private possessions now contained (in addition to the rose petal paternoster, the cloth, the other small gifts) a quadrans vetus that Guilhem bought from the Jewish goldsmiths in Beziers ("Why is it called an old quadrant?" he had asked, not wanting an answer), a merchant's calendar with illuminated initials and red letter days, folded twice and fitted into a fine leather case, a tiny portable altar, a little brazier with elegant metalwork, a ring, and the Book of Hours that Sylvia had tried to steal. Even now, when these items were not ancient, her possessions were suddenly worth a vast amount of money.

She wanted to declare them and she wanted to hide them and she wanted the whole thing not to have happened. She did that last time, however this time she would keep everything. For herself and for her child and because, from what Guilhem had said in the note, he really was repentant.

And besides, the curse had helped. A lot.

* * *

The bedroom partitions were burning. The smell of charred cork infused the air. The chairs had already burned and lounge disassembled: the team all lived in the office area. The desk chairs served a multitude of uses and the trestle table likewise.

The living area shrank as Cormac took up mesh floor and made it small for transit. It was not long before the platform was full to the ceiling and the next load was being assembled, ready to be pushed on, and the load after that. It was a rigorous operation and Cormac handled it inexorably.

Artemisia was worried about her timetable. These big things were the easy part of it. Sylvia had already snubbed her. "Do you want to go home near the beginning," Artemisia had asked, "Or later?"

"I'll go home when I'm ready," Sylvia had said.

And Ben was impossible to find and Luke was so obsessed with his calculations that she was stuck. She put Sylvia and Pauline down for early departure. Mac would be the last to go. He and Ben had both asked for that.

Artemisia copied the schedule several times and used up the last of her precious paper. She handed a copy out to each and every team member.

Luke nodded as he received it, during the staff meeting. "Good," he said. "One more thing out of the way. Tell the others not to disturb me. I think I might have something."

"I'm not going to get all this into the datastream," he warned Sylvia. "You're going to have to put it in as I do it, as much as you can." Sylvia nodded to Mac and Artemisia to rearrange her duties to encompass this.

"I can only do it until about lunchtime on the thirty-first," she worried. "After that I have to make sure everything's in place. What do I do if you have a big breakthrough after that?"

"I will have that breakthrough," Luke said, quietly satisfied. "It's all leading up to it, now. The rest will come back in here," and he tapped his forehead, significantly. "There's too much and too little time."

"It sounds exciting."

"It's what we came here for," replied Luke, jubilantly.

The midwinter day wasn't long enough to contain all the activity. The bonfire blazed all night, sending a signal to the region. Those whose task was to tend the bonfire didn't think of that. Instead they waited for the moment when work beneath them ended for the night and they were joined by the others for singing and campfire.

The more they fed to the bonfire, the more the empty caves echoed.

Bona and her brother watched, of course. Mac and Geoff chased them away, also of course.

The people in Saint-Guilhem regarded this as a new problem. Not just the fire. Berta told anyone who would listen that the fire showed that her children were being lured by the demons from under the hill. Fiz repeated this to anyone who would listen, and to some who were not paying him sufficient attention.

Fr Peire was worried and checked with Guilhem's household. He was not terribly surprised to discover that he had simply walked out. Their intermediary was gone.

"If the fires last, we'll send a party to talk to them," they agreed.

Not everyone thought this is was good idea. Some still felt that the hillfolk were dangerous they had lured Guilhem into sin, after all.

The good people of Saint-Guilhem talked with the castle folk and with the monks. Both told them that as long as the hillfolk finally stayed under their hill and had stopped coming down to the town, there was no problem. They both explained, as if to simpletons, that if there was no threat, it was not their jurisdiction. They had never seen these strangers as posing a threat. None of the townsfolk of Saint-Guilhem were happy with this response, not even the priest.

"It's now a waiting game," Peire announced gloomily.

Chapter Fifty: Endgame

There was no more observation. No more delta T or meteorology. No more scraps of plants or animals or observations of water and wind and sky. Luke calculated and thought and worked out the future with more and more fury. Sylvia's model had led to what Luke had been after, what the whole expedition was for: he could see how to change their reality. The sky was obscured by the smoke from the bonfire. It was like the end of the world.

* * *

Mac quietly and very cautiously set up his explosives. He checked and he double-checked and he made sure that the caps were not too warm and that he didn't drop anything. He set them up when the others weren't watching. The caps alone could take his eyes and hands, if he weren't careful, but this had to be done both he and Ben were agreed. It was why he was going to be the last out. No-one should get caught when the caves blew up.

Tony was concerned with his plants and finishing his documentation and making sure everything was right. He hadn't been included in the final lists, apart from hefting things onto Bottie when the time was right. This was because Artemisia had asked him, "What are you likely to remember?" She and Mac had both suggested that he be responsible for his own stuff, and then help at the end. Everyone else found this sensible. Tony found it vaguely insulting, but didn't care enough to complain.

The destruction of their possessions distressed him unutterably. Sylvia, on the other hand, took savage glee in burning objects. As each item went up in smoke something within her cheered.

The town still kept an eye on the burning and Fiz wondered loudly if it were hellfire.

"Don't be stupid," Fr Peire said. "It's a bonfire. A midwinter bonfire. They are pagans. Just like the ones in the stories of Charlemagne and of Guillaume."

"We don't want pagans," said Berta. "Or demons. Or fairies.

They have no rights here. They do not belong."

"We should go up there and look," said Fiz.

* * *

Ben shoved the last camera (which had unaccountably been left just outside the cave) and some wire he had picked up from Tony's patch into a sliver of space on the already-laden platform then checked the time. He had left his outfit at Mac's secret exit, for he wasn't certain of his next step. He joined the others, looking innocent. Living the lie.

Luke did a head count and came up one short. He looked around, puzzled. It took him a moment before he put a name to the missing team member, "Tony."

"He's not in his garden, for I've just been there. We need search parties. We need to get him back here, pronto."

"Find him and come back quickly we don't have much time," Luke said.

Ben paired Sylvia with Pauline, then Geoff with Artemisia. Mac and Luke stayed back to continue the work.

Ben dressed in the clothing he had left by Mac's hideaway. It included every layer of reproduction clothing he could find, because it was cold, because it meant they didn't have to be burned, and because…he didn't know. He was happier going out with extra layers, perhaps. It was like having Mac set the caves up with explosives: he liked being prepared for the worst. He even had his Batman belt set up with full Medieval everything knife, purse, the lot. He wore duplicates. Some of it was his, some Mac's, some Geoff's. It should have felt stupid, but it gave him a sense of security. Of a future that didn't consist of his career in tatters because of Theodore Lucas Mann announcing "Mischling" to the assembled throngs. He went out alone.

Ben found a patch of hillside and sat there quietly, looking across at the hill under which he had lived. He needed a space away from Sylvia and her torments. He had to make a decision. There was time.

His watch was with his goods, ready to be shipped back, but he knew time the way he knew the breath of air in these hills. It would be a full hour before anything happened.

At the end of that hour he was there, still, on the hillside with his purloined artefacts.

The next morning, he asked Guilhem-the-Silent if he needed a farm worker. The farmer angled his head and looked at the tall foreigner and nodded.

* * *

Luke went back first. Botty was opening twice for the occasion and Luke was the only person scheduled. He had demanded the first spot and asked that he be alone in it. He and the computer with his last calculations had been saved a spot on one of the fridges. He said that he wanted to welcome his team from the far end. Artemisia suspected that he wanted to make an entrance.

He stepped lightly onto Botty's platform, sitting cross-legged on two freezer-chests one above the other. Luke was like a guru about to prognosticate, with his shaggy beard and his hooded fervent eyes. Botty flickered and changed colour and chests and guru were gone to the future.

* * *

It was the burning that caused most of the people of Saint-Guilhem to come out on a cold winter's night. That unceasing red and black had caused the end of the year to feel like the end of the world ever since it began. Why after dark in mid-winter on a cold night was the moment everyone became angry was beyond reason. This is because the townsfolk were beyond reason. The infernal flames had to stop.

The group from Saint-Guilhem-le-Désert walked up the slender path carefully. Berta had been the one to persuade them. Louis led them, however. It was a large group. Most of the people of two parishes. Their flickering torches made the ground look irregular, so progress was slow. They made as much noise as they could.

"We need to sound like the big devils of hell. The folks in the hill won't be surprised by us if we are loud."

The aim was to scare the hillfolk away, not to surprise them. That was what Louis thought. Peire and Guilhem-the-smith simply wanted to talk to them and persuade them to bring a halt to their foul fire and maybe to leave. Fiz bubbled with mischief.

Pauline was hauling her last armful of stuff upstairs, for the bonfire. She emerged from the hole and noticed that the light had changed. She looked around and a multitude of flickers captured her gaze. She saw the trail of people with their fire and lanterns. She thought of lynch mobs and burning witches and she panicked.

"Mac they're coming!"

"Who's coming?" Mac had one last armful of material to add to Pauline's and then all the burning was complete. It had taken far longer than anyone expected.

"Marauding peasants! Look!" They looked together from the hilltop and saw the many small flames flicker slowly up the path.

Cormac told Pauline to find Sylvia and not to wait for their due time. "Go back the moment there's space," he said. While Pauline found her things and collected her travelling companion, Mac finished arming the explosives in the wall of the Botty's cave. He was very relieved when it was finished. Detonator caps were sensitive and he was so hurried that he was certain he was clumsy. Mac got through the wiring and the explosives and all the checks and double checks without destroying either himself or his surroundings. He heaved a sigh and went about the next bit of business. He ignored the timetable: he had to finish everything. Just as long as he made it to Botty in time and got home.

The caves were wired up. All it would take was detonation.

* * *

Artemisia had scheduled Geoff as her travel companion. They stood near their little corner of Botty, and worried. Just before they stepped onto their little patch of light, Geoff turned his body slightly so that he was looking into Artemisia's eyes. He asked "Marry me?"

He put something in her hand and stepped up into the light. She opened her hand. In it was a poesie ring that announced "Amor vincit omnia." She barely had time to wonder how he got it, to put it on and to grab her bags before his, "Now! Hurry!" reached her brain. She stepped onto the platform herself.

* * *

When he'd seen Artemisia and Geoff safely though, and had made sure that Tony was finally gone, Mac went upstairs one last time, to check that the bonfire had done its job and destroyed their daily lives. He found Bona there, with her brother, eyes taking in the dying flames of the bonfire as if it had been set just for them.

"Boo!" he said, making faces. They didn't go. "You gotta go," he said. "Please? Look at those people coming up the hillside. You can't be here when they arrive."

Bona's eyes followed his hand. Those eyes became very big.

"We have to go," she told her brother, urgently. "Everyone's coming! We're supposed to be asleep."

The children walked across the hilltop and Mac lost sight of them in the darkness. He heaved a sigh of relief.

When he got back inside, he went to pull out his lucky coin. It wasn't there. He must have lost it on that hilltop, near the bonfire. A 2009 Australian coin could not be left behind, so he wasted more precious time. Finally, he found it.

"I'm the last to go," he thought. "I took so long. I hope Tony went. Stupid idiot may have forgotten."

He didn't have time to check. All he had time for was to press his button and set off the chain of explosions.

"In case of problems," he said to himself, "Press red button."

He did just that, then he flung himself onto Botty's lighted platform as quickly as he could. He half-noted that he was joined by a female figure.

Timebot blinked out and there was no-one and then Botty himself folded himself up and disappeared to the future

The link with 1305 was severed. Guilhem no longer walked in step with Artemisia. Botty was now fully in the twenty-first century. It was finished.

* * *

The noise from the explosion spilled out from the caves. The trail of people stopped in confusion. Everyone turned to Fr Peire.

"Back," he said. "Everyone go home. We can return tomorrow, when it's light." The horde of marauding peasants obediently did what it was told and went home, to bed.

One marauding peasant, however, was determined to see for himself, tonight. Fiz couldn't wait until morning. Before he had moved ten paces, he felt a tug on his ear.

"You, boy, are going home and to bed. Now." Guilhem-the-smith's voice was inexorable and his right arm the strongest in the village. Fiz went.

* * *

When Botty's other half had finished its deliveries, Botty's light blinked out in the twenty-first century, his other half returned and folded again into himself.

"He's back," announced one of the technical people. "We're all done."

A cheer went up.

Artemisia noticed that the young scientist who had sent her to the past was there, to welcome her back. He looked worried. Geoff looked worried. She turned around at looked at the assembled team, to find out what had silenced them. She was unable to speak, herself. They had all emerged in Melbourne on the glowing platform, walked off it and went to the waiting room. The whole team.

Sylvia was missing. Ben was missing. Luke was missing.

"Where are they?" Tony asked.

"Wait," said Harvey, in his most golden and reassuring voice, "I'll be making an announcement in a moment."

Artemisia took a deep breath and reached for Geoff's hand. She knew Harvey's voice, now. She suspected that the missing members were not being debriefed.

As they all filed into the hall, a loudspeaker played Sylvia's bright song.

"I sent it back last datastream," Cormac said. "Just shows they looked at what we sent."

"But where is she?" Pauline fretted.

"Dunno."

Soon they were all assembled in chairs, looking out at the assembled scientists and journalists with a mixture of worry and defiance.

Harvey introduced himself and then each of them explaining their role in the expedition. It all took an unconscionable time. Artemisia was there, sitting next to Geoff. Then came Mac and Tony and Pauline. That was all.

"As you can see," he declared, "The expedition was a success. It was not, however, without losses. Professor Mann died in transit." The team shifted uncomfortably, remembering the melted refrigerator. "Drs Smith and Konig also perished, although, not, we suspect, in transit. Dr Smith was with Dr Adamson and their timing was very tight: Dr Adamson got through and is right here with us, but the wormhole closed before Dr Smith could reach Botty. There will be an inquiry. In the meantime, please celebrate these heroes, who have accomplished the impossible."

The Ancient Mariner spoke, his eyes as wild as ever. "And the big project?"

"We have much of it. Some was lost with Professor Mann and Dr Smith."

"How much?"

"That is not relevant right now. We have the time team back. They have advanced humankind's knowledge by an enormous amount." Harvey's voice didn't hide the fact that he was worried. "We shall debrief and then allow the travellers to see their family. Thank you all for coming today, to greet them."

Artemisia looked to where Harvey's hand had pointed.

There, sitting amidst the strangers, was Lucia, alive. Lucia with short curls and a radiant smile.

Artemisia smiled back.

More Great Releases from Satalyte Publishing

More Great Releases from Satalyte Publishing

THE DAGGER OF DRESNIA

THE TALISMANS:
BOOK ONE

SATIMA FLAVELL

Queen Ellyria just wants her sick triplet sons to live, each ruling over a third of the kingdom as their dying father wished. When she finds herself trapped in a deadly bargain with a Dark Spirit, she recruits a band of young mages to help – but a terrible curse takes over.

The Dark Spirit befriends her enemies and seduces her friends, and Ellyria soon finds that famine, pestilence, betrayal and bereavement are all in its arsenal.

Can Ellyria unite the elvish and mortal sides of her family and in so doing, save the kingdom?

Crisp, stylish prose, a nicely realised medieval world and an undercurrent of dark magic make The Dagger of Dresnia a good read for lovers of epic fantasy. It's refreshing to see an older female character on centre stage!
- Juliet Marillier Author of the Sevenwaters series

Available at all good book stores in both paperback and ebook formats.

Lightning Source UK Ltd.
Milton Keynes UK
UKOW05f1626210714

235496UK00002B/36/P